THE D. CASE

Also by Fruttero & Lucentini

THE SUNDAY WOMAN

THE D. CASE

The Truth about the Mystery of Edwin Drood

CHARLES DICKENS

CARLO FRUTTERO & FRANCO LUCENTINI

Translated from the Italian by Gregory Dowling

A HELEN

AND KURT

WOLFF BOOK

HARCOURT   NEW YORK

BRACE   SAN DIEGO

JOVANOVICH   LONDON

HBJ

© 1989 by Giulio Einaudi editore s.p.a., Torino
English translation copyright © 1992 by
Harcourt Brace Jovanovich, Inc.

Library of Congress Cataloging-in-Publication Data
Dickens, Charles, 1812–1870.
[Mystery of Edwin Drood]
The D. case / Charles Dickens, Carlo Fruttero & Franco Lucentini;
translated from the Italian by Gregory Dowling.
p.   cm.
Translation of the revisions and ending to Dickens's work
originally appearing as: La verità sul caso D.
"A Helen and Kurt Wolff Book."
I. Fruttero, Carlo.   II. Lucentini, Franco.   III. Title.
IV. Title: Truth about the mystery of Edwin Drood.
PR4564.A1   1992
823'.8—dc20   91-29169

The character of Hercule Poirot is used in this book
with the kind permission of Agatha Christie Ltd.

Designed by Lisa Peters
Printed in the United States of America
First United States edition
A B C D E

CONTENTS

PART ONE: *The April Number*

1. THE RUIN LIES THERE IN THE RAIN . . . 3
Chapter I. The Dawn . . . 17

2. THUS ENDS THE FIRST CHAPTER . . . 22
Chapter II. A Dean, and a Chapter Also . . . 29

3. ON THIS AMBIGUOUS NOTE . . . 46
Chapter III. The Nuns' House . . . 54

4. IF INSTEAD OF INVESTIGATORS . . . 71
Chapter IV. Mr. Sapsea . . . 80
Chapter V. Mr. Durdles and Friend . . . 94

5. THE FINAL SPEECH RECEIVES . . . 104

PART TWO: *The May and June Numbers*

6. ANYBODY WHO EVER SPENT . . . 113
Chapter VI. Philanthropy in Minor Canon Corner . . . 114
Chapter VII. More Confidences Than One . . . 129

7. THE MENACING CONCLUSION . . . 143
Chapter VIII. Daggers Drawn . . . 148
Chapter IX. Birds in the Bush . . . 162

CONTENTS

8. AFTER THE LIGHTNING SPURT . . . 184

Chapter X. Smoothing the Way . . . 194

Chapter XI. A Picture and a Ring . . . 215

Chapter XII. A Night with Durdles . . . 236

9. AT THE END OF THE IMPRINTING . . . 257

PART THREE: *The July and August Numbers*

10. WHAT IS THE ATMOSPHERE OF A CONVENTION . . . 271

Chapter XIII. Both at Their Best . . . 280

Chapter XIV. When Shall These Three Meet Again? . . . 296

11. THE THIN MELANCHOLY MAN . . . 316

Chapter XV. Impeached . . . 328

Chapter XVI. Devoted . . . 341

12. THE DEBATE ON THE "MYSTERY NUMBER" . . . 356

Chapter XVII. Philanthropy, Professional . . . 367
and Unprofessional

Chapter XVIII. A Settler in Cloisterham . . . 389

Chapter XIX. Shadow on the Sun-Dial . . . 402

Chapter XX. Divers Flights . . . 413

CONTENTS

PART FOUR: *The Last Number*

13. It should now be the fourth day . . . 439
Chapter XXI. A Gritty State of Things Comes On . . . 454
Chapter XXII. The Dawn Again . . . 479

14. We had reached the Circus Maximus . . . 504

15. If a visitor to the Roman Forum . . . 516

16. It is nine a.m., reader . . . 526

17. Waiting for Poirot . . . 540

18. The D. case . . . 551

Epilogue . . . 582

THE D. CASE

PART ONE

THE APRIL NUMBER

1.

T HE RUIN LIES THERE IN THE RAIN, a great fossilized eyesocket staring emptily at nothing, like a long-silenced witness; it is now no more than a traffic-island beset on all sides by raging motor vehicles. Some way off, a black and a grey umbrella stand and gaze at it in long puzzlement.

"I don't know," the grey umbrella says at last. "I think it's the anachronism that bothers me most. All these mechanised vehicles, this motorised intrusion . . ."

A solitary yellow-green van accelerates in pursuit of the wave that has just surged by, and for a few seconds the asphalt lies empty and glistening before them.

"Ah, but where does the anachronism begin, *mon cher*?" smiles the black umbrella. "Do you think that seventeenth-century coaches or fiacres, or horse-drawn omnibuses, would look any less incongruous? Any less . . . degrading?"

"You're right. Anything more recent than chariots is out of place here."

"Including our umbrellas, clearly."

Two bad-tempered little cars charge forward through the rain, jostling for position and duelling furiously with their horns, while the massed army of which they form the vanguard snarls and chafes still at the traffic-lights.

"Excuse me, did you say chariots?" a passing umbrella interposes. "But they never held races here. Besides . . ."

The next maddened herd of traffic roars forward, flinging up great spattering wings of water, shattering every drop in its path into myriads of glittering granulets.

"Besides, in this city . . ." The new arrival tries to speak again. But then resigns himself and waits. The thunderous roar fades into the perpetual dull rumble that passes for silence in this neighbourhood, and the rain is heard again drumming on their umbrellas, feebly re-asserting its own sonorous independence.

"Besides, in this city, if I remember correctly from my seminary days, the Lex Julia Municipalis of 45 B.C. forbade the circulation of any vehicle during daylight hours. The only exceptions were the fire-brigade and refuse-carts."

"Ah," says Grey Umbrella, somewhat piqued, "but this Lex: did they abide by it? Because from what *I* remember from school, the poet Juvenal complained that the traffic . . ."

Black Umbrella has meanwhile recognized the third umbrella (which is so shabby and bedraggled as to be of no definable colour) and greets it effusively.

"What a pleasure to meet you, *mon père*! I did know you were here too."

"I think we're all here, more or less. But I'm not quite sure when this blessed convention is supposed to open. At three o'clock? At five? They were rather vague at the hotel this morning."

"They advised us to be back by half past three," says Grey Umbrella, "and so we've kept our cab. Would you like to join us? You'll find it difficult to get another one in this rain."

"That would be most kind. Thank you very much."

All three climb into the taxi waiting there with its engine running, and as they drive away, the great ruin dissolves and vanishes behind them like a pointillist mirage.

What is this ruin? The perspicacious reader will have deduced from certain clues that it can only be the Colosseum. He will also have guessed that the three umbrellas must belong to three foreigners, who are specialists in some discipline as yet to be ascertained, and who have come to Rome for one of the many international conventions held here. They probably all arrived this very morning. The downpour, the fury of which now abates, took them by surprise while they were making a short tour of the city. But who are they?

One is apparently an English Roman-Catholic priest.

The other two, judging by their umbrellas, at least, also seem to be English. But it will have been noticed that the shorter one uses occasional French expressions. The clouded windows of the car frustrate any further attempt at identification. The reader will have to contain his curiosity until the taxi arrives at their hotel.

It is fortunate at least that they are not staying at the Excelsior or the Grand Hotel, or indeed any of the central hotels, which would be impossible to reach in this traffic. Instead, the taxi is now progressing (and even here "progressing" is a relative term) along suburban streets, down avenues, and through squares, all anonymous in their geometrical exactitude, but which all lead towards an unmistakable architectural clue: a monumental grey cube of a building with six storeyed rows of arches.

This tells us that we are skirting the EUR quarter of Rome, and we leave it now on our right as we make our way into the Cecchignola area, with its wilderness of cranes and almost virgin building-sites. We finally draw up at a parallelepiped which is almost as imposing in its proportions as the cube we passed earlier: the Hotel Urbis et Orbis, the name abbreviated on the towering signboard to a succinct U&O.

The building is of steel and crystal, and is surrounded by a park somewhat meagre in extent but rich in bushes and trees, benches and gravel-paths. A great red banner hung across the hotel's entrance pillars announces that . . .

No, it doesn't announce. The wind has flapped and wrapped it drunkenly around itself. We have to go into the lobby and look at a free-standing notice-board to read about the convention that is opening today:

COMPLETENESS IS ALL
An International Forum on the Completion
of Unfinished or Fragmentary Works
in Music and Literature

Schubert: *Sinfonie n. 8*	Livy: *Ab Urbe condita*
Bach: *Die Kunst der Fuge*	Poe: *The Narrative of A. G. Pym*
Puccini: *Turandot*	Dickens: *The Mystery of E. Drood*

The Italian notice is not ready yet, they tell us at the reception-desk, but the English one presents the Italian reader with no problems of translation. It is clearly the six works cited—beginning with Schubert's *Sinfonie n. 8* ("The Unfinished")—whose completion is to be discussed and planned.

The Art of the Fugue, Turandot, and *The Mystery of Edwin Drood* were all cut short by the death of their authors; whereas it was Poe himself, terrified perhaps by the phantom that suddenly looms at the end of Chapter 25, who

7

broke off the *Narrative of Arthur Gordon Pym of Nantucket* at
its very climax. Of the six, only Titus Livius's monumental
work was ever concluded, although we possess only LXV
books out of its CXLII. The organizers of the convention
wish to remedy this regrettable situation. But how can
they hope to succeed?

Or rather: How can they hope to succeed better than
their predecessors? For attempts have been made to complete all the works in question, with the exception of Livy's,
for which scholars have made do with ancient summaries.
Dickens's disturbing *Mystery*, for example: at least two
hundred different solutions have been devised for it.

But this is precisely the point. The very fact that the
solutions are so at variance with one another (one might
say in discord, in the case of the musical works) proves
that up to now the task has been handled in an amateurish
fashion, without the right tools, without any real method,
and above all without the backing of a strong organisation.
Here the circumstances will be very different. The convention has been arranged and is being run by highly methodical people, practised masters in the planning, programming,
and accomplishment of anything and everything. It is they
who have booked the entire Hotel Urbis et Orbis for a
week (four hundred rooms, four-and-a-half-star category),
attracting specialists from every age and country by means

of irresistible perquisites. They are paying. They are the sponsors.

Even the slowest reader cannot fail to catch on: yes, they are Japanese. No-one else could have conceived so bold and ambitious a programme of "integrative restorations." Of course, nobody ever gives something for nothing, and the sponsors are to receive, for the next fifty years, the royalties of the "integrated" works. But they expect a more immediate (if less pecuniary) return in terms of "image," especially since the two companies involved in the courageous joint-venture are by their very nature dedicated to completeness: one of them dominates the world-market in automobile spare-parts; the other produces a relentless supply of electronic components.

We have lost sight of our three umbrellas amidst the cosmopolitan crowd clogging the lobby of the U&O. But here they are again—closed now, of course—following the arrows on the arcades and pillars, and thus making their way to the bar of their particular section. The convention will be inaugurated in half an hour, and they just have time to warm themselves with a quick cappuccino.

The room they enter is dimly lit and caressed by velvety background music. Numerous other experts in their field sit at the bar and at the tables. They are together for the first time, but they are all known to one another, as indeed they will be to any devotee of fictional detection.

Noticing that their colleagues have already done so, Black Umbrella and Grey Umbrella pin their identification badges onto their lapels: "H. Poirot" and "Capt. Hastings." Shabby Umbrella pins his onto his cassock: "Father Brown." They are all sipping their cappuccini when a tall man, whose billowing cloak and singular cap identify him at once, comes up and examines their badges with a large magnifying-glass.

"May I make so bold? Holmes," he announces, and then introduces his companion, whose lapel-badge reads: "Dr Watson."

Yes, reader! Thanks to the initiative and ingenuity of Japanese industry, all or nearly all the world's best-known investigators are here assembled—masters of intuition and deduction, experts in strange co-incidences and suspicious omissions, supreme solvers of riddles!

There are other famous duos, apart from the two we have just identified: at one table sits Auguste Dupin, the founding father of all private eyes, alongside his inseparable though anonymous companion; by the window we can see Dr Thorndyke with his colleague Astley, and Nero Wolfe with his assistant Goodwin; while Philip Marlowe and Lew Archer clutch double bourbons at the bar. The lone detectives and occasional investigators such as Father Brown are far too numerous to be listed now. And, of course, there are plenty of representatives of the official police-forces. Scotland Yard naturally dominates, but not to the exclusion of the Parisian Préfecture de Police; nor, we are happy to say, to that of some of our own Questure.

Within the framework of the convention, all these people (including a colonel of the Carabinieri, who has just this moment turned up) constitute the "Drood work-group." It is up to them to disentangle this knottiest of cases, to solve the mystery that Dickens left at his death. When that has been done, it will be child's play for the computers of the two sponsoring companies to provide the world's readers with the completed novel.

At this point a smiling hostess (her name is Loredana) in a lavender-coloured dress enters and announces (in Basic English) that there will be a slight change in the programme.

The Italian reader—and the foreign reader, a second or two later—will no doubt mutter that this was only to be expected. It is fitting, perhaps inevitable, that the undisputed capital of ruins and restorations should have been chosen to host such a convention. But Rome is also the equally undisputed capital of strikes, muddles, and traffic-jams, a city whose airport rarely functions and whose town-

11

council is in permanent crisis. Thus it can come as no surprise that the mayor, the central figure in the solemn inauguration ceremony, is held up at an interminable council session at the Campidoglio; that the Minister of Culture is stuck at Lamezia Terme on account of the non-arrival of the plane from Catania; and that the plane from Tokyo with the sponsors on board has been diverted to Pisa.

Loredana announces all this very sweetly, continually brushing aside the long auburn hair that caresses her face. Her unruffled tones make it quite clear that she knows all there is to know about delays, hitches, and contretemps. The inauguration (hair to the right) will of course take place, but not until seven p.m. or thereabouts. Consequently the Cocktail Welcoming set for eight-thirty will be a Socialising Dinner. The first work-sessions, however, can begin at once, and she will now (hair to the left) escort the Drood group into the room reserved for them.

With her hair tossed back, the efficient young lady conducts her party into the U&O's subterranean depths, a vast labyrinthine warren of congress-rooms. Similar young ladies with similar smiles or semi-smiles on their lips are already leading the other parties to their respective rooms: the Schubert Room, J. S. Bach Room, etc.

Ours is the Dickens Room, and although it is naturally not as large as the music rooms or the Livy Room, it contains numerous rows of elegant black arm-chairs, all of which are fitted with adjustable trays for notebooks and with headphones for simultaneous translation. At the front is a platform bearing a long table and four chairs, four microphones, and four bottles of mineral water. Next to the table is a rostrum, which also has a microphone. Loredana mounts the rostrum and cheerfully informs us of another "slight problem." The simultaneous translation, she says, is guaranteed, but due to technical difficulties the only language available at the moment is Latin; but Latin is, after all (hair flicked forwards), the universal tongue.

This announcement is greeted with hostility by a certain H. Popeau, whom nobody appears to know, but it wins the warm approval of Porfiry Petrovich, the humanist investigator who intuited Raskolnikov's guilt and finally induced him to confess.

"Roma caput mundi," the colonel of the Carabinieri proclaims in the front row.

Everybody applauds as the first panel of three take their places at the table along with a man in a tweed jacket and with a vaguely Oxford accent, whom some mistake for Philo Vance.

But this is not the famous specialist in locked-room murders. Dr Wilmot, our hostess explains from the rostrum, is the editor of *The Dickensian*, the prestigious journal which since 1904 has published all that is best in Dickensian research and studies. As the leading authority in the field, he will chair this constructive debate. Anybody who wishes to contribute an observation or a question from the floor is welcome to do so, but should raise his hand first.

The young lady steps back while the chairman adjusts his bow-tie and clears his throat. But there is already a raised hand in the sixth row.

"Yes?" says the chairman.

The obscure participant, Popeau, asks: "Is this the sort of conference where everybody is assumed to know everything already?"

Loredana at once returns to the microphone. "No, no, on the contrary. I apologise for not saying so at once: the text of the MED will be read in its entirety by—"

"The text of what?" interrupts Popeau, whose deductive skills are perhaps not of the keenest.

"In specialist studies of *The Mystery of Edwin Drood*, this abbreviation is generally adopted," Dr Wilmot explains. And lest there still be any doubt, he adds: "M = Mystery, E = Edwin, D = Drood."

"Ah," the Carabinieri colonel says from the front row.

Loredana, who has just been handed a note by a messenger-boy, resumes: "So then, the complete text of the novel . . . that is, the complete text of the chapters we possess . . . will be read in its entirety in the course of the sessions. In that way, the participants as well as the panel . . ."

But the young lady seems to have lost the thread; seems to be no longer in control. Perhaps because she has just learned that it is she who must read aloud the complete text of the MED?

"The fact is," she explains in sudden embarrassment, "the sponsors . . . that is, the two organising companies, to make the readings as effective as possible, booked a well-known announcer, a highly talented actress and speaker, but unfortunately she . . ."

"Is unable, due to an indisposition and/or circumstances beyond her control, to arrive before tomorrow morning," the panel-member Auguste Dupin concludes, deducing these facts from the colour and format of the sheet of paper in Loredana's hand.

"Elementary, my dear Dupin," smiles Holmes, miffed that he did not say this first.

The third member of the panel is Jules Maigret, who lights his pipe (the luminous rectangular signs in the Dickens Room read, thank goodness, SMOKING) and addresses the hostess paternally. "Why don't you read the first chapter yourself, mademoiselle? I'm sure that everyone present . . ."

Enthusiastic applause ensues, a genuine ovation of sympathy and encouragement, and the hesitant girl is thus persuaded to remain on the rostrum. Dr Wilmot rises and hands her a booklet with an illustrated cover (the novel, he reminds everyone, appeared in monthly numbers, beginning in April 1870, and was broken off after the sixth number).

"Issue number one," Loredana reads, "Chapter One."

CHAPTER I

THE DAWN

AN ancient English Cathedral Tower? How can the ancient English Cathedral tower be here! The well-known massive grey square tower of its old Cathedral? How can that be here! There is no spike of rusty iron in the air, between the eye and it, from any point of the real prospect. What is the spike that intervenes, and who has set it up? Maybe, it is set up by the Sultan's orders for the impaling of a horde of Turkish robbers, one by one. It is so, for cymbals clash, and the Sultan goes by to his palace in long procession. Ten thousand scimitars flash in the sunlight, and thrice ten thousand dancing-girls strew flowers. Then, follow white elephants caparisoned in countless gorgeous colors, and infinite in number and attendants. Still, the Cathedral Tower rises in the background, where it cannot be, and still no writhing figure is on the grim spike. Stay! Is the spike so low a thing as the rusty spike on the top of a post of an old bedstead that has tumbled all awry? Some vague period of drowsy laughter must be devoted to the consideration of this possibility.

Shaking from head to foot, the man whose scattered consciousness has thus fantastically pieced itself together, at length rises, supports his trembling frame upon his arms, and looks around. He is in the meanest and closest of small rooms. Through the ragged window-curtain, the light of early day steals in from a miserable court. He lies, dressed, across a large unseemly bed, upon a bedstead that has indeed given way under the weight upon it. Lying, also dressed and also across the bed, not longwise, are a Chinaman, a Lascar, and a haggard woman. The two first are in a sleep or stupor; the last is blowing at a kind of pipe, to kindle it. And as she blows, and shading it with her lean hand, concentrates its red spark of light, it serves in the dim morning as a lamp to show him what he sees of her.

"Another?" says this woman, in a querulous, rattling whisper. "Have another?"

He looks about him, with his hand to his forehead.

"Ye've smoked as many as five since ye come in at midnight," the woman goes on, as she chronically complains. "Poor me, poor me, my head is so bad! Them two come in after ye. Ah, poor me, the business is slack, is slack! Few Chinamen about the Docks, and fewer Lascars, and no ships coming in, these say! Here's another ready for ye, deary. Ye'll remember like a good soul, won't ye, that the market price is dreffle high just now? More nor three shillings and sixpence for a thimbleful! And ye'll remember that nobody but me (and Jack Chinaman t'other side the court; but he can't do it as well as me) has the true secret of mixing it? Ye'll pay up according, deary, won't ye?"

She blows at the pipe as she speaks, and, occasionally bubbling at it, inhales much of its contents.

"O me, O me, my lungs is weak, my lungs is bad! It's nearly ready for ye, deary. Ah poor me, poor me, my poor hand shakes like to drop off! I see ye coming-to, and I ses to my poor self, 'I'll have another ready for him, and he'll bear in mind the market price of opium, and pay according.' O my poor head! I makes my pipes of old penny ink-bottles, ye see, deary—this is one—and I fits in a mouthpiece, this way, and I takes my mixter out of this thimble with this little horn spoon; and so I fills, deary. Ah, my poor nerves! I got Heavens-hard drunk for sixteen year afore I took to this; but this don't hurt me, not to speak of. And it takes away the hunger as well as wittles, deary."

She hands him the nearly-emptied pipe, and sinks back, turning over on her face.

He rises unsteadily from the bed, lays the pipe upon the hearth-stone, draws back the ragged curtain, and looks with repugnance at his three companions. He notices that the woman has opium-smoked herself into a strange likeness of the Chinaman. His form of cheek, eye, and temple, and his color, are repeated in her. Said Chinaman convulsively wrestles with one of his many Gods, or Devils, perhaps, and snarls horribly. The Lascar laughs and dribbles at the mouth. The hostess is still.

"What visions can *she* have?" the waking man muses, as he turns her face towards him, and stands looking down at it. "Visions of many butchers' shops, and public-houses, and much credit? Of an increase of hideous customers, and this horrible bedstead set upright again, and this horrible court swept clean? What can she rise to, under any quantity of opium, higher than that!—Eh?"

He bends down his ear, to listen to her mutterings.

19

"Unintelligible!"

As he watches the spasmodic shoots and darts that break out of her face and limbs, like fitful lightning out of a dark sky, some contagion in them seizes upon him: insomuch that he has to withdraw himself to a lean arm-chair by the hearth—placed there, perhaps, for such emergencies—and to sit in it, holding tight, until he has got the better of this unclean spirit of imitation.

Then he comes back, pounces on the Chinaman, and, seizing him with both hands by the throat, turns him violently on the bed. The Chinaman clutches the aggressive hands, resists, gasps, and protests.

"What do you say?"

A watchful pause.

"Unintelligible!"

Slowly loosening his grasp as he listens to the incoherent jargon with an attentive frown, he turns to the Lascar and fairly drags him forth upon the floor. As he falls, the Lascar starts into a half-risen attitude, glares with his eyes, lashes about him fiercely with his arms, and draws a phantom knife. It then becomes apparent that the woman has taken possession of his knife, for safety's sake; for, she too starting up, and restraining and expostulating with him, the knife is visible in her dress, not in his, when they drowsily drop back, side by side.

There has been chattering and clattering enough between them, but to no purpose. When any distinct word has been flung into the air, it has had no sense or sequence. Wherefore "unintelligible!" is

20

again the comment of the watcher, made with some reassured nodding of his head, and a gloomy smile. He then lays certain silver
money on the table, finds his hat, gropes his way down the broken
stairs, gives a good morning to some rat-ridden doorkeeper, in bed
in a black hutch beneath the stairs, and passes out.

That same afternoon, the massive grey square tower of an old
Cathedral rises before the sight of a jaded traveller. The bells are
going for daily vesper service, and he must needs attend it, one
would say, from his haste to reach the open cathedral door. The
choir are getting on their sullied white robes, in a hurry, when he
arrives among them, gets on his own robe, and falls into the procession filing in to service. Then, the Sacristan locks the iron-barred
gates that divide the sanctuary from the chancel, and all of the
procession having scuttled into their places, hide their faces; and
then the intoned words, "WHEN THE WICKED MAN———" rise among
groins of arches and beams of roof, awakening muttered thunder.

2.

THUS ENDS THE FIRST CHAPTER. Extremely short. And Loredana, who after some initial stumbling has acquired a certain graceful fluency, apparently wants to go straight on to the second, just as a young lady of 1870 would have done, with that same bound copy in her hands and the Victorian family circle hanging from her rosy lips. At last, a new Dickens! There had been nothing from his pen since 1865, when *Our Mutual Friend* came out, and his vast public of admirers, from the Queen downwards, had been waiting impatiently ever since.

But no-one here is listening for the sheer pleasure of it. Here—the reader must not forget—we are surrounded by a host of scrupulous, even fanatical, analysts. Their attitude is understandable: from the business point of view, they have a professional obligation to the Japanese sponsors; and on the level of personal prestige, none of the detectives wants a single detail of the interwoven mysteries of the MED to escape him. And, of course, as the reader well knows, there is a pinch of exhibitionism in one or two of these people.

So, with a wave of his hand, Dr Wilmot checks Loredana's eagerness, and invites Holmes, who has raised his magnifying-glass, to speak.

"There is one small point I would like to clear up," says the expert in fluorescent hounds. "The man who comes hurrying into the cathedral of X and who joins the choir in intoning 'When the wicked man': is this the same man we saw leaving the opium-den at dawn? I would have you note that the author does not say so explicitly."

The director of *The Dickensian* sighs. The proceedings are likely to be lengthy, with a quibbler of this calibre.

"An interesting point," he concedes courteously, "but I would prefer not to discuss it just now. For the moment we can take it for granted that the opium-addict and the chorist are the same person. Dickens does not reveal his name at once, and the character is thus introduced to us (in a highly effective way, if I may say so) enshrouded in an aura of mysterious ambiguity, or, if you prefer, of seeming duplicity. But," he adds with a faint smile, "if we will wait until the next chapter, the character's duplicity will become more obvious."

"Thank you." Holmes smiles back. "It is what I feared."

"Too obvious, too obvious," comes a raucous voice from the back.

This obscure pronouncement leaves everybody puzzled for a moment, and a lady without a name-badge takes advantage of this to address Father Brown directly.

"So the Wicked Man," she asks, "is supposed to be him? The opium-addict, I mean?"

"The allusion," says Father Brown into the microphone handed to him briskly by Loredana, "seems clear enough to me. But . . ."

"Too clear, too clear," the raucous voice again croaks from the back.

". . . but," the priest continues seraphically, "it is by no means a forced or artificial allusion. The evening service of the Anglican liturgy opens with this verse from Ezekiel (18:27), and Dickens's use of it is thus quite natural. I might add that the verse in its complete form opens up new possibilities: 'And when the wicked man turneth himself away from his wickedness that he hath committed, and doeth that which is lawful and right, he shall save his soul alive.' Therefore there is a hope of redemption for him, despite his evil secret."

The lady expresses surprise. "Why evil? My brother, who's a senior consultant in Arezzo, told me that in Dickens's time drug-addiction wasn't considered so very scandalous or reprehensible. They prescribed opium quite routinely as a pain-killer, and addicts weren't particularly ashamed of their vice."

Here tact seems called for. The lady has failed to understand that the opium-addict's secret has nothing to do with opium. And, once again, Popeau (who takes this opportunity to introduce himself as "an ex-high-ranking officer of the Préfecture de Paris and subsequently private investigator in the service of Mrs M. Belloc Lowndes") reveals that he has understood even less.

"Mais si secret il y a," he asks, "if there is a secret, is it not rather the one that *le sujet*, the subject, tries to learn from the lips of his companions in the den?"

The chairman clears his throat and turns to Maigret, who is filling his pipe with ostentatious concentration. "Your former colleague's interpretation is, perhaps . . ."

"Quite. But we must acknowledge that the text, especially when rendered . . . ehm . . . into Latin, can be misleading. Because, yes, it is true that the subject listens keenly to what his companions mutter in their fitful sleep; and it is also true that his first 'Unintelligible!,' through some cleverness on the author's part, might be occasioned by disappointment. But the gist lies in his 'gloomy smile,' and in his 'reassured' nodding. We must therefore conclude that it is he who has a terrible secret, and that he wished to ascertain whether it might have slipped out while he was under the influence of the opium."

"An open secret, an open secret," the raucous voice interrupts once again.

25

The reader undoubtedly wishes to know to whom this subversive voice belongs, but the man's name, alas, is not known. De Quincey, in his essay "On Murder Considered as One of the Fine Arts," calls him merely Toad in the Hole (which is a kind of sausage-pudding), but this nickname should not mislead us into underestimating him. Toad is in fact a fastidious connoisseur of murder, an insatiable gourmet of criminal mystery, who was so disgusted by the coarse level of London homicides at the beginning of the nineteenth century that he withdrew to the country for a while. An extremely demanding and hypercritical expert, from whom we must expect, unfortunately, further pungent interruptions.

But now Dupin, who has been showing signs of impatience, leans into the microphone: "I have nothing against allusions, first impressions, or connections, whether obvious or not, which might lead to results later on. But I would like to point out that so far no-one has posed the purely technical question of times and places. Where is this opium-den? Where is this cathedral? And at the time of the events, with the means of transport then existing, how long would it take to get from one to the other?"

A murmur of approval rises from that formidable gathering of time-table experts and clock-watchers, all accustomed to seeking out truth in the tiniest of chronological chinks. And the editor of *The Dickensian* satisfies their cu-

riosity at once: "The opium-den is in London. We know,
from reliable witnesses, that when Dickens was doing his
research for the book, he visited one such den, which he
then took as a model, with its hostess and its clients. It
was situated near the port, in the notorious district of
Shadwell, to be precise, in . . . But this is hardly relevant . . ."

But, reader, how could we omit the fact that the opium-
den was not only in Shadwell but on the corner of the
Ratcliff Highway, the scene of the *Ratcliff Road Murders*,
which De Quincey elevated to the "dignity of a national
event," thus restoring Toad's faith in crime? And how could
we fail to add that Dickens carried out his reconnaissance
in the company of a Scotland Yard officer, who under the
name of Bucket appears in another of his novels and is the
first-ever detective inspector in English literature?

Nor should we pass over the fact that a Baltimore col-
lector, after the writer's death, had the happy idea of visiting that den; he found the bedstead in the same "tumbled"
state as ever, bought it for a pound, and took it back with
him to the U.S.A., where it can still be seen.

"As for the cathedral town," Dr Wilmot goes on to
explain, "its fictitious name in the novel is Cloisterham.
But it is unanimously agreed among scholars that it is, in
fact, Rochester, where the great writer spent part of his
childhood, where he set some immortal scenes of *Pickwick*,

and where—or near where—he was to die on June 9, 1870. The novel is clearly set in the early 1840s, when the rail link with London was not fully established. From the MED itself we gather that the journey, some thirty-five miles, was made partly by train and partly by omnibus, and took three hours."

"But," observes the Carabinieri colonel, "that means that the culprit can't have left London before one o'clock, given that he arrived just in time for the service. What was he doing all that time in-between?"

"Good point," says Wilmot, "but one that has remained unanswered. It's a pity, the more so since we find the same situation in Chapter Twenty-two, the last we have. Once again, the . . . well, not exactly the culprit, let's say the suspect . . . emerges from the opium-den at dawn and returns to Cloisterham on an afternoon train—or, rather, an evening train. But we are told nothing of how he spent the intervening time."

Dr Wilmot looks around with a courteous smile, but his tone has the sharpness of a sickle poised to lop off all the upraised arms. "Speaking of time, we should perhaps be getting on, so if our kind assistant would care to resume her reading . . ."

For a moment the embarrassed flush rekindles Loredana's cheeks, but then she plucks up courage and begins: "Chapter Two . . ."

CHAPTER II

A DEAN, AND A CHAPTER ALSO

WHOSOEVER has observed that sedate and clerical bird, the rook, may perhaps have noticed that when he wings his way homeward towards nightfall, in a sedate and clerical company, two rooks will suddenly detach themselves from the rest, will retrace their flight for some distance, and will there poise and linger; conveying to mere man the fancy that it is of some occult importance to the body politic, that this artful couple should pretend to have renounced connection with it.

Similarly, service being over in the old cathedral with the square tower, and the choir scuffling out again, and divers venerable persons of rook-like aspect dispersing, two of these latter retrace their steps, and walk together in the echoing Close.

Not only is the day waning, but the year. The low sun is fiery and yet cold behind the monastery ruin, and the Virginia creeper on the cathedral wall has showered half its deep-red leaves down on the pavement. There has been rain this afternoon, and a wintry shudder goes among the little pools on the cracked uneven flagstones, and through the giant elm trees as they shed a gust of tears. Their fallen leaves lie strewn thickly about. Some of these leaves, in a timid rush, seek sanctuary within the low arched cathedral door;

but two men coming out, resist them, and cast them forth again with their feet; this done, one of the two locks the door with a goodly key, and the other flits away with a folio music book.

"Mr. Jasper was that, Tope?"

"Yes, Mr. Dean."

"He has stayed late."

"Yes, Mr. Dean. I have stayed for him, your Reverence. He has been took a little poorly."

"Say 'taken,' Tope—to the Dean," the younger rook interposes in a low tone with this touch of correction, as who should say: "You may offer bad grammar to the laity, or the humbler clergy, not to the Dean."

Mr. Tope, Chief Verger and Showman, and accustomed to be high with excursion parties, declines with a silent loftiness to perceive that any suggestion has been tendered to him.

"And when and how has Mr. Jasper been taken—for, as Mr. Crisparkle has remarked, it is better to say taken—taken—" repeats the Dean; "when and how has Mr. Jasper been Taken——"

"Taken, sir," Tope deferentially murmurs.

"——Poorly, Tope?"

"Why, sir, Mr. Jasper was that breathed——"

"I wouldn't say, 'That breathed,' Tope," Mr. Crisparkle interposes, with the same touch as before. "Not English—to the Dean."

"Breathed to that extent," the Dean (not unflattered by this indirect homage), condescendingly remarks, "would be preferable."

"Mr. Jasper's breathing was so remarkably short;" thus discreetly does Mr. Tope work his way round the sunken rock, "when he came in, that it distressed him mightily to get his notes out: which was perhaps the cause of his having a kind of fit on him after a little. His memory grew DAZED." Mr. Tope, with his eyes on the Reverend Mr. Crisparkle, shoots this word out, as if defying him to improve upon it: "and a dimness and giddiness crept over him as strange as ever I saw: though he didn't seem to mind it particularly, himself. However, a little time and a little water brought him out of his DAZE." Mr. Tope repeats the word and its emphasis, with the air of saying: "As I *have* made a success, I'll make it again."

"And Mr. Jasper has gone home quite himself, has he?" asked the Dean.

"Your Reverence, he has gone home quite himself. And I'm glad to see he's having his fire kindled up, for it's chilly after the wet, and the Cathedral had both a damp feel and a damp touch this afternoon, and he was very shivery."

They all three look towards an old stone gatehouse crossing the Close, with an arched thoroughfare passing beneath it. Through its latticed window, a fire shines out upon the fast-darkening scene, involving in shadow the pendent masses of ivy and creeper covering the building's front. As the deep Cathedral-bell strikes the hour, a ripple of wind goes through these at their distance, like a ripple of the solemn sound that hums through tomb and tower, broken niche and defaced statue, in the pile close at hand.

"Is Mr. Jasper's nephew with him?" the Dean asks.

"No, sir," replies the Verger, "but expected. There's his own solitary shadow betwixt his two windows—the one looking this way, and the one looking down into the High Street—drawing his own curtains now."

"Well, well," says the Dean, with a sprightly air of breaking up the little conference, "I hope Mr. Jasper's heart may not be too much set upon his nephew. Our affections, however laudable, in this transitory world, should never master us; we should guide them, guide them. I find I am not disagreeably reminded of my dinner, by hearing my dinner-bell. Perhaps, Mr. Crisparkle, you will, before going home, look in on Jasper?"

"Certainly, Mr. Dean. And tell him that you had the kindness to desire to know how he was?"

"Ay; do so, do so. Certainly. Wished to know how he was. By all means. Wished to know how he was."

With a pleasant air of patronage, the Dean as nearly cocks his quaint hat as a Dean in good spirits may, and directs his comely gaiters towards the ruddy dining-room of the snug old red-brick house where he is at present "in residence" with Mrs. Dean and Miss Dean.

Mr. Crisparkle, Minor Canon, fair and rosy, and perpetually pitching himself head-foremost into all the deep running water in the surrounding country; Mr. Crisparkle, Minor Canon, early riser, musical, classical, cheerful, kind, good-natured, social, contented, and boy-like; Mr. Crisparkle, Minor Canon and good man, lately "Coach" upon the chief Pagan high roads, but since promoted by a patron (grateful for a well-taught son) to his present Christian beat; betakes himself to the gate house, on his way home to his early tea.

"Sorry to hear from Tope that you have not been well, Jasper."

"Oh, it was nothing, nothing!"

"You look a little worn."

"Do I? Oh, I don't think so. What is better, I don't feel so. Tope has made too much of it, I suspect. It's his trade to make the most of everything appertaining to the Cathedral, you know."

"I may tell the Dean—I call expressly from the Dean—that you are all right again?"

The reply, with a slight smile, is: "Certainly; with my respects and thanks to the Dean."

"I'm glad to hear that you expect young Drood."

"I expect the dear fellow every moment."

"Ah! He will do you more good than a doctor, Jasper."

"More good than a dozen doctors. For I love him dearly, and I don't love doctors, or doctors' stuff."

Mr. Jasper is a dark man of some six-and-twenty, with thick, lustrous, well-arranged black hair and whisker. He looks older than he is, as dark men often do. His voice is deep and good, his face and figure are good, his manner is a little sombre. His room is a little sombre, and may have had its influence in forming his manner. It is mostly in shadow. Even when the sun shines brilliantly, it seldom touches the grand piano in the recess, or the folio music-books on the stand, or the bookshelves on the wall, or the unfinished picture of a blooming schoolgirl hanging over the chimneypiece; her flowing brown hair tied with a blue riband, and her beauty remarkable for a quite childish, almost babyish, touch of saucy discontent, comically conscious of itself. (There is not the least artistic merit in this picture, which is a mere daub; but it is clear that the painter had made it humorously—one might almost say, revengefully—like the original.)

"We shall miss you, Jasper, at the 'Alternate Musical Wednesdays' to-night; but no doubt you are best at home. Good-night. God bless you! 'Tell me, shep-herds te-e-ell me, tell me-e-e, have you seen (have you seen, have you seen, have you seen) my-y-y Flo-o-ora-a pass this way!' " Melodiously good Minor Canon the Reverend Septimus Crisparkle thus delivers himself, in musical rhythm, as he withdraws his amiable face from the doorway and conveys it down stairs.

Sounds of recognition and greeting pass between the Reverend Septimus and somebody else, at the stair-foot. Mr. Jasper listens, starts from his chair, and catches a young fellow in his arms, exclaiming:

"My dear Edwin!"

"My dear Jack! So glad to see you!"

"Get off your greatcoat, bright boy, and sit down here in your own corner. Your feet are not wet? Pull your boots off. Do pull your boots off."

"My dear Jack, I am as dry as a bone. Don't moddley-coddley, there's a good fellow. I like anything better than being moddley-coddleyed."

With the check upon him of being unsympathetically restrained in a genial outburst of enthusiasm, Mr. Jasper stands still, and looks on intently at the young fellow, divesting himself of his outer coat, hat, gloves, and so forth. Once for all, a look of intentness and intensity—a look of hungry, exacting, watchful, and yet devoted affection—is always, now and ever afterwards, on the Jasper face whenever the Jasper face is addressed in this direction. And whenever it is so addressed, it is never, on this occasion or on any other, dividedly addressed; it is always concentrated.

"Now I am right, and now I'll take my corner, Jack. Any dinner, Jack?"

Mr. Jasper opens a door at the upper end of the room, and discloses a small inner room pleasantly lighted and prepared, wherein a comely dame is in the act of setting dishes on table.

"What a jolly old Jack it is!" cries the young fellow, with a clap of his hands. "Look here, Jack; tell me; whose birthday is it?"

"Not yours, I know," Mr. Jasper answers, pausing to consider.

"Not mine, you know? No; not mine, *I* know! Pussy's!"

Fixed as the look the young fellow meets, is, there is yet in it some strange power of suddenly including the sketch over the chimneypiece.

"Pussy's, Jack! We must drink Many happy returns to her. Come, uncle; take your dutiful and sharp-set nephew in to dinner."

As the boy (for he is little more) lays a hand on Jasper's shoulder, Jasper cordially and gaily lands a hand on *his* shoulder, and so Marseillaise-wise they go in to dinner.

"And Lord! Here's Mrs. Tope!" cries the boy. "Lovelier than ever!"

"Never you mind me, Master Edwin," retorts the Verger's wife; "I can take care of myself."

"You can't. You're much too handsome. Give me a kiss, because it's Pussy's birthday."

"I'd Pussy you, young man, if I was Pussy, as you call her," Mrs. Tope blushingly retorts, after being saluted. "Your uncle's too much wrapt up in you, that's where it is. He makes so much of you, that it's my opinion you think you've only to call your Pussys by the dozen, to make 'em come."

"You forget, Mrs. Tope," Mr. Jasper interposes, taking his place at table with a genial smile, "and so do you, Ned, that Uncle and Nephew are words prohibited here by common consent and express agreement. For what we are going to receive His holy name be praised!"

"Done like the Dean! Witness, Edwin Drood! Please to carve, Jack, for I can't."

This sally ushers in the dinner. Little to the present purpose, or to any purpose, is said, while it is in course of being disposed of. At length the cloth is drawn, and a dish of walnuts and a decanter of rich-coloured sherry are placed upon the table.

"I say! Tell me, Jack," the young fellow then flows on: "do you really and truly feel as if the mention of our relationship divided us at all? *I* don't."

"Uncles as a rule, Ned, are so much older than their nephews," is the reply, "that I have that feeling instinctively."

"As a rule? Ah, may-be! But what is a difference in age of half a dozen years or so? And some uncles, in large families, are even younger than their nephews. By George, I wish it was the case with us!"

"Why?"

"Because if it was, I'd take the lead with you, Jack, and be as wise as Begone dull care that turned a young man grey, and begone dull care that turned an old man to clay.——Halloa, Jack! Don't drink."

"Why not?"

"Asks why not, on Pussy's birthday, and no Happy Returns proposed! Pussy, Jack, and many of 'em! Happy returns, I mean."

Laying an affectionate and laughing touch on the boy's extended hand, as if it were at once his giddy head and his light heart, Mr. Jasper drinks the toast in silence.

"Hip, hip, hip, and nine times nine, and one to finish with, and all that, understood. Hooray, hooray, hooray! And now, Jack, let's have a little talk about Pussy. Two pairs of nut-crackers? Pass me one, and take the other." Crack. "How's Pussy getting on, Jack?"

"With her music? Fairly."

"What a dreadfully conscientious fellow you are, Jack. But *I* know, Lord bless you! Inattentive, isn't she?"

"She can learn anything, if she will."

"*If* she will? Egad that's it. But if she won't?"

Crack. On Mr. Jasper's part.

"How's she looking, Jack?"

Mr. Jasper's concentrated face again includes the portrait as he returns: "Very like your sketch indeed."

"I *am* a little proud of it," says the young fellow, glancing up at the sketch with complacency, and then shutting one eye, and taking a corrected prospect of it over a level bridge of nut-cracker in the air: "Not badly hit off from memory. But I ought to have caught that expression pretty well, for I have seen it often enough."

Crack. On Edwin Drood's part.

Crack. On Mr. Jasper's part.

"In point of fact," the former resumes, after some silent dipping among his fragments of walnut with an air of pique, "I see it whenever I go to see Pussy. If I don't find it on her face, I leave it there. —You know I do, Miss Scornful Pert. Booh!" With a twirl of the nut-crackers at the portrait.

Crack. Crack. Crack. Slowly, on Mr. Jasper's part.

Crack. Sharply, on the part of Edwin Drood.

Silence on both sides.

"Have you lost your tongue, Jack?"

"Have you found yours, Ned?"

"No, but really; —isn't it, you know, after all?"

Mr. Jasper lifts his dark eyebrows inquiringly.

"Isn't it unsatisfactory to be cut off from choice in such a matter? There, Jack! I tell you! If I could choose, I would choose Pussy from all the pretty girls in the world."

"But you have not got to choose."

"That's what I complain of. My dead and gone father and Pussy's dead and gone father must needs marry us together by anticipation. Why the——Devil, I was going to say, if it had been respectful to their memory——couldn't they leave us alone?"

"Tut, tut, dear boy," Mr. Jasper remonstrates, in a tone of gentle deprecation.

"Tut, tut? Yes, Jack, it's all very well for *you. You* can take it easily. *Your* life is not laid down to scale, and lined and dotted out for you, like a surveyor's plan. *You* have no uncomfortable suspicion that you are forced upon anybody, nor has anybody an uncomfortable suspicion that she is forced upon you, or that you are forced upon her. *You* can choose for yourself. Life, for *you*, is a plum with the natural bloom on; it hasn't been over-carefully wiped off for *you*——"

"Don't stop, dear fellow. Go on."

"Can I anyhow have hurt your feelings, Jack?"

"How can you have hurt my feelings?"

"Good Heaven, Jack, you look frightfully ill! There's a strange film come over your eyes."

Mr. Jasper, with a forced smile, stretches out his right hand, as if at once to disarm apprehension and gain time to get better. After a while he says faintly:

"I have been taking opium for a pain—an agony—that some-times overcomes me. The effects of the medicine steal over me like a blight or a cloud, and pass. You see them in the act of passing; they will be gone directly. Look away from me. They will go all the sooner."

With a scared face, the younger man complies, by casting his eyes downward at the ashes on the hearth. Not relaxing his own gaze at the fire, but rather strengthening it with a fierce, firm grip upon his elbow-chair, the elder sits for a few moments rigid, and then, with thick drops standing on his forehead, and a sharp catch of his breath, becomes as he was before. On his so subsiding in his chair, his nephew gently and assiduously tends him while he quite recovers. When Jasper is restored, he lays a tender hand upon his nephew's shoulder, and, in a tone of voice less troubled than the purport of his words—indeed with something of raillery or banter in it—thus addresses him:

"There is said to be a hidden skeleton in every house; but you thought there was none in mine, dear Ned."

"Upon my life, Jack, I did think so. However, when I come to consider that even in Pussy's house—if she had one—and in mine—if I had one———"

"You were going to say (but that I interrupted you in spite of myself) what a quiet life mine is. No whirl and uproar around me, no distracting commerce or calculation, no risk, no change of place, myself devoted to the art I pursue, my business my pleasure."

"I really was going to say something of the kind, Jack; but you see, you, speaking of yourself, almost necessarily leave out much that I should have put in. For instance: I should have put in the foreground, your being so much respected as Lay Precentor, or Lay Clerk, or whatever you call it, of this Cathedral; your enjoying the reputation of having done such wonders with the choir; your choosing your society, and holding such an independent position in this queer old place; your gift of teaching (why, even Pussy, who don't like being taught, says there never was such a Master as you are!) and your connexion."

"Yes; I saw what you were tending to. I hate it."

"Hate it, Jack?" (Much bewildered.)

"I hate it. The cramped monotony of my existence grinds me away by the grain. How does our service sound to you?"

"Beautiful! Quite celestial."

"It often sounds to me quite devilish. I am so weary of it. The echoes of my own voice among the arches seem to mock me with my daily drudging round. No wretched monk who droned his life away in that gloomy place, before me, can have been more tired of it than I am. He could take for relief (and did take) to carving demons out of the stalls and seats and desks. What shall I do? Must I take to carving them out of my heart?"

"I thought you had so exactly found your niche in life, Jack," Edwin Drood returns, astonished, bending forward in his chair to lay a sympathetic hand on Jasper's knee, and looking at him with an anxious face.

"I know you thought so. They all think so."

"Well; I suppose they do," says Edwin, meditating aloud. "Pussy thinks so."

"When did she tell you that?"

"The last time I was here. You remember when. Three months ago."

"How did she phrase it?"

"Oh! She only said that she had become your pupil, and that you were made for your vocation."

The younger man glances at the portrait. The elder sees it in him.

"Anyhow, my dear Ned," Jasper resumes, as he shakes his head with a grave cheerfulness: "I must subdue myself to my vocation: which is much the same thing outwardly. It's too late to find another now. This is a confidence between us."

"It shall be sacredly preserved, Jack."

"I have reposed it in you, because———"

"I feel it, I assure you. Because we are fast friends, and because you love and trust me, as I love and trust you. Both hands, Jack."

As each stands looking into the other's eyes, and as the uncle holds the nephew's hands, the uncle thus proceeds:

"You know now, don't you, that even a poor monotonous chorister and grinder of music—in his niche—may be troubled with some stray sort of ambition, aspiration, restlessness, dissatisfaction, what shall we call it?"

"Yes, dear Jack."

"And you will remember?"

"My dear Jack, I only ask you, am I likely to forget what you have said with so much feeling?"

"Take it as a warning, then."

In the act of having his hands released, and of moving a step back, Edwin pauses for an instant to consider the application of these last words. The instant over, he says, sensibly touched:

"I am afraid I am but a shallow, surface kind of fellow, Jack, and that my headpiece is none of the best. But I needn't say I am young; and perhaps I shall not grow worse as I grow older. At all events, I hope I have something impressible within me, which feels — deeply feels — the disinterestedness of your painfully laying your inner self bare, as a warning to me."

Mr. Jasper's steadiness of face and figure becomes so marvellous that his breathing seems to have stopped.

"I couldn't fail to notice, Jack, that it cost you a great effort, and that you were very much moved, and very unlike your usual self. Of course I knew that you were extremely fond of me, but I really was not prepared for your, as I may say, sacrificing yourself to me, in that way."

Mr. Jasper, becoming a breathing man again without the smallest stage of transition between the two extreme states, lifts his shoulders, laughs, and waves his right arm.

"No; don't put the sentiment away, Jack; please don't; for I am very much in earnest. I have no doubt that that unhealthy state of mind which you have so powerfully described is attended with some real suffering, and is hard to bear. But let me reassure you, Jack, as to the chances of its overcoming Me. I don't think I am in the way of it. In some few months less than another year, you know, I shall carry Pussy off from school as Mrs. Edwin Drood. I shall then go engineering into the East, and Pussy with me. And although we have our little tiffs now, arising out of a certain unavoidable flatness that attends our love-making, owing to its end being all settled beforehand, still I have no doubt of our getting on capitally then, when it's done and can't be helped. In short, Jack, to go back to the old song I was freely quoting at dinner (and who knows old songs better than you!), my wife shall dance and I will sing, so merrily pass the day. Of Pussy's being beautiful there cannot be a doubt; —and when you are good besides, Little Miss Impudence," once more apostrophising the portrait, "I'll burn your comic likeness and paint your music-master another."

Mr. Jasper, with his hand to his chin, and with an expression of musing benevolence on his face, has attentively watched every animated look and gesture attending the delivery of these words. He remains in that attitude after they are spoken, as if in a kind of fascination attendant on his strong interest in the youthful spirit that he loves so well. Then, he says with a quiet smile:

"You won't be warned, then?"

"No, Jack."

"You can't be warned, then?"

"No, Jack, not by you. Besides that I don't really consider myself in danger, I don't like your putting yourself in that position."

"Shall we go and walk in the churchyard?"

"By all means. You won't mind my slipping out of it for half a moment to the Nuns' House, and leaving a parcel there? Only gloves for Pussy; as many pairs of gloves as she is years old today. Rather poetical, Jack?"

Mr. Jasper, still in the same attitude, murmurs: " 'Nothing half so sweet in life,' Ned!"

"Here's the parcel in my greatcoat pocket. They must be presented to-night, or the poetry is gone. It's against regulations for me to call at night, but not to leave a packet. I am ready, Jack!"

Mr. Jasper dissolves his attitude, and they go out together.

3.

ON THIS AMBIGUOUS NOTE Chapter Two concludes. We are sure, reader, you did not fail to notice the genial pun in the title, and also the delicious ecclesiastical scene which Dickens uses like a shuttle on which to weave the first threads of his plot. Such devices, we must not forget, constitute the very essence of the novelist's art, and his skill can be measured by how successfully he manages to "palm off the information" without seeming to do so, rather in the manner of a conjuror (and Dickens was a keen amateur conjuror, who never missed an opportunity to perform before spellbound audiences of children).

But the crime-specialists are already hard at work, assessing the wealth of information provided in Chapter Two. Let us listen to what they have to say.

Actually, they're not saying anything at the moment, because Holmes, after a word with the chairman, has left the platform and is taking a seat in the audience. Why? The famous detective, Dr Wilmot announces briefly, will make a statement clarifying this change of position at the end of Chapter Three. Holmes's place is taken by Porfiry Petrovich, the examining magistrate of the Criminal Investigations Office of St. Petersburg, who immediately saw to the heart of the matter in *Crime and Punishment*.

"So what do you think of Jasper's great secret? You're not going to tell us that it baffles you?" Toad attacks him at once. "He's insanely jealous of his nephew and has decided to get rid of him: that's all there is to it. A tuppeny-ha'penny mystery, like the instalments it came out in."

"Well, actually, here it says a shilling," Loredana murmurs, examining the cover of her issue.

The Czarist magistrate smiles at the girl through the smoke of his eternal cigarette, but he addresses Toad in a tone of sincere regret: "No, no, dear sir. I fear I must disagree. Dickens is a popular writer, but he is certainly not slipshod or superficial. And here you must allow me to mention Dostoevsky's admiration for him—an admiration raised even to the level of a cult. Indeed, in many of his works, and particularly in *The Insulted and the Injured*—Dr Wilmot will correct me if I'm wrong—we can detect a distinct Dickensian influence."

Dr Wilmot does not correct him, and the investigator, after apologising for the digression, proceeds: "In short, and this is my point, Jasper is by no means a mere run-of-the-mill hypocrite, hiding his sneer behind a smile;

no dime-a-dozen villain from some serial-novel (the story of Raskolnikov, too, I might add, was first published in instalments, in *Ruskij Jazyk*). Jasper is a complex and tormented man. His affection for Drood is sincere and spontaneous; there is nothing artificial about his attitude towards his nephew. His conscience struggles desperately against . . ."

Yes, no doubt, and we are sure that nobody wishes to interrupt this elaborate defence of Jasper (Jasper as a literary creation, that is, quite apart from any proven or presumed guilt on his part). But let us withdraw for one moment, reader, to consider the two schools of thought, as it were, that are forming within the convention, even before Drood is murdered (if he ever *does* get murdered).

The first could be called the Porfiry Petrovich School, of the *Porfirians*, who already consider the MED to be less a detective novel than a psychological thriller—if not indeed a psychiatric thriller, on account of the opium. The other school, which we will call the Christie School, or the *Agathists*, claim that the novel's detective-story intention is clear from the very beginning, and demand a surprise ending.

The fragments of sentences that ricochet from the Dickens Room tell us that battle between the two camps has already been joined.

". . . nature of the murderer. And, in my opinion, it is this that the author . . ."

". . . nothing against psychology, just so long as . . ."

". . . has got to be someone else, because in a real detective story the prime suspect is never . . ."

". . . unless he himself has fabricated the evidence that indicates his guilt, so that when it's proved false . . ."

"But this is Dickens, for God's sake, not some old hack like . . ."

"No need to get personal. Dickens is Dickens, we know, but he too . . ."

The debate continues heatedly until the chairman's repeated appeals finally re-establish order of a kind. When we return to the room, Loredana is writing a list on the blackboard near the platform, to Dupin's dictation.

UN-NAMED OPIUM ADDICT

LANDLADY OF THE DEN

TWO OTHER CLIENTS OF THE DEN

CHINAMAN (landlord of another den)

MR TOPE (Cathedral verger)

CHOIRBOYS

THE DEAN

DEAN'S WIFE

DEAN'S UNMARRIED DAUGHTER

REV. CRISPARKLE

JOHN JASPER (Choirmaster and Drood's uncle; perhaps the same person as the Opium Addict at the beginning and perhaps the Wicked Man of Ezekiel)

"PUSSY" (school-girl, Drood's fiancée; we have seen only her portrait)

EDWIN DROOD (Jasper's young nephew, an engineer, and Pussy's fiancé)

MRS TOPE (verger's wife and occasionally Jasper's charwoman)

"Fine," Dupin thanks her. "We now have a complete list of the characters in the first two chapters. Or, if you prefer, of the suspects."

"Suspects, suspects," the Agathist School says unanimously.

"Characters," protest the Porfirians, who consider that suspecting a school-girl or, worse still, the Dean and his daughter, would compromise the seriousness of the discussion.

The chairman gives the floor to Superintendent Battle of Scotland Yard, who although intimate with Poirot, has never belonged to a school of any sort. A stolid, positive man, for whom the only thing that counts is results.

"I remember," he says phlegmatically, "many years ago, I was talking to an inspector about the Waynflate case . . ."

"The Waynflate case, *parfaitement*," Poirot says, nodding.

". . . and as an example of persons who were not suspected but *suspectable* I listed the following: a young school-girl, a highly virtuous spinster-lady, and a high-ranking dignitary of the Anglican church."

"You refer to our characters?"

"No, no. I refer only to the fact that *anybody* can be a criminal."

This irrefutable statement is necessarily accepted by all, and the editor of *The Dickensian*, who knows every detail of everything that has been written on the Drood case, is summoned to the blackboard.

"In theory," Maigret says, handing him the chalk, "all these good people are 'suspectable' with regard to the case we are examining. But to simplify matters, could you cross out all those who have never been suspected by any of our predecessors?"

Wilmot crosses out the Dean and his wife and daughter. He also crosses out Rev. Crisparkle, the "two other clients of the den," and then, after a moment's hesitation, Drood. Then he stops.

"Of course," he says, "we must bear in mind that the 'reconstructions' attempted so far are by no means all on the same level. Many are even . . ."

"Of course."

"And so, it remains only to eliminate the Opium Addict: because, as I said, nobody has ever doubted that he and Jasper are . . . the same person."

"Yet you have not eliminated him," says Maigret, studying his pipe. "Why?"

"Ah," says Wilmot, "you put me in a difficult position, Inspector."

Any reader who likes to imagine Dr Wilmot sitting in Maigret's office, with Maigret facing him as Inspectors Lucas and Janvier fire relentless questions, is of course free to do so. But don't expect to find him brow-beaten and ready to "blow the gaff." His demeanour remains reticent, even evasive. He is not (he repeats) unwilling to furnish information on previous research, or about clues that have already been uncovered. Indeed, he is here for that very purpose. But, he insists, he thinks it better if certain over-audacious theories are left alone for the moment, "so as not to influence the normal course of the enquiry." This, he reaffirms, is "in the interests of justice, if I may put it like that."

And so, all that the staff of the Quai des Orfèvres manage to worm out of him is the suggestion that they might "keep an eye on Jasper's sudden transformations": at one moment he is normal, at another (could this be an effect of the opium he takes allegedly as medicine?) he is not, and at yet another he is, as Drood tells him at a certain point, "very unlike his usual self."

Maigret takes note of this. But it's not the uncle's transformations that strike him as peculiar in that conversation, he says; it is the nephew's gullibility. Can the young man really take Jasper's scarcely veiled threat as a sign of "fondness" for him? Does he really see nothing sinister in the invitation to "go and walk in the churchyard"?

The chairman throws his hands wide. "There's no denying that Drood's intelligence quotient appears to be well below average. However," he adds, nodding to the hostess, "let's hear the third chapter before we discuss this point further."

CHAPTER III

THE NUNS' HOUSE

FOR sufficient reasons which this narrative will itself unfold as it advances, a fictitious name must be bestowed upon the old Cathedral town. Let it stand in these pages as Cloisterham. It was once possibly known to the Druids by another name, and certainly to the Romans by another, and to the Saxons by another, and to the Normans by another; and a name more or less in the course of many centuries can be of little moment to its dusty chronicles.

An ancient city, Cloisterham, and no meet dwelling-place for any one with hankerings after the noisy world. A monotonous, silent city, deriving an earthy flavor throughout, from its cathedral crypt, and so abounding in vestiges of monastic graves, that the Cloisterham children grow small salad in the dust of abbots and abbesses, and make dirt-pies of nuns and friars; while every ploughman in its outlying fields renders to once puissant Lord Treasurers, Archbishops, Bishops, and such-like, the attention which the Ogre in the story-book desired to render to his unbidden visitor, and grinds their bones to make his bread.

A drowsy city, Cloisterham, whose inhabitants seem to suppose, with an inconsistency more strange than rare, that all its changes lie behind it, and that there are no more to come. A queer moral to derive from antiquity, yet older than any traceable antiquity. So silent are the streets of Cloisterham (though prone to echo on the smallest provocation), that of a summer-day the sunblinds of its shops dare to flap in the south wind; while the sun-browned tramps who pass along and stare, quicken their limp a little, that they may the sooner get beyond the confines of its oppressive respectability. This is a feat not difficult of achievement, seeing that the streets of Cloisterham city are little more than one narrow street by which you get into it and get out of it: the rest being mostly disappointing yards with pumps in them and no thoroughfare—exception made of the Cathedral-close, and a paved Quaker settlement, in color and general conformation very like a Quakeress's bonnet, up in a shady corner.

In a word, a city of another and a bygone time is Cloisterham, with its hoarse cathedral bell, its hoarse rooks hovering about the Cathedral tower, its hoarser and less distinct rooks in the stalls far beneath. Fragments of old wall, saint's chapel, chapter-house, convent, and monastery, have got incongruously or obstructively built into many of its houses and gardens, much as kindred jumbled notions have become incorporated into many of its citizens' minds. All things in it are of the past. Even its single pawnbroker takes in no pledges, nor has he for a long time, but offers vainly an unredeemed stock for sale, of which the costlier articles are dim and pale old watches apparently in a slow perspiration, tarnished sugar-tongs with ineffectual legs, and odd volumes of dismal books. The most abundant and the most agreeable evidences of progressing life in Cloisterham, are the evidences of vegetable life in its many gardens; even its drooping and despondent little theatre has its poor strip of garden, receiving the foul fiend, when he ducks from its stage into the infernal regions, among scarlet beans or oyster-shells, according to the season of the year.

In the midst of Cloisterham stands the Nuns' House; a venerable brick edifice whose present appellation is doubtless derived from the legend of its conventual uses. On the trim gate enclosing its old courtyard, is a resplendent brass plate flashing forth the legend: "Seminary for Young Ladies. Miss Twinkleton." The house-front is so old and worn, and the brass plate is so shining and staring, that the general result has reminded imaginative strangers of a battered old beau with a large modern eye-glass stuck in his blind eye.

Whether the nuns of yore, being of a submissive rather than a stiff-necked generation, habitually bent their contemplative heads to avoid collision with the beams in the low ceilings of the many chambers of their House; whether they sat in its long low windows, telling their beads for their mortification instead of making necklaces of them for their adornment; whether they were ever walled up alive in odd angles and jutting gables of the building for having some ineradicable leaven of busy Mother Nature in them which has kept the fermenting world alive ever since; these may be matters of interest to its haunting ghosts (if any), but constitute no item in Miss Twinkleton's half-yearly accounts. They are neither of Miss Twinkleton's inclusive regulars, nor of her extras. The lady who undertakes the poetical department of the establishment at so much (or so little) a quarter, has no pieces in her list of recitals bearing on such unprofitable questions.

As, in some cases of drunkenness, and in others of animal magnetism, there are two states of consciousness which never clash, but each of which pursues its separate course as though it were continuous instead of broken (thus if I hide my watch when I am drunk, I must be drunk again before I can remember where), so Miss Twinkleton has two distinct and separate phases of being. Every night, the moment the young ladies have retired to rest, does Miss Twinkleton smarten up her curls a little, brighten up her eyes a little, and become a sprightlier Miss Twinkleton than the young ladies have ever seen. Every night, at the same hour, does Miss Twinkleton resume the topics of the previous night, comprehending the tenderer scandal of Cloisterham, of which she has no knowledge whatever by day, and references to a certain season at Tunbridge Wells (airily called by Miss Twinkleton in this state of her existence "The Wells"), notably the season wherein a certain finished gentleman (compassionately called by Miss Twinkleton in this state of her existence, "Foolish Mr. Porters") revealed a homage of the heart, whereof Miss Twinkleton, in her scholastic state of existence, is as ignorant as a granite pillar. Miss Twinkleton's companion in both states of existence, and equally adaptable to either, is one Mrs. Tisher: a deferential widow with a weak back, a chronic sigh, and a suppressed voice, who looks after the young ladies' wardrobes, and leads them to infer that she has seen better days. Perhaps this is the reason why it is an article of faith with the servants, handed down from race to race, that the departed Tisher was a hairdresser.

The pet pupil of the Nuns' House is Miss Rosa Bud, of course called Rosebud; wonderfully pretty, wonderfully childish, wonderfully whimsical. An awkward interest (awkward because romantic) attaches to Miss Bud in the minds of the young ladies, on account of its being known to them that a husband has been chosen for her by will and bequest, and that her guardian is bound down to bestow her on that husband when he comes of age. Miss Twinkleton, in her seminarial state of existence, has combated the romantic aspect of this destiny by affecting to shake her head over it behind Miss Bud's dimpled shoulders, and to brood on the unhappy lot of that doomed little victim. But with no better effect—possibly some unfelt touch of foolish Mr. Porters has undermined the endeavour—than to evoke from the young ladies a unanimous bedchamber cry of "Oh! what a pretending old thing Miss Twinkleton is, my dear!"

The Nuns' House is never in such a state of flutter as when this allotted husband calls to see little Rosebud. (It is unanimously understood by the young ladies that he is lawfully entitled to this privilege, and that if Miss Twinkleton disputed it she would be instantly taken up and transported.) When his ring at the gate bell is expected, or takes place, every young lady who can, under any pretence, look out of window, looks out of window: while every young lady who is "practising," practises out of time; and the French class becomes so demoralized that the Mark goes round as briskly as the bottle at a convivial party in the last century.

On the afternoon of the day next after the dinner of two at the Gate House, the bell is rung with the usual fluttering results.

"Mr. Edwin Drood to see Miss Rosa."

This is the announcement of the parlour-maid in chief. Miss Twinkleton, with an exemplary air of melancholy on her, turns to the sacrifice, and says: "You may go down, my dear." Miss Bud goes down, followed by all eyes.

Mr. Edwin Drood is waiting in Miss Twinkleton's own parlour: a dainty room, with nothing more directly scholastic in it than a terrestrial and a celestial globe. These expressive machines imply (to parents and guardians) that even when Miss Twinkleton retires into the bosom of privacy, duty may at any moment compel her to become a sort of Wandering Jewess, scouring the earth and soaring through the skies in search of knowledge for her pupils.

The last new maid, who has never seen the young gentleman Miss Rosa is engaged to, and who is making his acquaintance between the hinges of the open door, left open for the purpose, stumbles guiltily down the kitchen stairs, as a charming little apparition with its face concealed by a little silk apron thrown over its head, glides into the parlour.

"Oh! It *is* so ridiculous!" says the apparition, stopping and shrinking. "Don't, Eddy!"

"Don't what, Rosa?"

"Don't come any nearer, please. It *is* so absurd."

"What is absurd, Rosa?"

"The whole thing is. It *is* so absurd to be an engaged orphan;

and it *is* so absurd to have the girls and the servants scuttling about after one, like mice in the wainscot; and it *is* so absurd to be called upon!"

The apparition appears to have a thumb in the corner of its mouth while making this complaint.

"You give me an affectionate reception, Pussy, I must say."

"Well, I will in a minute, Eddy, but I can't just yet. How are you?" (very shortly).

"I am unable to reply that I am much the better for seeing you, Pussy, inasmuch as I see nothing of you."

This second remonstrance brings a dark bright pouting eye out from a corner of the apron; but it swiftly becomes invisible again, as the apparition exclaims: "Oh! Good Gracious, you have had half your hair cut off!"

"I should have done better to have had my head cut off, I think," says Edwin, rumpling the hair in question, with a fierce glance at the looking-glass, and giving an impatient stamp. "Shall I go?"

"No; you needn't go just yet, Eddy. The girls would all be asking questions why you went."

"Once for all, Rosa, will you uncover that ridiculous little head of yours and give me a welcome?"

The apron is pulled off the childish head, as its wearer replies: "You're very welcome, Eddy. There! I'm sure that's nice. Shake hands. No, I can't kiss you, because I've got an acidulated drop in my mouth."

"Are you at all glad to see me, Pussy?"

"Oh, yes, I'm dreadfully glad. —Go and sit down. —Miss Twinkleton."

It is the custom of that excellent lady, when these visits occur, to appear every three minutes, either in her own person or in that of Mrs. Tisher, and lay an offering on the shrine of Propriety by affecting to look for some desiderated article. On the present occasion, Miss Twinkleton, gracefully gliding in and out, says, in passing: "How do you do, Mr. Drood? Very glad indeed to have the pleasure. Pray excuse me. Tweezers. Thank you!"

"I got the gloves last evening, Eddy, and I like them very much. They are beauties."

"Well, that's something," the affianced replies, half grumbling. "The smallest encouragement thankfully received. And how did you pass your birthday, Pussy?"

"Delightfully! Everybody gave me a present. And we had a feast. And we had a ball at night."

"A feast and a ball, eh? These occasions seem to go off tolerably well without me, Pussy."

"De-lightfully!" cries Rosa, in a quite spontaneous manner, and without the least pretence of reserve.

"Hah! And what was the feast?"

"Tarts, oranges, jellies, and shrimps."

"Any partners at the ball?"

"We danced with one another, of course, sir. But some of the girls made game to be their brothers. It *was* so droll!"

"Did anybody make game to be———"

"To be you? Oh dear yes!" cries Rosa, laughing with great enjoyment. "That was the first thing done."

"I hope she did it pretty well," says Edwin, rather doubtfully.

"Oh! It was excellent —I wouldn't dance with you, you know."

Edwin scarcely seems to see the force of this; begs to know if he may take the liberty to ask why?

"Because I was so tired of you," returns Rosa. But she quickly adds, and pleadingly too, seeing displeasure in his face: "Dear Eddy, you were just as tired of me, you know."

"Did I say so, Rosa?"

"Say so! Do you ever say so? No, you only showed it. Oh, she did it so well!" cries Rosa, in a sudden ecstasy with her counterfeit betrothed.

"It strikes me that she must be a devilish impudent girl," says Edwin Drood. "And so, Pussy, you have passed your last birthday in this old house."

"Ah, yes!" Rosa clasps her hands, looks down with a sigh, and shakes her head.

"You seem to be sorry, Rosa."

"I am sorry for the poor old place. Somehow, I feel as if it would miss me, when I am gone so far away, so young."

"Perhaps we had better stop short, Rosa?"

She looks up at him with a swift bright look; next moment shakes her head, sighs, and looks down again.

"That is to say, is it, Pussy, that we are both resigned?"

She nods her head again, and after a short silence, quaintly bursts out with: "You know we must be married, and married from here, Eddy, or the poor girls will be so dreadfully disappointed!"

For the moment there is more of compassion, both for her and for himself, in her affianced husband's face, than there is of love. He checks the look, and asks: "Shall I take you out for a walk, Rosa dear?"

Rosa dear does not seem at all clear on this point, until her face, which has been comically reflective, brightens. "Oh yes, Eddy; let us go for a walk! And I tell you what we'll do. You shall pretend that you are engaged to somebody else, and I'll pretend that I am not engaged to anybody, and then we shan't quarrel."

"Do you think that will prevent our falling out, Rosa?"

"I know it will. Hush! Pretend to look out of window. —Mrs. Tisher!"

Through a fortuitous concourse of accidents, the matronly Tisher heaves in sight, says, in rustling through the room like the legendary ghost of a Dowager in silken skirts: "I hope I see Mr. Drood well; though I needn't ask, if I may judge from his complexion? I trust I disturb no one; but there *was* a paper-knife— Oh, thank you, I am sure!" and disappears with her prize.

"One other thing you must do, Eddy, to oblige me," says Rosebud. "The moment we get into the street, you must put me outside, and keep close to the house yourself—squeeze and graze yourself against it."

"By all means, Rosa, if you wish it. Might I ask why?"

"Oh! because I don't want the girls to see you."

"It's a fine day; but would you like me to carry an umbrella up?"

"Don't be foolish, sir. You haven't got polished leather boots on," pouting, with one shoulder raised.

"Perhaps that might escape the notice of the girls, even if they did see me," remarks Edwin, looking down at his boots with a sudden distaste for them.

"Nothing escapes their notice, sir. And then I know what would happen. Some of them would begin reflecting on me by saying (for *they* are free) that they never will on any account engage themselves to lovers without polished leather boots. Hark! Miss Twinkleton. I'll ask for leave."

That discreet lady being indeed heard without, inquiring of nobody in a blandly conversational tone as she advances: "Eh? Indeed! Are you quite sure you saw my mother-of-pearl button-holder on the work-table in my room?" is at once solicited for walking leave, and graciously accords it. And soon the young couple go out of the Nuns' House, taking all precautions against the discovery of the so vitally defective boots of Mr. Edwin Drood: precautions, let us hope, effective for the peace of Mrs. Edwin Drood that is to be.

"Which way shall we take, Rosa?"

Rosa replies: "I want to go to the Lumps-of-Delight shop."

"To the———?"

"A Turkish sweetmeat, sir. My gracious me, don't you understand anything? Call yourself an Engineer, and not know *that*?"

"Why, how should I know it, Rosa?"

64

"Because I am very fond of them. But oh! I forgot what we are to pretend. No, you needn't know anything about them; never mind."

So, he is gloomily borne off to the Lumps-of-Delight shop, where Rosa makes her purchase, and, after offering some to him (which he rather indignantly declines), begins to partake of it with great zest: previously taking off and rolling up a pair of little pink gloves, like rose-leaves, and occasionally putting her little pink fingers to her rosy lips, to cleanse them from the Dust of Delight that comes off the Lumps.

"Now, be a good-tempered Eddy, and pretend. And so you are engaged?"

"And so I am engaged."

"Is she nice?"

"Charming."

"Tall?"

"Immensely tall!" Rosa being short.

"Must be gawky, I should think," is Rosa's quiet commentary.

"I beg your pardon; not at all," contradiction rising in him. "What is termed a fine woman; a splendid woman."

"Big nose, no doubt," is the quiet commentary again.

"Not a little one, certainly," is the quick reply. (Rosa's being a little one.)

"Long pale nose, with a red knob in the middle. *I* know the sort of nose," says Rosa, with a satisfied nod, and tranquilly enjoying the Lumps.

"You *don't* know the sort of nose, Rosa," with some warmth; "because it's nothing of the kind."

"Not a pale nose, Eddy?"

"No." Determined not to assent.

"A red nose? Oh! I don't like red noses. However; to be sure she can always powder it."

"She would scorn to powder it," says Edwin, becoming heated.

"Would she? What a stupid thing she must be! Is she stupid in everything?"

"No. In nothing."

After a pause, in which the whimsically wicked face has not been unobservant of him, Rosa says:

"And this most sensible of creatures likes the idea of being carried off to Egypt; does she, Eddy?"

"Yes. She takes a sensible interest in triumphs of engineering skill: especially when they are to change the whole condition of an undeveloped country."

"Lor!" says Rosa, shrugging her shoulders, with a little laugh of wonder.

"Do you object," Edwin inquires, with a majestic turn of his eyes downward upon the fairy figure: "do you object, Rosa, to her feeling that interest?"

"Object? My dear Eddy! But really. Doesn't she hate boilers and things?"

"I can answer for her not being so idiotic as to hate Boilers," he returns with angry emphasis; "though I cannot answer for her views about Things; really not understanding what Things are meant."

"But don't she hate Arabs, and Turks, and Fellahs, and people?"

"Certainly not." Very firmly.

"At least, she *must* hate the Pyramids? Come, Eddy?"

"Why should she be such a little—tall, I mean—Goose, as to hate the Pyramids, Rosa?"

"Ah! you should hear Miss Twinkleton," often nodding her head, and much enjoying the Lumps, "bore about them, and then you wouldn't ask. Tiresome old burying-grounds! Isises, and Ibises, and Cheopses, and Pharaohses; who cares about them? And then there was Belzoni or somebody, dragged out by the legs, half choked with bats and dust. All the girls say serve him right, and hope it hurt him, and wish he had been quite choked."

The two youthful figures, side by side, but not now arm-in-arm, wander discontentedly about the old Close; and each sometimes stops and slowly imprints a deeper footstep in the fallen leaves.

"Well!" says Edwin, after a lengthy silence. "According to custom. We can't get on, Rosa."

Rosa tosses her head, and says she don't want to get on..

"That's a pretty sentiment, Rosa, considering."

"Considering what?"

"If I say what, you'll go wrong again."

"*You'll* go wrong, you mean, Eddy. Don't be ungenerous."

"Ungenerous! I like that!"

"Then I *don't* like that, and so I tell you plainly," Rosa pouts.

"Now, Rosa, I put it to you. Who disparaged my profession, my destination—"

"You are not going to be buried in the Pyramids, I hope?" she interrupts, arching her delicate eyebrows. "You never said you were. If you are, why haven't you mentioned it to me? I can't find out your plans by instinct."

"Now, Rosa; you know very well what I mean, my dear."

"Well then, why did you begin with your detestable red-nosed Giantesses? And she would, she would, she would, she would, she WOULD powder it!" cries Rosa, in a little burst of comical contradictory spleen.

"Somehow or other, I never can come right in these discussions," says Edwin, sighing and becoming resigned.

"How is it possible, sir, that you ever can come right when you're always wrong? And as to Belzoni, I suppose he's dead; —I'm sure I hope he is—and how can his legs, or his chokes concern you?"

"It is nearly time for your return, Rosa. We have not had a very happy walk, have we?"

"A happy walk? A detestably unhappy walk, sir. If I go up stairs the moment I get in and cry till I can't take my dancing-lesson, you are responsible, mind!"

"Let us be friends, Rosa."

"Ah!" cries Rosa, shaking her head and bursting into real tears.

"I wish we *could* be friends! It's because we can't be friends, that we try one another so. I am a young little thing, Eddy, to have an old heartache; but I really, really have, sometimes. Don't be angry. I know you have one yourself, too often. We should both of us have done better, if What is to be had been left, What might have been. I am quite a serious little thing now, and not teasing you. Let each of us forbear, this one time, on our own account, and on the other's!"

Disarmed by this glimpse of a woman's nature in the spoilt child, though for an instant disposed to resent it as seeming to involve the enforced infliction of himself upon her, Edwin Drood stands watching her as she childishly cries and sobs, with both hands to the handkerchief at her eyes, and then—she becoming more composed, and indeed beginning in her young inconstancy to laugh at herself for having been so moved—leads her to a seat hard by, under the elm trees.

"One clear word of understanding, Pussy dear. I am not clever out of my own line—now I come to think of it I don't know that I am particularly clever in it—but I want to do right. There is not—there may be—I really don't see my way to what I want to say, but I must say it before we part—there is not any other young——"

"Oh no, Eddy! It's generous of you to ask me; but no, no, no!"

They have come very near to the Cathedral windows, and at this moment the organ and the choir sound out sublimely. As they sit listening to the solemn swell, the confidence of last night rises in young Edwin Drood's mind, and he thinks how unlike this music is, to that discordance.

"I fancy I can distinguish Jack's voice," is his remark in a low tone in connexion with the train of thought.

"Take me back at once, please," urges his Affianced, quickly laying her light hand upon his wrist. "They will all be coming out directly; let us get away. Oh, what a resounding chord! But don't let us stop to listen to it; let us get away!"

Her hurry is over, as soon as they have passed out of the Close. They go, arm-in-arm now, gravely and deliberately enough, along the old High Street, to the Nuns' House. At the gate, the street being within sight empty, Edwin bends down his face to Rosebud's.

She remonstrates, laughing, and is a childish schoolgirl again.

"Eddy, no! I'm too sticky to be kissed. But give me your hand, and I'll blow a kiss into that."

He does so. She breathes a light breath into it, and asks, retaining it and looking into it:

"Now say, what do you see?"

"See, Rosa?"

"Why, I thought you Egyptian boys could look into a hand and see all sorts of phantoms? Can't you see a happy Future?"

For certain, neither of them sees a happy Present, as the gate opens and closes, and one goes in and the other goes away.

4.

IF INSTEAD OF INVESTIGATORS we had here a bevy of literary critics and philologists (who would not do badly to cultivate the sharp persistence of the private eye), the reader can be certain that after a chapter like the previous one there would be no avoiding a learned lecture on comparing Dickens and Alessandro Manzoni.

But as it is, only the colonel of the Carabinieri patriotically evokes the name of the great Milanese writer: Weren't Edwin and Rosa *promessi sposi,* betrothed, and isn't there an echo of Monza's *Betrothed,* where nuns are walled up alive for following their . . . er, natural instincts?

A colonel of the Carabinieri always merits respect, and Dr Wilmot murmurs suitable thanks for the interesting suggestion. But in his reference to the torbid, prison-like aspects of convent life, the anti-clerical Dickens was probably inspired more by Diderot and Voltaire than by the pious Manzoni. As for the *promessi sposi,* "Eddy" and Rosebud's situation is somewhat different—if not, indeed, the opposite—from that of Renzo and Lucia.

On the other hand we know, the editor of *The Dicken-sian* adds, that this was the very first idea for the novel. Let us travel back to April 1869. Physically exhausted by lecture-tours in America and forced to rest by his doctor, Dickens has retired to his beautiful country-house at Gadshill and is sitting at his study-window, which has a distant view of the tower of the cathedral of Rochester/ Cloisterham. Those close to him are seriously worried by the state of his circulation. Yet his extraordinary creative energy shows no signs of flagging. He has not written a single page of a novel for four years. He feels, perhaps, professional envy towards his friend Wilkie Collins, who in fact is not quite so much a friend since the sensational success of *The Moonstone,* the bestseller of 1868.

And so in the rural peace of Kent, Dickens begins to look around for a plot. The first story which comes to him is that of two adolescents who not only love each other (or believe they do) but who, by the express desire of their deceased parents, must marry when they are of age. An original twist, in which the obstacle on the road towards love and the happy ending consists in the very fact that the love and happy ending have been so carefully provided for. A few weeks later, Dickens changes the plot radically, but without giving up his pair of lovers.

We will spare the reader the sarcastic asides that Philip Marlowe and Lew Archer exchange on the subject of the betrothed couple. These "tough guys" are extra edgy due to alcohol deprivation, and their only thought now is the solemn inauguration and the refreshment that they hope will flow freely afterwards.

But others have found clues of varying importance amidst the chapter's mawkish bickering and simpering. Poirot says nothing, but he is musing over what would seem to be an unimportant detail. Gadshill . . . Gadshill . . . He repeats it over and over to himself. Where has he heard that name before? Like all Anglicised foreigners, he has dutifully read his way through the Bard's works, including the sonnets, and now his diligence is rewarded. Gadshill. Why of course, in *Henry IV, Part One*! It's where Falstaff gets a richly merited thrashing by two "rogues in buckram" (buckram: a coarse cloth stiffened with paste): two rogues, who in his heroic-epic account of the "battle" swell first to four, then seven, then eleven . . . Ever since, "men in buckram" has proverbially meant "imaginary men." And now something gently stirs in Poirot's mind, like the drifting tendril of an aquatic plant: the vague idea bobs before him, of a connection between those chimerical assailants and the "sun-browned tramps" who pass through Cloisterham at a quickened pace. A mere tough of colour to emphasise the city's gruff provincialism? Or does this little detail mean that the culprit—provided, of course, there was a crime—is going to play the usual trick of trying to persuade the inept investigators to close the case, since the evil deed was clearly the work of some "passing malefactor"?

Porfiry Petrovich meanwhile has been ferreting his way down the labyrinthine passages of psychology.

PORFIRY PETROVICH, *with fervour:* Yes, two infantile characters, two innocent souls. But only up to a point. Edwin candidly admits that he is "not clever out of his own line," and, as is typical of young men of that age, we see he cannot understand or deal with the girl's caprices and mood-changes. But there are indications that she is more than a ridiculous featherhead. When she hears Jasper's voice singing in the cathedral, she is agitated, frightened; she begs Edwin to take her away from there at once. But goes into "ecstasy" at the memory of the ball and her girlfriend dressed as a young man. Is it pushing things too far to consider such behaviour as erotic disturbance, though obviously undirected and unconscious as yet, which is typical of young women of that age?

FATHER BROWN, *with a sigh:* Sex, sex, sex . . . Poor Dickens.

ARCHER, *through clenched teeth:* Come on, behind all that Victorian holier-than-thou stuff, Dickens was no plaster saint. He got that old rake Wilkie Collins to show him the seamy side of gay Paree. He secretly supported an actress, Ellen Lawless Ternan, thirty years younger than he. There may even have been some funny business with his sister-in-law.

FATHER BROWN, *curtly:* Pure slander.

WILMOT, *conciliatory:* Well, but one can hardly imagine that so full-blooded, prodigal, and exuberant a writer was without personal knowledge of certain . . . sides of life . . .

N. WOLFE *cuts the discussion short with an impatient gesture:* Gentlemen, gentlemen, we are overlooking the main clue slipped into this chapter. Miss Twinkleton! A writer like Dickens knew that every novelistic device can be made plausible and acceptable to the reader if it is presented at a distance, subtly anticipated in a different context. When we are told that Miss Twinkleton, a typical comic spinster, lives a double life, we should be on the alert at once. There are *two* Miss Twinkletons, the author tells us, two quite separate and distinct persons, each existing unknown to the other. And he gives us the crucial example of the watch which somebody hides while drunk, and which he can find only by becoming drunk again. This is a classic case of split personality, and if Dickens presents it to us so early in the book, and in a "light-hearted" context, I have little doubt that we will see it return sooner or later in a dramatic context, if not indeed in the final solution.

TOAD, *raucous, but with the air of one who is fully aware of what he is saying:* And a fine piece of plagiary that would be!

This word cannot be allowed to slip by unremarked, reader. Toad has a certain amount of prestige in these circles, but even he cannot be permitted to level an accusation of plagiarism against one of the most fecund and imaginative novelists of all time. Words of censure rain down from all sides, and the committer of sacrilege is insulted and invited to leave the room. The most loudly indignant, naturally, are those who have the least interest in the conference; who came, with mysteriously obtained invitations, to while away an afternoon.

When an elderly lawyer, a primary-school teacher, and a young activist without a cause start to raise the decibel level of the debate, the reader can be sure that utter confusion is now guaranteed. In vain does Dr Wilmot attempt to point out that this is a specific conference on a specific novel; in vain does he repeat that D'Annunzio's plagiaries, Victorian hypocrisy, the early stages of the industrial revolution, and Dickens's zodiac sign have little to do with the argument.

He is saved by Loredana, who stems the tide of chaos by reminding everyone of a great truth: Time is flying. There is now only half an hour until the inauguration. But no need to panic. If the participants will all go to their rooms to freshen up, they will find a surprise in the hotel's complimentary basket of fruit; a scroll tied with a yellow silk ribbon containing the text of the last two chapters— four and five—of the first, April number of the MED. This is a further example of the organisers' efficiency: photocopies have been produced on Japanese handmade-paper, each one numbered and signed by the author in facsimile, so that in the course of the evening everyone will have the chance to read and meditate upon them, and even discuss them—unless of course they should be drawn by the rival attraction of the Turkish-Brazilian orchestra, who are to play on the hotel's roof-terrace after the Socialising Dinner.

Archer and Marlowe spring to their feet, run their hands over their darkly-shadowed chins but decide not to bother with a second shave, and saunter off in search of the Inauguration Room. Or rather, of the room next to it. There, as their experience of conferences tells them, a row of barmen will undoubtedly be poised to set the glasses clinking and the bottles gurgling.

The other participants disperse to their rooms. Everybody has forgotten about Sherlock Holmes and the announcement he was going to make. A moment or two later, he gives a resigned shrug and follows the others in silence.

————

The solemn inauguration of a convention is in itself a triumph of completeness. There are at least a dozen television cameras filming every part, at least thirty photographers recording every possible image, however trivial. There is a complete array of dignitaries, all dressed in sober blues and dark-greys. The ladies, too, are complete, to the last lacquered detail, from foundation cream to nail varnish, from hairdos to high heels, and amidst the glitter of their jewellery they gaze at one another in reciprocal assessment and are satisfied.

The only thing that falls short of the occasion is our journalistic talents. For example, how can we do justice to the Eternal City's welcome, a welcome conveyed not by the mayor (who was unable to make it after all) but by the deputy-mayor, who belongs to another political party but still bears a 78% resemblance to the mayor? It is a speech complete with gratitude to the sponsors, respect for the illustrious speakers and participants, Classical quotations, and references to international co-operation, world-peace, and universal brotherhood.

And the speeches of the orators who follow him are no less complete. In a hundred ingenious ways, the concept of completeness is pulled to pieces and put together again, each speaker parading his repertoire of quotations, examples, metaphors, and theories. Plato and Dante, Pericles and the Renaissance, Leibniz and the Encyclopaedists, not to mention physics, astronomy, geometry, matrimony, the ecosystem, UNESCO, Interpol, a drop of water, a simple wild rose.

All orotund speeches, orotundly delivered. But why bother listening to them, reader, when Dickens's satirical genius offers us the very quintessence of pomposity in Mr Sapsea? Why not imitate the Drood work-group, as one by one they surreptitiously unroll their scrolls and settle down to read the last two chapters of the first number? Let's unroll with them.

CHAPTER IV

MR. SAPSEA

ACCEPTING the Jackass as the type of self-sufficient stupidity and conceit—a custom, perhaps, like some few other customs, more conventional than fair—then the purest Jackass in Cloisterham is Mr. Thomas Sapsea, Auctioneer.

Mr. Sapsea "dresses at" the Dean; has been bowed to for the Dean, in mistake; has even been spoken to in the street as My Lord, under the impression that he was the Bishop come down unexpectedly, without his chaplain. Mr. Sapsea is very proud of this, and of his voice, and of his style. He has even (in selling landed property), tried the experiment of slightly intoning in his pulpit, to make himself more like what he takes to be the genuine ecclesiastical article. So, in ending a Sale by Public Auction, Mr. Sapsea finishes off with an air of bestowing a benediction on the assembled brokers, which leaves the real Dean—a modest and worthy gentleman—far behind.

Mr. Sapsea has many admirers; indeed, the proposition is carried by a large local majority, even including non-believers in his wisdom, that he is a credit to Cloisterham. He possesses the great qualities of being portentous and dull, and of having a roll in his speech, and another roll in his gait; not to mention a certain gravely flowing action with his hands, as if he were presently going to Confirm the individual with whom he holds discourse. Much nearer sixty years of age than fifty, with a flowing outline of stomach, and horizontal creases in his waistcoat; reputed to be rich; voting at elections in the strictly respectable interest; morally satisfied that nothing but he himself has grown since he was a baby; how can dunder-headed Mr. Sapsea be otherwise than a credit to Cloisterham, and society?

Mr. Sapsea's premises are in the High Street, over against the Nuns' House. They are of about the period of the Nuns' House, irregularly modernized here and there, as steadily deteriorating generations found, more and more, that they preferred air and light to Fever and the Plague. Over the doorway, is a wooden effigy, about half life-size, representing Mr. Sapsea's father, in a curly wig and toga, in the act of selling. The chastity of the idea, and the natural appearance of the little finger, hammer, and pulpit, have been much admired.

Mr. Sapsea sits in his dull ground-floor sitting-room, giving first on his paved back yard, and then on his railed-off garden. Mr. Sapsea has a bottle of port wine on a table before the fire—the fire is an early luxury, but pleasant on the cool, chilly autumn evening—and is characteristically attended by his portrait, his eight-day clock, and his weather-glass. Characteristically, because he would uphold himself against mankind, his weather-glass against weather, and his clock against time.

By Mr. Sapsea's side on the table are a writing-desk and writing materials. Glancing at a scrap of manuscript, Mr. Sapsea reads it to himself with a lofty air, and then, slowly pacing the room with his thumbs in the arm-holes of his waistcoat, repeats it from memory: so internally, though with much dignity, that the word "Ethelinda" is alone audible.

There are three clean wineglasses in a tray on the table. His serving-maid entering, and announcing "Mr. Jasper is come, sir," Mr. Sapsea waves "Admit him" and draws two wineglasses from the rank, as being claimed.

"Glad to see you, sir. I congratulate myself on having the honor of receiving you here for the first time." Mr. Sapsea does the honors of his house in this wise.

"You are very good. The honor is mine and the self-congratulation is mine."

"You are pleased to say so, sir. But I do assure you that it is a satisfaction to me to receive you in my humble home. And that is what I would not say to everybody." Ineffable loftiness on Mr. Sapsea's part accompanies these words, as leaving the sentence to be understood: "You will not easily believe that your society can be a satisfaction to a man like myself; nevertheless, it is."

"I have for some time desired to know you, Mr. Sapsea."

"And I, sir, have long known you by reputation as a man of taste. Let me fill your glass. I will give you, sir," says Mr. Sapsea, filling his own:

> "When the French come over,
> May we meet them at Dover!"

This was a patriotic toast in Mr. Sapsea's infancy, and he is therefore fully convinced of its being appropriate to any subsequent era.

"You can scarcely be ignorant, Mr. Sapsea," observes Jasper, watching the auctioneer with a smile as the latter stretches out his legs before the fire, "that you know the world."

"Well, sir," is the chuckling reply, "I think I know something of it; something of it."

"Your reputation for that knowledge has always interested and surprised me, and made me wish to know you. For, Cloisterham is a little place. Cooped up in it myself, I know nothing beyond it, and feel it to be a very little place."

"If I have not gone to foreign countries, young man," Mr. Sapsea begins, and then stops: ——"You will excuse my calling you young man, Mr. Jasper? You are much my junior."

"By all means."

"If I have not gone to foreign countries, young man, foreign countries have come to me. They have come to me in the way of business, and I have improved upon my opportunities. Put it that I take an inventory, or make a catalogue. I see a French clock. I never saw him before, in my life, but instantly lay my finger on him and say 'Paris!' I see some cups and saucers of Chinese make, equally strangers to me personally: I put my finger on them, then and there, and I say 'Pekin, Nankin, and Canton.' It is the same with Japan, with Egypt, and with bamboo and sandal-wood from the East Indies; I put my finger on them all. I have put my finger on the North Pole before now, and said, 'Spear of Esquimaux make, for half a pint of pale sherry!' "

"Really? A very remarkable way, Mr. Sapsea, of acquiring a knowledge of men and things."

"I mention it, sir," Mr. Sapsea rejoins, with unspeakable complacency, "because, as I say, it don't do to boast of what you are; but show how you came to be it, and then you prove it."

"Most interesting. We were to speak of the late Mrs. Sapsea."

"We were, sir." Mr. Sapsea fills both glasses, and takes the decanter into safe keeping again. "Before I consult your opinion as a man of taste on this little trifle"—holding it up—"which is *but* a trifle, and still has required some thought, sir, some little fever of the brow, I ought perhaps to describe the character of the late Mrs. Sapsea, now dead three quarters of a year."

Mr. Jasper, in the act of yawning behind his wineglass, puts down that screen and calls up a look of interest. It is a little impaired in its expressiveness by his having a shut-up gape still to dispose of, with watering eyes.

"Half a dozen years ago, or so," Mr. Sapsea proceeds, "when I had enlarged my mind up to—I will not say to what it now is, for that might seem to aim at too much, but up to the pitch of wanting another mind to be absorbed in it—I cast my eye about me for a nuptial partner. Because, as I say, it is not good for man to be alone."

Mr. Jasper appears to commit this original idea to memory.

"Miss Brobity at that time kept, I will not call it the rival establishment to the establishment at the Nuns' House opposite, but I will call it the other parallel establishment down town. The world did have it that she showed a passion for attending my sales, when they took place on half-holidays, or in vacation time. The world did put it about, that she admired my style. The world did notice that as time flowed by, my style became traceable in the dictation-exercises of Miss Brobity's pupils. Young man, a whisper even sprang up in obscure malignity, that one ignorant and besotted Churl (a parent) so committed himself as to object to it by name. But I do not believe this. For is it likely that any human creature in his right senses would so lay himself open to be pointed at, by what I call the finger of scorn?"

Mr. Jasper shakes his head. Not in the least likely. Mr. Sapsea, in a grandiloquent state of absence of mind, seems to refill his visitor's glass, which is full already; and does really refill his own, which is empty.

"Miss Brobity's Being, young man, was deeply imbued with homage to Mind. She revered Mind, when launched, or, as I say, precipitated, on an extensive knowledge of the world. When I made my proposal, she did me the honor to be so overshadowed with a species of Awe, as to be able to articulate only the two words, 'Oh Thou!'—meaning myself. Her limpid blue eyes were fixed upon me, her semi-transparent hands were clasped together, pallor overspread her aquiline features, and, though encouraged to proceed, she never did proceed a word further. I disposed of the parallel establishment, by private contract, and we became as nearly one as could be expected under the circumstances. But she never could, and she never did, find a phrase satisfactory to her perhaps-too-favourable estimate of my intellect. To the very last (feeble action of liver), she addressed me in the same unfinished terms."

Mr. Jasper has closed his eyes as the auctioneer has deepened his voice. He now abruptly opens them, and says, in unison with the deepened voice, "Ah!"—rather as if stopping himself on the extreme verge of adding—"men!"

"I have been since," says Mr. Sapsea, with his legs stretched out, and solemnly enjoying himself with the wine and the fire, "what you behold me; I have been since a solitary mourner; I have been since, as I say, wasting my evening conversation on the desert air. I will not say that I have reproached myself; but there have been times when I have asked myself the question: What if her husband had been nearer on a level with her? If she had not had to look up quite so high, what might the stimulating action have been upon the liver?"

Mr. Jasper says, with an appearance of having fallen into dreadfully low spirits, that he "supposes it was to be."

"We can only suppose so, sir," Mr. Sapsea coincides. "As I say, Man proposes, Heaven disposes. It may or may not or be putting the same thought in another form; but that is the way I put it."

Mr. Jasper murmurs assent.

"And now, Mr. Jasper," resumes the auctioneer, producing his scrap of manuscript, "Mrs. Sapsea's monument having had full time to settle and dry, let me take your opinion, as a man of taste, on the inscription I have (as I before remarked, not without some little fever of the brow), drawn out for it. Take it in your own hand. The setting out of the lines requires to be followed with the eye, as well as the contents with the mind."

Mr. Jasper complying, sees and reads as follows:

ETHELINDA,
Reverential Wife of
MR. THOMAS SAPSEA
AUCTIONEER, VALUER, ESTATE AGENT, & c.,
OF THIS CITY,
Whose Knowledge of the World,
Though somewhat extensive,
Never brought him acquainted with
A SPIRIT
More capable of
LOOKING UP TO HIM.
STRANGER PAUSE
And ask thyself the Question,
CANST THOU DO LIKEWISE?
If not,
WITH A BLUSH RETIRE.

Mr. Sapsea having risen and stationed himself with his back to the fire, for the purpose of observing the effect of these lines on the countenance of a man of taste, consequently has his face towards the door, when his serving-maid, again appearing, announces, "Durdles is come, sir!" He promptly draws forth and fills the third wineglass, as being now claimed, and replies, "Show Durdles in."

"Admirable!" quoth Mr. Jasper, handing back the paper.

"You approve, sir?"

"Impossible not to approve. Striking, characteristic, and complete."

The auctioneer inclines his head, as one accepting his due and giving a receipt; and invites the entering Durdles to take off that glass of wine (handing the same), for it will warm him.

Durdles is a stonemason; chiefly in the gravestone, tomb, and monument way, and wholly of their color from head to foot. No man is better known in Cloisterham. He is the chartered libertine of the place. Fame trumpets him a wonderful workman—which, for aught that anybody knows, he may be (as he never works); and a wonderful sot—which everybody knows he is. With the Cathedral crypt he is better acquainted than any living authority; it may even be than any dead one. It is said that the intimacy of this acquaintance began in his habitually resorting to that secret place, to lock out the Cloisterham boy-populace, and sleep off the fumes of liquor: he having ready access to the Cathedral, as contractor for rough repairs. Be this as it may, he does know much about it, and, in the demolition of impedimental fragments of wall, buttress, and pavement, has seen strange sights. He often speaks of himself in the third person; perhaps being a little misty as to his own identity when he narrates; perhaps impartially adopting the Cloisterham nomenclature in reference to a character of acknowledged distinction. Thus he will say, touching his strange sights: "Durdles come upon the old chap," in reference to a buried magnate of ancient time and high degree, "by striking right into the coffin with his pick. The old chap gave Durdles a look with his open eyes, as much as to say 'Is your name Durdles? Why, my man, I've been waiting for you a Devil of a time!' And then he turned to powder." With a two-foot rule always in his pocket, and a mason's hammer all but always in his hand, Durdles goes continually sounding and tapping all about and about the Cathedral; and whenever he says to Tope: "Tope, here's another old 'un in here!" Tope announces it to the Dean as an established discovery.

In a suit of coarse flannel with horn buttons, a yellow necker-chief with draggled ends, an old hat more russet-colored than black, and laced boots of the hue of his stony calling, Durdles leads a hazy, gipsy sort of life, carrying his dinner about with him in a small bundle, and sitting on all manner of tombstones to dine. This dinner of Durdles's has become quite a Cloisterham institution: not only because of his never appearing in public without it, but because of its having been, on certain renowned occasions, taken into custody along with Durdles (as drunk and incapable), and ex-hibited before the Bench of Justices at the Town Hall. These occa-sions, however, have been few and far apart: Durdles being as seldom drunk as sober. For the rest, he is an old bachelor, and he lives in a little antiquated hole of a house that was never finished: supposed to be built, so far, of stones stolen from the city wall. To this abode

there is an approach, ankle-deep in stone chips, resembling a petri-
fied grove of tombstones, urns, draperies, and broken columns, in
all stages of sculpture. Herein, two journeymen incessantly chip,
while two other journeymen, who face each other, incessantly saw
stone; dipping as regularly in and out of their sheltering sentry-
boxes, as if they were mechanical figures emblematical of Time and
Death.

To Durdles, when he has consumed his glass of port, Mr. Jasper
entrusts that precious effort of his Muse. Durdles unfeelingly takes
out his two-foot rule, and measures the lines calmly, alloying them
with stone-grit.

"This is for the monument, is it, Mr. Sapsea?"

"The Inscription. Yes." Mr. Sapsea waits for its effect on a common mind.

"It'll come in to a eighth of a inch," says Durdles. "Your servant, Mr. Jasper. Hope I see you well."

"How are you, Durdles?"

"I've got a touch of the Tombatism on me, Mr. Jasper, but that
I must expect."

"You mean the Rheumatism," says Sapsea, in a sharp tone. (He
is nettled by having his composition so mechanically received.)

"No, I don't. I mean, Mr. Sapsea, the Tombatism. It's another
sort from Rheumatism. Mr. Jasper knows what Durdles means. You
get among them Tombs afore it's well light on a winter morning,
and keep on, as the Catechism says, a-walking in the same all the
days of your life, and *you'll* know what Durdles means."

"It is a bitter cold place," Mr. Jasper assents, with an antipathetic shiver.

"And if it's bitter cold for you, up in the chancel, with a lot of live breath smoking out about you, what the bitterness is to Durdles, down in the crypt among the earthy damps there, and the dead breath of the old 'uns," returns that individual, "Durdles leaves you to judge. —Is this to be put in hand at once, Mr. Sapsea?"

Mr. Sapsea, with an Author's anxiety to rush into publication, replies that it cannot be out of hand too soon.

"You had better let me have the key, then," says Durdles.

"Why, man, it is not to be put inside the monument!"

"Durdles knows where it's to be put, Mr. Sapsea; no man better. Ask 'ere a man in Cloisterham whether Durdles knows his work."

Mr. Sapsea rises, takes a key from a drawer, unlocks an iron safe let into the wall, and takes from it another key.

"When Durdles puts a touch or a finish upon his work, no matter where, inside or outside, Durdles likes to look at his work all round, and see that his work is a doing him credit," Durdles explains, doggedly.

The key proffered him by the bereaved widower being a large one, he slips his two-foot rule into a side pocket of his flannel trousers made for it, and deliberately opens his flannel coat, and opens the mouth of a large breast-pocket within it before taking the key to place in that repository.

"Why, Durdles!" exclaims Jasper, looking on amused. "You are undermined with pockets!"

"And I carries weight in 'em too, Mr. Jasper. Feel those;" producing two other large keys.

"Hand me Mr. Sapsea's likewise. Surely this is the heaviest of the three."

"You'll find 'em much of a muchness, I expect," says Durdles. "They all belong to monuments. They all open Durdles's work. Durdles keeps the keys of his work mostly. Not that they're much used."

"By the bye," it comes into Jasper's mind to say, as he idly examines the keys; "I have been going to ask you, many a day, and have always forgotten. You know they sometimes call you Stony Durdles, don't you?"

"Cloisterham knows me as Durdles, Mr. Jasper."

"I am aware of that, of course. But the boys sometimes——"

"Oh! If you mind them young Imps of boys——" Durdles gruffly interrupts.

"I don't mind them, any more than you do. But there was a discussion the other day among the Choir, whether Stony stood for Tony;" clinking one key against another.

("Take care of the wards, Mr. Jasper.")

"Or whether Stony stood for Stephen;" clinking with a change of keys.

("You can't make a pitch-pipe of 'em, Mr. Jasper.")

"Or whether the name comes from your trade. How stands the fact?"

Mr. Jasper weighs the three keys in his hand, lifts his head from his idly stooping attitude over the fire, and delivers the keys to Durdles with an ingenuous and friendly face.

But the stony one is a gruff one likewise, and that hazy state of his is always an uncertain state, highly conscious of its dignity, and prone to take offence. He drops his two keys back into his pocket one by one, and buttons them up; he takes his dinner-bundle from the chair-back on which he hung it when he came in; he distributes the weight he carries, by tying the third key up in it, as though he were an Ostrich, and liked to dine off cold iron; and he gets out of the room, deigning no word of answer.

Mr. Sapsea then proposes a hit at backgammon, which, seasoned with his own improving conversation, and terminating in a supper of cold roast beef and salad, beguiles the golden evening until pretty late. Mr. Sapsea's wisdom being, in its delivery to mortals, rather of the diffuse than the epigrammatic order, is by no means expended even then; but his visitor intimates that he will come back for more of the precious commodity on future occasions, and Mr. Sapsea lets him off for the present, to ponder on the instalment he carries away.

CHAPTER V

MR. DURDLES AND FRIEND

JOHN JASPER, on his way home through the Close, is brought to a standstill by the spectacle of Stony Durdles, dinner-bundle and all, leaning his back against the iron railing of the burial-ground enclosing it from the old cloister-arches; and a hideous small boy in rags flinging stones at him as a well-defined mark in the moonlight. Sometimes the stones hit him, and sometimes they miss him, but Durdles seems indifferent to either fortune. The hideous small boy, on the contrary, whenever he hits Durdles, blows a whistle of triumph through a jagged gap convenient for the purpose, in the front of his mouth, where half his teeth are wanting; and whenever he misses him, yelps out "Mulled agin!" and tries to atone for the failure by taking a more correct and vicious aim.

"What are you doing to the man?" demands Jasper, stepping out into the moonlight from the shade.

"Making a cock-shy of him," replies the hideous small boy.

"Give me those stones in your hand."

"Yes, I'll give 'em you down your throat, if you come a-kething hold of me," says the small boy, shaking himself loose, and backing. "I'll smash your eye, if you don't look out!"

"Baby-Devil that you are, what has the man done to you?"

"He won't go home."

"What is that to you?"

"He gives me 'apenny to pelt him home if I ketches him out too late," says the boy. And then chants, like a little savage, half stumbling and half dancing among the rags and laces of his dilapidated boots:

> "Widdy widdy wen!
> I—ket—ches—Im—out—ar—ter—ten,
> Widdy widdy wy!
> Then—E—don't—go—then—I—shy
> Widdy Widdy Wake-cock warning!"

—with a comprehensive sweep on the last word, and one more delivery at Durdles.

This would seem to be a poetical note of preparation, agreed upon, as a caution to Durdles to stand clear if he can, or to betake himself homeward.

John Jasper invites the boy with a beck of his head to follow him (feeling it hopeless to drag him, or coax him) and crosses to the iron railing where the Stony (and stoned) One is profoundly meditating.

"Do you know this thing, this child?" asks Jasper, at a loss for a word that will define this thing.

"Deputy," says Durdles, with a nod.

"Is that it's—his—name?"

"Deputy," assents Durdles.

"I'm man-servant up at the Travellers' Twopenny in Gas Works

Garding," this thing explains. "All us man-servants at Travellers Lodgings is named Deputy. When we're chock full and the Travellers is all a-bed I come out for my 'elth." Then withdrawing into the road, and taking aim, he resumes:

"Widdy Widdy wen!
I—ket—ches—Im—out—ar—ter—"

"Hold your hand," cries Jasper, "and don't throw while I stand so near him, or I'll kill you! Come, Durdles; let me walk home with you to-night. Shall I carry your bundle?"

"Not on any account," replies Durdles, adjusting it. "Durdles was making his reflections here when you come up, sir, surrounded by his works, like a poplar Author. —Your own brother-in-law;" introducing a sarcophagus within the railing, white and cold in the moonlight. "Mrs. Sapsea;" introducing the monument of that devoted wife. "Late Incumbent;" introducing the Reverend Gentleman's broken column. "Departed Assessed Taxes;" introducing a vase and towel, standing on what might represent a cake of soap. "Former pastrycook and muffin-maker, much respected;" introducing gravestone. "All safe and sound here, sir, and all Durdles's work! Of the common folk that is merely bundled up in turf and brambles, the less said, the better. A poor lot, soon forgot."

"This creature, Deputy, is behind us," says Jasper, looking back. "Is he to follow us?"

The relations between Durdles and Deputy are of a capricious kind; for, on Durdles's turning himself about with the slow gravity of beery soddenness, Deputy makes a pretty wide circuit into the road and stands on the defensive.

"You never cried Widdy Warning before you begun to-night," says Durdles, unexpectedly reminded of, or imagining, an injury.

"Yer lie, I did," says Deputy, in his only form of polite contradiction.

"Own brother, sir," observes Durdles, turning himself about again, and as unexpectedly forgetting his offence as he had recalled or conceived it; "own brother to Pete the Wild Boy! But I gave him an object in life."

"At which he takes aim?" Mr. Jasper suggests.

"That's it, sir," returns Durdles, quite satisfied; "at which he takes aim. I took him in hand and gave him an object. What was he before? A destroyer. What work did he do? Nothing but destruction. What did he earn by it? Short terms in Cloisterham Jail. Not a person, not a piece of property, not a winder, not a horse, nor a dog, nor a cat, nor a bird, nor a fowl, nor a pig, but what he stoned, for want of an enlightened object. I put that enlightened object before him, and now he can turn his honest half-penny by the three penn'orth a week."

"I wonder he has no competitors."

"He has plenty, Mr. Jasper, but he stones 'em all away. Now, I don't know what this scheme of mine comes to," pursues Durdles, considering about it with the same sodden gravity; "I don't know what you may precisely call it. It ain't a sort of a—scheme of a— National Education?"

"I should say not," replies Jasper.

"*I* should say not," assents Durdles; "then we won't try to give it a name."

"He still keeps behind us," repeats Jasper, looking over his shoulder; "is he to follow us?"

"We can't help going round by the Travellers' Twopenny, if we go the short way, which is the back way," Durdles answers, "and we'll drop him there."

So they go on; Deputy, as a rear rank of one, taking open order, and invading the silence of the hour and place by stoning every wall, post, pillar, and other inanimate object, by the deserted way.

"Is there anything new down in the crypt, Durdles?" asks John Jasper.

"Anything old, I think you mean," growls Durdles. "It ain't a spot for novelty."

"Any new discovery on your part, I meant."

"There's a old 'un under the seventh pillar on the left as you go down the broken steps of the little underground chapel as formerly was; I make him out (so fur as I've made him out yet) to be one of them old 'uns with a crook. To judge from the size of the passages in the walls, and of the steps and doors, by which they come and went, them crooks must have been a good deal in the way of the old 'uns! Two on 'em meeting promiscuous must have hitched one another by the mitre, pretty often, I should say."

Without any endeavour to correct the literality of this opinion, Jasper surveys his companion — covered from head to foot with old mortar, lime, and stone grit — as though he, Jasper, were getting imbued with a romantic interest in his weird life.

"Yours is a curious existence."

Without furnishing the least clue to the question, whether he receives this as a compliment or as quite the reverse, Durdles gruffly answers: "Yours is another."

"Well! Inasmuch as my lot is cast in the same old earthy, chilly, never-changing place, yes. But there is much more mystery and interest in your connexion with the cathedral than in mine. Indeed, I am beginning to have some idea of asking you to take me on as a sort of student, or free 'prentice, under you, and to let me go about with you sometimes, and see some of these odd nooks in which you pass your days."

The Stony One replies, in a general way, All right. Everybody knows where to find Durdles, when he's wanted. Which, if not strictly true, is approximately so, if taken to express that Durdles may always be found in a state of vagabondage somewhere.

"What I dwell upon most," says Jasper, pursuing his subject of romantic interest, "is the remarkable accuracy with which you would seem to find out where people are buried. —What is the matter? That bundle is in your way; let me hold it."

Durdles has stopped and backed a little (Deputy, attentive to all his movements, immediately skirmishing into the road) and was looking about for some ledge or corner to place his bundle on, when thus relieved of it.

"Just you give me my hammer out of that," says Durdles, "and I'll show you."

Clink, clink. And his hammer is handed him.

"Now, lookee here. You pitch your note, don't you, Mr. Jasper?"

"Yes."

"So I sound for mine. I take my hammer, and I tap." (Here he strikes the pavement, and the attentive Deputy skirmishes at a rather wider range, as supposing that his head may be in requisition.) "I tap, tap, tap. Solid! I go on tapping. Solid still! Tag again. Holloa! Hollow! Tap again, persevering. Solid in hollow! Tap, tap, tap, to try it better. Solid in hollow; and inside solid, hollow again! There you are! Old 'un crumbled away in stone coffin, in vault!"

"Astonishing!"

"I have even done this," says Durdles, drawing out his two-foot rule, (Deputy meanwhile skirmishing nearer, as suspecting that Treasure may be about to be discovered, which may somehow lead to his own enrichment, and the delicious treat of the discoverers being hanged by the neck, on his evidence, until they are dead). "Say that hammer of mine's a wall—my work. Two; four; and two is six," measuring on the pavement. "Six foot inside that wall is Mrs. Sapsea."

100

"Not really Mrs. Sapsea?"

"Say Mrs. Sapsea. Her wall's thicker, but say Mrs. Sapsea. Durdles taps that wall represented by that hammer, and says, after good sounding: 'Something betwixt us!' Sure enough, some rubbish has been left in that same six foot space by Durdles's men!"

Jasper opines that such accuracy "is a gift."

"I wouldn't have it as a gift," returns Durdles, by no means receiving the observation in good part. "I worked it out for myself. Durdles comes by *his* knowledge through grubbing deep for it, and having it up by the roots when it don't want to come. —Halloa you Deputy!"

"Widdy!" is Deputy's shrill response, standing off again.

"Catch that ha'penny. And don't let me see any more of you to-night, after we come to the Travellers' Twopenny."

"Warning!" returns Deputy, having caught the halfpenny, and appearing by this mystic word to express his assent to the arrangement.

They have but to cross what was once the vineyard, belonging to what was once the Monastery, to come into the narrow back lane wherein stands the crazy wooden house of two low stories currently known as the Travellers' Twopenny: —a house all warped and distorted, like the morals of the travellers, with scant remains of a lattice-work porch over the door, and also of a rustic fence before its stamped-out garden; by reason of the travellers being so bound to the premises by a tender sentiment (or so fond of having a fire by the roadside in the course of the day), that they can never be persuaded or threatened into departure, without violently possessing themselves of some wooden forget-me-not, and bearing it off.

The semblance of an inn is attempted to be given to this wretched place by fragments of conventional red curtaining in the windows, which rags are made muddily transparent in the night-season by feeble lights of rush or cotton dip burning dully in the close air of the inside. As Durdles and Jasper come near, they are addressed by an inscribed paper lantern over the door, setting forth the purport of the house. They are also addressed by some half-dozen other hideous small boys——whether twopenny lodgers or followers or hangers-on of such, who knows!——who, as if attracted by some carrion-scent of Deputy in the air, start into the moonlight, as vultures might gather in the desert, and instantly fall to stoning him and one another.

"Stop, you young brutes," cries Jasper, angrily, "and let us go by!"

This remonstrance being received with yells and flying stones, according to a custom of late years comfortably established among the police regulations of our English communities, where Christians are stoned on all sides, as if the days of Saint Stephen were revived, Durdles remarks of the young savages, with some point, that "they haven't got an object," and leads the way down the lane.

At the corner of the lane, Jasper, hotly enraged, checks his companion and looks back. All is silent. Next moment, a stone coming rattling at his hat, and a distant yell of "Wake-cock! Warning!" followed by a crow, as from some infernally-hatched Chanticleer,

102

apprising him under whose victorious fire he stands, he turns the corner into safety, and takes Durdles home: Durdles stumbling among the litter of his stony yard as if he were going to turn head foremost into one of the unfinished tombs.

John Jasper returns by another way to his gate house, and entering softly with his key, finds his fire still burning. He takes from a locked press, a peculiar-looking pipe which he fills—but not with tobacco—and, having adjusted the contents of the bowl, very carefully, with a little instrument, ascends an inner staircase of only a few steps, leading to two rooms. One of these is his own sleeping chamber: the other, is his nephew's. There is a light in each.

His nephew lies asleep, calm and untroubled. John Jasper stands looking down upon him, his unlighted pipe in his hand, for some time, with a fixed and deep attention. Then, hushing his footsteps, he passes to his own room, lights his pipe, and delivers himself to the Spectres it invokes at midnight.

5.

THE FINAL SPEECH RECEIVES particularly warm applause, almost an ovation; and for a second or two the members of the Drood work-group, who have finished reading almost at the same moment, are under the impression that it is Dickens who is being so vigorously clapped. After all, that was how the great writer was greeted when he toured the theatres, electrifying the audiences with his histrionic (and highly lucrative) readings from the more dramatic passages in his novels.

But it is only the inauguration drawing to its conclusion. None of those now trooping forward to the refreshments has paid with an entrance ticket. Do we need to dwell on the crowd that seethes around the long table, foraging, battling for the exotic titbits arrayed there? The reader is familiar with such scenes: the lunging arms, the swooping bodies, the jabbing elbows, the sloshed sauces and spilt drinks. We might as well move smoothly forward in space and time, to find the Drood work-group all together once again (give or take a detective or two) in an undisturbed side-room.

The plates have all been filled in the random, desperate haste of such occasions, and every diner now finds himself confronting a culinary puzzle. We hear such words as:

"A date—with a prawn inside? *Ça alors!*"

"Do I really want to know what lies beneath this greeney-grey goo?"

"The circumstantial evidence says pigeon, but the stuffing, beyond a shadow of a doubt, is mango."

"Salami with crème caramel topping?"

"The aim is laudable," Dr Wilmot observes, separating a banana fritter from its bed of sauerkraut, "that of culinary completeness. There's absolutely everything in this dinner."

"Cooking," states Nero Wolfe, who has decided to avoid surprises by limiting himself to a stick of raw celery, "is not a matter of chaotically combining comestibles. The art of cooking consists in calculation, in meticulous premeditation, just as with the art of the novel. Take Dickens. Take what he does with Giovanni Battista Belzoni (1778–1823), an Italian archaeologist who narrowly escaped death by suffocation in the second pyramid of Gizeh. Dickens has Rosa name him in Chapter Three, with a vague reference to the dangerous misadventure. Thus he prepares the ground for Durdles, who in his own way, in a comic and

105

strictly English context, is an archaeologist too, and who employs the same, so-to-speak, echographic methods. This in turn sets the stage for the murderer's probable modus operandi, and indeed, looking still further ahead, for the eventual discovery of the victim. Precisely the kind of subtlety required in haute cuisine."

DUPIN: Not to mention the subtlety of the keys. The idea of having a musicologist clink three keys, one against the other, so that he'll be able to recognize the right one, when he needs to, by its sound, strikes me as exquisite. Which I'm afraid I cannot say of this cocoa-coated pig's trotter.

TOAD: You call that subtlety? Burying Jasper beneath a mound of transparent evidence, like this poor little pepper-squashed frog? Just look at what happens: Jasper hits on the blatant pretext of the tombstone in order to visit Sapsea and thus meet Durdles and thus identifies the keys which will then open the tomb in which he plans to conceal the corpse! And then another "chance" nocturnal encounter with Durdles, and this time right outside the burialground!

WILMOT, *scooping up the shark-meat cubes oozing out of his pancake:* I should point out that this last co-incidence is not due to clumsiness or carelessness, of which Dickens is sometimes accused. It was forced upon the author, owing to the fact that the novel came out in instalments. He had concluded the first number with Chapter Four and had already written a good deal of the next number, in which the nocturnal encounter with Durdles took place in Chapter Eight. But at the last moment the printer realised that the issue wasn't long enough: they were six pages short of thirty-two. Hence the transformation of Chapter Eight into Five and its inclusion in the first instalment.

WOLFE: Haute cuisine once again! Whipping up something new in the face of the unforeseen is a gift only the greatest chefs possess. Because quite apart from this regrettable "co-incidence," there is another incongruous detail: on his way back from Sapsea's house in High Street, which is opposite the Nuns' House, Jasper had no need to pass the burial-ground . . .

This exercise in detective pedantry is greeted by appreciative if indistinct murmurs from the circle of full mouths.

WOLFE, *continuing:* . . . and yet I consider that the ending of the April number is clearly improved in this way: The character of Durdles is rounded out, and we make the acquaintance of the street urchin, Deputy. There is something Londonish about him, something not quite in keeping with the surroundings of the ancient cathedral, but he appears at just the right moment to set off the provincial respectability of Cloisterham. Dickens thereby assures us that this peaceful little town contains a stratum of society which is, if not exactly criminal, at least ready to dispose of the rules.

TOAD: But that doesn't stop the author piling up the evidence against Jasper! The shady uncle actually asks to be taken on as Durdles's apprentice, to learn all about tombs and burials. And when he comes home, we see him gaze upon his sleeping nephew with a peculiar concentration, and then "deliver himself to Spectres" which the pipe brings at midnight. What are these spectres if not his future crime? No, it's too easy, too . . . obvious.

HOLMES, who has found the Completeness dinner completely inedible and is holding nothing more than a glass of mineral water, seems to shudder at the word *spectres.* He sips his water and, looking rather pale, addresses Toad:

"Too obvious, you say? You find the case too easy, open-and-shut? Yes . . . So it would appear . . . And yet Conan Doyle, the man for whom I worked for so long, was not of that opinion. Indeed, in 1927, as a firm believer in spiritualism (chairman of the British Society for Spiritualist Research) he decided to devote a séance to the Drood case, with the intention of questioning Charles Dickens's spirit on the subject.

POIROT: You mean he asked Dickens directly who the murderer was?

HOLMES: Yes. He invoked the spirit of "Boz," as Dickens signed himself in his early journalist years.

POIROT: And Boz came, and answered?

HOLMES: Yes, my friend. He came. He answered.

ALL: And so what did he——?

But at that moment a slurred voice interrupts from the far end of the room.

"So that's where you all are!"

In comes Loredana, on rather unsteady legs.

ALL: For God's sake, Holmes!

HOLMES, *rapidly, almost under his breath:* Boz said that behind the mystery of Edwin Drood lay something that he would rather did not come to light. And during that séance I myself had——indeed, still have——the feeling that it might be better to proceed no further in this business.

POIROT: Not today, at any rate.

Then they all make their way out onto the terrace, where Loredana has been settled for some time now, in the company of Archer and Marlowe, drinking and dancing to Turkish-Brazilian rhythms.

PART TWO

THE MAY AND JUNE NUMBERS

6.

ANYBODY WHO EVER SPENT six or seven hours in an airport, waiting to see if there is the remotest possibility of the departure of flight AZ 437 to Frankfurt, knows that there is no arguing delays "due to technical difficulties." Such difficulties, by their very nature, cannot—*must* not—be explained to the common traveller, for that information would be useless if not actually harmful to him. Besides, the newsstand is always there (though not always open), should he need assistance in whiling away the hours. With luck, he may find something in the current-affairs magazines which is not depressing.

And here in fact is Issue No. 2 of the *Mystery of Edwin Drood*. It is dated May 1870, but has been on the newsstands since yesterday, April 30. What better occasion for dipping into a couple of chapters? We are not waiting for a plane to take off but for the Drood group to re-open their session—delayed due to technical difficulties—in the Dickens Room.

CHAPTER VI

PHILANTHROPY
IN MINOR CANON CORNER

THE REVEREND Septimus Crisparkle (Septimus, because six little brother Crisparkles before him went out, one by one, as they were born, like six weak little rushlights, as they were lighted), having broken the thin morning ice near Cloisterham Weir with his amiable head, much to the invigoration of his frame, was now assisting his circulation by boxing at a looking-glass with great science and prowess. A fresh and healthy portrait the looking-glass presented of the Reverend Septimus, feinting and dodging with the utmost artfulness, and hitting out from the shoulder with the utmost straightness, while his radiant features teemed with innocence, and soft-hearted benevolence beamed from his boxing-gloves.

It was scarcely breakfast time yet, for Mrs. Crisparkle—mother, not wife, of the Reverend Septimus—was only just down, and waiting for the urn. Indeed, the Reverend Septimus left off at this very moment to take the pretty old lady's entering face between his boxing-gloves and kiss it. Having done so with tenderness, the Reverend Septimus turned to again, countering with his left, and putting in his right, in a tremendous manner.

114

"I say, every morning of my life, that you'll do it at last, Sept,"
remarked the old lady, looking on; "and so you will."

"Do what, Ma dear?"

"Break the pier-glass, or burst a blood-vessel."

"Neither, please God, Ma dear. Here's wind, Ma. Look at this!"

In a concluding round of great severity, the Reverend Septimus
administered and escaped all sorts of punishment, and wound up by
getting the old lady's cap into Chancery—such is the technical term
used in scientific circles by the learned in the Noble Art—with a
lightness of touch that hardly stirred the lightest lavender or cherry
riband on it. Magnanimously releasing the defeated, just in time to
get his gloves into a drawer and feign to be looking out the window
in a contemplative state of mind when a servant entered, the Reverend Septimus then gave place to the urn and other preparations
for breakfast. These completed, and the two alone again, it was
pleasant to see (or would have been, if there had been any one to
see it, which there never was), the old lady standing to say the
Lord's Prayer aloud, and her son, Minor Canon nevertheless, standing with bent head to hear it, he being within five years of forty:
much as he had stood to hear the same words from the same lips
when he was within five months of four.

What is prettier than an old lady—except a young lady—when
her eyes are bright, when her figure is trim and compact, when her
face is cheerful and calm, when her dress is as the dress of a china
shepherdess: so dainty in its colors, so individually assorted to her-

self, so neatly moulded on her? Nothing is prettier, thought the good Minor Canon frequently, when taking his seat at table opposite his long-widowed mother. Her thought at such times may be condensed into the two words that oftenest did duty together in all her conversations: "My Sept!"

They were a good pair to sit breakfasting together in Minor Canon Corner, Cloisterham. For, Minor Canon Corner was a quiet place in the shadow of the Cathedral, which the cawing of the rooks, the echoing footsteps of rare passers, the sound of the Cathedral bell, or the roll of the Cathedral organ, seemed to render more quiet than absolute silence. Swaggering fighting men had had their centuries of ramping and raving about Minor Canon Corner, and beaten serfs had had their centuries of drudging and dying there, and powerful monks had had their centuries of being sometimes useful and sometimes harmful there, and behold they were all gone out of Minor Canon Corner, and so much the better. Perhaps one of the highest uses of their ever having been there, was, that there might be left behind, that blessed air of tranquillity which pervaded Minor Canon Corner, and that serenely romantic state of the mind—productive for the most part of pity and forbearance—which is engendered by a sorrowful story that is all told, or a pathetic play that is played out.

Red-brick walls harmoniously toned down in color by time, strong-rooted ivy, latticed windows, panelled rooms, big oaken beams in little places, and stone-walled gardens where annual fruit yet ripened upon monkish trees, were the principal surroundings of pretty old Mrs. Crisparkle and the Reverend Septimus as they sat at breakfast.

"And what, Ma dear," inquired the Minor Canon, giving proof of a wholesome and vigorous appetite, "does the letter say?"

The pretty old lady, after reading it, had just laid it down upon the breakfast-cloth. She handed it over to her son.

Now, the old lady was exceedingly proud of her bright eyes being so clear that she could read writing without spectacles. Her son was also so proud of the circumstance, and so dutifully bent on her deriving the utmost possible gratification from it, that he had invented the pretence that he himself could *not* read writing without spectacles. Therefore he now assumed a pair, of grave and prodigious proportions, which not only seriously inconvenienced his nose and his breakfast, but seriously impeded his perusal of the letter. For, he had the eyes of a microscope and a telescope combined, when they were unassisted.

"It's from Mr. Honeythunder, of course," said the old lady, folding her arms.

"Of course," assented her son. He then lamely read on:

> "Haven of Philanthropy,
> "Chief Offices, London, Wednesday.

"DEAR MADAM,

" 'I write in the——;' In the what's this? What does he write in?"

"In the chair," said the old lady.

The Reverend Septimus took off his spectacles, that he might see her face, as he exclaimed:

"Why, what should he write in?"

"Bless me, bless me, Sept," returned the old lady, "you don't see the context! Give it back to me, my dear."

Glad to get his spectacles off (for they always made his eyes water) her son obeyed: murmuring that his sight for reading manuscript got worse and worse daily.

" 'I write,' " his mother went on, reading very perspicuously and precisely, " 'from the chair, to which I shall probably be confined for some hours.' "

Septimus looked at the row of chairs against the wall, with a half-protesting and half-appealing countenance.

" 'We have,' " the old lady read on with a little extra emphasis, " 'a meeting of our Convened Chief Composite Committee of Central and District Philanthropists, at our Head Haven as above; and it is their unanimous pleasure that I take the chair.' "

Septimus breathed more freely, and muttered: "Oh! If he comes to *that,* let him."

" 'Not to lose a day's post, I take the opportunity of a long report being read, denouncing a public miscreant——' "

"It is a most extraordinary thing," interposed the gentle Minor Canon, laying down his knife and fork to rub his ear in a vexed manner, "that these Philanthropists are always denouncing somebody. And it is another most extraordinary thing that they are always so violently flush of miscreants!"

" 'Denouncing a public miscreant!' "—the old lady resumed, " 'to get our little affair of business off my mind. I have spoken with my two wards, Neville and Helena Landless, on the subject of their defective education, and they give in to the plan proposed; as I should have taken good care they did, whether they liked it or not.' "

"And it is another most extraordinary thing," remarked the Minor Canon in the same tone as before, "that these Philanthropists are so given to seizing their fellow-creatures by the scruff of the neck, and (as one may say) bumping them into the paths of peace. —I beg your pardon, Ma dear, for interrupting."

" 'Therefore, dear Madam, you will please prepare your son, the Rev. Mr. Septimus, to expect Neville as an inmate to be read with, on Monday next. On the same day Helena will accompany him to Cloisterham, to take up her quarters at the Nuns' House, the establishment recommended by yourself and son jointly. Please likewise to prepare for her reception and tuition there. The terms in both cases are understood to be exactly as stated to me in writing by yourself, when I opened a correspondence with you on this subject, after the honor of being introduced to you at your sister's house in town here. With compliments to the Rev. Mr. Septimus, I am, Dear Madam, Your affectionate brother (In Philanthropy), LUKE HONEY-THUNDER.' "

"Well, Ma," said Septimus, after a little more rubbing of his ear, "we must try it. There can be no doubt that we have room for an inmate, and that I have time to bestow upon him, and inclination too. I must confess to feeling rather glad that he is not Mr. Honeythunder himself. Though that seems wretchedly prejudiced—does it not?—for I never saw him. Is he a large man, Ma?"

"I should call him a large man, my dear," the old lady replied after some hesitation, "but that his voice is so much larger."

"Than himself?"

"Than anybody."

"Hah!" said Septimus. And finished his breakfast as if the flavor of the Superior Family Souchong, and also of the ham and toast and eggs, were a little on the wane.

Mrs. Crisparkle's sister, another piece of Dresden china, and matching her so neatly that they would have made a delightful pair of ornaments for the two ends of any capacious old-fashioned chimneypiece, and by right should never have been seen apart, was the childless wife of a clergyman holding Corporation preferment in London City. Mr. Honeythunder in his public character of Professor of Philanthropy had come to know Mrs. Crisparkle during the last re-matching of the china ornaments (in other words during her last annual visit to her sister), after a public occasion of a philanthropic nature, when certain devoted orphans of tender years had been glutted with plum buns, and plump bumptiousness. These were all the antecedents known in Minor Canon Corner of the coming pupils.

"I am sure you will agree with me, Ma," said Mr. Crisparkle, after thinking the matter over, "that the first thing to be done, is, to put these young people as much at their ease as possible. There is nothing disinterested in the notion, because we cannot be at our ease with them unless they are at their ease with us. Now, Jasper's nephew is down here at present; and like takes to like, and youth takes to youth. He is a cordial young fellow, and we will have him to meet the brother and sister at dinner. That's three. We can't think of asking him, without asking Jasper. That's four. Add Miss Twinkleton and the fairy bride that is to be, and that's six. Add our two selves, and that's eight. Would eight at a friendly dinner at all put you out, Ma?"

"Nine would, Sept," returned the old lady, visibly nervous.

"My dear Ma, I particularize eight."

"The exact size of the table and the room, my dear."

So it was settled that way; and when Mr. Crisparkle called with his mother upon Miss Twinkleton, to arrange for the reception of Miss Helena Landless at the Nuns' House, the two other invitations having reference to that establishment were proffered and accepted. Miss Twinkleton did, indeed, glance at the globes, as regretting that they were not formed to be taken out into society; but became reconciled to leaving them behind. Instructions were then despatched to the Philanthropist for the departure and arrival, in good time for dinner, of Mr. Neville and Miss Helena; and stock for soup became fragrant in the air of Minor Canon Corner.

In those days there was no railway to Cloisterham, and Mr. Sapsea said there never would be. Mr. Sapsea said more; he said there never should be. And yet, marvellous to consider, it has come to pass, in these days, that Express Trains don't think Cloisterham worth stopping at, but yell and whirl through it on their larger errands, casting the dust off their wheels as a testimony against its insignificance. Some remote fragment of Main Line to somewhere else, there was, which was going to ruin the Money Market if it failed, and Church and State if it succeeded, and (of course), the Constitution, whether or no; but even that had already so unsettled Cloisterham traffic, that the traffic, deserting the high road, came sneaking in from an unprecedented part of the country by a back stable-way, for many years labelled at the corner: "Beware of the Dog."

To this ignominious avenue of approach, Mr. Crisparkle repaired, awaiting the arrival of a short squat omnibus, with a disproportionate heap of luggage on the roof—like a little Elephant with infinitely too much Castle—which was then the daily service between Cloisterham and external mankind. As this vehicle lumbered up, Mr. Crisparkle could hardly see anything else of it for a large outside passenger seated on the box, with his elbows squared, and his hands on his knees, compressing the driver into a most uncomfortably small compass, and glowering about him with a strongly marked face.

"Is this Cloisterham?" demanded the passenger, in a tremendous voice.

"It is," replied the driver, rubbing himself as if he ached, after throwing the reins to the ostler. "And I never was so glad to see it."

"Tell your master to make his box seat wider then," returned the passenger. "Your master is morally bound—and ought to be legally, under ruinous penalties—to provide for the comfort of his fellow-man."

The driver instituted, with the palms of his hands, a superficial perquisition into the state of his skeleton; which seemed to make him anxious.

"Have I sat upon you?" asked the passenger.

"You have," said the driver, as if he didn't like it at all.

"Take that card, my friend."

"I think I won't deprive you on it," returned the driver, casting his eyes over it with no great favor, without taking it. "What's the good of it to me?"

"Be a Member of that Society," said the passenger.

"What shall I get by it?" asked the driver.

"Brotherhood," returned the passenger, in a ferocious voice.

"Thankee," said the driver, very deliberately, as he got down; "my mother was contented with myself, and so am I. I don't want no brothers."

"But you must have them," replied the passenger, also descending, "whether you like it or not. I am your brother."

"I say!" expostulated the driver, becoming more chafed in temper; "not too fur! The worm *will,* when——"

But here Mr. Crisparkle interposed, remonstrating aside, in a friendly voice: "Joe, Joe, Joe! Don't forget yourself, Joe, my good fellow!" and then, when Joe peaceably touched his hat, accosting the passenger with: "Mr. Honeythunder?"

"That is my name, sir."

"My name is Crisparkle."

"Reverend Mr. Septimus? Glad to see you, sir. Neville and Helena are inside. Having a little succumbed of late, under the pressure of my public labours, I thought I would take a mouthful of fresh air, and come down with them, and return at night. So you are the Reverend Mr. Septimus, are you?" surveying him on the whole with disappointment, and twisting a double eye-glass by its ribbon, as if he were roasting it; but not otherwise using it. "Hah! I expected to see you older, sir."

"I hope you will," was the good-humoured reply.

"Eh?" demanded Mr. Honeythunder.

"Only a poor little joke. Not worth repeating."

"Joke? Aye; I never see a joke," Mr. Honeythunder frowningly retorted. "A joke is wasted upon me, sir. Where are they! Helena and Neville, come here! Mr. Crisparkle has come down to meet you."

An unusually handsome lithe young fellow, and an unusually handsome lithe girl; much alike; both very dark, and very rich in color; she, of almost the gipsy type; something untamed about them both; a certain air upon them of hunter and huntress; yet withal a certain air of being the objects of the chase, rather than the followers. Slender, supple, quick of eye and limb; half shy, half defiant; fierce of look; an indefinable kind of pause coming and going on their whole expression, both of face and form, which might be equally likened to the pause before a crouch, or a bound. The rough mental notes made in the first five minutes by Mr. Crisparkle, would have read thus, *verbatim.*

He invited Mr. Honeythunder to dinner, with a troubled mind, (for the discomfiture of the dear old china shepherdess lay heavy on it), and gave his arm to Helena Landless. Both she and her brother, as they walked all together through the ancient streets, took great delight in what he pointed out of the Cathedral and the Monastery-ruin, and wondered——so his notes ran on——much as if they were beautiful barbaric captives brought from some wild tropical dominion. Mr. Honeythunder walked in the middle of the road, shouldering the natives out of his way, and loudly developing a scheme he had, for making a raid on all the unemployed persons in the United Kingdom, laying them every one by the heels in jail, and forcing them on pain of prompt extermination to become philanthropists.

Mrs. Crisparkle had need of her own share of philanthropy when she beheld this very large and very loud excrescence on the little party. Always something in the nature of a Boil upon the face of society, Mr. Honeythunder expanded into an inflammatory Wen in Minor Canon Corner. Though it was not literally true, as was facetiously charged against him by public unbelievers, that he called aloud to his fellow-creatures: "Curse your souls and bodies, come here and be blessed!" still his philanthropy was of that gunpowderous sort that the difference between it and animosity was hard to determine. You were to abolish military force, but you were first to bring all commanding officers who had done their duty, to trial by court martial for that offence, and shoot them. You were to abolish war, but were to make converts by making war upon them, and charging them with loving war as the apple of their eye. You were to have no capital punishment, but were first to sweep off the face of the earth all legislators, jurists, and judges, who were of the contrary opinion. You were to have universal concord, and were to get it by eliminating all the people who wouldn't, or conscientiously couldn't, be concordant. You were to love your brother as yourself, but after an indefinite interval of maligning him (very much as if you hated him), and calling him all manner of names. Above all things, you were to do nothing in private, or on your own account. You were to go to the offices of the Haven of Philanthropy, and put your name down as a Member and a Professing Philanthropist. Then, you were to pay up your subscription, get your card of membership and your riband and medal, and were evermore to live upon a platform, and evermore to say what Mr. Honeythunder said, and what the Treasurer said, and what the sub-Treasurer said, and what the Committee said, and what the sub-Committee said, and what the Secretary said, and what the Vice Secretary said. And this was usually said in the unanimously carried resolution under hand and seal, to the effect: "That this assembled Body of Professing Philanthropists views, with indignant scorn and contempt, not unmixed with utter detestation and loathing abhorrence,"—in short, the baseness of all those who do not belong to it, and pledges itself to make as many obnoxious statements as possible about them, without being at all particular as to facts.

The dinner was a most doleful breakdown. The philanthropist deranged the symmetry of the table, sat himself in the way of the waiting, blocked up the thoroughfare, and drove Mr. Tope (who assisted the parlour-maid), to the verge of distraction by passing plates and dishes on, over his own head. Nobody could talk to anybody, because he held forth to everybody at once, as if the company had no individual existence, but were a Meeting. He impounded the Reverend Mr. Septimus, as an official personage to be addressed, or kind of human peg to hang his oratorical hat on, and fell into the exasperating habit, common among such orators, of impersonating him as a wicked and weak opponent. Thus, he would ask: "And will you, sir, now stultify yourself by telling me"——and so forth, when the innocent man had not opened his lips, nor meant to open them. Or he would say: "Now see, sir, to what a position you are reduced. I will leave you no escape. After exhausting all the resources of fraud and falsehood, during years upon years; after exhibiting a combination of dastardly meanness with ensanguined daring, such as the world has not often witnessed; you have now the hypocrisy to bend the knee before the most degraded of mankind, and to sue and whine and howl for mercy!" Whereat the unfortunate Minor Canon would look, in part indignant and in part perplexed: while his worthy mother sat bridling, with tears in her eyes, and the remainder of the party lapsed into a sort of gelatinous state, in which there was no flavor or solidity, and very little resistance.

But the gush of philanthropy that burst forth when the departure of Mr. Honeythunder began to impend, must have been highly gratifying to the feelings of that distinguished man. His coffee was produced, by the special activity of Mr. Tope, a full hour before he wanted it. Mr. Crisparkle sat with his watch in his hand, for about the same period, lest he should overstay his time. The four young people were unanimous in believing that the Cathedral clock struck three-quarters, when it actually struck but one. Miss Twinkleton estimated the distance to the omnibus at five-and-twenty minutes' walk, when it was really five. The affectionate kindness of the whole circle hustled him into his great-coat, and shoved him out into the moonlight, as if he were a fugitive traitor with whom they sympathised, and a troop of horse were at the back door. Mr. Crisparkle and his new charge, who took him to the omnibus, were so fervent in their apprehensions of his catching cold, that they shut him up in it instantly and left him, with still half an hour to spare.

CHAPTER VII

MORE CONFIDENCES THAN ONE

"I KNOW very little of that gentleman, sir," said Neville to the Minor Canon as they turned back.

"You know very little of your guardian?" the Minor Canon repeated.

"Almost nothing."

"How came he——"

"To *be* my guardian? I'll tell you, sir. I suppose you know that we come (my sister and I) from Ceylon?"

"Indeed, no."

"I wonder at that. We lived with a stepfather there. Our mother died there, when we were little children. We have had a wretched existence. She made him our guardian, and he was a miserly wretch who grudged us food to eat, and clothes to wear. At his death, he passed us over to this man; for no better reason that I know of, than his being a friend or connexion of his, whose name was always in print and catching his attention."

"That was lately, I suppose?"

"Quite lately, sir. This stepfather of ours was a cruel brute as well as a grinding one. It was well he died when he did, or I might have killed him."

Mr. Crisparkle stopped short in the moonlight and looked at his hopeful pupil in consternation.

"I surprise you, sir?" he said, with a quick change to a submissive manner.

"You shock me; unspeakably shock me."

The pupil hung his head for a little while, as they walked on, and then said: "You never saw him beat your sister. I have seen him beat mine, more than once or twice, and I never forgot it."

"Nothing," said Mr. Crisparkle, "not even a beloved and beautiful sister's tears under dastardly ill-usage;" he became less severe, in spite of himself, as his indignation rose; "could justify those horrible expressions that you used."

"I am sorry I used them, and especially to you, sir. I beg to recall them. But permit me to set you right on one point. You spoke of my sister's tears. My sister would have let him tear her to pieces, before she would have let him believe that he could make her shed a tear."

Mr. Crisparkle reviewed those mental notes of his, and was neither at all surprised to hear it, nor at all disposed to question it.

"Perhaps you will think it strange, sir"—this was said in a hesitating voice—"that I should so soon ask you to allow me to confide in you, and to have the kindness to hear a word or two from me in my defence?"

"Defence?" Mr. Crisparkle repeated. "You are not on your defence, Mr. Neville."

"I think I am, sir. At least I know I should be, if you were better acquainted with my character."

"Well, Mr. Neville," was the rejoinder. "What if you leave me to find it out?"

"Since it is your pleasure, sir," answered the young man, with a quick change in his manner to sullen disappointment: "since it is your pleasure to check me in my impulse, I must submit."

There was that in the tone of this short speech which made the conscientious man to whom it was addressed, uneasy. It hinted to him that he might, without meaning it, turn aside a trustfulness beneficial to a mis-shapen young mind and perhaps to his own power of directing and improving it. They were within sight of the lights in his windows, and he stopped.

"Let us turn back and take a turn or two up and down, Mr. Neville, or you may not have time to finish what you wish to say to me. You are hasty in thinking that I mean to check you. Quite the contrary. I invite your confidence."

"You have invited it, sir, without knowing it, ever since I came here. I say 'ever since,' as if I had been here a week! The truth is, we came here (my sister and I) to quarrel with you, and affront you, and break away again."

"Really?" said Mr. Crisparkle, at a dead loss for anything else to say.

"You see, we could not know what you were beforehand, sir; could we?"

"Clearly not," said Mr. Crisparkle.

"And having liked no one else with whom we have ever been brought into contact, we had made up our minds not to like you."

"Really?" said Mr. Crisparkle again.

"But we do like you, sir, and we see an unmistakeable difference between your house and your reception of us, and anything else we have ever known. This—and my happening to be alone with you—and everything around us seeming so quiet and peaceful after Mr. Honeythunder's departure—and Cloisterham being so old and grave and beautiful, with the moon shining on it—these things inclined me to open my heart."

"I quite understand, Mr. Neville. And it is salutary to listen to such influences."

"In describing my own imperfections, sir, I must ask you not to suppose that I am describing my sister's. She has come out of the disadvantages of our miserable life, as much better than I am, as that Cathedral tower is higher than those chimnies."

Mr. Crisparkle in his own breast was not so sure of this.

"I have had, sir, from my earliest remembrance, to suppress a deadly and bitter hatred. This has made me secret and revengeful. I have been always tyrannically held down by the strong hand. This has driven me, in my weakness, to the resource of being false and mean. I have been stinted of education, liberty, money, dress, the very necessaries of life, the commonest pleasures of childhood, the commonest possessions of youth. This has caused me to be utterly wanting in I don't know what emotions, or remembrances, or good instincts——I have not even a name for the thing, you see——that you have had to work upon in other young men to whom you have been accustomed."

"This is evidently true. But this is not encouraging," thought Mr. Crisparkle as they turned again.

"And to finish with, sir: I have been brought up among abject and servile dependents, of an inferior race, and I may easily have contracted some affinity with them. Sometimes, I don't know but that it may be a drop of what is tigerish in their blood."

"As in the case of that remark just now," thought Mr. Crisparkle.

"In a last word of reference to my sister, sir (we are twin children), you ought to know, to her honor, that nothing in our misery ever subdued her, though it often cowed me. When we ran away from it (we ran away four times in six years, to be soon brought back and cruelly punished), the flight was always of her planning and leading. Each time she dressed as a boy, and showed the daring of a man. I take it we were seven years old when we first decamped; but I remember, when I lost the pocket-knife with which she was to have cut her hair short, how desperately she tried to tear it out, or bite it off. I have nothing further to say, sir, except that I hope you will bear with me and make allowance for me."

"Of that, Mr. Neville, you may be sure," returned the Minor Canon. "I don't preach more than I can help, and I will not repay your confidence with a sermon. But I entreat you to bear in mind, very seriously and steadily, that if I am to do you any good, it can only be with your own assistance; and that you can only render that, efficiently, by seeking aid from Heaven."

"I will try to do my part, sir."

"And, Mr. Neville, I will try to do mine. Here is my hand on it. May God bless our endeavours!"

They were now standing at his house-door, and a cheerful sound of voices and laughter was heard within.

"We will take one more turn before going in," said Mr. Crisparkle, "for I want to ask you a question. When you said you were in a changed mind concerning me, you spoke, not only for yourself, but for your sister too?"

"Undoubtedly I did, sir."

"Excuse me, Mr. Neville, but I think you have had no opportunity of communicating with your sister, since I met you. Mr. Honeythunder was very eloquent; but perhaps I may venture to say, without ill-nature, that he rather monopolized the occasion. May you not have answered for your sister without sufficient warrant?"

Neville shook his head with a proud smile.

"You don't know, sir, yet, what a complete understanding can exist between my sister and me, though no spoken word—perhaps hardly as much as a look—may have passed between us. She not only feels as I have described, but she very well knows that I am taking this opportunity of speaking to you, both for her and for myself."

Mr. Crisparkle looked in his face, with some incredulity; but his face expressed such absolute and firm conviction of the truth of what he said, that Mr. Crisparkle looked at the pavement, and mused, until they came to his door again.

"I will ask for one more turn, sir, this time," said the young man with a rather heightened color rising in his face. "But for Mr. Honeythunder's—I think you called it eloquence, sir?" (somewhat slyly).

"I—yes, I called it eloquence," said Mr. Crisparkle.

"But for Mr. Honeythunder's eloquence, I might have had no need to ask you what I am going to ask you. This Mr. Edwin Drood, sir: I think that's the name?"

"Quite correct," said Mr. Crisparkle. "D-r-double o-d."

"Does he—or did he—read with you, sir?"

"Never, Mr. Neville. He comes here visiting his relation, Mr. Jasper."

"Is Miss Bud his relation too, sir?"

("Now, why should he ask that, with sudden superciliousness!" thought Mr. Crisparkle.) Then he explained, aloud, what he knew of the little story of their betrothal.

"Oh! *That's* it, is it?" said the young man. "I understand his air of proprietorship now!"

This was said so evidently to himself, or to anybody rather than Mr. Crisparkle, that the latter instinctively felt as if to notice it would be almost tantamount to noticing a passage in a letter which he had read by chance over the writer's shoulder. A moment afterwards they re-entered the house.

Mr. Jasper was seated at the piano as they came into his drawing-room, and was accompanying Miss Rosebud while she sang. It was a consequence of his playing the accompaniment without notes, and of her being a heedless little creature very apt to go wrong, that he followed her lips most attentively, with his eyes as well as hands; carefully and softly hinting the key-note from time to time. Standing with an arm drawn round her, but with a face far more intent on Mr. Jasper than on her singing, stood Helena, between whom and her brother an instantaneous recognition passed, in which Mr. Crisparkle saw, or thought he saw, the understanding that had been spoken of, flash out. Mr. Neville then took his admiring station, leaning against the piano, opposite the singer; Mr. Crisparkle sat down by the china shepherdess; Edwin Drood gallantly furled and unfurled Miss Twinkleton's fan; and that lady passively claimed that sort of exhibitor's proprietorship in the accomplishment on view, which Mr. Tope, the Verger, daily claimed in the Cathedral service.

The song went on. It was a sorrowful strain of parting, and the fresh young voice was very plaintive and tender. As Jasper watched the pretty lips, and ever and again hinted the one note, as though it were a low whisper from himself, the voice became less steady, until all at once the singer broke into a burst of tears, and shrieked out, with her hands over her eyes: "I can't bear this! I am frightened! Take me away!"

With one swift turn of her lithe figure, Helena laid the little beauty on a sofa, as if she had never caught her up. Then, on one knee beside her, and with one hand upon her rosy mouth, while with the other she appealed to all the rest, Helena said to them:

"It's nothing; it's all over; don't speak to her for one minute, and she is well!"

Jasper's hands had, in the same instant, lifted themselves from the keys, and were now poised above them, as though he waited to resume. In that attitude he yet sat quiet: not even looking round, when all the rest had changed their places and were reassuring one another.

"Pussy's not used to an audience; that's the fact," said Edwin Drood. "She got nervous, and couldn't hold out. Besides, Jack, you are such a conscientious master, and require so much, that I believe you make her afraid of you. No wonder."

"No wonder," repeated Helena.

"There, Jack, you hear! You would be afraid of him, under similar circumstances, wouldn't you, Miss Landless?"

"Not under any circumstances," returned Helena.

Jasper brought down his hands, looked over his shoulder, and begged to thank Miss Landless for her vindication of his character. Then he fell to dumbly playing, without striking the notes, while his little pupil was taken to an open window for air, and was otherwise petted and restored. When she was brought back, his place was empty. "Jack's gone, Pussy," Edwin told her. "I am more than half afraid he didn't like to be charged with being the Monster who had frightened you." But she answered never a word, and shivered, as if they had made her a little too cold.

Miss Twinkleton now opining that indeed these were late hours, Mrs. Crisparkle, for finding ourselves outside the walls of the Nuns'

House, and that we who undertook the formation of the future wives and mothers of England (the last words in a lower voice, as requiring to be communicated in confidence) were really bound (voice coming up again) to set a better example than one of rakish habits, wrappers were put in requisition, and the two young cavaliers volunteered to see the ladies home. It was soon done, and the gate of the Nuns' House closed upon them.

The boarders had retired, and only Mrs. Tisher in solitary vigil awaited the new pupil. Her bedroom being within Rosa's, very little introduction or explanation was necessary, before she was placed in charge of her new friend, and left for the night.

"This is a blessed relief, my dear," said Helena. "I have been dreading all day, that I should be brought to bay at this time."

"There are not many of us," returned Rosa, "and we are good-natured girls; at least the others are; I can answer for them."

"I can answer for you," laughed Helena, searching the lovely little face with her dark fiery eyes, and tenderly caressing the small figure. "You will be a friend to me, won't you?"

"I hope so. But the idea of my being a friend to you seems too absurd, though."

"Why?"

"Oh! I am such a mite of a thing, and you are so womanly and handsome. You seem to have resolution and power enough to crush me. I shrink into nothing by the side of your presence even."

"I am a neglected creature, my dear, unacquainted with all accomplishments, sensitively conscious that I have everything to learn, and deeply ashamed to own my ignorance."

"And yet you acknowledge everything to me!" said Rosa.

"My pretty one, can I help it? There is a fascination in you."

"Oh! Is there though?" pouted Rosa, half in jest and half in earnest. "What a pity Master Eddy doesn't feel it more!"

Of course her relations towards that young gentleman had been already imparted, in Minor Canon Corner.

"Why, surely he must love you with all his heart!" cried Helena, with an earnestness that threatened to blaze into ferocity if he didn't.

"Eh? Oh, well, I suppose he does," said Rosa, pouting again; "I am sure I have no right to say he doesn't. Perhaps it's my fault. Perhaps I am not as nice to him as I ought to be. I don't think I am. But it *is* so ridiculous!"

Helena's eyes demanded what was.

"*We* are," said Rosa, answering as if she had spoken. "We are such a ridiculous couple. And we are always quarrelling."

"Why?"

"Because we both know we are ridiculous, my dear!" Rosa gave that answer as if it were the most conclusive answer in the world.

Helena's masterful look was intent upon her face for a few moments, and then she impulsively put out both her hands and said:

"You will be my friend and help me?"

"Indeed, my dear, I will," replied Rosa, in a tone of affectionate childishness that went straight and true to her heart; "I will be as good a friend as such a mite of a thing can be to such a noble creature as you. And be a friend to me, please; for I don't understand myself; and I want a friend who can understand me, very much indeed."

Helena Landless kissed her, and retaining both her hands, said: "Who is Mr. Jasper?"

Rosa turned aside her head in answering: "Eddy's uncle, and my music-master."

"You do not love him?"

"Ugh!" She put her hands up to her face, and shook with fear or horror.

"You know that he loves you?"

"Oh, don't, don't, don't!" cried Rosa, dropping on her knees, and clinging to her new resource. "Don't tell me of it! He terrifies me. He haunts my thoughts, like a dreadful ghost. I feel that I am never safe from him. I feel as if he could pass in through the wall when he is spoken of." She actually did look round, as if she dreaded to see him standing in the shadow behind her.

"Try to tell me more about it, darling."

"Yes, I will, I will. Because you are so strong. But hold me the while, and stay with me afterwards."

"My child! You speak as if he had threatened you in some dark way."

"He has never spoken to me about—that. Never."

"What has he done?"

"He has made a slave of me with his looks. He has forced me to understand him, without his saying a word; and he has forced me to keep silence, without his uttering a threat. When I play, he never moves his eyes from my hands. When I sing, he never moves his eyes from my lips. When he corrects me, and strikes a note, or a chord, or plays a passage, he himself is in the sounds, whispering that he pursues me as a lover, and commanding me to keep his secret. I avoid his eyes, but he forces me to see them without looking at them. Even when a glaze comes over them (which is sometimes the case), and he seems to wander away into a frightful sort of dream in which he threatens most, he obliges me to know it, and to know that he is sitting close at my side, more terrible to me then than ever."

"What is this imagined threatening, pretty one? What is threatened?"

"I don't know. I have never even dared to think or wonder what it is."

"And was this all, to-night?"

"This was all; except that to-night when he watched my lips so closely as I was singing, besides feeling terrified I felt ashamed and passionately hurt. It was as if he kissed me, and I couldn't bear it, but cried out. You must never breathe this to any one. Eddy is devoted to him. But you said to-night that you would not be afraid of him, under any circumstances, and that gives me—who am so much afraid of him—courage to tell only you. Hold me! Stay with me! I am too frightened to be left by myself."

The lustrous gipsy-face drooped over the clinging arms and bosom, and the wild black hair fell down protectingly over the childish form. There was a slumbering gleam of fire in the intense dark eyes, though they were then softened with compassion and admiration. Let whomsoever it most concerned, look well to it!

7.

THE MENACING CONCLUSION of Chapter Seven has left us perplexed. Someone would appear to be threatened by that gleam of fire in Helena Landless's eye, and this someone should "look well to it." But who is this someone? Logic would suggest Jasper. Yet we have the feeling that it is the reader who should be careful, who should "look well to it."

The author tells us that the person the gleam concerns (or rather: "most" concerns) could be anyone, but there is a hint of mockery, of playfulness, in the way he says it, as if he doesn't for one minute believe it himself.

"But of course it's Jasper," he seems to assure us, with the frank smile of one who plays fair. "Who else could it be?"

"Drood," we reply, not trusting Dickens. But we might have said any other name.

While waiting for the conference to start up again, let us have another look at the cast of characters. Whom can we classify as above, and whom below, suspicion?

Half-way through No. 2, John Jasper is more than ever
the prime suspect. The evidence against him was already
weighty, but now it is overwhelming. His behaviour becomes more sinister with every turn of the page. Rev. Crisparkle, on the other hand, can be excluded—and not just
because nobody has ever suspected him (Helena has never
been suspected either, if it comes to that). He is, in contrast to the "philanthropist" Honeythunder, the incarna-
tion of the ideas of tolerance and neighbourliness that
Dickens most cherished. Impossible for him to be a cold-
blooded murderer! For the same reason, we feel no possible suspicion can fall on the lawyer Grewgious, another
of Dickens's marvellous creations, who is about to make
his appearance. We exclude also (unless for solutions of a
paradoxical or burlesque kind) such comic characters as
Durdles, the Topes, Miss Twinkleton, or caricatures such
as the Dean and Mr Sapsea. Honeythunder himself, odious
as he is, is too grotesque to be suspected of anything other
than fraud and embezzlement against those in his charge.
Which means that apart from Rosa (whom we leave to the
study of Superintendent Battle), only the two Landlesses
remain as rival candidates to Jasper for potential murderer.

But while the evidence against Jasper is consistent and
detailed, the few facts that might cast suspicion on the
twins will not stand up to serious scrutiny. What weight
can be given to such heavy-handed, clumsy "evidence" as

their Oriental origins, their possible "mixed blood," their "wildness," or Neville's sudden infatuation with Rosa?

And yet, can we rule out the possibility that this is real evidence deliberately presented in such a way as to appear false? Dickens did not know Agatha Christie, of course, but he did know Wilkie Collins and his *Moonstone,* which was praised by T. S. Eliot as "the first, the longest, and the best of English detective novels."

So in the MED, too, we must be careful not to brush aside clues that are "too obvious"; and equally careful not to miss such clues as the author might have slipped in between the lines or hidden in digressions and simple colourful descriptions that would seem to bear no relation to the crime.

As for digressions, here is one on hypnotism and telepathy.

Dickens did not believe in spiritualism, and in his ghost-stories he never ceased to make fun of it. But he was extremely interested in paranormal psychology. He himself practised "mesmerism," as we know; and though he never succeeded in hypnotising his daughter Kate, not even from close-to, he was convinced that mesmeric powers could be exerted even from a distance, by telepathy. That is why Rosa, who is highly sensitive, fears that Jasper, with his magnetic powers, can reach her, even "passing in through the wall." And that is why Helena says that she does not

145

fear him: being magnetic and telepathic herself, not only has she recognised Jasper as a "colleague" (note how she looks at him in the Crisparkles' house while he secretly hypnotises Rosa), but probably she also judges herself to be stronger than he. Her eyes, remember, are described as intensely dark, and she has a "gipsy-face." And she comes from Ceylon.

Furthermore, telepathic communication seems to be habitual between the twins. They can understand each other without needing to exchange a word, as Crisparkle has already noted. Later, while teaching Neville, the Reverend will have the impression that "in teaching one, he was teaching two."

Returning to the end of Chapter Seven, then, we ask: Where is Neville during this scene between Helena and Rosa? And who is he with? The title of Chapter Eight suggests that he is already at daggers drawn, and a rapid glance through it confirms this surmise: the hot-blooded young man, mortally offended by his rival, is actually about to kill him in the presence of Jasper. But not only of Jasper. His sister is present too, if the telepathic link between them is operating. In this case, against whom could the "gleam of fire" in her eyes be directed, if not Drood?

Our hypothesis was not so wide the mark, after all. And our advice to Drood, could we give him any, would be to beware, above all, Helena.

We are now in the Dickens Room, where the session is at last about to begin. The technical difficulties, truly technical, have been solved: the sponsors, to save precious time, and tired of waiting for the famous announcer, have had a new relaying system put in, which is not only simultaneous but also subliminal. White-coated technicians have just completed the installation.

Loredana explains that everyone must now put on the headphones and listen attentively to a three- or four-second buzz (made up, in fact, of billions of subliminal bytes) which will imprint the entire second number of the MED on the brain. Attention.

"Zzz, zzz," and that's Chapters Six and Seven (which we already know). "Zzz, zzz," and that's Eight and Nine.

CHAPTER VIII

DAGGERS DRAWN

THE two young men, having seen the damsels, their charges, enter the courtyard of the Nuns' House, and finding themselves coldly stared at by the brazen door-plate, as if the battered old beau with the glass in his eye were insolent, look at one another, look along the perspective of the moonlit street, and slowly walk away together.

"Do you stay here long, Mr. Drood?" says Neville.

"Not this time," is the careless answer. "I leave for London again, to-morrow. But I shall be here, off and on, until next Midsummer; then I shall take my leave of Cloisterham, and England too; for many a long day, I expect."

"Are you going abroad?"

"Going to wake up Egypt a little," is the condescending answer.

"Are you reading?"

"Reading!" repeats Edwin Drood, with a touch of contempt. "No. Doing, working, engineering. My small patrimony was left a part of the capital of the Firm I am with, by my father, a former partner; and I am a charge upon the Firm until I come of age; and then I step into my modest share in the concern. Jack—you met him at dinner—is, until then, my guardian and trustee."

148

"I heard from Mr. Crisparkle of your other good fortune."

"What do you mean by my other good fortune?"

Neville has made his remark in a watchfully advancing, and yet furtive and shy manner, very expressive of that peculiar air already noticed, of being at once hunter and hunted. Edwin has made his retort with an abruptness not at all polite. They stop and interchange a rather heated look.

"I hope," says Neville, "there is no offence, Mr. Drood, in my innocently referring to your betrothal?"

"By George!" cries Edwin, leading on again at a somewhat quicker pace. "Everybody in this chattering old Cloisterham refers to it. I wonder no Public House has been set up, with my portrait for the sign of The Betrothed's Head. Or Pussy's portrait. One or the other."

"I am not accountable for Mr. Crisparkle's mentioning the matter to me, quite openly," Neville begins.

"No; that's true; you are not," Edwin Drood assents.

"But," resumes Neville, "I am accountable for mentioning it to you. And I did so, on the supposition that you could not fail to be highly proud of it."

Now, there are these two curious touches of human nature working the secret springs of this dialogue. Neville Landless is already enough impressed by Little Rosebud, to feel indignant that Edwin Drood (far below her) should hold his prize so lightly. Edwin Drood is already enough impressed by Helena, to feel indignant that Helena's brother (far below her) should dispose of him so coolly, and put him out of the way so entirely.

However, the last remark had better be answered. So, says Edwin:

"I don't know, Mr. Neville" (adopting that mode of address from Mr. Crisparkle), "that what people are proudest of, they usually talk most about; I don't know either, that what they are proudest of, they most like other people to talk about. But I live a busy life, and I speak under correction by you readers, who ought to know everything, and I dare say do."

By this time they have both become savage; Mr. Neville out in the open; Edwin Drood under the transparent cover of a popular tune, and a stop now and then to pretend to admire picturesque effects in the moonlight before him.

"It does not seem to me very civil in you," remarks Neville, at length, "to reflect upon a stranger who comes here, not having had your advantages, to try to make up for lost time. But, to be sure, *I* was not brought up in 'busy life,' and my ideas of civility were formed among Heathens."

"Perhaps, the best civility, whatever kind of people we are brought up among," retorts Edwin Drood, "is to mind our own business. If you will set me that example, I promise to follow it."

"Do you know that you take a great deal too much upon yourself," is the angry rejoinder; "and that in the part of the world I come from, you would be called to account for it?"

"By whom, for instance?" asks Edwin Drood, coming to a halt, and surveying the other with a look of disdain.

But, here a startling right hand is laid on Edwin's shoulder, and Jasper stands between them. For, it would seem that he, too, has strolled round by the Nuns' House, and has come up behind them on the shadowy side of the road.

"Ned, Ned, Ned!" he says. "We must have no more of this. I don't like this. I have overheard high words between you two. Remember, my dear boy, you are almost in the position of host to-night. You belong, as it were, to the place, and in a manner represent it towards a stranger. Mr. Neville is a stranger, and you should respect the obligations of hospitality. And, Mr. Neville:" laying his left hand on the inner shoulder of that young gentleman, and thus walking on between them, hand to shoulder on either side: "you will pardon me; but I appeal to you to govern your temper too. Now, what is amiss? But why ask! Let there be nothing amiss, and the question is superfluous. We are all three on a good understanding, are we not?"

After a silent struggle between the two young men who shall speak last, Edwin Drood strikes in with: "So far as I am concerned, Jack, there is no anger in me."

"Nor in me," says Neville Landless, though not so freely; or perhaps so carelessly. "But if Mr. Drood knew all that lies behind me, far away from here, he might know better how it is that sharp-edged words have sharp edges to wound me."

"Perhaps," says Jasper, in a smoothing manner, "we had better not qualify our good understanding. We had better not say anything having the appearance of a remonstrance or condition; it might not seem generous. Frankly and freely, you see there is no anger in Ned. Frankly and freely, there is no anger in you, Mr. Neville?"

"None at all, Mr. Jasper." Still, not quite so frankly or so freely; or, be it said once again, not quite so carelessly perhaps.

"All over then! Now, my bachelor gate-house is a few yards from here, and the heater is on the fire, and the wine and glasses are on the table, and it is not a stone's throw from Minor Canon Corner. Ned, you are up and away to-morrow. We will carry Mr. Neville in with us, to take a stirrup-cup."

"With all my heart, Jack."

"And with all mine, Mr. Jasper." Neville feels it impossible to say less, but would rather not go. He has an impression upon him that he has lost hold of his temper; feels that Edwin Drood's coolness, so far from being infectious, makes him red hot.

Mr. Jasper, still walking in the centre, hand to shoulder on either side, beautifully turns the Refrain of a drinking-song, and they all go up to his rooms. There, the first object visible, when he adds the light of a lamp to that of the fire, is the portrait over the chimney-piece. It is not an object calculated to improve the understanding between the two young men, as rather awkwardly reviving the subject of their difference. Accordingly, they both glance at it consciously, but say nothing. Jasper, however (who would appear from his conduct to have gained but an imperfect clue to the cause of their late high words), directly calls attention to it.

"You recognize that picture, Mr. Neville?" shading the lamp to throw the light upon it.

"I recognize it, but it is far from flattering the original."

"Oh, you are hard upon it! It was done by Ned, who made me a present of it."

"I am sorry for that, Mr. Drood." Neville apologizes, with a real intention to apologize; "if I had known I was in the artist's presence——"

"Oh, a joke, sir, a mere joke," Edwin cuts in, with a provoking yawn. "A little humoring of Pussy's points! I'm going to paint her gravely, one of these days, if she's good."

The air of leisurely patronage and indifference with which this is said, as the speaker throws himself back in a chair and clasps his hands at the back of his head, as a rest for it, is very exasperating to the excitable and excited Neville. Jasper looks observantly from the one to the other, slightly smiles, and turns his back to mix a jug of mulled wine at the fire. It seems to require much mixing and compounding.

"I suppose, Mr. Neville," says Edwin, quick to resent the indignant protest against himself in the face of young Landless, which is fully as visible as the portrait, or the fire, or the lamp: "I suppose that if you painted the picture of your lady love——"

"I can't paint," is the hasty interruption.

"That's your misfortune, and not your fault. You would if you could. But if you could, I suppose you would make her (no matter what she was in reality), Juno, Minerva, Diana, and Venus, all in one. Eh?"

"I have no lady love, and I can't say."

"If I were to try my hand," says Edwin, with a boyish boastfulness getting up in him, "on a portrait of Miss Landless — in earnest, mind you; in earnest — you should see what I could do!"

"My sister's consent to sit for it being first got, I suppose? As it never will be got, I am afraid I shall never see what you can do. I must bear the loss."

Jasper turns round from the fire, fills a large goblet glass for Neville, fills a large goblet glass for Edwin, and hands each his own; then fills for himself, saying:

"Come, Mr. Neville, we are to drink to my Nephew, Ned. As it is his foot that is in the stirrup — metaphorically — our stirrup-cup is to be devoted to him. Ned, my dearest fellow, my love!"

Jasper sets the example of nearly emptying his glass, and Neville follows it. Edwin Drood says "Thank you both very much," and follows the double example.

"Look at him!" cries Jasper, stretching out his hand admiringly and tenderly, though rallyingly too. "See where he lounges so easily, Mr. Neville! The world is all before him where to choose. A life of stirring work and interest, a life of change and excitement, a life of domestic ease and love! Look at him!"

Edwin Drood's face has become quickly and remarkably flushed by the wine; so has the face of Neville Landless. Edwin still sits thrown back in his chair, making that rest of clasped hands for his head.

"See how little he heeds it all!" Jasper proceeds in a bantering vein. "It is hardly worth his while to pluck the golden fruit that hangs ripe on the tree for him. And yet consider the contrast, Mr. Neville. You and I have no prospect of stirring work and interest, or of change and excitement, or of domestic ease and love. You and I have no prospect (unless you are more fortunate than I am, which may easily be), but the tedious, unchanging round of this dull place."

"Upon my soul, Jack," says Edwin, complacently, "I feel quite apologetic for having my way smoothed as you describe. But you know what I know, Jack, and it may not be so very easy as it seems, after all. May it, Pussy?" To the portrait, with a snap of his thumb and finger. "We have got to hit it off yet; haven't we, Pussy? You know what I mean, Jack."

His speech has become thick and indistinct. Jasper, quiet and self-possessed, looks to Neville, as expecting his answer or comment. When Neville speaks, *his* speech is also thick and indistinct.

"It might have been better for Mr. Drood to have known some hardships," he says, defiantly.

"Pray," retorts Edwin, turning merely his eyes in that direction, "pray why might it have been better for Mr. Drood to have known some hardships?"

"Aye," Jasper assents with an air of interest; "let us know why?"

"Because they might have made him more sensible," says Neville, "of good fortune that is not by any means necessarily the result
of his own merits."

Mr. Jasper quickly looks to his nephew for his rejoinder.

"Have *you* known hardships, may I ask?" says Edwin Drood,
sitting upright.

Mr. Jasper quickly looks to the other for his retort.

"I have."

"And what have they made *you* sensible of?"

Mr. Jasper's play of eyes between the two, holds good throughout the dialogue, to the end.

"I have told you once before to-night."

"You have done nothing of the sort."

"I tell you I have. That you take a great deal too much upon
yourself."

"You added something else to that, if I remember?"

"Yes, I did say something else."

"Say it again."

"I said that in the part of the world I come from, you would be
called to account for it."

"Only there?" cries Edwin Drood, with a contemptuous laugh.
"A long way off, I believe? Yes; I see! That part of the world is at a
safe distance."

"Say here, then," rejoins the other, rising in a fury. "Say anywhere! Your vanity is intolerable, your conceit is beyond endurance,
you talk as if you were some rare and precious prize, instead of a

common boaster. You are a common fellow, and a common boaster."

"Pooh, pooh," says Edwin Drood, equally furious, but more collected; "how should you know? You may know a black common fellow, or a black common boaster, when you see him (and no doubt you have a large acquaintance that way); but you are no judge of white men."

This insulting allusion to his dark skin infuriates Neville to that violent degree, that he flings the dregs of his wine at Edwin Drood, and is in the act of flinging the goblet after it, when his arm is caught in the nick of time by Jasper.

"Ned, my dear fellow!" he cries in a loud voice; "I entreat you, I command you, to be still!" There has been a rush of all the three, and a clattering of glasses and overturning of chairs. "Mr. Neville, for shame! Give this glass to me. Open your hand, sir. I WILL have it!"

But Neville throws him off, and pauses for an instant, in a raging passion, with the goblet yet in his uplifted hand. Then, he dashes it down under the grate, with such force that the broken splinters fly out again in a shower; and he leaves the house.

When he first emerges into the night air, nothing around him is still or steady; nothing around him shows like what it is; he only knows that he stands with a bare head in the midst of a blood-red whirl, waiting to be struggled with, and to struggle to the death.

But, nothing happening, and the moon looking down upon him as if he were dead after a fit of wrath, he holds his steam-hammer beating head and heart, and staggers away. Then, he becomes half conscious of having heard himself bolted and barred out, like a dangerous animal; and thinks what shall he do?

Some wildly passionate ideas of the river, dissolve under the spell of the moonlight on the Cathedral and the graves, and the remembrance of his sister, and the thought of what he owes to the good man who has but that very day won his confidence and given him his pledge. He repairs to Minor Canon Corner, and knocks softly at the door.

It is Mr. Crisparkle's custom to sit up last of the early household, very softly touching his piano and practising his favourite parts in concerted vocal music. The south wind that goes where it lists, by way of Minor Canon Corner on a still night, is not more subdued than Mr. Crisparkle at such times, regardful of the slumbers of the china shepherdess.

His knock is immediately answered by Mr. Crisparkle himself. When he opens the door, candle in hand, his cheerful face falls, and disappointed amazement is in it.

"Mr. Neville! In this disorder! Where have you been?"

"I have been to Mr. Jasper's, sir. With his nephew."

"Come in."

The Minor Canon props him by the elbow with a strong hand (in a strictly scientific manner, worthy of his morning trainings), and turns him into his own little book-room, and shuts the door.

"I have begun ill, sir. I have begun dreadfully ill."

"Too true. You are not sober, Mr. Neville."

"I am afraid I am not, sir, though I can satisfy you at another time that I have had very little indeed to drink, and that it overcame me in the strangest and most sudden manner."

"Mr. Neville, Mr. Neville," says the Minor Canon, shaking his head with a sorrowful smile; "I have heard that said before."

"I think—my mind is much confused, but I think—it is equally true of Mr. Jasper's nephew, sir."

"Very likely," is the dry rejoinder.

"We quarrelled, sir. He insulted me most grossly. He had heated that tigerish blood I told you of to-day, before then."

"Mr. Neville," rejoins the Minor Canon, mildly, but firmly: "I request you not to speak to me with that clenched right hand. Unclench it, if you please."

"He goaded me, sir," pursues the young man, instantly obeying, "beyond my power of endurance. I cannot say whether or no he meant it at first, but he did it. He certainly meant it at last. In short, sir," with an irrepressible outburst, "in the passion into which he lashed me, I would have cut him down if I could, and I tried to do it."

"You have clenched that hand again," is Mr. Crisparkle's quiet commentary.

"I beg your pardon, sir."

"You know your room, for I showed it to you before dinner; but I will accompany you to it once more. Your arm, if you please. Softly, for the house is all a-bed."

Scooping his hand into the same scientific elbow-rest as before, and backing it up with the inert strength of his arm, as skilfully as a Police Expert, and with an apparent repose quite unattainable by Novices, Mr. Crisparkle conducts his pupil to the pleasant and orderly old room prepared for him. Arrived there, the young man throws himself into a chair, and, flinging his arms upon his reading-table, rests his head upon them with an air of wretched self-reproach.

The gentle Minor Canon has had it in his thoughts to leave the room, without a word. But, looking round at the door, and seeing this dejected figure, he turns back to it, touches it with a mild hand, and says "Good night!" A sob is his only acknowledgment. He might have had many a worse; perhaps, could have had few better.

Another soft knock at the outer door, attracts his attention as he goes down stairs. He opens it to Mr. Jasper, holding in his hand the pupil's hat.

"We have had an awful scene with him," says Jasper, in a low voice.

"Has it been so bad as that?"

"Murderous!"

Mr. Crisparkle remonstrates: "No, no, no. Do not use such strong words."

"He might have laid my dear boy dead at my feet. It is no fault of his, that he did not. But that I was, through the mercy of God, swift and strong with him, he would have cut him down on my hearth."

The phrase smites home. "Ah!" thinks Mr. Crisparkle. "His own words!"

"Seeing what I have seen to-night, and hearing what I have heard," adds Jasper, with great earnestness, "I shall never know peace of mind when there is danger of those two coming together with no one else to interfere. It was horrible. There is something of the tiger in his dark blood."

"Ah!" thinks Mr. Crisparkle. "So he said!"

"You, my dear sir," pursues Jasper, taking his hand, "even you, have accepted a dangerous charge."

"You need have no fear for me, Jasper," returns Mr. Crisparkle, with a quiet smile. "I have none for myself."

"I have none for myself," returns Jasper, with an emphasis on the last pronoun, "because I am not, nor am I in the way of being, the object of his hostility. But you may be, and my dear boy has been. Good night!"

Mr. Crisparkle goes in, with the hat that has so easily, so almost imperceptibly, acquired the right to be hung up in his hall; hangs it up; and goes thoughtfully to bed.

CHAPTER IX

BIRDS IN THE BUSH

ROSA, having no relation that she knew of in the world, had, from the seventh year of her age, known no home but the Nuns' House, and no mother but Miss Twinkleton. Her remembrance of her own mother was of a pretty little creature like herself (not much older than herself it seemed to her), who had been brought home in her father's arms, drowned. The fatal accident had happened at a party of pleasure. Every fold and color in the pretty summer dress, and even the long wet hair, with scattered petals of ruined flowers still clinging to it, as the dead young figure, in its sad, sad beauty lay upon the bed, were fixed indelibly in Rosa's recollection. So were the wild despair and the subsequent bowed-down grief of her poor young father, who died brokenhearted on the first anniversary of that hard day.

The betrothal of Rosa grew out of the soothing of his year of mental distress by his fast friend and old college companion, Drood: who likewise had been left a widower in his youth. But he, too, went the silent road into which all earthly pilgrimages merge, some sooner, and some later; and thus the young couple had come to be as they were.

The atmosphere of pity surrounding the little orphan girl when she first came to Cloisterham, had never cleared away. It had taken brighter hues as she grew older, happier, prettier; now it had been golden, now roseate, and now azure; but it had always adorned her with some soft light of its own. The general desire to console and caress her, had caused her to be treated in the beginning as a child much younger than her years; the same desire had caused her to be still petted when she was a child no longer. Who should be her favorite, who should anticipate this or that small present, or do her this or that small service; who should take her home for the holidays; who should write to her the oftenest when they were separated, and whom she would most rejoice to see again when they were reunited; even these gentle rivalries were not without their slight dashes of bitterness in the Nuns' House. Well for the poor Nuns in their day, if they hid no harder strife under their veils and rosaries!

Thus Rosa had grown to be an amiable, giddy, wilful, winning little creature; spoilt, in the sense of counting upon kindness from all around her; but not in the sense of repaying it with indifference. Possessing an exhaustless well of affection in her nature, its sparkling waters had freshened and brightened the Nuns' House for years, and yet its depths had never yet been moved: what might betide when that came to pass; what developing changes might fall upon the heedless head, and light heart then; remained to be seen.

By what means the news that there had been a quarrel between the two young men over-night, involving even some kind of onslaught by Mr. Neville upon Edwin Drood, got into Miss Twinkleton's establishment before breakfast, it is impossible to say. Whether it was brought in by the birds of the air, or came blowing in with the very air itself, when the casement windows were set open; whether the baker brought it kneaded into the bread, or the milkman delivered it as part of the adulteration of his milk; or the housemaids, beating the dust out of their mats against the gateposts, received it in exchange deposited on the mats by the town atmosphere; certain it is that the news permeated every gable of the old building before Miss Twinkleton was down, and that Miss Twinkleton herself received it through Mrs. Tisher, while yet in the act of dressing; or (as she might have expressed the phrase to a parent or guardian of a mythological turn), of sacrificing to the Graces.

Miss Landless's brother had thrown a bottle at Mr. Edwin Drood.

Miss Landless's brother had thrown a knife at Mr. Edwin Drood.

A knife became suggestive of a fork, and Miss Landless's brother had thrown a fork at Mr. Edwin Drood.

As in the governing precedent of Peter Piper, alleged to have picked the peck of pickled pepper, it was held physically desirable to have evidence of the existence of the peck of pickled pepper which Peter Piper was alleged to have picked: so, in this case, it was held psychologically important to know Why Miss Landless's brother threw a bottle, knife, or fork—or bottle, knife, *and* fork—for the cook had been given to understand it was all three—at Mr. Edwin Drood?

Well, then. Miss Landless's brother had said he admired Miss Bud. Mr. Edwin Drood had said to Miss Landless's brother that he

164

had no business to admire Miss Bud. Miss Landless's brother had then "up'd" (this was the cook's exact information), with the bottle, knife, fork, and decanter (the decanter now coolly flying at every-body's head, without the least introduction), and thrown them all at Mr. Edwin Drood.

Poor little Rosa put a forefinger into each of her ears when these rumours began to circulate, and retired into a corner, beseeching not to be told any more; but Miss Landless, begging permission of Miss Twinkleton to go and speak with her brother, and pretty plainly showing that she would take it if it were not given, struck out the more definite course of going to Mr. Crisparkle's for accurate intel-ligence.

When she came back (being first closeted with Miss Twinkleton, in order that anything objectionable in her tidings might be retained by that discreet filter), she imparted to Rosa only, what had taken place; dwelling with a flushed cheek on the provocation her brother had received, but almost limiting it to that last gross affront as crowning "some other words between them," and, out of consid-eration for her new friend, passing lightly over the fact that the other words had originated in her lover's taking things in general so very easily . To Rosa direct, she brought a petition from her brother that she would forgive him; and, having delivered it with sisterly earnestness, made an end of the subject.

It was reserved for Miss Twinkleton to tone down the public mind of the Nuns' House. That lady, therefore, entering in a stately manner what plebeians might have called the school-room, but what,

in the patrician language of the head of the Nuns' House, was eu-
phuistically, not to say round-aboutedly, denominated "the apartment allotted to study," and saying with a forensic air, "Ladies!" all
rose. Mrs. Tisher at the same time grouped herself behind her chief,
as representing Queen Elizabeth's first historical female friend at
Tilbury Fort. Miss Twinkleton then proceeded to remark that Rumour, Ladies, had been represented by the Bard of Avon—needless
were it to mention the immortal SHAKESPEARE, also called the Swan
of his native river, not improbably with some reference to the ancient superstition that that bird of graceful plumage (Miss Jennings
will please stand upright) sang sweetly on the approach of death,
for which we have no ornithological authority, —Rumour, Ladies,
had been represented by that bard—hem!—

> "who drew
> The celebrated Jew,"

as painted full of tongues. Rumour in Cloisterham (Miss Ferdinand
will honour me with her attention) was no exception to the great
limner's portrait of Rumour elsewhere. A slight *fracas* between two
young gentlemen occurring last night within a hundred miles of
these peaceful walls (Miss Ferdinand, being apparently incorrigible,
will have the kindness to write out this evening, in the original
language, the first four fables of our vivacious neighbour, Monsieur
La Fontaine) had been very grossly exaggerated by Rumour's voice.
In the first alarm and anxiety arising from our sympathy with a
sweet young friend, not wholly to be dissociated from one of the

gladiators in the bloodless arena in question (the impropriety of Miss Reynolds's appearing to stab herself in the hand with a pin, is far too obvious, and too glaringly unlady-like, to be pointed out), we descended from our maiden elevation to discuss this uncongenial and this unfit theme. Responsible inquiries having assured us that it was but one of those "airy nothings" pointed at by the Poet (whose name and date of birth Miss Giggles will supply within half an hour), we would now discard the subject, and concentrate our minds upon the grateful labours of the day.

But the subject so survived all day, nevertheless, that Miss Ferdinand got into new trouble by surreptitiously clapping on a paper moustache at dinner-time, and going through the motions of aiming a water-bottle at Miss Giggles, who drew a table-spoon in defence.

Now, Rosa thought of this unlucky quarrel a great deal, and thought of it with an uncomfortable feeling that she was involved in it, as cause, or consequence, or what not, through being in a false position altogether as to her marriage engagement. Never free from such uneasiness when she was with her affianced husband, it was not likely that she would be free from it when they were apart. To-day, too, she was cast in upon herself, and deprived of the relief of talking freely with her new friend, because the quarrel had been with Helena's brother, and Helena undisguisedly avoided the subject as a delicate and difficult one to herself. At this critical time, of all times, Rosa's guardian was announced as having come to see her.

Mr. Grewgious had been well selected for his trust, as a man of incorruptible integrity, but certainly for no other appropriate quality discernible on the surface. He was an arid, sandy man, who, if he had been put into a grinding-mill, looked as if he would have ground immediately into high-dried snuff. He had a scanty flat crop of hair, in color and consistency like some very mangy yellow fur tippet; it was so unlike hair, that it must have been a wig, but for the stupendous improbability of anybody's voluntarily sporting such a head. The little play of feature that his face presented, was cut deep into it, in a few hard curves that made it more like work; and he had certain notches in his forehead, which looked as though Nature had been about to touch them into sensibility or refinement, when she had impatiently thrown away the chisel, and said: "I really cannot be worried to finish off this man; let him go as he is."

With too great length of throat at his upper end, and too much ankle-bone and heel at his lower; with an awkward and hesitating manner; with a shambling walk, and with what is called a near sight—which perhaps prevented his observing how much white cotton stocking he displayed to the public eye, in contrast with his black suit—Mr. Grewgious still had some strange capacity in him of making on the whole an agreeable impression.

Mr. Grewgious was discovered by his ward, much discomfitted by being in Miss Twinkleton's company in Miss Twinkleton's own sacred room. Dim forebodings of being examined in something, and not coming well out of it, seemed to oppress the poor gentleman when found in these circumstances.

"My dear, how do you do? I am glad to see you. My dear, how much improved you are. Permit me to hand you a chair, my dear."

Miss Twinkleton rose at her little writing-table, saying, with general sweetness, as to the polite Universe: "Will you permit me to retire?"

"By no means, madam, on my account. I beg that you will not move."

"I must entreat permission to *move*," returned Miss Twinkleton, repeating the word with a charming grace; "but I will not withdraw, since you are so obliging. If I wheel my desk to this corner window, shall I be in the way?"

"Madam! In the way!"

"You are very kind. Rosa, my dear, you will be under no restraint, I am sure."

Here Mr. Grewgious, left by the fire with Rosa, said again: "My dear, how do you do? I am glad to see you, my dear." And having waited for her to sit down, sat down himself.

"My visits," said Mr. Grewgious, "are, like those of the angels—not that I compare myself to an angel."

"No, sir," said Rosa.

"Not by any means," assented Mr. Grewgious. "I merely refer to my visits, which are few and far between. The angels, are, we know very well, upstairs."

Miss Twinkleton looked round with a kind of stiff stare.

"I refer, my dear," said Mr. Grewgious, laying his hand on Rosa's, as the possibility thrilled through his frame of his otherwise seeming to take the awful liberty of calling Miss Twinkleton my dear; "I refer to the other young ladies."

Miss Twinkleton resumed her writing.

Mr. Grewgious, with a sense of not having managed his opening point quite as neatly as he might have desired, smoothed his head from back to front as if he had just dived, and were pressing the water out—this smoothing action, however superfluous, was habitual with him—and took a pocket-book from his coat-pocket, and a stump of black-lead pencil from his waistcoat pocket.

"I made," he said, turning the leaves: "I made a guiding memorandum or so—as I usually do, for I have no conversational powers whatever—to which I will, with your permission, my dear, refer. 'Well and happy.' Truly. You are well and happy, my dear? You look so."

"Yes, indeed, sir," answered Rosa.

"For which," said Mr. Grewgious, with a bend of his head towards the corner window, "our warmest acknowledgments are due, and I am sure are rendered, to the maternal kindness and the constant care and consideration of the lady whom I have now the honor to see before me."

This point, again, made but a lame departure from Mr. Grewgious, and never got to its destination; for, Miss Twinkleton, feeling that the courtesies required her to be by this time quite outside the conversation, was biting the end of her pen, and looking upward, as waiting for the descent of an idea from any member of the Celestial Nine who might have one to spare.

Mr. Grewgious smoothed his smooth head again, and then made

another reference to his pocket-book; lining out 'well and happy' as disposed of.

" 'Pounds, shillings, and pence' is my next note. A dry subject for a young lady, but an important subject too. Life is pounds, shillings, and pence. Death is————" A sudden recollection of the death of her two parents seemed to stop him, and he said in a softer tone, and evidently inserting the negative as an after-thought: "Death is *not* pounds, shillings, and pence."

His voice was as hard and dry as himself, and Fancy might have ground it straight, like himself, into high-dried snuff. And yet, through the very limited means of expression that he possessed, he seemed to express kindness. If Nature had but finished him off, kindness might have been recognisable in his face at this moment. But if the notches in his forehead wouldn't fuse together, and if his face would work and couldn't play, what could he do, poor man!

" 'Pounds, shillings, and pence.' You find your allowance always sufficient for your wants, my dear?"

Rosa wanted for nothing, and therefore it was ample.

"And you are not in debt?"

Rosa laughed at the idea of being in debt. It seemed, to her inexperience, a comical vagary of the imagination. Mr. Grewgious stretched his near sight to be sure that this was her view of the case. "Ah!" he said, as comment, with a furtive glance towards Miss Twinkleton, and lining out pounds, shillings, and pence: "I spoke of having got among the angels! So I did!"

171

Rosa felt what his next memorandum would prove to be, and was blushing and folding a crease in her dress with one embarrassed hand, long before he found it.

" 'Marriage.' Hem!" Mr. Grewgious carried his smoothing hand down over his eyes and nose, and even chin, before drawing his chair a little nearer, and speaking a little more confidentially: "I now touch, my dear, upon the point that is the direct cause of my troubling you with the present visit. Otherwise, being a particularly Angular man, I should not have intruded here. I am the last man to intrude into a sphere for which I am so entirely unfitted. I feel, on these premises, as if I was a bear——with the cramp——in a youthful Cotillon."

His ungainliness gave him enough of the air of his simile to set Rosa off laughing heartily.

"It strikes you in the same light," said Mr. Grewgious, with perfect calmness. "Just so. To return to my memorandum. Mr. Edwin has been to and fro here, as was arranged. You have mentioned that, in your quarterly letters to me. And you like him, and he likes you."

"I *like* him very much, sir," rejoined Rosa.

"So I said, my dear," returned her guardian, for whose ear the timid emphasis was much too fine. "Good. And you correspond."

"We write to one another," said Rosa, pouting, as she recalled their epistolary differences.

"Such is the meaning that I attach to the word 'correspond' in this application, my dear," said Mr. Grewgious. "Good. All goes

172

well, time works on, and at this next Christmas time it will become necessary, as a matter of form, to give the exemplary lady in the corner window, to whom we are so much indebted, business notice of your departure in the ensuing half-year. Your relations with her, are far more than business relations no doubt; but a residue of business remains in them, and business is business ever. I am a particularly Angular man," proceeded Mr. Grewgious, as if it suddenly occurred to him to mention it, "and I am not used to give anything away. If, for these two reasons, some competent Proxy would give *you* away, I should take it very kindly."

Rosa intimated, with her eyes on the ground, that she thought a substitute might be found, if required.

"Surely, surely," said Mr. Grewgious. "For instance, the gentleman who teaches Dancing here—he would know how to do it with graceful propriety. He would advance and retire in a manner satisfactory to the feelings of the officiating clergyman, and of yourself, and the bridegroom, and all parties concerned. I am—I am a particularly Angular man," said Mr. Grewgious, as if he had made up his mind to screw it out at last: "and should only blunder."

Rosa sat still and silent. Perhaps her mind had not got quite so far as the ceremony yet, but was lagging on the way there.

"Memorandum, 'Will.' Now, my dear," said Mr. Grewgious, referring to his notes, disposing of 'marriage' with his pencil, and taking a paper from his pocket: "although I have before possessed you with the contents of your father's will, I think it right at this time to leave a certified copy of it in your hands. And although Mr.

Edwin is also aware of its contents, I think it right at this time likewise to place a certified copy of it in Mr. Jasper's hands——"

"Not in his own?" asked Rosa, looking up quickly. "Cannot the copy go to Eddy himself?"

"Why, yes, my dear, if you particularly wish it; but I spoke of Mr. Jasper as being his trustee."

"I do particularly wish it, if you please," said Rosa, hurriedly and earnestly; "I don't like Mr. Jasper to come between us, in any way."

"It is natural, I suppose," said Mr. Grewgious, "that your young husband should be all in all. Yes. You observe that I say, I suppose. The fact is, I am a particularly Unnatural man, and I don't know from my own knowledge."

Rosa looked at him with some wonder.

"I mean," he explained, "that young ways were never my ways. I was the only offspring of parents far advanced in life, and I half believe I was born advanced in life myself. No personality is intended towards the name you will so soon change, when I remark that while the general growth of people seem to have come into existence, buds, I seem to have come into existence a chip. I was a chip—and a very dry one—when I first became aware of myself. Respecting the other certified copy, your wish shall be complied with. Respecting your inheritance, I think you know all. It is an annuity of two hundred and fifty pounds. The savings upon that annuity, and some other items to your credit, all duly carried to account, with vouchers, will place you in possession of a lump-sum of money, rather exceeding Seventeen Hundred Pounds. I am empowered to advance the cost of your preparations for your marriage out of that fund. All is told."

"Will you please tell me," said Rosa, taking the paper with a prettily knitted brow, but not opening it: "whether I am right in what I am going to say? I can understand what you tell me, so very much better than what I read in law-writings. My poor papa and Eddy's father made their agreement together, as very dear and firm and fast friends, in order that we, too, might be very dear and firm and fast friends after them?"

"Just so."

"For the lasting good of both of us, and the lasting happiness of both of us?"

"Just so."

"That we might be to one another even much more than they had been to one another?"

"Just so."

"It was not bound upon Eddy, and it was not bound upon me, by any forfeit, in case———"

"Don't be agitated, my dear. In the case that it brings tears into your affectionate eyes even to picture to yourself—in the case of your not marrying one another—no, no forfeiture on either side. You would then have been my ward until you were of age. No worse would have befallen you. Bad enough perhaps!"

"And Eddy?"

"He would have come into his partnership derived from his

father, and into its arrears to his credit (if any), on attaining his majority, just as now."

Rosa with her perplexed face and knitted brow, bit the corner of her attested copy, as she sat with her head on one side, looking abstractedly on the floor, and smoothing it with her foot.

"In short," said Mr. Grewgious, "this betrothal is a wish, a sentiment, a friendly project, tenderly expressed on both sides. That it was strongly felt, and that there was a lively hope that it would prosper, there can be no doubt. When you were both children, you began to be accustomed to it, and it *has* prospered. But circumstances alter cases; and I made this visit to-day, partly, indeed principally, to discharge myself to the duty of telling you, my dear, that two young people can only be betrothed in marriage (except as a matter of convenience, and therefore mockery and misery), of their own free will, their own attachment, and their own assurance (it may or may not prove a mistaken one, but we must take our chance of that), that they are suited to each other and will make each other happy. It is to be supposed, for example, that if either of your fathers were living now, and had any mistrust on that subject, his mind would not be changed by the change of circumstances involved in the change of your years? Untenable, unreasonable, inconclusive, and preposterous!"

Mr. Grewgious said all this, as if he were reading it aloud; or, still more, as if he were repeating a lesson. So expressionless of any approach to spontaneity were his face and manner.

"I have now, my dear," he added, blurring out 'Will' with his

176

pencil, "discharged myself of what is doubtless a formal duty in this case, but still a duty in such a case. Memorandum, 'Wishes:' My dear, is there any wish of yours that I can further?"

Rosa shook her head, with an almost plaintive air of hesitation in want of help.

"Is there any instruction that I can take from you with reference to your affairs?"

"I—I should like to settle them with Eddy first, if you please," said Rosa, plaiting the crease in her dress.

"Surely. Surely," returned Mr. Grewgious. "You two should be of one mind in all things. Is the young gentleman expected shortly?"

"He has gone away only this morning. He will be back at Christmas."

"Nothing could happen better. You will, on his return at Christmas, arrange all matters of detail with him; you will then communicate with me; and I will discharge myself (as a mere business acquittance) of my business responsibilities towards the accomplished lady in the corner window. They will accrue at that season." Blurring pencil once again. "Memorandum 'Leave.' Yes. I will now, my dear, take my leave."

"Could I," said Rosa, rising, as he jerked out of his chair in his ungainly way: "could I ask you, most kindly to come to me at Christmas, if I had anything particular to say to you?"

"Why, certainly, certainly," he rejoined; apparently—if such a word can be used of one who had no apparent lights or shadows about him—complimented by the question. "As a particularly An-

gular man, I do not fit smoothly into the social circle, and consequently I have no other engagement at Christmas-time than to partake,
on the twenty-fifth, of a boiled turkey and celery sauce with a—
with a particularly Angular clerk I have the good fortune to possess,
whose father, being a Norfolk farmer, sends him up (the turkey up),
as a present to me, from the neighbourhood of Norwich. I should
be quite proud of your wishing to see me, my dear. As a professional
Receiver of rents, so very few people *do* wish to see me, that the
novelty would be bracing."

For his ready acquiescence, the grateful Rosa put her hands
upon his shoulders, stood on tiptoe, and instantly kissed him.

"Lord bless me!" cried Mr. Grewgious. "Thank you, my dear!
The honor is almost equal to the pleasure. Miss Twinkleton, Madam,
I have had a most satisfactory conversation with my ward, and I will
now release you from the incumbrance of my presence."

"Nay, sir," rejoined Miss Twinkleton, rising with a gracious condescension: "say not incumbrance. Not so, by any means. I cannot
permit you to say so."

"Thank you, madam. I have read in the newspapers," said Mr.
Grewgious, stammering a little, "that when a distinguished visitor
(not that I am one: far from it), goes to a school (not that this is
one: far from it), he asks for a holiday, or some sort of grace. It
being now the afternoon in the—College—of which you are the
eminent head, the young ladies might gain nothing, except in name,
by having the rest of the day allowed them. But if there is any young
lady at all under a cloud, might I solicit——?"

"Ah, Mr. Grewgious, Mr. Grewgious!" cried Miss Twinkleton, with a chastely-rallying forefinger. "Oh, you gentlemen, you gentlemen! Fie for shame, that you are so hard upon us poor maligned disciplinarians of our sex, for your sakes! But as Miss Ferdinand is at present weighed down by an incubus"—Miss Twinkleton might have said a pen-and-ink-ubus of writing out Monsieur La Fontaine—"go to her, Rosa, my dear, and tell her the penalty is remitted, in deference to the intercession of your guardian, Mr. Grewgious."

Miss Twinkleton here achieved a curtsey, suggestive of marvels happening to her respected legs, and which she came out of nobly, three yards behind her starting-point.

As he held it incumbent upon him to call on Mr. Jasper before leaving Cloisterham, Mr. Grewgious went to the Gate House, and climbed its postern stair. But Mr. Jasper's door being closed, and presenting on a slip of paper the word "Cathedral," the fact of its being service-time was borne into the mind of Mr. Grewgious. So, he descended the stair again, and, crossing the Close, paused at the great western folding-door of the Cathedral, which stood open on the fine and bright, though short-lived, afternoon, for the airing of the place.

"Dear me," said Mr. Grewgious, peeping in, "it's like looking down the throat of Old Time."

Old Time heaved a mouldy sigh from tomb and arch and vault; and gloomy shadows began to deepen in corners; and damps began to rise from green patches of stone; and jewels, cast upon the pavement of the nave from stained glass by the declining sun, began to perish. Within the grill-gate of the chancel, up the steps surmounted loomingly by the fast darkening organ, white robes could be dimly seen, and one feeble voice, rising and falling in a cracked monotonous mutter, could at intervals be faintly heard. In the free outer air, the river, the green pastures, and the brown arable lands, the teeming hills and dales, were reddened by the sunset: while the distant little windows in windmills and farm homesteads, shone, patches of bright beaten gold. In the Cathedral, all became grey, murky, and sepulchral, and the cracked monotonous mutter went on like a dying voice, until the organ and the choir burst forth, and drowned it in a sea of music. Then, the sea fell, and the dying voice made another feeble effort, and then the sea rose high, and beat its life out, and lashed the roof, and surged among the arches, and pierced the heights of the great tower; and then the sea was dry, and all was still.

Mr. Grewgious had by that time walked to the chancel-steps, where he met the living waters coming out.

"Nothing is the matter?" Thus Jasper accosted him, rather quickly. "You have not been sent for?"

"Not at all, not at all. I came down of my own accord. I have been to my pretty ward's, and am now homeward bound again."

"You found her thriving?"

"Blooming indeed. Most blooming. I merely came to tell her, seriously, what a betrothal by deceased parents is."

"And what is it—according to your judgment?"

Mr. Grewgious noticed the whiteness of the lips that asked the question, and put it down to the chilling account of the Cathedral.

"I merely came to tell her that it could not be considered binding, against any such reason for its dissolution as a want of affection, or want of disposition to carry it into effect, on the side of either party."

"May I ask, had you any especial reason for telling her that?"

Mr. Grewgious answered somewhat sharply: "The especial reason of doing my duty, sir. Simply that." Then he added: "Come, Mr. Jasper; I know your affection for your nephew, and that you are quick to feel on his behalf. I assure you that this implies not the least doubt of, or disrespect to, your nephew."

"You could not," returned Jasper, with a friendly pressure of his arm, as they walked on side by side, "speak more handsomely."

Mr. Grewgious pulled off his hat to smooth his head, and, having smoothed it, nodded it contentedly, and put his hat on again.

"I will wager," said Jasper, smiling—his lips were still so white that he was conscious of it, and bit and moistened them while speaking: "I will wager that she hinted no wish to be released from Ned."

"And you will win your wager, if you do," retorted Mr. Grewgious. "We should allow some margin for little maidenly delicacies in a young motherless creature, under such circumstances, I suppose; it is not in my line; what do you think?"

"There can be no doubt of it."

"I am glad you say so. Because," proceeded Mr. Grewgious, who had all this time very knowingly felt his way round to action on his remembrance of what she had said of Jasper himself: "because she seems to have some little delicate instinct that all preliminary arrangements had best be made between Mr. Edwin Drood and herself, don't you see? She don't want us, don't you know?"

Jasper touched himself on the breast, and said, somewhat indistinctly: "You mean me."

Mr. Grewgious touched himself on the breast, and said: "I mean us. Therefore, let them have their little discussions and councils together, when Mr. Edwin Drood comes back here at Christmas, and then you and I will step in, and put the final touches to the business."

"So, you settled with her that you would come back at Christmas?" observed Jasper. "I see! Mr. Grewgious, as you quite fairly said just now, there is such an exceptional attachment between my nephew and me, that I am more sensitive for the dear, fortunate, happy, happy fellow than for myself. But it is only right that the young lady should be considered, as you have pointed out, and that I should accept my cue from you. I accept it. I understood that at Christmas they will complete their preparations for May, and that their marriage will be put in final train by themselves, and that nothing will remain for us but to put ourselves in train also, and have everything ready for our formal release from our trusts, on Edwin's birthday."

"That is my understanding," assented Mr. Grewgious, as they shook hands to part. "God bless them both!"

"God save them both!" cried Jasper.

"I said, bless them," remarked the former, looking back over his shoulder.

"I said, save them," returned the latter. "Is there any difference?"

8.

AFTER THE LIGHTNING SPURT of subliminal transmission, a prolonged
silence descends upon the room. One by one, with slow,
somnolent movements, the participants take off their
headphones and sit as if stunned, their eyes glassy, their
lips tight. Dr Wilmot is the only one not to make use of
the miraculous appliance, because, of course, he knows the
MED by heart; he looks about him in surprise, wondering
at the sudden lack of loquacity in the audience.

This austere literary scholar, cut off from the practi-
calities of life, and in particular from the manifestations of
modern technology, has no idea that the people around
him are in fact communicating among themselves—mentally. The reader may know something of the phenomenon:
after an intense subliminal bombardment, a sort of telepathic network establishes itself, however briefly, between
the subjects, especially if it is their first experience of the
kind. In this particular case, the text itself, with its allu-

sions to the paranormal talents that Jasper and the twins possess, may have contributed to the intensity of the effect.

But mental conversation has its drawbacks. The interlocutors' thoughts become so interwoven and entangled—far more than in any spoken debate—that it is impossible to sort out who is thinking what. Here, for example, is how this morning's session opens (as reported in the verbal transcriptions provided later by the technicians):

i dont like that rosa one bit and i wouldnt be surprised if * but what did jasper put in the wine? opium doesnt have that effect at all * on the other hand helena * on the other hand rosa * the timing does correspond in fact, which means that gleam of fire * come off it! dickens cant expect * id pick loredana over either helena or rosa * but he really did believe in telepathy just as he did in premonitions and such phenomena as * mamma mia! * clairvoyance * mamma mia! now i see it all! i understand everything! thats why the dogs didnt * remember they came from ceylon * that loredana really * i didnt get a wink last night with that mattress * i tell you, i see it all! the false vagabond! the jug by the window! the hand that * that loredana, id love to * but ceylon isnt * and yet from the literary point of view * the murderer! thats how * india is still india: the sikhs, the thugs, and god knows what other * come back, you british soldier come you back to mandalay * underneath that lavender dress of hers * now look here! * thats how the deed was done! because my brother once told me * and that sharp knife he used to cut off her hair? * damned pâté they gave us last night * a malay kriss perhaps *

because from the literary point of view, as i was saying * we could do it on the bed in the opium-den * now look here, thats enough of these porno thoughts * the marvellous character of grewgious, which also inspired steven-son * come on, honey, dont get up-tight * the cathedral in the * i see it all! the dogs, the window, the * the cathedral in the twilight

A hopelessly unravelled babble, as one can see, and not merely because various contributions to the discussion come spilling out one on top of the other. There is, in addition, the unwelcome intrusion of mental remarks that have nothing whatsoever to do with the case, quite apart from being in questionable taste, some of them. And what is to be made of the repeated reference to certain dogs, a jug by a window, and a "false vagabond," who may be the real murderer? No, that is surely some kind of hallucination, triggered in an overheated mind[1] by the talk of clairvoy-ance. The clairvoyant claims to "see everything." But what this hallucinatory "everything" may be, is anyone's guess. There is no shortage of vagabonds in Cloisterham, as we know, but in the whole of the MED there is not a single dog, and no jug situated near a window.

Fortunately the record of this session is not all chaos.

---

[1] Most likely the lady whose brother is a senior consultant in Arezzo. Note that the moment she leaves the room, quite clearly in a state of mental disturbance, the phenomenon ceases. The lady is not seen again at the U&O.

Here and there, through the static, voices become recognisable, and the progress of the debate can be followed, more or less. But (the reader will understand) we must use caution in attributing thoughts to persons. The opinions of the Drood work-group, after the imprinting of the second number, can be roughly catalogued as follows:

THE PORFIRIANS: Immense admiration for the character of Grewgious, who among other things would inspire R. L. Stevenson in his creation of the immortal figure of Mr Utterson in *The Strange Case of Dr Jekyll and Mr Hyde*. Dickens is here at the height of his powers, observes Magistrate Petrovich. Wolfe, whose taste is the best, expresses his appreciation of other memorable passages: the description of the cathedral "in double perspective" at sunset; Miss Twinkleton's address to her pupils, which plays down the news of the altercation between Drood and Neville.

FATHER BROWN: And so the author was by no means exhausted, or "at a crisis," as some have claimed. Those who have considered and those who still do consider the MED to be not only an incomplete novel but an inferior one don't know what they're talking about. In the case of Wilkie Collins, who privately judged it as "Dickens's last laboured effort, the melancholy work of a worn-out brain," one must bear in mind the fact that the two writers had been on bad terms for some time.

THE AGATHISTS: It is not the literary value of the work

that is in question but its detective plot. From that point of view, Collins could well have been right. Because if Dickens's intention was that the murderer turn out to be the prime suspect, well then, to put it frankly, this so-called mystery . . .

But here there is a divergence of opinion, and the group of Agathists must be divided into pessimists and optimists.

PESSIMISTS: The second (May) issue leaves us with no alternative to Jasper's guilt. The arrival of the twins merely reinforces it. Up to that point, the reader could imagine the uncle's crime remaining in its Platonic state of intention, an opium-induced flight of fantasy. This is no longer possible. Because it is perfectly clear that Neville, with or without Helena, is a character of convenience, brought in with the sole purpose of providing the villain with an innocent person on whom suspicion can be diverted. And indeed, Jasper sets to work without wasting a minute: 1) With diabolic intuition he gathers that his nephew and the newcomer dislike each other on sight. 2) He follows them furtively in the darkness, and as soon as he hears them arguing, he steps in, ostensibly to pacify, but 3) when he discovers that the dispute is over Rosa, he smiles in a patiently devilish manner and at once prepares a drugged wine, which stirs the two young men up again, rousing them almost to violence. 4) Immediately afterwards, he hurries round to Crisparkle to tell him about the quarrel, making it sound as dramatic as possible, and putting him on his guard against the homicidal temperament of that young man and his "dark blood." 5) By now he is so certain that his murder will go undetected, that in Grewgious's presence he quite openly and ominously plays on the words "bless" and "save." The only trouble is that 6) a perfect crime to him can only be a disappointment to us!

HOLMES: Better a disappointment than . . . I don't know, I'm more convinced than ever that we would do best to leave these things alone, not to pry any more deeply into this matter . . . Someone here has raised an issue that perturbs me greatly.[1]

OPTIMISTS: The ending is not so obvious, and the twins are by no means characters of convenience. Dickens has taken care to give them not only a wonderful aura of the picturesque but also all the qualifications for possible guilt. Both have a mysterious past of suffering, humiliation, cruel treatment, and rebellion. The brother used to go round armed with a knife, and quite possibly still does so, and by his own admission he can be provoked into killing someone, even if only in the heat of the moment. He is surly, touchy to an extreme, and tormented by a racial and social inferiority complex. His sister is equally fearsome. A girl

---

[1] We attribute this snatch to Holmes, on account of his declaration the previous evening. But the meaning of the last sentence is not clear to us.

able to tear out her own hair in order to disguise herself as a man will stop at nothing; and she herself says that she is afraid of nobody. The twins are fully convincing as "reserve" villains.

MAIGRET: If they convince me at all, it is as providers of *coups de théâtre* of the (puff, puff)[1] classic kind. Their arrival from Ceylon is the first of such coups. Their mysterious past presages more to come. They are orphans, but we are told nothing else of their family. That cruel stepfather of theirs (puff, puff), will he turn up again? Perhaps some amazing disclosure of relationship is in the offing, some extraordinary scene of recognition. And a dark complexion, it leaves the way open for highly exotic developments, things that have to do with the secrets, sects, rites (puff, puff) of the Far East.

DUPIN: A real coup could come about through telepathy. The twins, though not together, may flare up with implacable hatred against Edwin at the same moment, may plan and carry out their crime by telepathic accord. This would catch the reader completely by surprise, who would then thank Dickens for putting him off the scent with all that evidence pointing to Jasper—poor Jasper, as we would then have to call him.

---

[1] It is interesting to note that Maigret, while thinking, continues to pull on his pipe *mentally*.

TOAD: Putting one off the scent is one thing; cheating is another! Forget about the telepathy and consider the milkman. You'll have noticed there's a milkman in this second instalment. What could be easier than to find a motive for him—he, too, is madly in love with Rosa, or Edwin once caught him watering down the milk and is blackmailing him—and have the modus operandi involve, say, his cart and bottles? I would be perfectly satisfied with a solution of that sort—provided the author also explains to me, in meticulous detail, just why Jasper has behaved in the peculiar way he's been made to behave. Because, and I'll say it again, putting one off the scent is one thing . . .

FATHER BROWN *and/or* PORFIRY PETROVICH: It never entered Dickens's head to cheat as a writer. His plots, true, are often complicated to the point of incoherence. Which means that the culprit could turn out to be Neville, after all. But involving Helena would be really too far-fetched; the motive of telepathically shared hatred just doesn't hold water.

MARLOWE *or* ARCHER: These prigs just won't admit that the girl, who's clearly lesbian as well as telepathic, has taken a fancy to sweet swooning Rosa. And this gives her a wonderful extra motive. Dickens, of course, with his fuddy-duddy, whiskered readers, couldn't spell all that out.

ARCHER *or* MARLOWE: But the winks and nods are like semaphore signals. All the hugging and kissing and you're so fascinating, you give me courage, hold me, stay with me. No, this is not your usual sweet-sixteen soppiness. One woman is tough, authoritarian, protective, clearly butch in looks and manners; the other never misses a chance to play cutesy coquette kitten, who constantly needs to be saved and cuddled. Old Boz knew more about life than some think! And he knew enough about his public of hypocritical moralists to be sure that there were plenty of readers out there who would get the idea.

HASTINGS: Well, maybe I'm a hypocritical moralist myself, but this seems to me a bit strong. What do you think, Poirot?

POIROT: . . . .[1]

LOREDANA, *aloud, passing a hand over her forehead:* What . . . where . . . what time is it?

WILMOT, *still without the foggiest idea of what is happening:* It is exactly nine minutes past eleven. But . . .

So only three minutes have elapsed, reader, since the beginning of this singular session, and the members of the Drood work-group have practically nothing left to say to one another. Archer and Marlowe stand up, humming softly,

---

[1] Poirot hasn't contributed to the debate so far, and even now he doesn't reply. One might conclude that the Drood case no longer interests him. Or, instead, could it be that his "little grey cells" are working so fast that not even the ultrahigh frequencies of the Japanese psycho-receivers can pick them up?

sure that a coffee-break, fully merited, is in the offing. But Watson, who has observed Dr Wilmot's bewilderment, realises that the scholar was left out of the telepathic circuit and proceeds to fill him in. Loredana, meanwhile, has gone to the technicians' room and now returns with the print-out of the debate.

WILMOT, *looking through the pages:* Fine . . . I'd say that we could pass on to the third issue, that is, the June number.

But the proposal is met with a general tramping of feet; the idea of a coffee-break has clearly infected everyone. And it is a break which flows on into lunch and aperitifs, then spills over into the garden-paths and the lobby's arm-chairs. There are even those who adopt the Roman custom of the siesta and return to their rooms.

The technicians use this intermission to make some adjustments in the equipment, so that the side-effects produced by the subliminal imprinting that morning can be avoided. The frequency of the impulses is reduced, the transmission-time lengthened. Thus, when the conference resumes in the afternoon, the transmission of the third number—that is, Chapters Ten, Eleven, and Twelve—takes a full minute.

CHAPTER X

SMOOTHING THE WAY

IT has been often enough remarked that women have a curious power of divining the characters of men, which would seem to be innate and instinctive; seeing that it is arrived at through no patient process of reasoning, that it can give no satisfactory or sufficient account of itself, and that it pronounces in the most confident manner even against accumulated observation on the part of the other sex. But it has not been quite so often remarked that this power (fallible, like every other human attribute), is for the most part absolutely incapable of self-revision; and that when it has delivered an adverse opinion which by all human lights is subsequently proved to have failed, it is undistinguishable from prejudice, in respect of its determination not to be corrected. Nay, the very possibility of contradiction or disproof, however remote, communicates to this feminine judgment from the first, in nine cases out of ten, the weakness attendant on the testimony of an interested witness: so personally and strongly does the fair diviner connect herself with her divination.

"Now, don't you think, Ma dear," said the Minor Canon to his mother one day as she sat at her knitting in his little book-room, "that you are rather hard on Mr. Neville?"

"No, I do *not*, Sept," returned the old lady.

"Let us discuss it, Ma."

"I have no objection to discuss it, Sept. I trust, my dear, I am always open to discussion." There was a vibration in the old lady's cap, as though she internally added: "and I should like to see the discussion that would change *my* mind!"

"Very good, Ma," said her conciliatory son. "There is nothing like being open to discussion."

"I hope not, my dear," returned the old lady, evidently shut to it.

"Well! Mr. Neville, on that unfortunate occasion, commits himself under provocation."

"And under mulled wine," added the old lady.

"I must admit the wine. Though I believe the two young men were much alike in that regard."

"I don't!" said the old lady.

"Why not, Ma?"

"Because I *don't*," said the old lady. "Still, I am quite open to discussion."

"But, my dear Ma, I cannot see how we are to discuss, if you take that line."

"Blame Mr. Neville for it, Sept, and not me," said the old lady, with stately severity.

"My dear Ma! Why Mr. Neville?"

"Because," said Mrs. Crisparkle, retiring on first principles, "he came home intoxicated, and did great discredit to this house, and showed great disrespect to this family."

"That is not to be denied, Ma. He was then, and he is now, very sorry for it."

"But for Mr. Jasper's well-bred consideration in coming up to me next day, after service, in the Nave itself, with his gown still on, and expressing his hope that I had not been greatly alarmed or had my rest violently broken, I believe I might never have heard of that disgraceful transaction," said the old lady.

"To be candid, Ma, I think I should have kept it from you if I could: though I had not decidedly made up my mind. I was following Jasper out, to confer with him on the subject, and to consider the expediency of his and my jointly hushing the thing up on all accounts, when I found him speaking to you. Then it was too late."

"Too late, indeed, Sept. He was still as pale as gentlemanly ashes at what had taken place in his rooms over-night."

"If I *had* kept it from you, Ma, you may be sure it would have been for your peace and quiet, and for the good of the young men, and in my best discharge of my duty according to my lights."

The old lady immediately walked across the room and kissed him; saying, "Of course, my dear Sept, I am sure of that."

"However, it became the town-talk," said Mr. Crisparkle, rubbing his ear, as his mother resumed her seat, and her knitting, "and passed out of my power."

"And I said then, Sept," returned the old lady, "that I thought ill of Mr. Neville. And I say now, that I think ill of Mr. Neville. And I said then, and I say now, that I hope Mr. Neville may come to good, but I don't believe he will." Here the cap vibrated again, considerably.

"I am sorry to hear you say so, Ma———"

"I am sorry to say so, my dear," interposed the old lady, knitting on firmly, "but I can't help it."

"———For," pursued the Minor Canon, "it is undeniable that Mr. Neville is exceedingly industrious and attentive, and that he improves apace, and that he has—I hope I may say—an attachment to me."

"There is no merit in the last article, my dear," said the old lady, quickly; "and if he says there is, I think the worse of him for the boast."

"But, my dear Ma, he never said there was."

"Perhaps not," returned the old lady; "still, I don't see that it greatly signifies."

There was no impatience in the pleasant look with which Mr. Crisparkle contemplated the pretty old piece of china as it knitted; but there was, certainly, a humorous sense of its not being a piece of china to argue with very closely.

"Besides, Sept. Ask yourself what he would be without his sister. You know what an influence she has over him; you know what a capacity she has; you know that whatever he reads with you, he reads with her. Give her her fair share of your praise, and how much do you leave for him?"

At these words Mr. Crisparkle fell into a little reverie, in which he thought of several things. He thought of the times he had seen the brother and sister together in deep converse over one of his old college books; now, in the rimy mornings, when he made those sharpening pilgrimages to Cloisterham Weir; now, in the sombre evenings, when he faced the wind at sunset, having climbed his favourite outlook, a beetling fragment of monastery ruin; and the two studious figures passed below him along the margin of the river, in which the town fires and lights already shone, making the landscape bleaker. He thought how the consciousness had stolen upon him that in teaching one, he was teaching two; and how he had almost insensibly adapted his explanations to both minds—that with which his own was daily in contact, and that which he only approached through it. He thought of the gossip that had reached him from the Nuns' House, to the effect that Helena, whom he had mistrusted as so proud and fierce, submitted herself to the fairy-bride (as he called her), and learnt from her what she knew. He thought of the picturesque alliance between those two, externally so very different. He thought—perhaps most of all—could it be that these things were yet but so many weeks old, and had become an integral part of his life?

As, whenever the Reverend Septimus fell a-musing, his good mother took it to be an infallible sign that he "wanted support," the blooming old lady made all haste to the dining-room closet, to produce from it the support embodied in a glass of Constantia and a home-made biscuit. It was a most wonderful closet, worthy of Cloisterham and of Minor Canon Corner. Above it, a portrait of

Handel in a flowing wig beamed down at the spectator, with a knowing air of being up to the contents of the closet, and a musical air of intending to combine all its harmonies in one delicious fugue. No common closet with a vulgar door on hinges, openable all at once, and leaving nothing to be disclosed by degrees, this rare closet had a lock in mid-air, where two perpendicular slides met: the one falling down, and the other pushing up. The upper slide, on being pulled down (leaving the lower a double mystery), revealed deep shelves of pickle-jars, jam-pots, tin canisters, spice-boxes, and agreeably outlandish vessels of blue and white, the luscious lodgings of preserved tamarinds and ginger. Every benevolent inhabitant of this retreat had his name inscribed upon his stomach. The pickles, in a uniform of rich brown double-breasted, buttoned coat, and yellow or sombre drab continuations, announced their portly forms, in printed capitals, as Walnut, Gherkin, Onion, Cabbage, Cauliflower, Mixed, and other members of that noble family. The jams, as being of a less masculine temperament, and as wearing curlpapers, announced themselves in feminine calligraphy, like a soft whisper, to be Raspberry, Gooseberry, Apricot, Plum, Damson, Apple, and Peach. The scene closing on these charmers, and the lower slide ascending, oranges were revealed, attended by a mighty japanned sugar-box, to temper their acerbity if unripe. Home-made biscuits waited at the Court of these Powers, accompanied by a goodly fragment of plum-cake, and various slender ladies' fingers, to be dipped into sweet wine and kissed. Lowest of all, a compact leaden vault enshrined the sweet wine and a stock of cordials: whence issued whispers of Seville

Orange, Lemon, Almond, and Carraway-seed. There was a crowning air upon this closet of closets, of having been for ages hummed through by the Cathedral bell and organ, until those venerable bees had made sublimated honey of everything in store; and it was always observed that every dipper among the shelves (deep, as has been noticed, and swallowing up head, shoulders, and elbows), came forth again mellow-faced, and seeming to have undergone a saccharine transfiguration.

The Reverend Septimus yielded himself up quite as willing a victim to a nauseous medicinal herb-closet, also presided over by the china shepherdess, as to this glorious cupboard. To what amazing infusions of gentian, peppermint, gilliflower, sage, parsley, thyme, rue, rosemary, and dandelion, did his courageous stomach submit itself! In what wonderful wrappers enclosing layers of dried leaves, would he swathe his rosy and contented face, if his mother suspected him of a toothache! What botanical blotches would he cheerfully stick upon his cheek, or forehead, if the dear old lady convicted him of an imperceptible pimple there! Into this herbaceous penitentiary, situated on an upper staircase-landing: a low and narrow whitewashed cell, where bunches of dried leaves hung from rusty hooks in the ceiling, and were spread out upon shelves, in company with portentous bottles: would the Reverend Septimus submissively be led, like the highly-popular lamb who has so long and unresistingly been led to the slaughter, and there would he, unlike that lamb, bore nobody but himself. Not even doing that much, so that the old lady were busy and pleased, he would quietly swallow what was given him, merely taking a corrective dip of hands and face into the great bowl of dried rose-leaves, and into the other great bowl of dried lavender, and then would go out, as confident in the sweetening powers of Cloisterham Weir and a wholesome mind, as Lady Macbeth was hopeless of those of all the seas that roll.

In the present instance the good Minor Canon took his glass of Constantia with an excellent grace, and, so supported to his mother's satisfaction, applied himself to the remaining duties of the day. In their orderly and punctual progress they brought round Vesper Service and twilight. The Cathedral being very cold, he set off for a brisk trot after service; the trot to end in a charge at his favorite fragment of ruin, which was to be carried by storm, without a pause for breath.

He carried it in a masterly manner, and, not breathed even then, stood looking down upon the river. The river at Cloisterham is sufficiently near the sea to throw up oftentimes a quantity of sea-weed. An unusual quantity had come in with the last tide, and this, and the confusion of the water, and the restless dipping and flapping of the noisy gulls, and an angry light out seaward beyond the brown-sailed barges that were turning black, foreshadowed a stormy night. In his mind he was contrasting the wild and noisy sea with the quiet harbour of Minor Canon Corner, when Helena and Neville Landless passed below him. He had had the two together in his thoughts all day, and at once climbed down to speak to them together. The footing was rough in an uncertain light for any tread save that of a good climber; but the Minor Canon was as good a climber as most men, and stood beside them before many good climbers would have been half-way down.

"A wild evening, Miss Landless! Do you not find your usual walk with your brother too exposed and cold for the time of year? Or at all events, when the sun is down, and the weather is driving in from the sea?"

Helena thought not. It was their favorite walk. It was very retired.

"It is very retired," assented Mr. Crisparkle, laying hold of his opportunity straightway, and walking on with them. "It is a place of all others where one can speak without interruption, as I wish to do. Mr. Neville, I believe you tell your sister everything that passes between us?"

"Everything, sir."

"Consequently," said Mr. Crisparkle, "your sister is aware that I have repeatedly urged you to make some kind of apology for that unfortunate occurrence which befell, on the night of your arrival here."

In saying it he looked to her, and not to him; therefore it was she, and not he, who replied:

"Yes."

"I call it unfortunate, Miss Helena," resumed Mr. Crisparkle, "forasmuch as it certainly has engendered a prejudice against Neville. There is a notion about, that he is a dangerously passionate fellow, of an uncontrollable and furious temper: he is really avoided as such."

"I have no doubt he is, poor fellow," said Helena, with a look of proud compassion at her brother, expressing a deep sense of his being ungenerously treated. "I should be quite sure of it, from your saying so; but what you tell me is confirmed by suppressed hints and references that I meet with every day."

"Now," Mr. Crisparkle again resumed, in a tone of mild though firm persuasion, "is not this to be regretted, and ought it not to be amended? These are early days of Neville's in Cloisterham, and I have no fear of his outliving such a prejudice, and proving himself to have been misunderstood. But how much wiser to take action at once, than to trust to uncertain time! Besides; apart from its being politic, it is right. For there can be no question that Neville was wrong."

"He was provoked," Helena submitted.

"He was the assailant," Mr. Crisparkle submitted.

They walked on in silence, until Helena raised her eyes to the Minor Canon's face, and said, almost reproachfully: "Oh, Mr. Crisparkle, would you have Neville throw himself at young Drood's feet, or at Mr. Jasper's, who maligns him every day! In your heart you cannot mean it. From your heart you could not do it, if his case were yours."

"I have represented to Mr. Crisparkle, Helena," said Neville, with a glance of deference towards his tutor, "that if I could do it from my heart, I would. But I cannot, and I revolt from the pretence. You forget, however, that to put the case to Mr. Crisparkle as his own, is to suppose Mr. Crisparkle to have done what I did."

203

"I ask his pardon," said Helena.

"You see," remarked Mr. Crisparkle, again laying hold of his opportunity, though with a moderate and delicate touch, "you both instinctively acknowledge that Neville did wrong! Then why stop short, and not otherwise acknowledge it?"

"Is there no difference," asked Helena, with a little faltering in her manner, "between submission to a generous spirit, and submission to a base or trivial one?"

Before the worthy Minor Canon was quite ready with his argument in reference to this nice distinction, Neville struck in:

"Help me to clear myself with Mr. Crisparkle, Helena. Help me to convince him that I cannot be the first to make concessions without mockery and falsehood. My nature must be changed before I can do so, and it is not changed. I am sensible of inexpressible affront, and deliberate aggravation of inexpressible affront, and I am angry. The plain truth is, I am still as angry when I recall that night as I was that night."

"Neville," hinted the Minor Canon, with a steady countenance, "you have repeated that former action of your hands, which I so much dislike."

"I am sorry for it, sir, but it was involuntary. I confessed that I was still as angry."

"And I confess," said Mr. Crisparkle, "that I hoped for better things."

"I am sorry to disappoint you, sir, but it would be far worse to deceive you, and I should deceive you grossly if I pretended that you had softened me in this respect. The time may come when your powerful influence will do even that with the difficult pupil whose antecedents you know; but it has not come yet. Is this so, and in spite of my struggles against myself, Helena?"

She, whose dark eyes were watching the effect of what he said on Mr. Crisparkle's face, replied—to Mr. Crisparkle: not to him: "It is so." After a short pause, she answered the slightest look of inquiry conceivable, in her brother's eyes, with as slight an affirmative bend of her own head; and he went on:

"I have never yet had the courage to say to you, sir, what in full openness I ought to have said when you first talked with me on this subject. It is not easy to say, and I have been withheld by a fear of its seeming ridiculous, which is very strong upon me down to this last moment, and might, but for my sister, prevent my being quite open with you even now. —I admire Miss Bud, sir, so very much, that I cannot bear her being treated with conceit or indifference; and even if I did not feel that I had an injury against young Drood on my own account, I should feel that I had an injury against him on hers."

Mr. Crisparkle, in utter amazement, looked at Helena for corroboration, and met in her expressive face full corroboration, and a plea for advice.

"The young lady of whom you speak is, as you know, Mr. Neville, shortly to be married," said Mr. Crisparkle, gravely; "therefore your admiration, if it be of that special nature which you seem to indicate, is outrageously misplaced. Moreover, it is monstrous that you should take upon yourself to be the young lady's champion against her chosen husband. Besides, you have seen them only once. The young lady has become your sister's friend; and I wonder that your sister, even on her behalf, has not checked you in this irrational and culpable fancy."

"She has tried, sir, but uselessly. Husband or no husband, that fellow is incapable of the feeling with which I am inspired towards the beautiful young creature whom he treats like a doll. I say he is as incapable of it, as he is unworthy of her. I say she is sacrificed in being bestowed upon him. I say that I love her, and despise and hate him!" This with a face so flushed, and a gesture so violent, that his sister crossed to his side, and caught his arm, remonstrating, "Neville, Neville!"

Thus recalled to himself, he quickly became sensible of having lost the guard he had set upon his passionate tendency, and covered his face with his hand, as one repentant, and wretched.

Mr. Crisparkle, watching him attentively, and at the same time meditating how to proceed, walked on for some paces in silence. Then he spoke:

"Mr. Neville, Mr. Neville, I am sorely grieved to see in you more traces of a character as sullen, angry, and wild, as the night now closing in. They are of too serious an aspect to leave me the resource of treating the infatuation you have disclosed, as undeserving serious consideration. I give it very serious consideration, and I speak to you accordingly. This feud between you and young Drood must not go on. I cannot permit it to go on, any longer, knowing what I now know from you, and you living under my roof. Whatever prejudiced and unauthorized constructions your blind and envious wrath may put upon his character, it is a frank, good-natured character. I know I can trust to it for that. Now, pray observe what I am about to say. On reflection, and on your sister's representation, I am willing to admit that, in making peace with young Drood, you have a right to be met half way. I will engage that you shall be, and even that young Drood shall make the first advance. This condition fulfilled, you will pledge me the honor of a Christian gentleman that the quarrel is for ever at an end on your side. What may be in your heart when you give him your hand, can only be known to the Searcher of all hearts; but it will never go well with you, if there be any treachery there. So far, as to that; next as to what I must again speak of as your infatuation. I understand it to have been confided to me, and to be known to no other person save your sister and yourself. Do I understand aright?"

Helena answered in a low voice: "It is only known to us three who are here together."

"It is not at all known to the young lady, your friend?"

"On my soul, no!"

"I require you, then, to give me your similar and solemn pledge, Mr. Neville, that it shall remain the secret it is, and that you will take no other action whatsoever upon it than endeavouring (and that most earnestly) to erase it from your mind. I will not tell you that it will soon pass; I will not tell you that it is the fancy of the moment; I will not tell you that such caprices have their rise and fall among the young and ardent every hour; I will leave you undisturbed in the belief that it has few parallels or none, that it will abide with you a long time, and that it will be very difficult to conquer. So much the more weight shall I attach to the pledge I require from you, when it is unreservedly given."

The young man twice or thrice essayed to speak, but failed.

"Let me leave you with your sister, whom it is time you took home," said Mr. Crisparkle. "You will find me alone in my room by-and-by."

"Pray do not leave us yet," Helena implored him. "Another minute."

"I should not," said Neville, pressing his hand upon his face, "have needed so much as another minute, if you had been less patient with me, Mr. Crisparkle, less considerate of me, and less unpretendingly good and true. Oh, if in my childhood I had known such a guide!"

"Follow your guide now, Neville," murmured Helena, "and follow him to Heaven!"

There was that in her tone which broke the good Minor Canon's voice, or it would have repudiated her exaltation of him. As it was, he laid a finger on his lips, and looked towards her brother.

"To say that I give both pledges, Mr. Crisparkle, out of my

innermost heart, and to say that there is no treachery in it, is to say nothing!" Thus Neville, greatly moved. "I beg your forgiveness for my miserable lapse into a burst of passion."

"Not mine, Neville, not mine. You know with whom forgiveness lies, as the highest attribute conceivable. Miss Helena, you and your brother are twin children. You came into this world with the same dispositions, and you passed your younger days together surrounded by the same adverse circumstances. What you have overcome in yourself, can you not overcome in him? You see the rock that lies in his course. Who but you can keep him clear of it?"

"Who but you, sir?" replied Helena. "What is my influence, or my weak wisdom, compared with yours!"

"You have the wisdom of Love," returned the Minor Canon, "and it was the highest wisdom ever known upon this earth, remember. As to mine—but the less said of that commonplace commodity the better. Good night!"

She took the hand he offered her, and gratefully and almost reverently raised it to her lips.

"Tut!" said the Minor Canon, softly, "I am much overpaid!" And turned away.

Retracing his steps towards the Cathedral Close, he tried, as he went along in the dark, to think out the best means of bringing to pass what he had promised to effect, and what must somehow be done. "I shall probably be asked to marry them," he reflected, "and I would they were married and gone! But this presses first." He debated principally, whether he should write to young Drood, or

209

whether he should speak to Jasper. The consciousness of being popular with the whole Cathedral establishment inclined him to the
latter course, and the well-timed sight of the lighted gatehouse decided him to take it. "I will strike while the iron is hot," he said,
"and see him now."

Jasper was lying asleep on a couch before the fire, when, having
ascended the postern-stair, and received no answer to his knock at
the door, Mr. Crisparkle gently turned the handle and looked in.
Long afterwards he had cause to remember how Jasper sprang from
the couch in a delirious state between sleeping and waking, crying
out: "What is the matter? Who did it?"

"It is only I, Jasper. I am sorry to have disturbed you."

The glare of his eyes settled down into a look of recognition,
and he moved a chair or two, to make a way to the fireside.

"I was dreaming at a great rate, and am glad to be disturbed
from an indigestive after-dinner sleep. Not to mention that you are
always welcome."

"Thank you. I am not confident," returned Mr. Crisparkle as he
sat himself down in the easy chair placed for him, "that my subject
will at first sight be quite as welcome as myself; but I am a minister
of peace, and I pursue my subject in the interests of peace. In a
word, Jasper, I want to establish peace between these two young
fellows."

A very perplexed expression took hold of Mr. Jasper's face; a
very perplexing expression too, for Mr. Crisparkle could make nothing of it.

"How?" was Jasper's inquiry, in a low and slow voice, after a silence.

"For the 'How' I come to you. I want to ask you to do me the great favor and service of interposing with your nephew (I have already interposed with Mr. Neville), and getting him to write you a short note, in his lively way, saying that he is willing to shake hands. I know what a good-natured fellow he is, and what influence you have with him. And without in the least defending Mr. Neville, we must all admit that he was bitterly stung."

Jasper turned that perplexed face towards the fire. Mr. Crisparkle continuing to observe it, found it even more perplexing than before, inasmuch as it seemed to denote (which could hardly be) some close internal calculation.

"I know that you are not prepossessed in Mr. Neville's favor," the Minor Canon was going on, when Jasper stopped him:

"You have cause to say so. I am not, indeed."

"Undoubtedly, and I admit his lamentable violence of temper, though I hope he and I will get the better of it between us. But I have exacted a very solemn promise from him as to his future demeanour towards your nephew, if you do kindly interpose; and I am sure he will keep it."

"You are always responsible and trustworthy, Mr. Crisparkle. Do you really feel sure that you can answer for him so confidently?"

"I do."

The perplexed and perplexing look vanished.

"Then you relieve my mind of a great dread, and a heavy weight," said Jasper; "I will do it."

Mr. Crisparkle, delighted by the swiftness and completeness of his success, acknowledged it in the handsomest terms.

"I will do it," repeated Jasper, "for the comfort of having your guarantee against my vague and unfounded fears. You will laugh — but do you keep a Diary?"

"A line for a day; not more."

"A line for a day would be quite as much as my uneventful life would need, Heaven knows," said Jasper, taking a book from a desk; "but that my Diary is, in fact, a Diary of Ned's life too. You will laugh at this entry; you will guess when it was made:

> 'Past midnight. —After what I have just now seen, I have a morbid dread upon me of some horrible consequences resulting to my dear boy, that I cannot reason with or in any way contend against. All my efforts are vain. The demoniacal passion of this Neville Landless, his strength in his fury, and his savage rage for the destruction of its object, appal me. So profound is the impression, that twice since have I gone into my dear boy's room, to assure myself of his sleeping safely, and not lying dead in his blood.'

"Here is another entry next morning:

> 'Ned up and away. Light-hearted and unsuspicious as ever. He laughed when I cautioned him, and said he was as good a man as Neville Landless any day. I told him that might be, but he was not as bad a man. He continued to make light of it, but I travelled with him as far as I could, and left him most unwillingly. I am unable to shake off these

212

dark intangible presentiments of evil—if feelings founded upon staring facts are to be so called.'

"Again and again," said Jasper, in conclusion, twirling the leaves of the book before putting it by, "I have relapsed into these moods, as other entries show. But I have now your assurance at my back, and shall put it in my book, and make it an antidote to my black humours."

"Such an antidote, I hope," returned Mr. Crisparkle, "as will induce you before long to consign the black humours to the flames. I ought to be the last to find any fault with you this evening, when you have met my wishes so freely; but I must say, Jasper, that your devotion to your nephew has made you exaggerative here."

"You are my witness," said Jasper, shrugging his shoulders, "what my state of mind honestly was, that night, before I sat down to write, and in what words I expressed it. You remember objecting to a word I used, as being too strong? It was a stronger word than any in my Diary."

"Well, well. Try the antidote," rejoined Mr. Crisparkle, "and may it give you a brighter and better view of the case! We will discuss it no more, now. I have to thank you for myself, and I thank you sincerely."

"You shall find," said Jasper, as they shook hands, "that I will not do the thing you wish me to do, by halves. I will take care that Ned, giving way at all, shall give way thoroughly."

On the third day after this conversation, he called on Mr. Crisparkle with the following letter:

213

"MY DEAR JACK,

"I am touched by your account of your interview with Mr. Crisparkle, whom I much respect and esteem. At once I openly say that I forgot myself on that occasion quite as much as Mr. Landless did, and that I wish that byegone to be a byegone, and all to be right again.

"Look here, dear old boy. Ask Mr. Landless to dinner on Christmas Eve (the better the day the better the deed), and let there be only we three, and let us shake hands all round there and then, and say no more about it.

"My Dear Jack,

"Ever your most affectionate,

"EDWIN DROOD.

"P.S.—Love to Miss Pussy at the next music lesson."

"You expect Mr. Neville, then?" said Mr. Crisparkle.

"I count upon his coming," said Mr. Jasper.

CHAPTER XI

A PICTURE AND A RING

BEHIND the most ancient part of Holborn, London, where certain gabled houses some centuries of age still stand looking on the public way, as if disconsolately looking for the Old Bourne that has long run dry, is a little nook composed of two irregular quadrangles, called Staple Inn. It is one of those nooks, the turning into which out of the clashing street, imparts to the relieved pedestrian the sensation of having put cotton in his ears, and velvet soles on his boots. It is one of those nooks where a few smoky sparrows twitter in smoky trees, as though they called to one another, "Let us play at country," and where a few feet of garden mould and a few yards of gravel enable them to do that refreshing violence to their tiny understandings. Moreover, it is one of those nooks which are legal nooks; and it contains a little Hall, with a little lantern in its roof: to what obstructive purposes devoted, and at whose expense, this history knoweth not.

In the days when Cloisterham took offence at the existence of a railroad afar off, as menacing that sensitive constitution, the property of us Britons. The odd fortune of which sacred institutions it is to be in exactly equal degrees croaked about, trembled for, and boasted of, whatever happens to anything, anywhere in the world:

in those days no neighbouring architecture of lofty proportions had arisen to overshadow Staple Inn. The westering sun bestowed bright glances on it, and the south-west wind blew into it unimpeded.

Neither wind nor sun, however, favored Staple Inn, one December afternoon towards six o'clock, when it was filled with fog, and candles shed murky and blurred rays through the windows of all its then-occupied sets of chambers; notably, from a set of chambers in a corner house in the little inner quadrangle, presenting in black and white over its ugly portal the mysterious inscription:

P
J   T
1747.

In which set of chambers, never having troubled his head about the inscription, unless to bethink himself at odd times on glancing up at it, that haply it might mean Perhaps John Thomas, or Perhaps Joe Tyler, sat Mr. Grewgious writing by his fire.

Who could have told, by looking at Mr. Grewgious, whether he had ever known ambition or disappointment? He had been bred to the Bar, and had laid himself out for chamber practice; to draw deeds; "convey the wise it call," as Pistol says. But Conveyancing and he had made such a very indifferent marriage of it that they had separated by consent—if there can be said to be separation where there has never been coming together.

No. Coy Conveyancing would not come to Mr. Grewgious. She

was wooed, not won, and they went their several ways. But an Arbitration being blown towards him by some unaccountable wind, and he gaining great credit in it as one indefatigable in seeking out right and doing right, a pretty fat Receivership was next blown into his pocket by a wind more traceable to its source. So, by chance, he had found his niche. Receiver and Agent now, to two rich estates, and deputing their legal business, in an amount worth having, to a firm of solicitors on the floor below, he had snuffed out his ambition (supposing him to have ever lighted it) and had settled down with his snuffers for the rest of his life under the dry vine and fig-tree of P. J. T., who planted in seventeen-forty-seven.

Many accounts and account-books, many files of correspondence, and several strong boxes, garnished Mr. Grewgious's room. They can scarcely be represented as having lumbered it, so conscientious and precise was their orderly arrangement. The apprehension of dying suddenly, and leaving one fact or one figure with any incompleteness or obscurity attaching to it, would have stretched Mr. Grewgious stone dead any day. The largest fidelity to a trust was the life-blood of the man. There are sorts of life-blood that course more quickly, more gaily, more attractively; but there is no better sort in circulation.

There was no luxury in his room. Even its comforts were limited to its being dry and warm, and having a snug though faded fireside. What may be called its private life was confined to the hearth, and an easy chair, and an old-fashioned occasional round table that was brought out upon the rug after business hours, from a corner where it elsewise remained turned up like a shining mahogany shield. Behind it, when standing thus on the defensive, was a closet, usually containing something good to drink. An outer room was the clerk's room; Mr. Grewgious's sleeping-room was across the common stair; and he held some not empty cellarage at the bottom of the common stair. Three hundred days in the year, at least, he crossed over to the hotel in Furnival's Inn for his dinner, and after dinner crossed back again, to make the most of these simplicities until it should become broad business day once more, with P. J. T., date seventeen-forty-seven.

As Mr. Grewgious sat and wrote by his fire that afternoon, so did the clerk of Mr. Grewgious sit and write by *his* fire. A pale, puffy-faced, dark-haired person of thirty, with big dark eyes that wholly wanted lustre, and a dissatisfied doughy complexion, that seemed to ask to be sent to the baker's, this attendant was a mysterious being, possessed of some strange power over Mr. Grewgious. As though he had been called into existence, like a fabulous Familiar, by a magic spell which had failed when required to dismiss him, he stuck tight to Mr. Grewgious's stool, although Mr. Grewgious's comfort and convenience would manifestly have been advanced by dispossessing him. A gloomy person with tangled locks, and a general air of having been reared under the shadow of that baleful tree of Java which has given shelter to more lies than the whole botanical kingdom, Mr. Grewgious, nevertheless, treated him with unaccountable consideration.

"Now, Bazzard," said Mr. Grewgious, on the entrance of his clerk: looking up from his papers as he arranged them for the night: "what is in the wind besides fog?"

"Mr. Drood," said Bazzard.

"What of him?"

"Has called," said Bazzard.

"You might have shown him in."

"I am doing it," said Bazzard.

The visitor came in accordingly.

"Dear me!" said Mr. Grewgious, looking round his pair of office candles. "I thought you had called and merely left your name, and gone. How do you do, Mr. Edwin? Dear me, you're choking!"

"It's this fog," returned Edwin; "and it makes my eyes smart, like Cayenne pepper."

"Is it really so bad as that? Pray undo your wrappers. It's fortunate I have so good a fire; but Mr. Bazzard has taken care of me."

"No I haven't," said Mr. Bazzard at the door.

"Ah! Then it follows that I must have taken care of myself without observing it," said Mr. Grewgious. "Pray be seated in my chair. No. I beg! Coming out of such an atmosphere, in *my* chair."

Edwin took the easy chair in the corner; and the fog he had brought in with him, and the fog he took off with his great-coat and neck-shawl, was speedily licked up by the eager fire.

"I look," said Edwin, smiling, "as if I had come to stop."

"—By-the-by," cried Mr. Grewgious; "excuse my interrupting

you; do stop. The fog may clear in an hour or two. We can have dinner in from just across Holborn. You had better take your cayenne pepper here than outside; pray stop and dine."

"You are very kind," said Edwin, glancing about him, as though attracted by the notion of a new and relishing sort of gipsy-party.

"Not at all," said Mr. Grewgious; "*you* are very kind to join issue with a bachelor in chambers, and take pot-luck. And I'll ask," said Mr. Grewgious, dropping his voice, and speaking with a twinkling eye, as if inspired with a bright thought: "I'll ask Bazzard. He mightn't like it else. Bazzard!"

Bazzard reappeared.

"Dine presently with Mr. Drood and me."

"If I am ordered to dine, of course I will, sir," was the gloomy answer.

"Save the man!" cried Mr. Grewgious. "You're not ordered; you're invited."

"Thank you, sir," said Bazzard; "in that case I don't care if I do."

"That's arranged. And perhaps you wouldn't mind," said Mr. Grewgious, "stepping over to the hotel in Furnival's, and asking them to send in materials for laying the cloth. For dinner we'll have a tureen of the hottest and strongest soup available, and we'll have the best made-dish that can be recommended, and we'll have a joint (such as a haunch of mutton), and we'll have a goose, or a turkey, or any little stuffed thing of that sort that may happen to be in the bill of fare—in short, we'll have whatever there is on hand."

These liberal directions Mr. Grewgious issued with his usual air of reading an inventory, or repeating a lesson, or doing anything else by rote. Bazzard, after drawing out the round table, withdrew to execute them.

"I was a little delicate, you see," said Mr. Grewgious, in a lower tone, after his clerk's departure, "about employing him in the foraging or commissariat department. Because he mightn't like it."

"He seems to have his own way, sir," remarked Edwin.

"His own way?" returned Mr. Grewgious. "Oh dear no! Poor fellow, you quite mistake him. If he had his own way, he wouldn't be here."

"I wonder where he would be!" Edwin thought. But he only thought it, because Mr. Grewgious came and stood himself with his back to the other corner of the fire, and his shoulder-blades against the chimneypiece, and collected his skirts for easy conversation.

"I take it, without having the gift of prophecy, that you have done me the favor of looking in to mention that you are going down yonder—where I can tell you, you are expected—and to offer to execute any little commission from me to my charming ward, and perhaps to sharpen me up a bit in any proceedings? Eh, Mr. Edwin?"

"I called, sir, before going down, as an act of attention."

"Of attention!" said Mr. Grewgious. "Ah! of course, not of impatience?"

"Impatience, sir?"

Mr. Grewgious had meant to be arch—not that he in the remotest degree expressed that meaning—and had brought himself into scarcely supportable proximity with the fire, as if to burn the fullest effect of his archness into himself, as other subtle impressions are burnt into hard metals. But his archness suddenly flying before the composed face and manner of his visitor, and only the fire remaining, he started and rubbed himself.

"I have lately been down yonder," said Mr. Grewgious, rearranging his skirts; "and that was what I referred to, when I said I could tell you you are expected."

"Indeed, sir! Yes; I knew that Pussy was looking out for me."

"Do you keep a cat down there?" asked Mr. Grewgious.

Edwin coloured a little, as he explained: "I call Rosa Pussy."

"Oh, really," said Mr. Grewgious, smoothing down his head; "that's very affable."

Edwin glanced at his face, uncertain whether or no he seriously objected to the appellation. But Edwin might as well have glanced at the face of a clock.

"A pet name, sir," he explained again.

"Umps," said Mr. Grewgious, with a nod. But with such an extraordinary compromise between an unqualified assent and a qualified dissent, that his visitor was much disconcerted.

"Did PRosa——" Edwin began, by way of recovering himself.

"PRosa?" repeated Mr. Grewgious.

"I was going to say Pussy, and changed my mind; —did she tell you anything about the Landlesses?"

"No," said Mr. Grewgious. "What is the Landlesses? An estate? A villa? A farm?"

"A brother and sister. The sister is at the Nuns' House, and has become a great friend of P——"

"PRosa's," Mr. Grewgious struck in, with a fixed face.

"She is a strikingly handsome girl, sir, and I thought she might have been described to you, or presented to you, perhaps?"

"Neither," said Mr. Grewgious. "But here is Bazzard."

Bazzard returned, accompanied by two waiters—an immoveable waiter, and a flying waiter; and the three brought in with them as much fog as gave a new roar to the fire. The flying waiter, who had brought everything on his shoulders, laid the cloth with amazing rapidity and dexterity; while the immoveable waiter, who had brought nothing, found fault with him. The flying waiter then highly polished all the glasses he had brought, and the immoveable waiter looked through them. The flying waiter then flew across Holborn for the soup, and flew back again, and then took another flight for the made-dish, and flew back again, and then took another flight for the joint and poultry, and flew back again, and between whiles took supplementary flights for a great variety of articles, as it was discovered from time to time that the immoveable waiter had forgotten them all. But let the flying waiter cleave the air as he might, he was always reproached on his return by the immoveable waiter for bringing fog with him, and being out of breath. At the conclusion of the repast, by which time the flying waiter was severely blown, the immoveable waiter gathered up the tablecloth under his arm with a grand air, and having sternly (not to say with indignation) looked on at the flying waiter while he set clean glasses round, directed a valedictory glance towards Mr. Grewgious, conveying: "Let it be clearly understood between us that the reward is mine, and that Nil is the claim of this slave," and pushed the flying waiter before him out of the room.

It was like a highly finished miniature painting representing My Lords of the Circumlocutional Department, Commandership-in-Chief of any sort, Government. It was quite an edifying little picture to be hung on the line in the National Gallery.

As the fog had been the proximate cause of this sumptuous repast, so the fog served for its general sauce. To hear the out-door clerks, sneezing, wheezing, and beating their feet on the gravel was a zest far surpassing Doctor Kitchener's. To bid, with a shiver, the unfortunate flying waiter shut the door before he had opened it, was a condiment of a profounder flavour than Harvey. And here let it be noticed, parenthetically, that the leg of this young man in its application to the door, evinced the finest sense of touch: always preceding himself and tray (with something of an angling air about it), by some seconds: and always lingering after he and the tray had disappeared like Macbeth's leg when accompanying him off the stage with reluctance to the assassination of Duncan.

The host had gone below to the cellar, and had brought up bottles of ruby, straw-colored, and golden, drinks, which had ripened long ago in lands where no fogs are, and had since lain slumbering in the shade. Sparkling and tingling after so long a nap, they pushed at their corks to help the corkscrew (like prisoners helping rioters to force their gates), and danced out gaily. If P. J. T. in seventeen-forty-seven, or in any other year of his period, drank such wines—then, for a certainty, P. J. T. was Pretty Jolly Too.

Externally, Mr. Grewgious showed no signs of being mellowed by these glowing vintages. Instead of his drinking them, they might have been poured over him in his high-dried snuff form, and run to waste, for any lights and shades they caused to flicker over his face. Neither was his manner influenced. But, in his wooden way, he had observant eyes for Edwin; and when, at the end of dinner, he motioned Edwin back to his own easy chair in the fireside corner, and Edwin luxuriously sank into it after very brief remonstrance, Mr. Grewgious, as he turned his seat round towards the fire too, and smoothed his head and face, might have been seen looking at his visitor between his smoothing fingers.

"Bazzard!" said Mr. Grewgious, suddenly turning to him.

"I follow you, sir," returned Bazzard; who had done his work of consuming meat and drink, in a workmanlike manner, though mostly in speechlessness.

"I drink to you, Bazzard; Mr. Edwin, success to Mr. Bazzard!"

"Success to Mr. Bazzard!" echoed Edwin, with a totally unfounded appearance of enthusiasm, and with the unspoken addition: "What in, I wonder!"

"And May!" pursued Mr. Grewgious—"I am not at liberty to be definite—May!—my conversational powers are so very limited that I know I shall not come well out of this—May!—it ought to be put imaginatively, but I have no imagination—May!—the thorn of anxiety is as nearly the mark as I am likely to get—May it come out at last!"

Mr. Bazzard, with a frowning smile at the fire, put a hand into his tangled locks, as if the thorn of anxiety were there; then into his waistcoat, as if it were there; then into his pockets, as if it were there. In all these movements he was closely followed by the eyes of Edwin, as if that young gentleman expected to see the thorn in action. It was not produced, however, and Mr. Bazzard merely said: "I follow you, sir, and I thank you."

"I am going," said Mr. Grewgious, jingling his glass on the table, with one hand, and bending aside under cover of the other, to whisper to Edwin, "to drink to my ward. But I put Bazzard first. He mightn't like it else."

This was said with a mysterious wink; or what would have been a wink if, in Mr. Grewgious's hands, it could have been quick enough. So Edwin winked responsively, without the least idea what he meant by doing so.

"And now," said Mr. Grewgious, "I devote a bumper to the fair and fascinating Miss Rosa. Bazzard, the fair and fascinating Miss Rosa!"

"I follow you, sir," said Bazzard, "and I pledge you!"

"And so do I!" said Edwin.

"Lord bless me!" cried Mr. Grewgious, breaking the blank silence which of course ensued: though why these pauses *should* come upon us when we have performed any small social rite, not directly inducive of self-examination or mental despondency, who can tell! "I am a particularly Angular man, and yet I fancy (if I may use the word, not having a morsel of fancy), that I could draw a picture of a true lover's state of mind, to-night."

"Let us follow you, sir," said Bazzard, "and have the picture."

"Mr. Edwin will correct it where it's wrong," resumed Mr. Grewgious, "and will throw in a few touches from the life. I dare say it is wrong in many particulars, and wants many touches from the life, for I was born a Chip, and have neither soft sympathies nor soft experiences. Well! I hazard the guess that the true lover's mind is completely permeated by the beloved object of his affections. I hazard the guess that her dear name is precious to him, cannot be heard or repeated without emotion, and is preserved sacred. If he has any distinguishing appellation of fondness for her, it is reserved for her, and is not for common ears. A name that it would be a privilege to call her by, being alone with her own bright self, it would be a liberty, a coldness, an insensibility, almost a breach of good faith, to flaunt elsewhere."

It was wonderful to see Mr. Grewgious sitting bolt upright, with his hands on his knees, continuously chopping this discourse out of himself: much as a charity boy with a very good memory might get his catechism said: and evincing no correspondent emotion whatever, unless in a certain occasional little tingling perceptible at the end of his nose.

"My picture," Mr. Grewgious proceeded, "goes on to represent (under correction from you, Mr. Edwin,) the true lover as ever impatient to be in the presence or vicinity of the beloved object of his affections; as caring very little for his ease in any other society; and as constantly seeking that. If I was to say seeking that, as a bird seeks its nest, I should make an ass of myself, because that would trench upon what I understand to be poetry; and I am so far from trenching upon poetry at any time, that I never, to my knowledge, got within ten thousand miles of it. And I am besides totally unacquainted with the habits of birds, except the birds of Staple Inn, who seek their nests on ledges, and in gutter-pipes and chimney-pots, not constructed for them by the beneficent hand of Nature. I beg, therefore, to be understood as foregoing the bird's-nest. But my picture does represent the true lover as having no existence separable from that of the beloved object of his affections, and as living at once a doubled life and a halved life. And if I do not clearly express what I mean by that, it is either for the reason that having no conversational powers, I cannot express what I mean, or that having no meaning, I do not mean what I fail to express. Which, to the best of my belief, is not the case."

Edwin had turned red and turned white, as certain points of this picture came into the light. He now sat looking at the fire, and bit his lip.

"The speculations of an Angular man," resumed Mr. Grewgious, still sitting and speaking exactly as before, "are probably erroneous on so globular a topic. But I figure to myself (subject, as before, to Mr. Edwin's correction), that there can be no coolness, no lassitude, no doubt, no indifference, no half fire and half smoke state of mind, in a real lover. Pray am I at all near the mark in my picture?"

As abrupt in his conclusion as in his commencement and progress, he jerked this inquiry at Edwin, and stopped when one might have supposed him in the middle of his oration.

"I should say, sir," stammered Edwin, "as you refer the question to me——"

"Yes," said Mr. Grewgious, "I refer it to you, as an authority."

"I should say then, sir," Edwin went on, embarrassed, "that the picture you have drawn, is generally correct; but I submit that perhaps you may be rather hard upon the unlucky lover."

"Likely so," assented Mr. Grewgious, "likely so. I am a hard man in the grain."

"He may not show," said Edwin, "all he feels; or he may not——"

There he stopped so long, to find the rest of his sentence, that Mr. Grewgious rendered his difficulty a thousand times the greater, by unexpectedly striking in with:

"No to be sure; he *may* not!"

After that, they all sat silent; the silence of Mr. Bazzard being occasioned by slumber.

"His responsibility is very great though," said Mr. Grewgious, at length, with his eyes on the fire.

Edwin nodded assent, with *his* eyes on the fire.

"And let him be sure that he trifles with no one," said Mr. Grewgious; "neither with himself, nor with any other."

Edwin bit his lip again, and still sat looking at the fire.

"He must not make a plaything of a treasure. Woe betide him if he does! Let him take that well to heart," said Mr. Grewgious.

Though he said these things in short sentences, much as the supposititious charity boy just now referred to, might have repeated a verse or two from the Book of Proverbs, there was something dreamy (for so literal a man) in the way in which he now shook his right forefinger at the live coals in the grate, and again fell silent.

But not for long. As he sat upright and stiff in his chair, he suddenly rapped his knees, like the carved image of some queer Joss or other coming out of its reverie, and said: "We must finish this bottle, Mr. Edwin. Let me help you. I'll help Bazzard, too, though he *is* asleep. He mightn't like it else."

He helped them both, and helped himself, and drained his glass, and stood it bottom upward on the table, as though he had just caught a bluebottle in it.

"And now, Mr. Edwin," he proceeded, wiping his mouth and hands upon his handkerchief: "to a little piece of business. You received from me, the other day, a certified copy of Miss Rosa's father's will. You knew its contents before, but you received it from me as a matter of business. I should have sent it to Mr. Jasper, but for Miss Rosa's wishing it to come straight to you, in preference. You received it?"

"Quite safely, sir."

"You should have acknowledged its receipt," said Mr. Grewgious, "business being business all the world over. However, you did not."

"I meant to have acknowledged it when I first came in this evening, sir."

"Not a business-like acknowledgment," returned Mr. Grew-gious; "however, let that pass. Now, in that document you have observed a few words of kindly allusion to its being left to me to discharge a little trust, confided to me in conversation, at such a time as I in my discretion may think best."

"Yes, sir."

"Mr. Edwin, it came into my mind just now, when I was looking at the fire, that I could, in my discretion, acquit myself of that trust at no better time than the present. Favor me with your attention, half a minute."

He took a bunch of keys from his pocket, singled out by the candle-light the key he wanted, and then, with a candle in his hand, went to a bureau or escritoire, unlocked it, touched the spring of a little secret drawer, and took from it an ordinary ring-case made for a single ring. With this in his hand, he returned to his chair. As he held it up for the young man to see, his hand trembled.

"Mr. Edwin, this rose of diamonds and rubies delicately set in gold, was a ring belonging to Miss Rosa's mother. It was removed from her dead hand, in my presence, with such distracted grief as I hope it may never be my lot to contemplate again. Hard man as I am, I am not hard enough for that. See how bright these stones shine!" opening the case. "And yet the eyes that were so much brighter, and that so often looked upon them with a light and a proud heart, have been ashes among ashes, and dust among dust, some years! If I had any imagination (which it is needless to say I have not), I might imagine that the lasting beauty of these stones was almost cruel."

He closed the case again as he spoke.

"This ring was given to the young lady who was drowned so early in her beautiful and happy career, by her husband, when they first plighted their faith to one another. It was he who removed it from her unconscious hand, and it was he who, when his death drew very near, placed it in mine. The trust in which I received it, was, that, you and Miss Rosa growing to manhood and womanhood, and your betrothal prospering and coming to maturity, I should give it to you to place upon her finger. Failing those desired results, it was to remain in my possession."

Some trouble was in the young man's face, and some indecision was in the action of his hand, as Mr. Grewgious, looking steadfastly at him, gave him the ring.

"Your placing it on her finger," said Mr. Grewgious, "will be the solemn seal upon your strict fidelity to the living and the dead. You are going to her, to make the last irrevocable preparations for your marriage. Take it with you."

The young man took the little case, and placed it in his breast.

"If anything should be amiss, if anything should be even slightly wrong, between you; if you should have any secret consciousness that you are committing yourself to this step for no higher reason than because you have long been accustomed to look forward to it; then," said Mr. Grewgious, "I charge you once more, by the living and by the dead, to bring that ring back to me!"

Here Bazzard awoke himself by his own snoring; and, as is usual in such cases, sat apoplectically staring at vacancy, as defying vacancy to accuse him of having been asleep.

"Bazzard!" said Mr. Grewgious, harder than ever.

"I follow you, sir," said Bazzard, "and I have been following you."

"In discharge of a trust, I have handed Mr. Edwin Drood a ring of diamonds and rubies. You see?"

Edwin reproduced the little case, and opened it; and Bazzard looked into it.

"I follow you both, sir," returned Bazzard, "and I witness the transaction."

Evidently anxious to get away and be alone, Edwin Drood now resumed his outer clothing, muttering something about time and appointments. The fog was reported no clearer (by the flying waiter, who alighted from a speculative flight in the coffee interest), but he went out into it; and Bazzard, after his manner, "followed" him.

Mr. Grewgious, left alone, walked softly and slowly to and fro, for an hour and more. He was restless to-night, and seemed dispirited.

"I hope I have done right," he said. "The appeal to him seemed necessary. It was hard to lose the ring, and yet it must have gone from me very soon."

He closed the empty little drawer with a sigh, and shut and locked the escritoire, and came back to the solitary fireside.

"Her ring," he went on. "Will it come back to me? My mind hangs about her ring very uneasily to-night. But that is explainable. I have had it so long, and I have prized it so much! I wonder——"

He was in a wondering mood as well as a restless; for, though he checked himself at that point, and took another walk, he resumed his wondering when he sat down again.

"I wonder (for the ten thousandth time, and what a weak fool I, for what can it signify now!) whether he confided the charge of their orphan child to me, because he knew——Good God, how like her mother she has become!"

"I wonder whether he ever so much as suspected that some one doted on her, at a hopeless, speechless distance, when he struck in and won her. I wonder whether it ever crept into his mind who that unfortunate some one was!"

"I wonder whether I shall sleep to-night! At all events, I will shut out the world with the bedclothes, and try."

Mr. Grewgious crossed the staircase to his raw and foggy bed-room, and was soon ready for bed. Dimly catching sight of his face in the misty looking-glass, he held his candle to it for a moment.

"A likely some one, *you*, to come into anybody's thoughts in such an aspect!" he exclaimed. "There, there! there! Get to bed, poor man, and cease to jabber!"

With that, he extinguished his light, pulled up the bedclothes around him, and with another sigh shut out the world. And yet there are such unexplored romantic nooks in the unlikeliest men, that even old tinderous and touch-woody P. J. T. Possibly Jabbered Thus, at some odd times, in or about seventeen-forty-seven.

CHAPTER XII

A NIGHT WITH DURDLES

WHEN Mr. Sapsea has nothing better to do, towards evening, and finds the contemplation of his own profundity becoming a little monotonous in spite of the vastness of the subject, he often takes an airing in the Cathedral Close and thereabout. He likes to pass the churchyard with a swelling air of proprietorship, and to encourage in his breast a sort of benignant-landlord feeling, in that he has been bountiful towards that meritorious tenant, Mrs. Sapsea, and has publicly given her a prize. He likes to see a stray face or two looking in through the railings, and perhaps reading his inscription. Should he meet a stranger coming from the churchyard with a quick step, he is morally convinced that the stranger is "with a blush retiring," as monumentally directed.

Mr. Sapsea's importance has received enhancement, for he has become Mayor of Cloisterham. Without mayors and many of them, it cannot be disputed that the whole framework of society—Mr. Sapsea is confident that he invented that forcible figure—would fall to pieces. Mayors have been knighted for "going up" with addresses: explosive machines intrepidly discharging shot and shell into the English Grammar. Mr. Sapsea may "go up" with an address. Rise, Sir Thomas Sapsea! Of such is the salt of the earth.

Mr. Sapsea has improved the acquaintance of Mr. Jasper, since their first meeting to partake of port, epitaph, backgammon, beef, and salad. Mr. Sapsea has been received at the Gate House with kindred hospitality; and on that occasion Mr. Jasper seated himself at the piano and sang to him, tickling his ears—figuratively, long enough to present a considerable area for tickling. What Mr. Sapsea likes in that young man, is, that he is always ready to profit by the wisdom of his elders, and that he is sound, sir, at the core. In proof of which, he sent to Mr. Sapsea that evening, no kickshaw ditties, favorites with national enemies, but gave him the genuine George the Third home-brewed; exhorting him (as "my brave boys") to reduce to a smashed condition all other islands but this island, and all continents, peninsulas, isthmuses, promontories, and other geographical forms of land soever, besides sweeping the seas in all directions. In short, he rendered it pretty clear that Providence made a distinct mistake in originating so small a nation of hearts of oak, and so many other verminous peoples.

Mr. Sapsea, walking slowly this moist evening near the churchyard with his hands behind him, on the look out for a blushing and retiring stranger, turns a corner, and comes instead into the goodly presence of the Dean, conversing with the Verger and Mr. Jasper. Mr. Sapsea makes his obeisance, and is instantly stricken far more ecclesiastical than any Archbishop of York, or Canterbury.

"You are evidently going to write a book about us, Mr. Jasper," quoth the Dean; "to write a book about us. Well! We are very ancient, and we ought to make a good book. We are not so richly endowed in possessions as in age; but perhaps you will put *that* in your book, among other things, and call attention to our wrongs."

Mr. Tope, as in duty bound, is greatly entertained by this.

"I really have no intention at all, sir," replies Jasper, "of turning author, or archæologist. It is but a whim of mine. And even for my whim, Mr. Sapsea here is more accountable than I am."

"How so, Mr. Mayor?" says the Dean, with a nod of good-natured recognition of his Fetch. "How is that, Mr. Mayor?"

"I am not aware," Mr. Sapsea remarks, looking about him for information, "to what the Very Reverend the Dean does me the honor of referring." And then falls to studying his original in minute points of detail.

"Durdles," Mr. Tope hints.

"Ay!" the Dean echoes; "Durdles, Durdles!"

"The truth is, sir," explains Jasper, "that my curiosity in the man was first really stimulated by Mr. Sapsea. Mr. Sapsea's knowledge of mankind, and power of drawing out whatever is recluse or odd around him, first led to my bestowing a second thought upon the man: though of course I had met him constantly about. You would not be surprised by this, Mr. Dean, if you had seen Mr. Sapsea deal with him in his own parlor, as I did."

"Oh!" cries Sapsea, picking up the ball thrown to him with ineffable complacency and pomposity; "yes, yes. The Very Reverend the Dean refers to that? Yes. I happened to bring Durdles as a Character."

"A character, Mr. Sapsea, that with a few skilful touches you turn inside out," says Jasper.

"Nay, not quite that," returns the lumbering auctioneer. "I may have a little influence over him, perhaps; and a little insight into his character, perhaps. The Very Reverend the Dean will please to bear in mind that I have seen the world." Here Mr. Sapsea gets a little behind the Dean, to inspect his coat-buttons.

"Well!" says the Dean, looking about him to see what has become of his copyist: "I hope, Mr. Mayor, you will use your study and knowledge of Durdles to the good purpose of exhorting him not to break our worthy and respected Choir-Master's neck; we cannot afford it; his head and voice are much too valuable to us."

Mr. Tope is again highly entertained, and, having fallen into respectful convulsions of laughter, subsides into a deferential murmur, importing that surely any gentleman would deem it a pleasure and an honor to have his neck broken, in return for such a compliment from such a source.

"I will take it upon myself, sir," observes Sapsea, loftily, "to answer for Mr. Jasper's neck. I will tell Durdles to be careful of it. He will mind what *I* say. How is it at present endangered?" he inquires, looking about him with magnificent patronage.

"Only by my making a moonlight expedition with Durdles among the tombs, vaults, towers, and ruins," returns Jasper. "You remember suggesting when you brought us together, that, as a lover of the picturesque, it might be worth my while?"

"*I* remember!" replies the auctioneer. And the solemn idiot really believes that he does remember.

"Profiting by your hint," pursues Jasper, "I have had some day-rambles with the extraordinary old fellow, and we are to make a moonlight hole-and-corner exploration to-night."

"And here he is," says the Dean.

Durdles, with his dinner-bundle in his hand, is indeed beheld slouching towards them. Slouching nearer, and perceiving the Dean, he pulls off his hat, and is slouching away with it under his arm, when Mr. Sapsea stops him.

"Mind you take care of my friend," is the injunction Mr. Sapsea lays upon him.

"What friend o' yourn is dead?" asks Durdles. "No orders has come in for any friend o' yourn."

"I mean my live friend, there."

"Oh! Him?" says Durdles. "He can take care of himself, can Mister Jarsper."

"But do you take care of him too," says Sapsea.

Whom Durdles (there being command in his tone), surlily surveys from head to foot.

"With submission to his Reverence the Dean, if you'll mind what concerns you, Mr. Sapsea, Durdles he'll mind what concerns him."

"You're out of temper," says Mr. Sapsea, winking to the company to observe how smoothly he will manage him. "My friend concerns me, and Mr. Jasper is my friend. And you are my friend."

"Don't you get into a bad habit of boasting," retorts Durdles, with a grave cautionary nod. "It'll grow upon you."

"You are out of temper," says Sapsea again; reddening, but again winking to the company.

"I own to it," returns Durdles; "I don't like liberties."

Mr. Sapsea winks a third wink to the company, as who should say: "I think you will agree with me that I have settled *his* business;" and stalks out of the controversy.

Durdles then gives the Dean a good evening, and adding, as he puts his hat on, "You'll find me at home, Mister Jarsper, as agreed, when you want me; I'm a going home to clean myself," soon slouches out of sight. This going home to clean himself is one of the man's incomprehensible compromises with inexorable facts; he, and his hat, and his boots, and his clothes, never showing any trace of cleaning, but being uniformly in one condition of dust and grit.

The lamplighter now dotting the quiet Close with specks of light, and running at a great rate up and down his little ladder with that object—his little ladder under the sacred shadow of whose inconvenience generations had grown up, and which all Cloisterham would have stood aghast at the idea of abolishing—the Dean withdraws to his dinner, Mr. Tope to his tea, and Mr. Jasper to his piano. There, with no light but that of the fire, he sits chanting choir-music in a low and beautiful voice, for two or three hours; in short, until it has been for some time dark, and the moon is about to rise.

Then, he closes his piano softly, softly changes his coat for a pea-jacket with a goodly wicker-cased bottle in its largest pocket, and, putting on a low-crowned flap-brimmed hat, goes softly out. Why does he move so softly to-night? No outward reason is apparent for it. Can there be any sympathetic reason crouching darkly within him?

Repairing to Durdles's unfinished house, or hole in the city wall, and seeing a light within it, he softly picks his course among the gravestones, monuments, and stony lumber of the yard, already touched here and there, sidewise, by the rising moon. The two journeymen have left their two great saws sticking in their blocks of stone; and two skeleton journeymen out of the Dance of Death might be grinning in the shadow of their sheltering sentry-boxes, about to slash away at cutting out the gravestones of the next two people destined to die in Cloisterham. Likely enough, the two think little of that now, being alive, and perhaps merry. Curious, to make a guess at the two; —or say at one of the two!

"Ho! Durdles!"

The light moves, and he appears with it at the door. He would seem to have been "cleaning himself" with the aid of a bottle, jug, and tumbler; for no other cleansing instruments are visible in the bare brick room with rafters overhead and no plastered ceiling, into which he shows his visitor.

"Are you ready?"

"I am ready, Mister Jarsper. Let the old uns come out if they dare, when we go among their tombs. My spirits is ready for 'em."

"Do you mean animal spirits, or ardent?"

242

"The one's the t'other," answers Durdles, "and I mean 'em both."

He takes a lantern from a hook, puts a match or two in his pocket wherewith to light it, should there be need, and they go out together, dinner-bundle and all.

Surely an unaccountable sort of expedition! That Durdles himself, who is always prowling among old graves and ruins, like a Ghoule—that he should be stealing forth to climb, and dive, and wander without an object, is nothing extraordinary; but that the Choir Master or any one else should hold it worth his while to be with him, and to study moonlight effects in such company, is another affair. Surely an unaccountable sort of expedition therefore!

" 'Ware that there mound by the yard-gate, Mister Jarsper."

"I see it. What is it?"

"Lime."

Mr. Jasper stops, and waits for him to come up, for he lags behind. "What you call quick-lime?"

"Ay!" says Durdles; "quick enough to eat your boots. With a little handy stirring, quick enough to eat your bones."

They go on, presently passing the red windows of the Travellers' Twopenny, and emerging into the clear moonlight of the Monks' Vineyard. This crossed, they come to Minor Canon Corner: of which the greater part lies in shadow until the moon shall rise higher in the sky.

The sound of a closing house-door strikes their ears, and two men come out. These are Mr. Crisparkle and Neville. Jasper, with a strange and sudden smile upon his face, lays the palm of his hand upon the breast of Durdles, stopping him where he stands.

At that end of Minor Canon Corner the shadow is profound in the existing state of the light: at that end, too, there is a piece of old dwarf wall, breast high, the only remaining boundary of what was once a garden, but is now the thoroughfare. Jasper and Durdles would have turned this wall in another instant; but, stopping so short, stand behind it.

"Those two are only sauntering," Jasper whispers; "they will go out into the moonlight soon. Let us keep quiet here, or they will detain us, or want to join us, or what not."

Durdles nods assent, and falls to munching some fragments from his bundle. Jasper folds his arms upon the top of the wall, and, with his chin resting on them, watches Neville, as though his eye were at the trigger of a loaded rifle, and he had covered him, and were going to fire. A sense of destructive power is so expressed in his face, that even Durdles pauses in his munching, and looks at him, with an unmunched something in his cheek.

Meanwhile Mr. Crisparkle and Neville walk to and fro, quietly talking together. What they say, cannot be heard consecutively; but Mr. Jasper has already distinguished his own name more than once.

"This is the first day of the week," Mr. Crisparkle can be distinctly heard to observe, as they turn back; "and the last day of the week is Christmas Eve."

"You may be certain of me, sir."

244

The echoes were favorable at those points, but as the two approach, the sound of their talking becomes confused again. The word "confidence," shattered by the echoes, but still capable of being pieced together, is uttered by Mr. Crisparkle. As they draw still nearer, this fragment of a reply is heard: "Not deserved yet, but shall be, sir." As they turn away again, Jasper again hears his own name, in connexion with the words from Mr. Crisparkle: "Remember that I said I answered for you confidently." Then the sound of their talk becomes confused again; they halting for a little while, and some earnest action on the part of Neville succeeding. When they move once more, Mr. Crisparkle is seen to look up at the sky, and to point before him. They then slowly disappear; passing out into the moonlight at the opposite end of the Corner.

It is not until they are gone, that Mr. Jasper moves. But then he turns to Durdles, and bursts into a fit of laughter. Durdles, who still has that suspended something in his cheek, and who sees nothing to laugh at, stares at him until Mr. Jasper lays his face down on his arms to have his laugh out. Then Durdles bolts the something, as if desperately resigning himself to indigestion.

Among those secluded nooks there is very little stir or movement after dark. There is little enough in the high-tide of the day, but there is next to none at night. Besides that the cheerfully frequented High Street lies nearly parallel to the spot (the old Cathedral rising between the two), and is the natural channel in which the Cloisterham traffic flows, a certain awful hush pervades the ancient pile, the cloisters, and the churchyard, after dark, which not many people care to encounter. Ask the first hundred citizens of Cloisterham, met at random in the streets at noon, if they believed in Ghosts, they would tell you no; but put them to choose at night between these eerie Precincts and the thoroughfare of shops, and you would find that ninety-nine declared for the longer round and the more frequented way. The cause of this is not to be found in any local superstition that attaches to the Precincts—albeit a mysterious lady, with a child in her arms and a rope dangling from her neck, has been seen flitting about there by sundry witnesses as intangible as herself—but it is to be sought in the innate shrinking of dust with the breath of life in it, from dust out of which the breath of life has passed; also in the widely diffused, and almost as widely unacknowledged, reflection: "If the dead do, under any circumstances, become visible to the living, these are such likely surroundings for the purpose that I, the living, will get out of them as soon as I can."

Hence, when Mr. Jasper and Durdles pause to glance around them, before descending into the crypt by a small side door of which the latter has a key, the whole expanse of moonlight in their view is utterly deserted. One might fancy that the tide of life was stemmed by Mr. Jasper's own Gatehouse. The murmur of the tide is heard beyond; but no wave passes the archway, over which his lamp burns red behind his curtain, as if the building were a Lighthouse.

They enter, locking themselves in, descend the rugged steps, and are down in the Crypt. The lantern is not wanted, for the moonlight strikes in at the groined windows, bare of glass, the broken frames for which cast patterns on the ground. The heavy pillars which support the roof engender masses of black shade, but between them there are lanes of light. Up and down these lanes, they walk, Durdles discoursing of the "old uns" he yet counts on disinterring, and slapping a wall, in which he considers "a whole family on 'em" to be stoned and earthed up, just as if he were a familiar friend of the family. The taciturnity of Durdles is for the time overcome by Mr. Jasper's wicker bottle, which circulates freely; —in the sense, that is to say, that its contents enter freely into Mr. Durdles's circulation, while Mr. Jasper only rinses his mouth once, and casts forth the rinsing.

They are to ascend the great Tower. On the steps by which they rise to the Cathedral, Durdles pauses for new store of breath. The steps are very dark, but out of the darkness they can see the lanes of light they have traversed. Durdles seats himself upon a step. Mr. Jasper seats himself upon another. The odour from the wicker bottle (which has somehow passed into Durdles's keeping), soon intimates that the cork has been taken out; but this is not ascertainable through the sense of sight, since neither can descry the other. And yet, in talking, they turn to one another, as though their faces could commune together.

"This is good stuff, Mister Jarsper!"

"It is very good stuff, I hope. I bought it on purpose."

"They don't show, you see, the old uns don't, Mister Jarsper!"

"It would be a more confused world than it is, if they could."

"Well, it *would* lead towards a mixing of things," Durdles acquiesces: pausing on the remark, as if the idea of ghosts had not previously presented itself to him in a merely inconvenient light, domestically, or chronologically. "But do you think there may be Ghosts of other things, though not of men and women?"

"What things? Flower-beds and watering-pots? Horses and harness?"

"No. Sounds."

"What sounds?"

"Cries."

"What cries do you mean? Chairs to mend?"

"No. I mean screeches. Now, I'll tell you, Mister Jarsper. Wait a bit till I put the bottle right." Here the cork is evidently taken out again, and replaced again. "There! *Now* it's right! This time last year, only a few days later, I happened to have been doing what was correct by the season, in the way of giving it the welcome it had a right to expect, when them townboys set on me at their worst. At length I gave 'em the slip, and turned in here. And here I fell asleep. And what woke me? The ghost of a cry. The ghost of one terrific shriek, which shriek was followed by the ghost of the howl of a dog: a long dismal woeful howl, such as a dog gives when a person's dead. That was *my* last Christmas Eve."

"What do you mean?" is the very abrupt, and, one might say, fierce retort.

"I mean that I made inquiries everywhere about, and that no living ears but mine heard either that cry or that howl. So I say they was both ghosts; though why they came to me, I've never made out."

"I thought you were another kind of man," says Jasper, scornfully.

"So I thought, myself," answers Durdles with his usual composure; "and yet I was picked out for it."

Jasper had risen suddenly, when he asked him what he meant, and he now says, "Come; we shall freeze here; lead the way."

Durdles complies, not over-steadily; opens the door at the top of the steps with the key he has already used; and so emerges on the Cathedral level, in a passage at the side of the chancel. Here, the moonlight is so very bright again that the colors of the nearest stained-glass window are thrown upon their faces. The appearance of the unconscious Durdles, holding the door open for his companion to follow, as if from the grave, is ghastly enough, with a purple band across his face, and a yellow splash upon his brow; but he bears the close scrutiny of his companion in an insensible way, although it is prolonged while the latter fumbles among his pockets for a key confided to him that will open an iron gate so to enable them to pass to the staircase of the great tower.

"That and the bottle are enough for you to carry," he says, giving it to Durdles; "hand your bundle to me; I am younger and longer-winded than you." Durdles hesitates for a moment between bundle and bottle; but gives the preference to the bottle as being by far the better company, and consigns the dry weight to his fellow-explorer.

Then they go up the winding staircase of the great tower, toilsomely, turning and turning, and lowering their heads to avoid the stairs above, or the rough stone pivot around which they twist. Durdles has lighted his lantern, by drawing from the cold hard wall a spark of that mysterious fire which lurks in everything, and, guided by this speck, they clamber up among the cobwebs and the dust. Their way lies through strange places. Twice or thrice they emerge into level low-arched galleries, whence they can look down into the moonlit nave; and where Durdles, waving his lantern, shows the dim angels' heads upon the corbels of the roof, seeming to watch their progress. Anon, they turn into narrower and steeper staircases, and the night air begins to blow upon them, and the chirp of some startled jackdaw or frightened rook precedes the heavy beating of wings in a confined space, and the beating down of dust and straws upon their heads. At last, leaving their light behind a stair—for it blows fresh up here—they look down on Cloisterham, fair to see in the moonlight: its ruined habitations and sanctuaries of the dead, at the tower's base: its moss-softened red-tiled roofs and red-brick houses of the living, clustered beyond: its river winding down from the mist on the horizon, as though that were its source, and already heaving with a restless knowledge of its approach towards the sea.

Once again, an unaccountable expedition this! Jasper (always moving softly with no visible reason) contemplates the scene, and especially that stillest part of it which the Cathedral overshadows. But he contemplates Durdles quite as curiously, and Durdles is by times conscious of his watchful eyes.

Only by times, because Durdles is growing drowsy. As aëronauts lighten the load they carry, when they wish to rise, similarly Durdles has lightened the wicker bottle in coming up. Snatches of sleep surprise him on his legs, and stop him in his talk. A mild fit of calenture seizes him, in which he deems that the ground, so far below, is on a level with the tower, and would as lief walk off the tower into the air as not. Such is his state when they begin to come down. And as aëronauts make themselves heavier when they wish to descend, similarly Durdles charges himself with more liquid from the wicker bottle, that he may come down the better.

The iron gate attained and locked—but not before Durdles has tumbled twice, and cut an eyebrow open once—they descend into the crypt again, with the intent of issuing forth as they entered. But, while returning among those lanes of light, Durdles becomes so very uncertain, both of foot and speech, that he half drops, half throws himself down, by one of the heavy pillars, scarcely less heavy than itself, and indistinctly appeals to his companion for forty winks of a second each.

"If you will have it so, or must have it so," replies Jasper, "I'll not leave you here. Take them, while I walk to and fro."

Durdles is asleep at once; and in his sleep he dreams a dream.

It is not much of a dream, considering the vast extent of the domains of dreamland, and their wonderful productions; it is only remarkable for being unusually restless, and unusually real. He dreams of lying there, asleep, and yet counting his companion's footsteps as he walks to and fro. He dreams that the footsteps die away into distance of time and of space, and that something touches him, and that something falls from his hand. Then something clinks and gropes about, and he dreams that he is alone for so long a time, that the lanes of light take new directions as the moon advances in her course. From succeeding unconsciousness, he passes into a dream of slow uneasiness from cold; and painfully awakes to a perception of the lanes of light—really changed, much as he had dreamed—and Jasper walking among them, beating his hands and feet.

"Holloa!" Durdles cries out, unmeaningly alarmed.

"Awake at last?" says Jasper, coming up to him. "Do you know that your forties have stretched into thousands?"

"No."

"They have though."

"What's the time?"

"Hark! The bells are going in the Tower!"

They strike four quarters, and then the great bell strikes.

"Two!" cries Durdles, scrambling up; "why didn't you try to wake me, Mister Jarsper?"

"I did. I might as well have tried to wake the dead: —your own family of dead, up in the corner there."

"Did you touch me?"

"Touch you? Yes. Shook you."

As Durdles recalls that touching something in his dream, he

252

looks down on the pavement, and sees the key of the crypt door lying close to where he himself lay.

"I dropped you, did I?" he says, picking it up, and recalling that part of his dream. As he gathers himself again into an upright position, or into a position as nearly upright as he ever maintains, he is again conscious of being watched by his companion.

"Well?" says Jasper, smiling. "Are you quite ready? Pray don't hurry."

"Let me get my bundle right, Mister Jarsper, and I'm with you."

As he ties it afresh, he is once more conscious that he is very narrowly observed.

"What do you suspect me of, Mister Jarsper?" he asks, with drunken displeasure. "Let them as has any suspicions of Durdles, name 'em."

"I've no suspicions of you, my good Mr. Durdles; but I have suspicions that my bottle was filled with something stiffer than either of us supposed. And I also have suspicions," Jasper adds, taking it from the pavement and turning it bottom upward, "that it's empty."

Durdles condescends to laugh at this. Continuing to chuckle when his laugh is over, as though remonstrant with himself on his drinking powers, he rolls to the door and unlocks it. They both pass out, and Durdles relocks it, and pockets his key.

"A thousand thanks for a curious and interesting night," says Jasper, giving him his hand; "you can make your own way home?"

"I should think so!" answers Durdles. "If you was to offer Durdles the affront to show him his way home, he wouldn't go home.

> Durdles wouldn't go home till morning,
> And *then* Durdles wouldn't go home,

Durdles wouldn't." This, with the utmost defiance.

"Good-night, then."

"Good-night, Mister Jarsper."

Each is turning his own way, when a sharp whistle rends the silence, and the jargon is yelped out:

> "Widdy widdy wen!
> I—ket—ches—Im—out—ar—ter—ten.
> Widdy widdy wy!
> Then—E—don't—go—then—I—shy—
> Widdy Widdy Wake-cock warning!"

Instantly afterwards, a rapid fire of stones rattles at the Cathedral wall, and the hideous small boy is beheld opposite, dancing in the moonlight.

"What! Is that baby-devil on the watch there!" cries Jasper in a fury: so quickly roused, and so violent, that he seems an older devil himself. "I shall shed the blood of that Impish wretch! I know I shall do it!" Regardless of the fire, though it hits him more than once, he rushes at Deputy, collars him, and tries to bring him across. But Deputy is not to be so easily brought across. With a diabolical insight into the strongest part of his position, he is no sooner taken by the throat than he curls up his legs, forces his assailant to hang him, as it were, and gurgles in his throat, and screws his body, and twists, as already undergoing the first agonies of strangulation. There is nothing for it but to drop him. He instantly gets himself together, backs over to Durdles, and cries to his assailant, gnashing the great gap in front of his mouth with rage and malice:

"I'll blind yer, s'elp me! I'll stone yer eyes out, s'elp me! If I don't have yer eyesight, bellows me!" At the same time dodging behind Durdles, and snarling at Jasper, now from this side of him, and now from that: prepared, if pounced upon, to dart away in all manner of curvilinear directions, and, if run down after all, to grovel in the dust, and cry: "Now, hit me when I'm down! Do it!"

"Don't hurt the boy, Mister Jarsper," urges Durdles, shielding him. "Recollect yourself."

"He followed us to-night, when we first came here!"

"Yer lie, I didn't!" replies Deputy, in his one form of polite contradiction.

"He has been prowling near us ever since!"

"Yer lie, I haven't," returns Deputy. "I'd only jist come out for my 'elth when I see you two a coming out of the Kinfreederel. If—

"I—ket—ches—I'm—out—ar—ter—ten,"

(with the usual rhythm and dance, though dodging behind Durdles), "it ain't *my* fault, is it?"

"Take him home, then," retorts Jasper, ferociously, though with a strong check upon himself, "and let my eyes be rid of the sight of you!"

Deputy, with another sharp whistle, at once expressing his relief, and his commencement of a milder stoning of Mr. Durdles, begins stoning that respectable gentleman home, as he if were a reluctant ox. Mr. Jasper goes to his Gate House, brooding. And thus, as everything comes to an end, the unaccountable expedition comes to an end—for the time.

9.

A T THE END OF THE IMPRINTING, Dr Wilmot lowers his hands, which had been folded under his chin in a pose of Oxfordian detachment.

"Subliminal listening is a wonderful achievement, I'm sure," he says, turning to the hostess and handing her the original edition of the instalment, "but I wonder, Loredana, if you would be so kind as to re-read the last sentence for us?"

Flattered at being so familiarly addressed by Dr Wilmot, she reads with great intensity and expression: "And thus, as everything comes to an end, the unaccountable expedition comes to an end—for the time."

WILMOT: Perfect, thank you. We are thus at the end of this instalment and also of the expedition . . . for the time. But what *is* this time? I feel we would do well to establish it precisely both within and without the novel.

ALL, *although not fully understanding him:* Right.

WILMOT: If we consider the events of the narration,

when Jasper returns home it is about half past two in the morning. And the night is that between Sunday the 18th and Monday the 19th of December.

LOREDANA, *clearing her throat uncertainly, apologetically:* Ahem.

WILMOT: What is it, signorina?

LOREDANA: I think it must be the night between Monday and Tuesday. Because at the beginning of the expedition we heard the Reverend Crisparkle say to Neville: "This is the first day of the week, and the last day of the week is Christmas Eve."

There is a general murmur of "Yes," "That's right," "The first day's Monday," etc., among the public (but not from Father Brown). The editor of *The Dickensian* waits for it to subside before replying.

"You're a careful reader and most valuable assistant, Loredana. But," he adds, pointing to a shelf on the wall, "I see the two volumes of the *Shorter Oxford English Dictionary* over there. Would you mind looking up the word Monday?"

The room is gripped by breathless suspense while the young lady, pale with anxiety, flips backwards and forwards through the *Shorter OED*. When at last she locates the word, she flushes scarlet.

"Monday: *second* day of the week," she stammers, crushed.

258

The chairman consoles her as best he can, while Father Brown, who has also come forward reassuringly, explains from the platform what lies behind this error.

"It is not the young lady's fault," he says, "that in our modern age consecrated to the weekend, the Lord's day has become the last one. For the Church, however, it has always been the first, and remains so in all major dictionaries, and there is no doubt that it was the first for Dickens, too: especially when putting words into the mouth of a churchman. It is therefore firmly established that the first expedition took place on Monday night."

This is the advantage of conventions, reader. How many of us, reading the MED by ourselves, would have made Loredana's mistake? And thus we would have placed the presumable "second expedition" of Christmas night between Sunday and Monday rather than between Saturday and Sunday. An unimportant detail? Nothing is unimportant in a murder mystery.

WILMOT: Particularly if it comes in instalments and is destined to be tragically broken off halfway through. That is why I say we must take into consideration the novel's internal as well as external chronology. Shall we have another look at the instalment?

By now fully recovered, Loredana eagerly takes it up again, and the chairman continues: "The last line finds us on December 19. The year could be 1842. Christmas is six days away. But what is the month and what is the year on the first line?"

The girl opens the booklet to the first page. But after a moment she closes it again and looks at Dr Wilmot questioningly. He nods, and she finally looks at the top of the cover page.

"June 1870," she reads. And, after an awed pause, remarks: "Just eight days before his death!"

WILMOT: Exactly. The third number is the last published in the author's lifetime. The next three will come out regularly, but posthumously. It's a point we would do well to bear in mind.

The mysterious Popeau, who has managed to worm his way into the panel, between Gideon Fell and Dr Thorndyke, interposes with his usual acrimony. "I fail to see what possible difference this makes. It strikes me as a complete waste of time. Why don't we get on and examine the evidence?"

"But may not this consideration of posthumousness affect the weight, the reliability, of the evidence?" Poirot asks from the floor. "Was it this to which you wished to draw our attention, Monsieur Wilmot?"

WILMOT: Yes. In the sense that the sum of the evidence, as it can be established up until Monday, December

19, 1842, in the novel, and up until Wednesday, June 1, 1870, in real life, is in fact . . .

POPEAU: Objection, monsieur! Previously you stated, on the basis of observations connected with the railway, that the novel "could be" set in 1842. Now it definitely is. How do you account for this?

POIROT: I imagine that in the meantime Dr Wilmot, like myself, has consulted his Perpetual Gregorian calendar, and thus ascertained that in 1842, December 19 fell on a Monday.

WILMOT: Quite right. But we were talking about the evidence. The evidence contained in the three numbers that had already come out (and which had sold on the order of 100,000 copies each) could not, of course, be modified or suppressed. But this does not apply to the later numbers. The fourth and fifth were in the editor's hands, and the author had already gone through the proofs—but he could always go through them again and make changes. And the sixth was only partly written. Now, we know from various witnesses that on June 1 (when he returned from London to Gadshill to finish the sixth number), Dickens was having trouble with the story's development. "I don't see how I can get myself out of this maze," he confided in particular to William Wills. It is thus conceivable that he had it in mind to alter some of the evidence, which because of its precision had tied his hands too much. That he wished to leave himself freer as regards the development of the plot, and also to prepare his surprise-ending better.

POPEAU: Objection! We do not know that the ending was going to be a surprise.

TOAD: I agree. I am more convinced than ever that the book would have ended with page upon tedious page of Jasper's torments of conscience, and the loss of that troubles me not one jot.

WILMOT: We have already discussed this. There are those, like Dickens's daughter, who believe that the writer was more interested in "the tragic secrets of the human heart" than "the intricate working out of his plot" and the traditional uncovering of the culprit. And there are those who believe the opposite. But Dickens himself wrote to James T. Field, his American publisher, in these words: "At Nos. 5 or 6 the story will turn upon an interest suspended until the end." To me, suspense until the end means a surprise ending.

The chairman's calm, impartial reply is rewarded with lively applause. Porfiry Petrovich, the colonel of the Carabinieri, and Toad himself step forward to shake his hand. And Loredana's eyes continually return to him with a greater intensity than is perhaps in keeping with her professional capacity. . . . But the speakers, Thorndyke and Fell, who are specialists in questions of scientific investigation, are already examining the "evidence that cannot be changed" of the third number.

Extrasensory perception. When teaching Neville, the Rev. Crisparkle has the strange sensation that Helena is listening to him as well. She also seems to have some mesmeric influence over him: after his first assessment of her as no less dangerous than her brother, he ends up considering her to be a kind of saint. But in Dr Fell's opinion, this is not necessarily caused by paranormal abilities. Helena may simply be using her feminine wiles to win the young churchman over, even to the point of mawkish displays of piety which seem quite out of place in a character such as hers. It remains to be seen what her purpose is.

Neville's hands. "You have repeated that former action of your hands, which I so much dislike," says Crisparkle, when his pupil, fired by hatred for Drood, clenches his hands convulsively. And note, observes Thorndyke, that the author says hands and not fists, betokening a less specific state of aggressiveness. This piece of evidence will be important should an eventual autopsy of Drood's body reveal that he was strangled before being thrown from the tower (if that is what is to happen). But in that case—Dr Wilmot fair-mindedly anticipating a detail—it will also be necessary to establish how he was strangled: that is, by a pair of hands or by a certain scarf that we will see around Jasper's neck in the next number.

Medicinal herbs. Unlike the special food closet, which is kept scrupulously locked, Mrs Crisparkle's "nauseous medicinal herb-closet" is accessible to anybody; and among other things it contains bottles of "a remedy against tooth-ache" (i.e., laudanum). Why does the author devote two whole pages to a description intended to introduce (and disguise) this clue? Probably — this is the opinion of both speakers — to establish right away that Neville, too, could obtain drugs.

Ambiguous cry. "What is the matter? Who did it?" Jasper cries out on being woken from a dream which, he tells Crisparkle, was produced by indigestion. In fact, it must have been his usual opium "vision." But "Who did it?" implies the fear that a certain act, so far only medi-tated, has indeed been committed. Or could it be that Jasper is so bent on killing his nephew himself that he would hate anybody else's stealing the crime from him?

Ring. Will it be used as a means of identification? Fa-ther Brown, no expert in matters of chemistry, asks whether a ring such as the one described would be proof against the action of quicklime. Dr Thorndyke cites various cases of corpses half-consumed by CaO (calcium oxide), but whose rings remained intact. Gideon Fell adds that even without rings or other forms of jewellery, human remains found in quicklime have been identified by the nails in the shoes.

Mayor's powers. At the panel's request, the chairman lists these powers, reciting from memory the immortal pages of *The Pickwick Papers* re G. Nupkins Esq., mayor of Ipswich. In small towns like Ipswich and Rochester, the mayor was also chief of police. This is why Jasper flatters Sapsea so assiduously, and does his best to turn him against the "half-caste" Neville. Not only to avert future suspicion. Jasper may also reckon that Neville may come off worse in the struggle he is so busily preparing, and then it will be Drood who gets into trouble with the law.

The quicklime deposit. Another double-edged clue. Jasper shows a certain interest in this lime; but if he wants to get rid of a corpse, he already has access to Mrs Sapsea's tomb. Besides, the deposit, as the author carefully specifies, is "by the gate" of Durdles's yard, not far from Crisparkle's house. It is therefore quite possible that Neville, too, has seen it and thought about it.

Eye and trigger. Jasper's eye fills with a sudden destructive hatred when he sees Helena's twin from far off. But this hatred seems hardly explicable as jealousy for a rival who is, after all, only a secondary rival. It is not clear why the author emphasises this point. "Unless," Loredana murmurs to herself, not daring to speak up again in the debate, "it's a way of suggesting that the uncle is actually on his nephew's side, despite appearances?" The Carabinieri colonel meanwhile puts Dr Wilmot in some difficulty with a technical question. "At the time of the novel," he inquires, "did one fire with one's eye to the trigger instead of to the sights? Or is this just an error on Dickens's part?"[1]

Ghostly cry. The speakers refuse to pronounce in any way on the nature and possible significance of this cry. But they take note of the date, *Christmas Eve,* on which Durdles claims to have heard it the previous year.

The tower and the keys. What can have been the purpose of the mysterious expedition? Everybody agrees—except Toad, who ironically says that Jasper really does intend to write a *Guide to Cloisterham,* which will earn him fame and fortune, but is reluctant to admit it—that the choir-master's aims were: 1) to inspect the stairs and the galleries that lead to the tower; 2) once up there, to study in the moonlight the best place from which to hurl someone down; and 3) to take the key to the Sapsea tomb off Durdles, after drugging him. All three aims appear to have been achieved, though there is some doubt with regard to the key. Or, rather, to the keys, since . . .

---

[1] The text (page 244) states that Jasper watches Neville "as though his eye were at the trigger of a loaded rifle, and he had covered him, and were going to fire."

LOREDANA, *whom there is no holding now:* But if he intended to go back up the tower with his victim, if that was the plan, wouldn't he need the keys also to the crypt and the tower?

POPEAU, *scornfully: Mais voyons, ma pauvre fille!* As choirmaster, Jasper has free run of the sacristy and can take Tope's keys. But what I do not understand is how Durdles could possibly have failed to realise that the key to the tomb was stolen.

POIROT: Jasper could have taken it for only a few minutes. The time needed to . . .

POPEAU, *sarcastically:* . . . go and open the tomb straightaway? In the hope that Durdles would not notice before Christmas? *Mais voyons, mon pauvre monsieur!*

POIROT, *mellifluously:* I meant the time needed for Jasper to make an impression of the key, with the wax he presumably brought with him. But this is a simple hypothesis of Hercule Poirot, which he hardly dares submit to the great Hercule Popeau! *Sensation and prolonged buzz of voices in the room.* In the hotel register, I noticed that not only do you have a surname very similar to my own, but you are actually called Hercule like myself. And our backgrounds are strangely analogous: you are a former high-ranking officer in the French police, it appears; and I in the Belgian police. I must confess that the coincidence strikes me as suspicious.

POPEAU, *furious:* You call *me* suspicious? If anyone has any explaining to do, it is you! . . .

WILMOT, *glancing diplomatically at the clock:* It's getting late. I suggest that in true Dickensian fashion we leave the sequel until the July and August numbers.

PART THREE

THE JULY AND AUGUST NUMBERS

10.

W HAT IS THE ATMOSPHERE OF A
CONVENTION—national or international—on the morning of the third day?

Not what one would call vibrant, reader; not what one
would call euphoric. There has been too much talk, both
serious and frivolous, and too much smoke, whether passive or active. Some have not yet accustomed or resigned
themselves to the hotel's mattresses and cuisine; some are
beginning to feel the first prickings of impatience towards
certain colleagues, a secret feeling distantly related to homicidal fury; and some (a minority, fortunately) can be found
staring at a door-handle or table-corner with the glazed
eyes of one no longer able to suppress the fatal question:
"What in hell am I doing here?"

And last night, nobody was able to leave the U&O.
Sumptuous dinners had been planned in picturesque Roman trattorias, to be followed by picturesque Roman
folkdancing on the Oppian Hill. But just as they were about
to leave, the . . . what do we call them? completers?

271

completists? completionists? found themselves confronting a hostile mob that had invaded the garden and was blocking the entrance-hall.

Who were these trouble-makers being kept under the uncertain rein of a few puzzled policemen? The papers this morning describe them as Byronic integralists and fanatical Mitteleuropeans, all demonstrating with loudspeakers, banners, leaflets, and even bonfires, against the exclusion of their favourite works from the convention. COMPLETE DON JUAN! the banners read; HOW DOES THE MAN WITHOUT QUALITIES END?; FINISH AMERIKA!

There was no violence, although a group of Kafkian extremists did try—without success—to break into the U&O via a service door. From our group, the Carabinieri colonel went out to parley. He managed to negotiate a compromise: the demonstrators would remain outside the building, the convention-members inside.

"What kind of compromise do you call that?" came a cry from all sides. A scholar from Fribourg made a detailed comparison with the siege of the Castle of Sant'Angelo as fancifully described by Cellini. Meanwhile the rage of the dissidents without began to infect people within, causing dramatic revolts among the different work-groups.

"Puccini's music makes me sick!" proclaimed a Danish musicologist, to general consternation. The clamor and the chaos reached their peak when a Latinist from Pirna (formerly East Germany) proposed that they complete the *Sa-tyricon* or reconstruct the comedies of Plautus "rather than Livy's *Roman History*, which is far too long as it is."

These iconoclastic pronouncements (there were even some, reader, for whom Leoncavallo, the *Unfinished Symphony*, and "O Sole Mio" were all much of a muchness) received more coverage in the press than they deserved. But they served to draw attention away from the Drood group, and thus prevented the reporters and photographers, whose interest in completeness could not compare with their thirst for scandal and gossip, from sinking their teeth into a story far juicier.

After the session, despite Dr Wilmot's request that the matter be tabled for the time being, several of our investigators surrounded Poirot and the preposterous impostor Popeau, bombarding them both with questions. The embarrassing truth gradually emerged: Popeau was preposterous perhaps, but no impostor; no, it was Poirot—or his absent-minded (cunning?) creator—who had usurped the other's name and credentials, making only the slightest modifications.[1]

---

[1] Created almost twenty years before Poirot by Mrs. Marie Adelaide Belloc Lowndes (1868–1948), Hercule Popeau rose to high rank in the French police. In 1918, after a brief period in counter-espionage, he reappeared as an Anglicised private detective in a series of melodramatic tales by the author (sister of the better-known Hilaire Belloc, but in her day famous enough in her own right; her novel *The Lodger*, of 1913,

But we are not here to do the media's job for them, reader. Therefore we will dwell neither on the illustrious plagiarist's ignominy nor on his humble victim's triumph. Instead, we will summarise the discussion that ensued, which the chairman, with his usual tact, managed to divert from the specific case, directing it to the subject of plagiarism in general.

WILMOT: There is, after all, a kind of plagiarism that is totally unconscious: a name, an idea, a situation, the starting point for a plot, which a writer forgets that he has absorbed from another writer, and which years later he may use as his own in perfectly good faith.

LATINIST FROM JUAN-LES-PINS, *who, disgusted by the treachery of his colleague from Pirna, has come to join the Drood group:* Among the ancients there was, of course, no such thing as copyright, and nothing to compare with the literary market of today, so the question didn't even arise. Consequently there is nothing in Latin that corresponds to our meaning of the word plagiarism. The term *plagiarius* (from the Greek *plágios*, "oblique, sly") was applied to a man who harboured runaway slaves or who reduced a free man to a condition of servility.

WOLFE: Today, however, copyright is an esssential part

---

was made into a celebrated film by Hitchcock). Hercule Poirot, complete with pension, moustaches, and little grey cells, did not appear until 1920, in *The Mysterious Affair at Styles*, Agatha Christie's first detective novel.

of the Rights of Man! Any violation of it means royalties lost or stolen, money that ends up in another writer's pocket.

HOLMES: But these are petty quarrels, unworthy of gentlemen. Borrowings and exchanges, themes and characters that cross from work to work, have always been part and parcel of the literary game.

WILMOT: An example of which can be found in the character Grewgious, the immortal solicitor whom Stevenson was to borrow and develop in *Jekyll and Hyde*, but who in turn was derived from a character in Sterne's *Tristram Shandy*.

LOREDANA: You know so much, Dr Wilmot!

MARLOWE AND ARCHER, *in low voices:* You'll find us even better-equipped, doll . . .

LOREDANA, *aside:* They're just jealous.

WILMOT, *spurred on by the woman's admiration:* There's more. In yet another novel, Stevenson used the idea of a wicked uncle planning to kill his nephew by making him fall from an ancient tower on a stormy night.

MARLOWE AND ARCHER, *low and mocking:* You know so much, Dr Wilmot!

LOREDANA, *through gritted teeth:* Peasants!

P. PETROVICH: But in *The Strange Case of Dr. Jekyll and Mr. Hyde*, in my opinion, Stevenson borrows much more from the MED than an isolated character or a series of external circumstances. He takes the novel's basic theme!

The idea of an individual who, like all of us, is a mixture of good and evil, and whose personality is tragically split by drugs. The two halves, the good and the evil, not only behave independently of each other, but do not even *know* what the other half is doing. In this sense, the MED could easily be called *The Strange Case of Mr Jasper and the Wicked Man*.

MAIGRET: I imagine that this explanation has been put forward by someone before us?

WILMOT: More than once, with variations. And, Inspector, this is why your question yesterday put me in some difficulty. I could not tell you how Jasper and the Opium-Addict, alias the Wicked Man, were and at the same time *were not* the same person, without anticipating the brilliant solution that Magistrate Petrovich has now come up with entirely on his own.

TOAD: That's what you call a brilliant solution? After all those promises of a surprise ending? If that's it, I'm leaving; I'll go and join the protestors outside!

LOREDANA: That would not be gentlemanly, Mr Toad. If you have a better idea, all you need do is put it forward, and I'm sure Dr Wilmot *(gazing so fondly at Wilmot that Toad himself is left dumbfounded)* will not fail to take it into consideration.

WILMOT: But tomorrow, I think. For the moment I would just like to mention that some of the Jekyll-type solutions are quite surprising in their own way, not to say quietly spectacular.

FATHER BROWN: You're not going to tell us that the wicked Jasper turns out to be a foot shorter than the good Jasper, like Hyde?

WILMOT: No, everything remains on the psychological plane. For example, in the most recent of these solutions,[1] Jasper finally returns to the crime in an opium-haze, and recounts it in detail, but without in the least suspecting that it was he who committed it.

TOAD: That would be more plagiarism. And plagiarism against a friend. Because the device was used by Wilkie Collins in *The Moonstone*, although the crime there was the theft of a diamond and not the murder of a rival.

WILMOT, *clearing his throat:* This is true. But another "Jekyllian," the American Edmund Wilson,[2] found a way round this problem. According to him, Jasper did not plan the murder of his nephew and carry it out under the influence of opium, but in a state of auto-hypnosis. And his memory would return under the influence of Helena's telehypnosis.

FATHER BROWN, *also clearing his throat:* I don't see how

---

[1] Charles Forsyte, *The Decoding of Edwin Drood,* London, 1980.
[2] E. Wilson, "The Two Scrooges" (in *The Wound and the Bow,* 1939). Another authoritative "Jekyllian" is J. B. Priestley, in his biography of Dickens (1961).

277

this makes much difference. Indeed, I wonder whether direct plagiarism might not be better than indirect imitation. "Inferior poets imitate, mature ones steal," says T. S. Eliot, whom we have already quoted.

POIROT, *cheered by this quotation: Parfaitement!*

THE MAN IN BLACK:[1] Up to a point, Poirot, up to a point. What do you think, Porfiry?

P. PETROVICH: As a Czarist magistrate, I am bound to condemn every crime against property, including literary property. On the other hand, it is also true that the artist *"prend son bien où il le trouve,"* as Molière declared in his self-defence. But there are limits.

POPEAU: I should hope so!

P. PETROVICH: Even in classical antiquity, which was extremely tolerant in this matter, a certain Ephorus, a pupil of Isocrates, was singled out for public censure when no fewer than three thousand lines in his works were discovered to have been copied directly from other authors.

WILMOT: But we mustn't put the cart before the horse. Before we accuse Dickens of plagiarism, we should first consider other solutions. After all, the idea that Jasper suf-

---

[1] This participant is an extremely thin man, dressed entirely in black. During the work sessions, he always sits in the back row, never joining in the debate. In the breaks, too, he keeps to himself, wandering around the garden with a melancholy air, and stopping every so often to look disapprovingly at the rose-bushes (which are rather badly kept, to tell the truth).

fered a personality split under the influence of opium or hypnosis is only one of *two* possibilities presented so far in the Drood case. In the other possibility, opium and hypnosis remain secondary elements, a red herring, since the villain is not Jasper.

TOAD: You have thrown me a life-line, Dr Wilmot! Tell us at once who this . . .

WILMOT, *raising his hand:* As I have already said, my dear friend, I do not wish to influence the normal course of the enquiry. Besides, it is getting late, the hotel is still besieged, and I would like to go to bed.

LOREDANA: Yes, let's all turn in. A comfortable bed awaits everybody here——*in a very low voice, intended only for the editor of* The Dickensian, *but not low enough to escape Poirot's keen ears*——and mine is on the second floor, No. 11, at the end of the second corridor and to the right.

This, reader, is a rough account of the events of yesterday evening at the U&O. This is what the members of our group——with the possible exception of two of them—— pondered over during the night, or perhaps even dreamt about. And this gives you an indication of the spirit in which they faced the new day and the discussion of the first two chapters of the July number.

CHAPTER XIII

BOTH AT THEIR BEST

MISS TWINKLETON'S establishment was about to undergo a serene hush. The Christmas recess was at hand. What had once, and at no remote period, been called, even by the erudite Miss Twinkleton herself, "the half;" but what was now called, as being more elegant, and more strictly collegiate; "the term," would expire to-morrow. A noticeable relaxation of discipline had for some few days pervaded the Nuns' House. Club suppers had occurred in the bedrooms, and a dressed tongue had been carved with a pair of scissors, and handed round with the curling-tongs. Portions of marmalade had likewise been distributed on a service of plates constructed of curlpaper; and cowslip wine had been quaffed from the small squat measuring glass in which little Rickitts (a junior of weakly constitution), took her steel drops daily. The housemaids had been bribed with various fragments of riband, and sundry pairs of shoes, more or less down at heel, to make no mention of crumbs in the beds; the airiest costumes had been worn on these festive occasions; and the daring Miss Ferdinand had even surprised the company with a sprightly solo on the comb-and-curlpaper, until suffocated in her own pillow by two flowing-haired executioners.

Nor were these the only tokens of dispersal. Boxes appeared in the bedrooms (where they were capital at other times), and a surprising amount of packing took place, out of all proportion to the amount packed. Largesse, in the form of odds and ends of cold cream and pomatum, and also of hairpins, was freely distributed among the attendants. On charges of inviolable secrecy, confidences were interchanged respecting golden youth of England expected to call, "at home," on the first opportunity. Miss Giggles (deficient in sentiment) did indeed profess that she, for her part, acknowledged such homage by making faces at the golden youth; but this young lady was outvoted by an immense majority.

On the last night before a recess, it was always expressly made a point of honor that nobody should go to sleep, and that Ghosts should be encouraged by all possible means. This compact invariably broke down, and all the young ladies went to sleep very soon, and got up very early.

The concluding ceremony came off at twelve o'clock on the day of departure; when Miss Twinkleton, supported by Mrs. Tisher, held a Drawing-Room in her own apartment (the globes already covered with brown holland), where glasses of white wine, and plates of cut pound-cake were discovered on the table. Miss Twinkleton then said, Ladies, another revolving year had brought us round to that festive period at which the first feelings of our nature bounded in our—— Miss Twinkleton was annually going to add "bosoms," but annually stopped on the brink of that expression, and substituted "hearts." Hearts; our hearts. Hem! Again a revolving year, ladies, had brought us to a pause in our studies—let us hope our greatly advanced studies—and, like the mariner in his bark, the warrior in his tent, the captive in his dungeon, and the traveller in his various conveyances, we yearned for home. Did we say, on such an occasion, in the opening words of Mr. Addison's impressive tragedy:

> "The dawn is overcast, the morning lowers,
> And heavily in clouds brings on the day,
> The great, th' important day——"?

Not so. From horizon to zenith all was *couleur de rose*, for all was redolent of our relations and friends. Might *we* find *them* prospering as *we* expected; might *they* find *us* prospering as *they* expected! Ladies, we would now, with our love to one another, wish one another good-bye, and happiness, until we met again. And when the time should come for our resumption of those pursuits which (here a general depression set in all round), pursuits which, pursuits which; —then let us ever remember what was said by the Spartan General, in words too trite for repetition, at the battle it was superfluous to specify.

The handmaidens of the establishment, in their best caps, then handed the trays, and the young ladies sipped and crumbled, and the bespoken coaches began to choke the street. Then, leave-taking was not long about, and Miss Twinkleton, in saluting each young lady's cheek, confided to her an exceedingly neat letter, addressed to her next friend at law, "with Miss Twinkleton's best compliments" in the corner. This missive she handed with an air as if it had not the least connexion with the bill, but were something in the nature of a delicate and joyful surprise.

So many times had Rosa seen such dispersals, and so very little did she know of any other Home, that she was contented to remain where she was, and was even better contented than ever before, having her latest friend with her. And yet her latest friendship had a blank place in it of which she could not fail to be sensible. Helena Landless, having been a party to her brother's revelation about Rosa, and having entered into that compact of silence with Mr. Crisparkle, shrank from any allusion to Edwin Drood's name. Why she so avoided it, was mysterious to Rosa, but she perfectly perceived the fact. But for the fact, she might have relieved her own little perplexed heart of some of its doubts and hesitations, by taking Helena into her confidence. As it was, she had no such vent: she could only ponder on her own difficulties, and wonder more and more why this avoidance of Edwin's name should last, now that she knew—for so much Helena had told her—that a good understanding was to be re-established between the two young men, when Edwin came down.

It would have made a pretty picture, so many pretty girls kissing Rosa in the cold porch of the Nuns' House, and that sunny little creature peeping out of it (unconscious of sly faces carved on spout and gable peeping at her), and waving farewells to the departing coaches, as if she represented the spirit of rosy youth abiding in the place to keep it bright and warm in its desertion. The hoarse High Street became musical with the cry, in various silvery voices, "Good-bye, Rosebud, Darling!" and the effigy of Mr. Sapsea's father over the opposite doorway, seemed to say to mankind: "Gentlemen, favor me with your attention to this charming little last lot left behind, and bid with a spirit worthy of the occasion!" Then the staid street, so unwontedly sparkling, youthful, and fresh for a few rippling moments, ran dry, and Cloisterham was itself again.

If Rosebud in her bower now waited Edwin Drood's coming with an uneasy heart, Edwin for his part was uneasy too. With far less force of purpose in his composition than the childish beauty, crowned by acclamation fairy queen of Miss Twinkleton's establishment, he had a conscience, and Mr. Grewgious had pricked it. That gentleman's steady convictions of what was right and what was wrong in such a case as his, were neither to be frowned aside, nor laughed aside. They would not be moved. But for the dinner in Staple Inn, and but for the ring he carried in the breast-pocket of his coat, he would have drifted into their wedding-day without another pause for real thought, loosely trusting that all would go well, left alone. But that serious putting him on his truth to the living and the dead had brought him to a check. He must either give the ring to Rosa, or he must take it back. Once put into this narrowed way of action, it was curious that he began to consider Rosa's claims upon him more unselfishly than he had ever considered them before, and began to be less sure of himself than he had ever been in all his easygoing days.

"I will be guided by what she says, and by how we get on," was his decision, walking from the Gate House to the Nuns' House.

"Whatever comes of it, I will bear his words in mind, and try to be true to the living and the dead."

Rosa was dressed for walking. She expected him. It was a bright frosty day, and Miss Twinkleton had already graciously sanctioned fresh air. Thus they got out together before it became necessary for either Miss Twinkleton, or the Deputy High Priest, Mrs. Tisher, to lay even so much as one of those usual offerings on the shrine of Propriety.

"My dear Eddy," said Rosa, when they had turned out of the High Street, and had got among the quiet walks in the neighbourhood of the Cathedral and the river: "I want to say something very serious to you. I have been thinking about it for a long, long time."

"I want to be serious with you too, Rosa dear. I mean to be serious and earnest."

"Thank you, Eddy. And you will not think me unkind because I begin, will you? You will not think I speak for myself only, because I speak first? That would not be generous, would it? And I know you are generous!"

He said, "I hope I am not ungenerous to you, Rosa." He called her Pussy no more. Never again.

"And there is no fear," pursued Rosa, "of our quarrelling, is there? Because, Eddy," clasping her hand on his arm, "we have so much reason to be very lenient to each other!"

"We will be, Rosa."

"That's a dear good boy! Eddy, let us be courageous. Let us change to brother and sister from this day forth."

"Never be husband and wife?"

"Never!"

Neither spoke again for a little while. But after that pause he said, with some effort:

"Of course I know that this has been in both our minds, Rosa, and of course I am in honor bound to confess freely that it does not originate with you."

"No, nor with you, dear," she returned, with pathetic earnestness. "It has sprung up between us. You are not truly happy in our engagement; I am not truly happy in it. O, I am so sorry, so sorry!" And there she broke into tears.

"I am deeply sorry too, Rosa. Deeply sorry for you."

"And I for you, poor boy! And I for you!"

This pure young feeling, this gentle and forbearing feeling of each towards the other, brought with it its reward in a softening light that seemed to shine on their position. The relations between them did not look wilful, or capricious, or a failure, in such a light; they became elevated into something more self-denying, honorable, affectionate, and true.

"If we knew yesterday," said Rosa, as she dried her eyes, "and we did know yesterday, and on many, many yesterdays, that we were far from right together in those relations which were not of our own choosing, what better could we do to-day than change them? It is natural that we should be sorry, and you see how sorry we both are; but how much better to be sorry now than then!"

"When, Rosa?"

"When it would be too late. And then we should be angry, besides."

Another silence fell upon them.

"And you know," said Rosa, innocently, "you couldn't like me then; and you can always like me now, for I shall not be a drag upon you, or a worry to you. And I can always like you now, and your sister will not tease or trifle with you. I often did when I was not your sister, and I beg your pardon for it."

"Don't let us come to that, Rosa; or I shall want more pardoning than I like to think of."

"No, indeed, Eddy; you are too hard, my generous boy, upon yourself. Let us sit down, brother, on these ruins, and let me tell you how it was with us. I think I know, for I have considered about it very much since you were here, last time. You liked me, didn't you? You thought I was a nice little thing?"

"Everybody thinks that, Rosa."

"Do they?" She knitted her brow musingly for a moment, and then flashed out with the bright little induction: "Well; but say they do. Surely it was not enough that you should think of me, only as other people did; now, was it?"

The point was not to be got over. It was not enough.

"And that is just what I mean; that is just how it was with us," said Rosa. "You liked me very well, and you had grown used to me, and had grown used to the idea of our being married. You accepted the situation as an inevitable kind of thing, didn't you? It was to be, you thought, and why discuss or dispute it."

It was new and strange to him to have himself presented to himself so clearly, in a glass of her holding up. He had always patronized her, in his superiority to her share of woman's wit. Was that but another instance of something radically amiss in the terms on which they had been gliding towards a life-long bondage?

"All this that I say of you, is true of me as well, Eddy. Unless it was, I might not be bold enough to say it. Only, the difference between us was, that by little and little there crept into my mind a habit of thinking about it, instead of dismissing it. My life is not so busy as yours, you see, and I have not so many things to think of. So I thought about it very much, and I cried about it very much too (though that was not your fault, poor boy); when all at once my guardian came down, to prepare for my leaving the Nuns' House. I tried to hint to him that I was not quite settled in my mind, but I hesitated and failed, and he didn't understand me. But he is a good, good man. And he put before me so kindly, and yet so strongly, how seriously we ought to consider, in our circumstances, that I resolved to speak to you the next moment we were alone and grave. And if I seemed to come to it easily just now, because I came to it all at once, don't think it was so really, Eddy, for O, it was very, very hard, and O, I am very, very sorry!"

Her full heart broke into tears again. He put his arm about her waist, and they walked by the river-side together.

"Your guardian has spoken to me too, Rosa dear. I saw him before I left London." His right hand was in his breast, seeking the ring; but he checked it as he thought: "If I am to take it back, why should I tell her of it?"

"And that made you more serious about it, didn't it, Eddy? And if I had not spoken to you, as I have, you would have spoken to me? I hope you can tell me so? I don't like it to be *all* my doing, though it *is* so much better for us."

"Yes, I should have spoken; I should have put everything before you; I came intending to do it. But I never could have spoken to you as you have spoken to me, Rosa."

"Don't say you mean so coldly or unkindly, Eddy, please, if you can help it."

"I mean so sensibly and delicately, so wisely and affectionately."

"That's my dear brother!" She kissed his hand in a little rapture. "The dear girls will be dreadfully disappointed," added Rosa, laughing, with the dew-drops glistening in her bright eyes. "They have looked forward to it so, poor pets!"

"Ah! But I fear it will be a worse disappointment to Jack," said Edwin Drood, with a start. "I never thought of Jack!"

Her swift and intent look at him as he said the words, could no more be recalled than a flash of lightning can. But it appeared as though she would have instantly recalled it, if she could; for she looked down, confused, and breathed quickly.

"You don't doubt it's being a blow to Jack, Rosa?"

She merely replied, and that, evasively and hurriedly: Why should she? She had not thought about it. He seemed, to her, to have so little to do with it.

"My dear child! Can you suppose that any one so wrapped up in another—Mrs. Tope's expression: not mine—as Jack is in me, could fail to be struck all of a heap by such a sudden and complete change in my life? I say sudden, because it will be sudden to *him,* you know."

She nodded twice or thrice, and her lips parted as if she would have assented. But she uttered no sound, and her breathing was no slower.

"How shall I tell Jack!" said Edwin, ruminating. If he had been less occupied with the thought, he must have seen her singular emotion. "I never thought of Jack. It must be broken to him, before the town crier knows it. I dine with the dear fellow to-morrow and next day—Christmas Eve and Christmas Day—but it would never do to spoil his feast days. He always worries about me, and moddley-coddleys in the merest trifles. The news is sure to overset him. How on earth shall this be broken to Jack!"

"He must be told, I suppose?" said Rosa.

"My dear Rosa! Who ought to be in our confidence, if not Jack?"

"My guardian promised to come down, if I should write and ask him. I am going to do so. Would you like to leave it to him?"

"A bright idea!" cried Edwin. "The other trustee. Nothing more natural. He comes down, he goes to Jack, he relates what we have agreed upon, and he states our case better than we could. He has already spoken feelingly to you, he has already spoken feelingly to me, and he'll put the whole thing feelingly to Jack. That's it! I am not a coward, Rosa, but to tell you a secret, I am a little afraid of Jack."

"No, no! You are not afraid of him?" cried Rosa, turning white and clasping her hands.

"Why, sister Rosa, sister Rosa, what do you see from the turret?" said Edwin, rallying her. "My dear girl!"

"You frightened me."

"Most unintentionally, but I am as sorry as if I had meant to do it. Could you possibly suppose for a moment, from any loose way of speaking of mine, that I was literally afraid of the dear fond fellow? What I mean is, that he is subject to a kind of paroxysm, or fit—I saw him in it once—and I don't know but that so great a surprise, coming upon him direct from me whom he is so wrapped up in, might bring it on perhaps. Which—and this is the secret I was going to tell you—is another reason for your guardian's making the communication. He is so steady, precise, and exact, that he will talk Jack's thoughts into shape, in no time: whereas with me Jack is always impulsive and hurried, and, I may say, almost womanish."

Rosa seemed convinced. Perhaps from her own very different point of view of "Jack," she felt comforted and protected by the interposition of Mr. Grewgious between herself and him.

And now, Edwin Drood's right hand closed again upon the ring in its little case, and again was checked by the consideration: "It is certain, now, that I am to give it back to him; then why should I tell her of it?" That pretty sympathetic nature which could be so sorry for him in the blight of their childish hopes of happiness together, and could so quietly find itself alone in a new world to weave fresh wreaths of such flowers as it might prove to bear, the old world's flowers being withered, would be grieved by those sorrowful jewels; and to what purpose? Why should it be? They were but a sign of broken joys and baseless projects; in their very beauty, they were (as the unlikeliest of men had said), almost a cruel satire on the loves, hopes, plans, of humanity, which are able to forecast nothing, and are so much brittle dust. Let them be. He would restore them to her guardian when he came down; he in his turn would restore them to the cabinet from which he had unwillingly taken them; and there, like old letters or old vows, or other records of old aspirations come to nothing, they would be disregarded, until, being valuable, they were sold into circulation again, to repeat their former round.

Let them be. Let them lie unspoken of, in his breast. However distinctly or indistinctly he entertained these thoughts, he arrived at the conclusion, Let them be. Among the mighty store of wonderful chains that are for ever forging, day and night, in the vast ironworks of time and circumstance, there was one chain forged in the moment of that small conclusion, riveted to the foundations of heaven and earth, and gifted with invincible force to hold and drag.

They walked on by the river. They began to speak of their separate plans. He would quicken his departure from England, and she would remain where she was, at least as long as Helena remained. The poor dear girls should have their disappointment broken to them gently, and, as the first preliminary, Miss Twinkleton should be confided in by Rosa, even in advance of the reappearance of Mr. Grewgious. It should be made clear in all quarters that she and Edwin were the best of friends. There had never been so serene an understanding between them since they were first affianced. And yet there was one reservation on each side; on hers, that she intended through her guardian to withdraw herself immediately from the tuition of her music-master; on his, that he did already entertain some wandering speculations whether it might ever come to pass that he would know more of Miss Landless.

The bright frosty day declined as they walked and spoke together. The sun dipped in the river far behind them, and the old city lay red before them, as their walk drew to a close. The moaning water cast its seaweed duskily at their feet, when they turned to leave its margin; and the rooks hovered above them with hoarse cries, darker splashes in the darkening air.

"I will prepare Jack for my flitting soon," said Edwin, in a low voice, "and I will but see your guardian when he comes, and then go before they speak together. It will be better done without my being by. Don't you think so?"

"Yes."

"We know we have done right, Rosa?"

"Yes."

"We know we are better so, even now?"

"And shall be far, far, better so, by-and-bye."

Still, there was that lingering tenderness in their hearts towards the old positions they were relinquishing, that they prolonged their parting. When they came among the elm trees by the cathedral, where they had last sat together, they stopped, as by consent, and Rosa raised her face to his, as she had never raised it in the old days; —for they were old already.

"God bless you, dear! Good-bye!"

"God bless you, dear! Good-bye!"

They kissed each other, fervently.

"Now, please take me home, Eddy, and let me be by myself."

"Don't look round, Rosa," he cautioned her, as he drew her arm through his, and led her away. "Didn't you see Jack?"

"No! Where?"

"Under the trees. He saw us, as we took leave of each other. Poor fellow! he little thinks we have parted. This will be a blow to him, I am much afraid!"

She hurried on, without resting, and hurried on until they had passed under the Gate House into the street; once there, she asked:

"Has he followed us? You can look without seeming to. Is he behind?"

"No. Yes! he is! He has just passed out under the gateway. The dear sympathetic old fellow likes to keep us in sight. I am afraid he will be bitterly disappointed!"

She pulled hurriedly at the handle of the hoarse old bell, and the gate soon opened. Before going in, she gave him one last wide wondering look, as if she would have asked him with imploring emphasis: "O! don't you understand?" And out of that look he vanished from her view.

CHAPTER XIV

WHEN SHALL THESE THREE MEET AGAIN?

CHRISTMAS EVE in Cloisterham. A few strange faces in the streets; a few other faces, half strange and half familiar, once the faces of Cloisterham children, now the faces of men and women who come back from the outer world at long intervals to find the city wonderfully shrunken in size, as if it had not washed by any means well in the meanwhile. To these, the striking of the cathedral clock, and the cawing of the rooks from the cathedral tower, are like voices of their nursery time. To such as these, it has happened in their dying hours afar off, that they have imagined their chamber floor to be strewn with the autumnal leaves fallen from the elm trees in the Close: so have the rustling sounds and fresh scents of their earliest impressions, revived, when the circle of their lives was very nearly traced, and the beginning and the end were drawing close together.

Seasonable tokens are about. Red berries shine here and there in the lattices of Minor Canon Corner; Mr. and Mrs. Tope are daintily sticking sprigs of holly into the carvings and sconces of the cathedral stalls, as if they were sticking them into the coat-button-holes of the Dean and Chapter. Lavish profusion is in the shops:

296

particularly in the articles of currants, raisins, spices, candied peel, and moist sugar. An unusual air of gallantry and dissipation is abroad; evinced in an immense bunch of mistletoe hanging in the greengrocer's shop doorway, and a poor little Twelfth Cake, culminating in the figure of a Harlequin—such a very poor little Twelfth Cake, that one would rather call it a Twenty Fourth Cake, or a Forty Eighth Cake—to be raffled for at the pastrycook's, terms one shilling per member. Public amusements are not wanting. The Wax-Work which made so deep an impression on the reflective mind of the Emperor of China is to be seen by particular desire during Christmas Week only, on the premises of the bankrupt livery-stable keeper up the lane; and a new grand comic Christmas pantomime is to be produced at the Theatre: the latter heralded by the portrait of Signor Jacksonini the clown, saying "How do you do to-morrow?" quite as large as life, and almost as miserably. In short, Cloisterham is up and doing: though from this description the High School and Miss Twinkleton's are to be excluded. From the former establishment, the scholars have gone home, every one of them in love with one of Miss Twinkleton's young ladies (who knows nothing about it); and only the handmaidens flutter occasionally in the windows of the latter. It is noticed, by-the-bye, that these damsels become, within the limits of decorum, more skittish when thus entrusted with the concrete representation of their sex, than when dividing the representation with Miss Twinkleton's young ladies.

Three are to meet at the Gate House to-night. How does each one of the three get through the day?

———

Neville Landless, though absolved from his books for the time by Mr. Crisparkle—whose fresh nature is by no means insensible to the charms of a holiday—reads and writes in his quiet room, with a concentrated air, until it is two hours past noon. He then sets himself to clearing his table, to arranging his books, and to tearing up and burning his stray papers. He makes a clean sweep of all untidy accumulations, puts all his drawers in order, and leaves no note or scrap of paper undestroyed, save such memoranda as bear directly on his studies. This done, he turns to his wardrobe, selects a few articles of ordinary wear—among them, change of stout shoes and socks for walking—and packs these in a knapsack. This knapsack is new, and he bought it in the High Street yesterday. He also purchased, at the same time and at the same place, a heavy walking-stick: strong in the handle for the grip of the hand, and iron-shod. He tries this, swings it, poises it, and lays it by, with the knapsack, on a window-seat. By this time his arrangements are complete.

He dresses for going out, and is in the act of going—indeed has left his room, and has met the Minor Canon on the staircase, coming out of his bedroom upon the same story—when he turns back again for his walking-stick, thinking he will carry it now. Mr. Crisparkle, who has passed on the staircase, sees it in his hand on his immediately reappearing, takes it from him, and asks him with a smile how he chooses a stick?

"Really I don't know that I understand the subject," he answers. "I chose it for its weight."

"Much too heavy, Neville; *much* too heavy."

"To rest upon in a long walk, sir?"

"Rest upon?" repeats Mr. Crisparkle, throwing himself into pedestrian form. "You don't rest upon it; you merely balance with it."

"I shall know better, with practice, sir. I have not lived in a walking country, you know."

"True," says Mr. Crisparkle. "Get into a little training, and we will have a few score miles together. I should leave you nowhere now. Do you come back before dinner?"

"I think not, as we dine early."

Mr. Crisparkle gives him a bright nod and a cheerful good-bye: expressing (not without intention), absolute confidence and ease.

Neville repairs to the Nuns' House, and requests that Miss Landless may be informed that her brother is there, by appointment. He waits at the gate, not even crossing the threshold; for he is on his parole not to put himself in Rosa's way.

His sister is at least as mindful of the obligation they have taken on themselves, as he can be, and loses not a moment in joining him. They meet affectionately, avoid lingering there, and walk towards the upper inland country.

"I am not going to tread upon forbidden ground, Helena," says Neville, when they have walked some distance and are turning; "you will understand in another moment that I cannot help referring to——what shall I say——my infatuation."

"Had you not better avoid it, Neville? You know that I can hear nothing."

"You can hear, my dear, what Mr. Crisparkle has heard, and heard with approval."

"Yes; I can hear so much."

"Well, it is this. I am not only unsettled and unhappy myself, but I am conscious of unsettling and interfering with other people. How do I know that, but for my unfortunate presence, you, and——and——the rest of that former party, our engaging guardian excepted, might be dining cheerfully in Minor Canon Corner to-morrow? Indeed it probably would be so. I can see too well that I am not high in the old lady's opinion, and it is easy to understand what an irksome clog I must be upon the hospitalities of her orderly house——especially at this time of year——when I must be kept asunder from this person, and there is such a reason for my not being brought into contact with that person, and an unfavorable reputation has preceded me with such another person, and so on. I have put this very gently to Mr. Crisparkle, for you know his self-denying ways, but still I have put it. What I have laid much greater stress upon at the same time, is, that I am engaged in a miserable struggle with myself, and that a little change and absence may enable me to come through it the better. So, the weather being bright and hard, I am going on a walking expedition, and intend taking myself out of everybody's way (my own included, I hope), to-morrow morning."

"When to come back?"

"In a fortnight."

"And going quite alone?"

"I am much better without company, even if there were any one but you to bear me company, my dear Helena."

"Mr. Crisparkle entirely agrees, you say?"

"Entirely. I am not sure but that at first he was inclined to think it rather a moody scheme, and one that might do a brooding mind harm. But we took a moonlight walk, last Monday night, to talk it over at leisure, and I represented the case to him as it really is. I showed him that I do want to conquer myself, and that, this evening well got over, it is surely better that I should be away from here just now, than here. I could hardly help meeting certain people walking together here, and that could do no good, and is certainly not the way to forget. A fortnight hence, that chance will probably be over, for the time; and when it again arises for the last time, why, I can again go away. Further, I really do feel hopeful of bracing exercise and wholesome fatigue. You know that Mr. Crisparkle allows such things their full weight in the preservation of his own sound mind in his own sound body, and that his just spirit is not likely to maintain one set of natural laws for himself and another for me. He yielded to my view of the matter, when convinced that I was honestly in earnest, and so, with his full consent, I start tomorrow morning. Early enough to be not only out of the streets, but out of hearing of the bells, when the good people go to church."

Helena thinks it over, and thinks well of it. Mr. Crisparkle doing so, she would do so; but she does originally, out of her own mind, think well of it, as a healthy project, denoting a sincere endeavour, and an active attempt at self-correction. She is inclined to pity him, poor fellow, for going away solitary on the great Christmas festival; but she feels it much more to the purpose to encourage him. And she does encourage him.

He will write to her?

He will write to her every alternate day, and tell her all his adventures.

Does he send clothes on, in advance of him?

"My dear Helena, no. Travel like a pilgrim, with wallet and staff. My wallet—or my knapsack—is packed, and ready for strapping on; and here is my staff!"

He hands it to her; she makes the same remark as Mr. Crispar-kle, that it is very heavy; and gives it back to him, asking what wood it is? Iron-wood.

Up to this point, he has been extremely cheerful. Perhaps, the having to carry his case with her, and therefore to present it in its brightest aspect, has roused his spirits. Perhaps, the having done so with success, is followed by a revulsion. As the day closes in, and the city lights begin to spring up before them, he grows depressed.

"I wish I were not going to this dinner, Helena."

"Dear Neville, is it worth while to care much about it? Think how soon it will be over."

"How soon it will be over," he repeats, gloomily. "Yes. But I don't like it."

There may be a moment's awkwardness, she cheeringly represents to him, but it can only last a moment. He is quite sure of himself.

"I wish I felt as sure of everything else, as I feel of myself," he answers her.

"How strangely you speak, dear! What do you mean?"

"Helena, I don't know. I only know that I don't like it. What a strange dead weight there is in the air!"

She calls his attention to those copperous clouds beyond the river, and says that the wind is rising. He scarcely speaks again, until he takes leave of her, at the gate of the Nuns' House. She does not immediately enter, when they have parted, but remains looking after him along the street. Twice, he passes the Gate House, reluctant to enter. At length, the cathedral clock chiming one quarter, with a rapid turn he hurries in.

And so *he* goes up the postern stair.

Edwin Drood passes a solitary day. Something of deeper moment than he had thought, has gone out of his life; and in the silence of his own chamber he wept for it last night. Though the image of Miss Landless still hovers in the background of his mind, the pretty little affectionate creature, so much firmer and wiser than he had supposed, occupies its stronghold. It is with some misgiving of his own unworthiness that he thinks of her, and of what they might have been to one another, if he had been more in earnest some time ago; if he had set a higher value on her; if, instead of accepting his lot in life as an inheritance of course, he had studied the right way to its appreciation and enhancement. And still, for all this, and though there is a sharp heartache in all this, the vanity and caprice of youth sustain that handsome figure of Miss Landless in the background of his mind.

That was a curious look of Rosa's when they parted at the gate. Did it mean that she saw below the surface of his thoughts, and down into their twilight depths? Scarcely that, for it was a look of astonished and keen inquiry. He decides that he cannot understand it, though it was remarkably expressive.

As he only waits for Mr. Grewgious now, and will depart immediately after having seen him, he takes a sauntering leave of the ancient city and its neighbourhood. He recalls the time when Rosa and he walked here or there, mere children, full of the dignity of being engaged. Poor children! he thinks, with a pitying sadness.

Finding that his watch has stopped, he turns into the jeweller's shop, to have it wound and set. The jeweller is knowing on the subject of a bracelet, which he begs leave to submit, in a general and quite aimless way. It would suit (he considers) a young bride, to perfection; especially if of a rather diminutive style of beauty. Finding the bracelet but coldly looked at, the jeweller invites attention to a tray of rings for gentlemen; here is a style of ring, now, he remarks—a very chaste signet—which gentlemen are much given to purchasing, when changing their condition. A ring of a very responsible appearance. With the date of their wedding-day engraved inside, several gentlemen have preferred it to any other kind of memento.

The rings are as coldly viewed as the bracelet. Edwin tells the tempter that he wears no jewellery but his watch and chain, which were his father's; and his shirt-pin.

"That I was aware of," is the jeweller's reply, "for Mr. Jasper dropped in for a watch-glass the other day, and, in fact, I showed these articles to him, remarking that if he *should* wish to make a present to a gentleman relative, on any particular occasion— But he said with a smile that he had an inventory in his mind of all the jewellery his gentleman relative ever wore; namely, his watch and chain, and his shirt-pin." Still (the jeweller considers) that might not apply to all times, though applying to the present time. "Twenty minutes past two, Mr. Drood, I set your watch at. Let me recommend you not to let it run down, sir."

Edwin takes his watch, puts it on, and goes out, thinking: "Dear old Jack! If I were to make an extra crease in my neck-cloth, he would think it worth noticing!"

He strolls about and about, to pass the time until the dinner hour. It somehow happens that Cloisterham seems reproachful to him to-day; has fault to find with him, as if he had not used it well; but is far more pensive with him than angry. His wonted carelessness is replaced by a wistful looking at, and dwelling upon, all the old landmarks. He will soon be far away, and may never see them again, he thinks. Poor youth! Poor youth!

As dusk draws on, he paces the Monks' Vineyard. He has walked to and fro, full half an hour by the cathedral chimes, and it has closed in dark, before he becomes quite aware of a woman crouching on the ground near a wicket gate in a corner. The gate commands a cross bye-path, little used in the gloaming; and the figure must have been there all the time, though he has but gradually and lately made it out.

He strikes into that path, and walks up to the wicket. By the light of a lamp near it, he sees that the woman is of a haggard appearance, and that her weazen chin is resting on her hands, and that her eyes are staring—with an unwinking, blind sort of steadfastness—before her.

Always kindly, but moved to be unusually kind this evening, and having bestowed kind words on most of the children and aged people he has met, he at once bends down, and speaks to this woman.

"Are you ill?"

"No, deary," she answers, without looking at him, and with no departure from her strange blind stare.

"Are you blind?"

"No, deary."

"Are you lost, homeless, faint? What is the matter, that you stay here in the cold so long, without moving?"

By slow and stiff efforts, she appears to contract her vision until it can rest upon him; and then a curious film passes over her, and she begins to shake.

He straitens himself, recoils a step, and looks down at her in a dread amazement; for he seems to know her.

"Good Heaven!" he thinks, next moment. "Like Jack that night!"

As he looks down at her, she looks up at him, and whimpers: "My lungs is weakly; my lungs is dreffle bad. Poor me, poor me, my cough is rattling dry!" And coughs in confirmation, horribly.

"Where do you come from?"

"Come from London, deary." (Her cough still rending her.)

"Where are you going to?"

"Back to London, deary. I came here, looking for a needle in a haystack, and I ain't found it. Look'ee, deary; give me three and sixpence, and don't you be afeard for me. I'll get back to London then, and trouble no-one. I'm in a business. —Ah, me! It's slack, it's slack, and times is very bad!—but I can make a shift to live by it."

"Do you eat opium?"

"Smokes it," she replies with difficulty, still racked by her cough. "Give me three and sixpence, and I'll lay it out well, and get back. If you don't give me three and sixpence, don't give me a brass farden. And if you do give me three and sixpence, deary, I'll tell you something."

He counts the money from his pocket, and puts it in her hand. She instantly clutches it tight, and rises to her feet with a croaking laugh of satisfaction.

"Bless ye! Harkee, dear genl'mn. What's your Chris'en name?"

"Edwin."

"Edwin, Edwin, Edwin," she repeats, trailing off into a drowsy repetition of the word; and then asks suddenly: "Is the short of that name, Eddy?"

"It is sometimes called so," he replies, with the color starting to his face.

"Don't sweethearts call it so?" she asks, pondering

"How should I know!"

"Haven't you a sweetheart, upon your soul?"

"None."

She is moving away, with another "Bless ye, and thank'ee, deary!" when he adds: "You were to tell me something; you may as well do so."

"So I was, so I was. Well, then. Whisper. You be thankful that your name ain't Ned."

He looks at her, quite steadily, as he asks: "Why?"

"Because it's a bad name to have just now."

"How a bad name?"

"A threatened name. A dangerous name."

"The proverb says that threatened men live long," he tells her, lightly.

"Then Ned—so threatened is he, wherever he may be while I am a talking to you, deary—should live to all eternity!" replies the woman.

She has leaned forward, to say it in his ear, with her forefinger shaking before his eyes, and now huddles herself together, and with another "Bless ye, and thank'ee!" goes away in the direction of the Travellers' Lodging House.

This is not an inspiriting close to a dull day. Alone, in a seques-
tered place, surrounded by vestiges of old time and decay, it rather
has a tendency to call a shudder into being. He makes for the better-
lighted streets, and resolves as he walks on to say nothing of this to-
night, but to mention it to Jack (who alone calls him Ned), as an
odd coincidence, to-morrow; of course only as a coincidence, and
not as anything better worth remembering.

Still, it holds to him, as many things much better worth remembering never did. He has another mile or so, to linger out before the
dinner-hour; and, when he walks over the bridge and by the river,
the woman's words are in the rising wind, in the angry sky, in the
troubled water, in the flickering lights. There is some solemn echo
of them, even in the cathedral chime, which strikes a sudden surprise to his heart as he turns in under the archway of the Gate
House.

And so *he* goes up the postern stair.

John Jasper passes a more agreeable and cheerful day than either
of his guests. Having no music-lessons to give in the holiday season,
his time is his own, but for the cathedral services. He is early among
the shopkeepers, ordering little table luxuries that his nephew likes.
His nephew will not be with him long, he tells his provision-dealers,
and so must be petted and made much of. While out on his hospi-
table preparations, he looks in on Mr. Sapsea; and mentions that
dear Ned, and that inflammable young spark of Mr. Crisparkle's, are
to dine at the Gate House to-day, and make up their difference. Mr.

Sapsea is by no means friendly towards the inflammable young spark. He says that his complexion is "Un-English." And when Mr. Sapsea has once declared anything to be Un-English, he considers that thing everlastingly sunk in the bottomless pit.

John Jasper is truly sorry to hear Mr. Sapsea speak thus, for he knows right well that Mr. Sapsea never speaks without a meaning, and that he has a subtle trick of being right. Mr. Sapsea (by a very remarkable coincidence) is of exactly that opinion.

Mr. Jasper is in beautiful voice this day. In the pathetic supplication to have his heart inclined to keep this law, he quite astonishes his fellows by his melodious power. He has never sung difficult music with such skill and harmony, as in this day's Anthem. His nervous temperament is occasionally prone to take difficult music a little too quickly; to-day, his time is perfect.

These results are probably attained through a grand composure of the spirits. The mere mechanism of his throat is a little tender, for he wears, both with his singing-robe and with his ordinary dress, a large black scarf of strong close-woven silk, slung loosely round his neck. But his composure is so noticeable, that Mr. Crisparkle speaks of it as they come out from Vespers.

"I must thank you, Jasper, for the pleasure with which I have heard you to-day. Beautiful! Delightful! You could not have so out-done yourself, I hope, without being wonderfully well."

"I *am* wonderfully well."

"Nothing unequal," says the Minor Canon, with a smooth motion of his hand: "nothing unsteady, nothing forced, nothing avoided;

all thoroughly done in a masterly manner, with perfect self-command."

"Thank you. I hope so, if it is not too much to say."

"One would think, Jasper, you had been trying a new medicine for that occasional indisposition of yours."

"No, really? That's well observed; for I have."

"Then stick to it, my good fellow," says Mr. Crisparkle, clapping him on the shoulder with friendly encouragement, "stick to it."

"I will."

"I congratulate you," Mr. Crisparkle pursues, as they come out of the cathedral, "on all accounts."

"Thank you again. I will walk round to the Corner with you, if you don't object; I have plenty of time before my company come; and I want to say a word to you, which I think you will not be displeased to hear."

"What is it?"

"Well. We were speaking, the other evening, of my black humours."

Mr. Crisparkle's face falls, and he shakes his head deploringly.

"I said, you know, that I should make you an antidote to those black humours; and you said you hoped I would consign them to the flames."

"And I still hope so, Jasper."

"With the best reason in the world! I mean to burn this year's Diary at the year's end."

"Because you———?" Mr. Crisparkle brightens greatly as he thus begins.

"You anticipate me. Because I feel that I have been out of sorts, gloomy, bilious, brain-oppressed, whatever it may be. You said I had been exaggerative. So I have."

Mr. Crisparkle's brightened face brightens still more.

"I couldn't see it then, because I *was* out of sorts; but I am in a healthier state now, and I acknowledge it with genuine pleasure I made a great deal of a very little; that's the fact."

"It does me good," cries Mr. Crisparkle, "to hear you say it!"

"A man leading a monotonous life," Jasper proceeds, "and getting his nerves, or his stomach, out of order, dwells upon an idea until it loses its proportions. That was my case with the idea in question. So I shall burn the evidence of my case, when the book is full, and begin the next volume with a clearer vision."

"This is better," says Mr. Crisparkle, stopping at the steps of his own door to shake hands, "than I could have hoped!"

"Why, naturally," returns Jasper. "You had but little reason to hope that I should become more like yourself. You are always training yourself to be, mind and body, as clear as crystal, and you always are, and never change; whereas, I am a muddy, solitary, moping weed. However, I have got over that mope. Shall I wait, while you ask if Mr. Neville has left for my place? If not, he and I may walk round together."

"I think," says Mr. Crisparkle, opening the entrance door with his key, "that he left some time ago; at least I know he left, and I think he has not come back. But I'll enquire. You won't come in?"

"My company wait," says Jasper, with a smile.

The Minor Canon disappears, and in a few moments returns. As he thought, Mr. Neville has not come back; indeed, as he remembers now, Mr. Neville said he would probably go straight to the Gate House.

"Bad manners in a host!" says Jasper. "My company will be there before me! What will you bet that I don't find my company embracing?"

"I will bet—or I would, if I ever did bet," returns Mr. Crisparkle, "that your company will have a gay entertainer this evening."

Jasper nods, and laughs Good Night!

He retraces his steps to the cathedral door, and turns down past it to the Gate House. He sings, in a low voice and with delicate expression, as he walks along. It still seems as if a false note were not within his power to-night, and as if nothing could hurry or retard him. Arriving thus, under the arched entrance of his dwelling, he pauses for an instant in the shelter to pull off that great black scarf, and hang it in a loop upon his arm. For that brief time, his face is knitted and stern. But it immediately clears, as he resumes his singing, and his way.

And so *he* goes up the postern stair.

———

The red light burns steadily all the evening in the lighthouse on the margin of the tide of busy life. Softened sounds and hum of traffic pass it and flow on irregularly into the lonely Precincts; but very little else goes by, save violent rushes of wind. It comes on to blow a boisterous gale.

The Precincts are never particularly well lighted; but the strong blasts of wind blowing out many of the lamps (in some instances shattering the frames too, and bringing the glass rattling to the ground), they are unusually dark to-night. The darkness is augmented and confused, by flying dust from the earth, dry twigs from the trees, and great ragged fragments from the rooks' nests up in the tower. The trees themselves so toss and creak, as this tangible part of the darkness madly whirls about, that they seem in peril of being torn out of the earth: while ever and again a crack, and a rushing fall, denote that some large branch has yielded to the storm.

No such power of wind has blown for many a winter-night. Chimneys topple in the streets, and people hold to posts and corners, and to one another, to keep themselves upon their feet. The violent rushes abate not, but increase in frequency and fury until at midnight, when the streets are empty, the storm goes thundering along them, rattling at all the latches, and tearing at all the shutters, as if warning the people to get up and fly with it, rather than have the roofs brought down upon their brains.

Still, the red light burns steadily. Nothing is steady but the red light.

All through the night, the wind blows, and abates not. But early in the morning when there is barely enough light in the east to dim the stars, it begins to lull. From that time, with occasional wild charges, like a wounded monster dying, it drops and sinks; and at full daylight it is dead.

It is then seen that the hands of the cathedral clock are torn off; that lead from the roof has been stripped away, rolled up, and blown into the Close; and that some stones have been displaced upon the summit of the great tower. Christmas morning though it be, it is necessary to send up workmen, to ascertain the extent of the damage done. These, led by Durdles, go aloft; while Mr. Tope and a crowd of early idlers gather down in Minor Canon Corner, shading their eyes and watching for their appearance up there.

This cluster is suddenly broken and put aside by the hands of Mr. Jasper; all the gazing eyes are brought down to the earth by his loudly enquiring of Mr. Crisparkle, at an open window:

"Where is my nephew?"

"He has not been here. Is he not with you?"

"No. He went down to the river last night, with Mr. Neville, to look at the storm, and has not been back. Call Mr. Neville!"

"He left this morning, early."

"Left this morning, early? Let me in, let me in!"

There is no more looking up at the tower, now. All the assembled eyes are turned on Mr. Jasper, white, half-dressed, panting, and clinging to the rail before the Minor Canon's house.

II.

The thin melancholy man in black, who aroused our curiosity yesterday, today sits at the speakers' table, together with Superintendent Battle and short, stolid Inspector Bucket, both from Scotland Yard.[1] Who can it be? Either through absent-mindedness or because of his love of black (in strange contrast with his love of roses), he has pinned his plastic name-badge *underneath* his lapel, so we are unable to identify him for the reader.

But almost everyone is looking, instead, at the non-regulation beige-tweed dress Loredana is wearing. The cameo-brooch and the arrangement of her hair in a bun behind her neck heighten the generally British—even Oxfordian—effect of the ensemble.

---

[1] The reader will remember that Bucket appears in *Bleak House* (1853), and is the first detective in English fiction. Dickens modelled him partly on his friend Inspector Charles F. Field, with whom he visited the opium den we have already referred to. A typical trait of Bucket is the way he points at suspects with his forefinger, then places it at his ear as if to listen to their reply.

Dr Wilmot's aplomb, meanwhile, is nonchalantly ac-centuated by a yellow cashmere scarf, and his bow-tie is a little less askew than usual.

He starts off the proceedings: "Halfway through the fourth number, the suspense begins, the suspense that the author had promised to maintain until the end, when the reader would learn not only by whom but, first of all, *whether* Rosa's ex-fiancé had been murdered."

MAN IN BLACK: Excuse me, but wasn't the suspense supposed to begin from the fifth or sixth number?

WILMOT: No. In all probability, Dickens intended the real suspense to begin with the arrival of a new and mys-terious character, a certain Datchery, who doesn't appear until the August number. However, at this point, accord-ing to most critics, the author's problem was not to speed things up but, rather, to slow them down. This is what he meant when he said that he was having trouble with the plot: miscalculating the distribution of events, he had over-loaded the first six instalments, and now was finding it difficult to fill the remaining six.

MAN IN BLACK: Excuse me again, but this strikes me as absurd. For a writer like Dickens, who was naturally prolix and, if I might say so, supremely digressive, the problem could hardly be how to fill six more instalments. Which means, in my opinion, that . . . But what do you think, Superintendent?

317

BATTLE: I don't know who this mysterious Datchery is, but I agree that the story must be far more complicated than it might appear from the first part.

MAN IN BLACK: Inspector Bucket?

BUCKET: I think so too. There's the whole opium business; there's the double, maybe triple personality of the presumed murderer; there's a highly elaborate murder-method . . . But these are all things that have been explained if not over-explained, and we already know that the motive is jealousy. What's the problem, then? If the murderer is Jasper, all you need is a reasonably bright policeman, and Jasper will confess in a twinkling: You got me dead to rights, officer, yes, I admit it all, your honour. And then—the rope.

MAN IN BLACK: Exactly. Which means that if the author says he's having trouble with the plot as soon as the sixth number, we can deduce that Jasper isn't the culprit.

TOAD: Hear hear!

MAN IN BLACK: Unless—and I wouldn't exclude this possibility—unless Jasper is in some way *working with the twins*.

WILMOT, *interrupting the audience's comments and exclamations:* This hypothesis has never before been put forward. But as it comes from Richard Cuff, we must of course take it seriously. Thank you, Sergeant Cuff.

LOREDANA, *with most un-Oxbridgean excitement:* Sergeant Cuff! So it's you, then!

Loredana is an expert on *The Moonstone,* having seen it twice on television, but even those less familiar with it know that the novel's intriguing mystery is solved by the sergeant from Scotland Yard. It should be pointed out, here, that in *Old* Scotland Yard (before its transformation into *Great* Scotland Yard and its subsequent move under the name of *New* Scotland Yard to the Thames embankment and then later to Victoria Street), a sergeant of the Detective Force was a high-ranking investigator. Wilmot has not chosen today's panel haphazardly: for the fourth number (or the "mystery number," as the author himself called it), it can truly be said that Scotland Yard has descended in force on Cloisterham, to carry out a highly professional on-the-spot investigation. Let us therefore follow the three officers as they make their watchful, invisible way around the ancient town.

It is the afternoon of December 23. In Mrs. Twinkleton's college, all the girls have left with the exception of Helena and Rosa. The latter, dressed to go out, is now alone in her "bower," waiting for Drood. And here is Drood, who has just arrived from London and come to pick her up. Off they go for their customary walk towards the Cathedral. The scene of clarification between the two is more or less expected and tells the investigators nothing they did not already know.

After Edwin's reference to his uncle's worrisome "paroxysms," Rosa discovers that the uncle in question is spying on them from under the trees. The chapter concludes with their farewell at the gate. While Jasper continues to spy on them, Drood obtusely refuses to see anything more than affectionate concern in this. When Drood leaves her, Rosa follows him with a wondering look, which seems to say, "O! don't you understand?"

"Too stupid to last long," is Bucket's cynical remark. In the course of the twenty instalments (two of which are double issues) of *Bleak House,* the man became hardened to the daily horrors of the struggle for existence in the slums of London.

Battle agrees. "Yes, he's a classic case of the character who's too good for his own good. He always turns up in suspense novels and films, and the readers just can't wait for him to get the chop. Still, we have no proof that he's wrong about Jasper's following them. Jasper's reasons for keeping Drood under such close watch may have nothing to do with jealousy."

Cuff nods but continues to gaze up at the windows of the college, beyond the locked gate. "I wonder," he says, "why Rosa was alone while she waited for Drood. Where was Helena? All the other girls had gone; they were the only two left. Wouldn't it have been natural for two friends like that to stick together, chatting and exchanging confidences? Instead . . . Which makes me think . . . I don't know, but I have a feeling we won't see them together again, from now on."

"Christmas Eve in Cloisterham. A few strange faces in the streets; a few other faces . . ." Et cetera.

The hasty reader will find nothing other than a lively passage of local colour in this opening of Chapter Fourteen. But Bucket, who knows Dickens's methods as well as anybody, realises at once that the reference to new faces is not a casual one. And indeed, looking around himself, he quickly spots an old acquaintance of his (and ours).

"Lascar Sal's here," he murmurs, pointing her out to his colleagues. "I'll follow her. We'll meet up again later."

The other two detectives also split up, one to keep an eye on Neville and the other on Drood. (As for Jasper, whom they've already seen pass by in his new black silk scarf, they know he'll be occupied in the Cathedral for the rest of the afternoon.)

But on his way to Minor Canon Corner, Cuff passes in front of the town's theatre, and he stops for a moment to study the big coloured posters announcing a comic pantomime with Signor Jacksonini: HOW DO YOU DO TO-MOR-

ROW? Yet another allusion—and a macabre one, hidden as it is in a clown's wisecrack. Yorick's skull is not too distant. Nor is Banquo's ghost, if we can judge by the title of the chapter.

But then, in contrast with this subtlety, the scene in the canon's house is so blatantly and clumsily suggestive as to act in Neville's favour rather than against him. The vindictive (though converted) young man going off to meet his ex-rival and mortal offender, armed with a heavy stick! And Crisparkle, out of delicacy (has he gone soft in the head?), says nothing? And Neville, who has been busy this afternoon destroying "his stray papers" (what papers? what have they got to do with all this?), tells him that he needs a change of air so he'll be off very early the next day! Is any reader, even the most ingenuous one, likely to be fooled by "clues" such as these?

Whistling "The Last Rose of Summer,"[1] Sergeant Cuff notes down, without batting an eyelid: "Heavy iron-shod walking-stick. Destruction of papers except for studies. Wish to make self untraceable next few days, perhaps to avoid immediate questioning, and see how dust settles."

But let the reader not smile. He would do better to follow Cuff, who in turn is following the twins on their

---

[1] In Collins's novel, the sergeant, in addition to his love of roses, is in the habit of whistling "The Last Rose of Summer" in moments of great concentration.

322

pre-evening walk; and listen again to their conversation. At first blush, it seemed "normal" to us, too: no underlying currents, nothing to draw the attention of the clue-seeker. But when we watch and hear again in playback, there is in fact something very peculiar about the whole scene.

If Neville is really leaving the next day in order to keep away from Rosa, why should he hesitate to say this to his sister? Since she deplores this infatuation of his, she should be entirely in favour of that course of action. Why, then, does she have to think so hard about it? Neville appears relieved, even euphoric, when his enigmatic twin finally announces that if Crisparkle agrees to the plan, she does, too. After this, however, it takes only a comment on her part about the weight of the stick to cause a "revulsion" in him, which makes him taciturn and depressed for the remainder of the walk. "I wish I were not going to this dinner, Helena," he says at last, when they are almost back at the gate of the Nuns' House.

Now, as we know, the whole point of the dinner is to make peace with Drood. This is what everyone has been waiting for, the last two weeks. It was this that occasioned Helena's big scene in front of Crisparkle, just the other day, with her exhortations to virtue and invocations of Heaven. So if there was one subject that the twins should touch on during their walk, it is this. But they don't mention it until the end, and then for no more than half a minute, and in such terms that make one wonder what it is they are really talking about. Let's hear it through again:

NEVILLE, *depressed:* I wish I were not going to this dinner, Helena.

HELENA, *airily:* Dear Neville, is it worth while to care much about it? Think how soon it will be over.

NEVILLE, *gloomily:* How soon it will be over. Yes. But I don't like it.

HELENA, *encouraging him:* There may be a moment's awkwardness, but it can only last a moment. You are quite sure of yourself.

NEVILLE, *portentously:* I wish I felt as sure of everything else, as I feel of myself.

HELENA, *raising an eyebrow:* How strangely you speak, dear! What do you mean?

NEVILLE, *frowning:* Helena, I don't know. I only know that I don't like it. What a strange dead weight there is in the air!

There is not a single word in this dialogue, Cuff notes, that can be applied to the reconciliation with Drood without some forcing, some twisting. But there is not a single word that does not apply easily to Drood's *murder,* if that is what these "Anglo-Cingalese" twins (or whatever they are) have come from Ceylon to commit. As an expert in criminal cases with a background of Oriental intrigue, Cuff knows that this is possible.[1] But he also knows that in that case the murder would have to be a ritual one, which means either strangulation or suffocation, without the shedding of blood. The scene between the twins would therefore have to be interpreted as follows:

Neville will strangle the victim with his bare hands, or with a cord, in the manner of the thugs; they agreed on this some time ago. But at the last moment he fears he might not be up to it, and that is why he is taking the stick with him. His sister strongly disapproves, for ritual reasons. It is clear that she is the governing mind here, and that it was not part of her plan (which may or may not include getting rid of the body in the calcium oxide) that Neville should leave Cloisterham immediately after the crime. But he feels he can't cope, so she has no choice but to accept his decision. The fact that Crisparkle approves of his tour—indeed, even encourages it—will make it seem less suspicious. But the real problem is that Neville seems to have lost the unquestioning fanatical faith that still inspires Helena. It is not only Drood's murder that he does not like, but "everything else": who knows what further chain of vendettas or terrorist actions he has allowed him-

---

[1] The three Brahmins who kill Ablewhite in *The Moonstone* come directly from Seringapatam.

self to be dragged into? That is why his sister accuses him of "speaking strangely"; and that is what lies behind the long doubtful stare she directs at him when he leaves her.

"Poor me, poor me!"

The woman from the Shadwell opium-den, known to the police under the nick-name of Lascar Sal or Sally the Opium Eater, was no different in life from the woman presented to us in the novel. When Dickens met her—trembling, emaciated, hoarse, and racked by a perpetual cough—her appearance was that of a woman of some sixty or seventy years. The poor creature was in fact twenty-six.[1]

"My lungs is weakly; my lungs is dreffle bad," she whimpers amidst her hacking cough.

But it is not self-pity, or an attempt to win Drood's sympathy (or the sympathy of the two invisible policemen in the background). It is, rather, a resigned self-assessment, a wretched but scrupulous account of herself that she keeps in her more lucid moments, in order to establish what stage she has reached in her downward path.

At the moment, for example, she needs three and sixpence for the drug, and if she can get it from this young

---

[1] Several careless commentators, and even some translators, speak of the "old woman of the opium den," since she is given no name. But Dickens never gives her age, and never uses the word "old" to describe her.

man, so much the better. If not, so much the worse. In any case, she makes her own way; she is not one to go round bothering people, asking them for help. In London, as she makes quite clear, she has her own "business," which supports her, although times are bad and business is slack.

"It's slack, it's slack!"

Even Bucket has to pay tribute to this last vestige of dignity, of obstinate independence, as he watches her depart with her three and sixpence in the direction of that den of sinners, the Travellers' Twopenny.

Meanwhile, Battle stays and watches Drood walk off (since it seems that no-one can walk off, in Chapters Thirteen and Fourteen, without someone watching them).

"Poor youth! Poor youth!" he repeats with the author. "He's really quite a nice chap, you know. A pity I can't stay around here to save him."

"A pity we can't stay and see who does him in," says Bucket cynically, addressing Cuff as well, since Cuff has arrived at that moment.

It's time, in fact, for the three policemen to return to the Dickens Room, where everybody is awaiting the results of their investigation. In the meantime, the keener conference members, such as Toad, have already begun to discuss Chapters Fifteen and Sixteen. Which means, reader, we had better sit down and read them attentively ourselves.

CHAPTER XV

IMPEACHED

NEVILLE LANDLESS had started so early and walked at so good a pace, that when the church bells began to ring in Cloisterham for morning service, he was eight miles away. As he wanted his breakfast by that time, having set forth on a crust of bread, he stopped at the next roadside tavern to refresh.

Visitors in want of breakfast—unless they were horses or cattle, for which class of guests there was preparation enough in the way of water-trough and hay—were so unusual at the sign of The Tilted Wagon, that it took a long time to get the wagon into the track of tea and toast and bacon. Neville, in the interval, sitting in a sanded parlor, wondering in how long a time after he had gone, the sneezy fire of damp fagots would begin to make somebody else warm.

Indeed, The Tilted Wagon, as a cool establishment on the top of a hill, where the ground before the door was puddled with damp hoofs and trodden straw; where a scolding landlady slapped a moist baby (with one red sock on and one wanting), in the bar; where the cheese was cast aground upon a shelf, in company with a mouldy tablecloth and a green-handled knife, in a sort of cast-iron canoe; where the pale-faced bread shed tears of crumb over its shipwreck in another canoe; where the family linen, half washed and half dried, led a public life of lying about; where everything to drink was drunk out of mugs, and everything else was suggestive of a rhyme to mugs; The Tilted Wagon, all these things considered, hardly kept its painted promise of providing good entertainment for Man and Beast. However, Man, in the present case, was not critical, but took what entertainment he could get, and went on again after a longer rest than he needed.

He stopped at some quarter of a mile from the house, hesitating whether to pursue the road, or to follow a cart-track between two high hedgerows, which led across the slope of a breezy heath, and evidently struck into the road again by-and-bye. He decided in favor of this latter track, and pursued it with some toil; the rise being steep, and the way worn into deep ruts.

He was labouring along, when he became aware of some other pedestrians behind him. As they were coming up at a faster pace than his, he stood aside, against one of the high banks, to let them pass. But their manner was very curious. Only four of them passed. Other four slackened speed, and loitered as intending to follow him when he should go on. The remainder of the party (half a dozen perhaps), turned, and went back at a great rate.

He looked at the four behind him, and he looked at the four before him. They all returned his look. He resumed his way. The four in advance went on, constantly looking back; the four in the rear came closing up.

When they all ranged out from the narrow track upon the open slope of the heath, and this order was maintained, let him diverge as he would to either side, there was no longer room to doubt that he was beset by these fellows. He stopped, as a last test; and they all stopped.

"Why do you attend upon me in this way?" he asked the whole body. "Are you a pack of thieves?"

"Don't answer him," said one of the number; he did not see which. "Better be quiet."

"Better be quiet?" repeated Neville. "Who said so?"

Nobody replied.

"It's good advice, which ever of you skulkers gave it," he went on angrily. "I will not submit to be penned in between four men there, and four men there. I wish to pass, and I mean to pass, those four in front."

They were all standing still: himself included.

"If eight men, or four men, or two men, set upon one," he proceeded, growing more enraged, "the one has no chance but to set his mark upon some of them. And by the Lord I'll do it, if I am interrupted any further!"

Shouldering his heavy stick, and quickening his pace, he shot on to pass the four ahead. The largest and strongest man of the number changed swiftly to the side on which he came up, and dexterously closed with him and went down with him; but not before the heavy stick had descended smartly.

"Let him be!" said this man in a suppressed voice, as they struggled together on the grass. "Fair play! His is the build of a girl to

330

mine, and he's got a weight strapped to his back besides. Let him alone. I'll manage him."

After a little rolling about, in a close scuffle which caused the faces of both to be besmeared with blood, the man took his knee from Neville's chest, and rose, saying: "There! Now take him arm-in-arm, any two of you!"

It was immediately done.

"As to our being a pack of thieves, Mr. Landless," said the man, as he spat out some blood, and wiped more from his face: "you know better than that, at midday. We wouldn't have touched you, if you hadn't forced us. We're going to take you round to the high road, anyhow, and you'll find help enough against thieves there, if you want it. Wipe his face somebody; see how it's a-trickling down him!"

When his face was cleansed, Neville recognized in the speaker, Joe, driver of the Cloisterham omnibus, whom he had seen but once, and that on the day of his arrival.

"And what I recommend you for the present, is, don't talk, Mr. Landless. You'll find a friend waiting for you, at the high road— gone ahead by the other way when we split into two parties—and you had much better say nothing till you come up with him. Bring that stick along, somebody else, and let's be moving!"

Utterly bewildered, Neville stared around him and said not a word. Walking between his two conductors, who held his arms in theirs, he went on, as in a dream, until they came again into the high road, and into the midst of a little group of people. The men who had turned back, were among the group; and its central figures were Mr. Jasper and Mr. Crisparkle. Neville's conductors took him up to the Minor Canon, and there released him, as an act of deference to that gentleman.

"What is all this, sir? What is the matter? I feel as if I had lost my senses!" cried Neville, the group closing in around him.

"Where is my nephew?" asked Mr. Jasper, wildly.

"Where is your nephew?" repeated Neville. "Why do you ask me?"

"I ask you," retorted Jasper, "because you were the last person in his company, and he is not to be found."

"Not to be found!" cried Neville, aghast.

"Stay, stay," said Mr. Crisparkle. "Permit me, Jasper. Mr. Neville, you are confounded; collect your thoughts; it is of great importance that you should collect your thoughts; attend to me."

"I will try, sir, but I seem mad."

"You left Mr. Jasper's last night, with Edwin Drood?"

"Yes."

"At what hour?"

"Was it at twelve o'clock?" asked Neville, with his hand to his confused head, and appealing to Jasper.

"Quite right," said Mr. Crisparkle; "the hour Mr. Jasper has already named to me. You went down to the river together?"

"Undoubtedly. To see the action of the wind there."

"What followed? How long did you stay there?"

"About ten minutes; I should say not more. We then walked together to your house, and he took leave of me at the door."

"Did he say that he was going down to the river again?"

"No. He said that he was going straight back."

The bystanders looked at one another, and at Mr. Crisparkle. To whom, Mr. Jasper, who had been intensely watching Neville, said, in a low distinct suspicious voice: "What are those stains upon his dress?"

All eyes were turned towards the blood upon his clothes.

"And here are the same stains upon this stick!" said Jasper, taking it from the hand of the man who held it. "I know the stick to be his, and he carried it last night. What does this mean?"

"In the name of God, say what it means, Neville!" urged Mr. Crisparkle.

"That man and I," said Neville, pointing out his late adversary, "had a struggle for the stick just now, and you may see the same marks on him, sir. What was I to suppose, when I found myself molested by eight people? Could I dream of the true reason when they would give me none at all?"

They admitted that they had thought it discreet to be silent, and that the struggle had taken place. And yet the very men who had seen it, looked darkly at the smears which the bright cold air had already dried.

"We must return, Neville," said Mr. Crisparkle; "of course you will be glad to come back to clear yourself?"

"Of course, sir."

"Mr. Landless will walk at my side," the Minor Canon continued, looking around him. "Come, Neville!"

They set forth on the walk back; and the others, with one exception, straggled after them at various distances. Jasper walked on
the other side of Neville, and never quitted that position. He was
silent, while Mr. Crisparkle more than once repeated his former
questions, and while Neville repeated his former answers; also, while
they both hazarded some explanatory conjectures. He was obsti-
nately silent, because Mr. Crisparkle's manner directly appealed to
him to take some part in the discussion, and no appeal would move
his fixed face. When they drew near to the city, and it was suggested
by the Minor Canon that they might do well in calling on the Mayor
at once, he assented with a stern nod; but he spake no word until
they stood in Mr. Sapsea's parlor.

Mr. Sapsea being informed by Mr. Crisparkle of the circumstances under which they desired to make a voluntary statement
before him, Mr. Jasper broke silence by declaring that he placed his
whole reliance, humanly speaking, on Mr. Sapsea's penetration. There
was no conceivable reason why his nephew should have suddenly
absconded, unless Mr. Sapsea could suggest one, and then he would
defer. There was no intelligible likelihood of his having returned to
the river, and been accidentally drowned in the dark, unless it should
appear likely to Mr. Sapsea, and then again he would defer. He
washed his hands as clean as he could, of all horrible suspicions,

unless it should appear to Mr. Sapsea that some such were inseparable from his last companion before his disappearance (not on good
terms with previously), and then, once more, he would defer. His
own state of mind, he being distracted with doubts, and labouring
under dismal apprehensions, was not to be safely trusted; but Mr.
Sapsea's was.

Mr. Sapsea expressed his opinion that the case had a dark look;
in short (and here his eyes rested full on Neville's countenance), an
Un-English complexion. Having made this grand point, he wandered into a denser haze and maze of nonsense than even a mayor
might have been expected to disport himself in, and came out of it
with the brilliant discovery that to take the life of a fellow-creature
was to take something that didn't belong to you. He wavered whether
or no he should at once issue his warrant for the committal of
Neville Landless to jail, under circumstances of grave suspicion; and
he might have gone so far as to do it but for the indignant protest
of the Minor Canon: who undertook for the young man's remaining
in his own house, and being produced by his own hands, whenever
demanded. Mr. Jasper then understood Mr. Sapsea to suggest that
the river should be dragged, that its banks should be rigidly examined, that particulars of the disappearance should be sent to all outlying places and to London, and that placards and advertisements
should be widely circulated imploring Edwin Drood, if for any unknown reason he had withdrawn himself from his uncle's home and
society, to take pity on that loving kinsman's sore bereavement and

distress, and somehow inform him that he was yet alive. Mr. Sapsea was perfectly understood, for this was exactly his meaning (though he had said nothing about it); and measures were taken towards all these ends immediately.

It would be difficult to determine which was the more oppressed with horror and amazement: Neville Landless, or John Jasper. But that Jasper's position forced him to be active, while Neville's forced him to be passive, there would have been nothing to choose between them. Each was bowed down and broken.

With the earliest light of the next morning, men were at work upon the river, and other men — most of whom volunteered for the service — were examining the banks. All the livelong day, the search went on; upon the river, with barge and pole, and drag and net; upon the muddy and rushy shore, with jack-boot, hatchet, spade, rope, dogs, and all imaginable appliances. Even at night, the river was specked with lanterns, and lurid with fires; far-off creeks, into which the tide washed as it changed, had their knots of watchers, listening to the lapping of the stream, and looking out for any burden it might bear; remote shingly causeways near the sea, and lonely points off which there was a race of water, had their unwonted flaring cressets and rough-coated figures when the next day dawned; but no trace of Edwin Drood revisited the light of the sun.

All that day, again, the search went on. Now, in barge and boat; and now ashore among the osiers, or tramping amidst mud and stakes and jagged stones in low-lying places, where solitary watermarks and signals of strange shapes showed like spectres, John Jasper worked and toiled. But to no purpose; for still no trace of Edwin Drood revisited the light of the sun.

Setting his watches for that night again, so that vigilant eyes should be kept on every change of tide, he went home exhausted. Unkempt and disordered, bedaubed with mud that had dried upon him, and with much of his clothing torn to rags, he had but just dropped into his easy chair, when Mr. Grewgious stood before him.

"This is strange news," said Mr. Grewgious.

"Strange and fearful news."

Jasper had merely lifted up his heavy eyes to say it, and now dropped them again as he drooped, worn out, over one side of his easy chair.

Mr. Grewgious smoothed his head and face, and stood looking at the fire.

"How is your ward?" asked Jasper, after a time, in a faint, fatigued voice.

"Poor little thing! You may imagine her condition."

"Have you seen his sister?" enquired Jasper, as before.

"Whose?"

The curtness of the counter-question, and the cool slow manner in which, as he put it, Mr. Grewgious moved his eyes from the fire to his companion's face, might at any other time have been exasperating. In his depression and exhaustion, Jasper merely opened his eyes to say: "The suspected young man's."

"Do you suspect him?" asked Mr. Grewgious.

"I don't know what to think. I cannot make up my mind."

"Nor I," said Mr. Grewgious. "But as you spoke of him as the suspected young man, I thought you *had* made up your mind. —I have just left Miss Landless."

"What is her state?"

"Defiance of all suspicion, and unbounded faith in her brother."

"Poor thing!"

"However," pursued Mr. Grewgious, "it is not of her that I came to speak. It is of my ward. I have a communication to make that will surprise you. At least, it has surprised me."

Jasper, with a groaning sigh, turned wearily in his chair.

"Shall I put it off till to-morrow?" said Mr. Grewgious. "Mind! I warn you, that I think it will surprise you!"

More attention and concentration came into John Jasper's eyes as they caught sight of Mr. Grewgious smoothing his head again, and again looking at the fire; but now, with a compressed and determined mouth.

"What is it?" demanded Jasper, becoming upright in his chair.

"To be sure," said Mr. Grewgious, provokingly slowly and internally, as he kept his eyes on the fire: "I might have known it sooner; she gave me the opening; but I am such an exceedingly Angular man, that it never occurred to me; I took all for granted."

"What is it?" demanded Jasper, once more.

Mr. Grewgious, alternately opening and shutting the palms of his hands as he warmed them at the fire, and looking fixedly at him sideways, and never changing either his action or his look in all that followed, went on to reply.

"This young couple, the lost youth and Miss Rosa, my ward, though so long betrothed, and so long recognizing their betrothal, and so near being married———"

Mr. Grewgious saw a staring white face, and two quivering white lips, in the easy chair, and saw two muddy hands gripping its sides. But for the hands, he might have thought he had never seen the face.

"———This young couple came gradually to the discovery, (made on both sides pretty equally, I think), that they would be happier and better, both in their present and their future lives, as affectionate friends, or say rather as brother and sister, than as husband and wife."

Mr. Grewgious saw a lead-coloured face in the easy chair, and on its surface dreadful starting drops or bubbles, as if of steel.

"This young couple formed at length the healthy resolution of interchanging their discoveries, openly, sensibly, and tenderly. They met for that purpose. After some innocent and generous talk, they agreed to dissolve their existing, and their intended, relations, for ever and ever."

Mr. Grewgious saw a ghastly figure rise, open-mouthed, from the easy chair, and lift its outspread hands towards its head.

"One of this young couple, and that one your nephew, fearful, however, that in the tenderness of your affection for him you would be bitterly disappointed by so wide a departure from his projected life, forbore to tell you the secret, for a few days, and left it to be disclosed by me, when I should come down to speak to you, and he would be gone. I speak to you, and he is gone."

Mr. Grewgious saw the ghastly figure throw back its head, clutch its hair with its hands, and turn with a writhing action from him.

"I have now said all I have to say: except that this young couple parted, firmly, though not without tears and sorrow, on the evening when you last saw them together."

Mr. Grewgious heard a terrible shriek, and saw no ghastly figure, sitting or standing; saw nothing but a heap of torn and miry clothes upon the floor.

Not changing his action even then, he opened and shut the palms of his hands as he warmed them, and looked down at it.

CHAPTER XVI

DEVOTED

WHEN John Jasper recovered from his fit or swoon, he found himself being tended by Mr. and Mrs. Tope, whom his visitor had summoned for the purpose. His visitor, wooden of aspect, sat stiffly in a chair, with his hands upon his knees, watching his recovery.

"There! You've come to, nicely now, sir," said the tearful Mrs. Tope; "you were thoroughly worn out, and no wonder!"

"A man," said Mr. Grewgious, with his usual air of repeating a lesson, "cannot have his rest broken, and his mind cruelly tormented, and his body overtaxed by fatigue, without being thoroughly worn out."

"I fear I have alarmed you?" Jasper apologized faintly, when he was helped into his easy chair.

"Not at all, I thank you," answered Mr. Grewgious.

"You are too considerate."

"Not at all, I thank you," answered Mr. Grewgious again.

"You must take some wine, sir," said Mrs. Tope, "and the jelly that I had ready for you, and that you wouldn't put your lips to at noon, though I warned you what would come of it, you know, and you not breakfasted; and you must have a wing of the roast fowl that has been put back twenty times if it's been put back once. It

341

shall all be on table in five minutes, and this good gentleman belike will stop and see you take it."

This good gentleman replied with a snort, which might mean yes, or no, or anything, or nothing, and which Mrs. Tope would have found highly mystifying, but that her attention was divided by the service of the table.

"You will take something with me?" said Jasper, as the cloth was laid.

"I couldn't get a morsel down my throat, I thank you," answered Mr. Grewgious.

Jasper both ate and drank almost voraciously. Combined with the hurry in his mode of doing it, was an evident indifference to the taste of what he took, suggesting that he ate and drank to fortify himself against any other failure of the spirits, far more than to gratify his palate. Mr. Grewgious in the meantime sat upright, with no expression in his face, and a hard kind of imperturbably polite protest all over him: as though he would have said, in reply to some invitation to discourse: "I couldn't originate the faintest approach to an observation on any subject whatever, I thank you."

"Do you know," said Jasper, when he had pushed away his plate and glass, and had sat meditating for a few minutes: "do you know that I find some crumbs of comfort in the communication with which you have so much amazed me?"

"*Do* you?" returned Mr. Grewgious; pretty plainly adding the unspoken clause: "I don't, I thank you!"

"After recovering from the shock of a piece of news of my dear boy, so entirely unexpected, and so destructive of all the castles I had built for him; and after having had time to think of it; yes."

"I shall be glad to pick up your crumbs," said Mr. Grewgious, dryly.

"Is there not, or is there—if I deceive myself, tell me so, and shorten my pain—is there not, or is there, hope that, finding himself in this new position, and becoming sensitively alive to the awkward burden of explanation, in this quarter, and that, and the other, with which it would load him, he avoided the awkwardness, and took to flight?"

"Such a thing might be," said Mr. Grewgious, pondering.

"Such a thing has been. I have read of cases in which people, rather than face a seven days' wonder, and have to account for themselves to the idle and impertinent, have taken themselves away, and been long unheard of."

"I believe such things have happened," said Mr. Grewgious, pondering still.

"When I had, and could have, no suspicion," pursued Jasper, eagerly following the new track, "that the dear lost boy had withheld anything from me—most of all, such a leading matter as this—what gleam of light was there for me in the whole black sky? When I supposed that his intended wife was here, and his marriage close at hand, how could I entertain the possibility of his voluntarily leaving this place, in a manner that would be so unaccountable, capricious, and cruel? But now that I know what you have told me, is there no little chink through which day pierces? Supposing him to

have disappeared of his own act, is not his disappearance more accountable and less cruel? The fact of his having just parted from
your ward, is in itself a sort of reason for his going away. It does
not make his mysterious departure the less cruel to me, it is true;
but it relieves it of cruelty to her."

Mr. Grewgious could not but assent to this.

"And even as to me," continued Jasper, still pursuing the new
track, with ardour, and, as he did so, brightening with hope: "he
knew that you were coming to me; he knew that you were entrusted
to tell me what you have told me; if your doing so has awakened a
new train of thought in my perplexed mind, it reasonably follows
that, from the same premises, he might have foreseen the inferences
that I should draw. Grant that he did foresee them; and even the
cruelty to me—and who am I!—John Jasper, Music-Master!—
vanishes."

Once more, Mr. Grewgious could not but assent to this.

"I have had my distrusts, and terrible distrusts they have been,"
said Jasper; "but your disclosure, overpowering as it was at first—
showing me that my own dear boy had had a great disappointing
reservation from me, who so fondly loved him—kindles hope within
me. You do not extinguish it when I state it, but admit it to be a
reasonable hope. I begin to believe it possible:" here he clasped his
hands: "that he may have disappeared from among us of his own
accord, and that he may yet be alive and well!"

Mr. Crisparkle came in at the moment. To whom Mr. Jasper
repeated:

"I begin to believe it possible that he may have disappeared of his own accord, and may yet be alive and well!"

Mr. Crisparkle taking a seat, and enquiring: "Why so?" Mr. Jasper repeated the arguments he had just set forth. If they had been less plausible than they were, the good Minor Canon's mind would have been in a state of preparation to receive them, as exculpatory of his unfortunate pupil. But he, too, did really attach great importance to the lost young man's having been, so immediately before his disappearance, placed in a new and embarrassing relation towards every one acquainted with his projects and affairs; and the fact seemed to him to present the question in a new light.

"I stated to Mr. Sapsea, when we waited on him," said Jasper: as he really had done: "that there was no quarrel or difference between the two young men at their last meeting. We all know that their first meeting was, unfortunately, very far from amicable; but all went smoothly and quietly when they were last together at my house. My dear boy was not in his usual spirits; he was depressed—I noticed that—and I am bound henceforth to dwell upon the circumstance the more, now that I know there was a special reason for his being depressed: a reason, moreover, which may possibly have induced him to absent himself."

"I pray to Heaven it may turn out so!" exclaimed Mr. Crisparkle.

"*I* pray to Heaven it may turn out so!" repeated Jasper. "You know—and Mr. Grewgious should now know likewise—that I took a great prepossession against Mr. Neville Landless, arising out of his furious conduct on that first occasion. You know that I came to you, extremely apprehensive, on my dear boy's behalf, of his mad violence. You know that I even entered in my Diary, and showed the entry to you, that I had dark forebodings against him. Mr. Grewgious ought to be possessed of the whole case. He shall not, through any suppression of mine, be informed of a part of it, and kept in ignorance of another part of it. I wish him to be good enough to understand that the communication he has made to me has hopefully influenced my mind, in spite of its having been, before this mysterious occurrence took place, profoundly impressed against young Landless."

This fairness troubled the Minor Canon much. He felt that he was not as open in his own dealing. He charged against himself reproachfully that he had suppressed, so far, the two points of a second strong outbreak of temper against Edwin Drood on the part of Neville, and of the passion of jealousy having, to his own certain knowledge, flamed up in Neville's breast against him. He was convinced of Neville's innocence of any part in the ugly disappearance, and yet so many little circumstances combined so woefully against him, that he dreaded to add two more to their cumulative weight. He was among the truest of men; but he had been balancing in his mind, much to its distress, whether his volunteering to tell these two fragments of truth, at this time, would not be tantamount to a piecing together of falsehood in the place of truth.

However, here was a model before him. He hesitated no longer. Addressing Mr. Grewgious, as one placed in authority by the revelation he had brought to bear on the mystery (and surpassingly Angular Mr. Grewgious became when he found himself in that un-expected position), Mr. Crisparkle bore his testimony to Mr. Jasper's strict sense of justice, and, expressing his absolute confidence in the complete clearance of his pupil from the least taint of suspicion, sooner or later, avowed that his confidence in that young gentleman had been formed, in spite of his confidential knowledge that his temper was of the hottest and fiercest, and that it was directly incensed against Mr. Jasper's nephew, by the circumstance of his romantically supposing himself to be enamoured of the same young lady. The sanguine reaction manifest in Mr. Jasper was proof even against this unlooked-for declaration. It turned him paler; but he repeated that he would cling to the hope he had derived from Mr. Grewgious; and that if no trace of his dear boy were found, leading to the dreadful inference that he had been made away with, he would cherish until the last stretch of possibility, the idea, that he might have absconded of his own wild will.

Now, it fell out that Mr. Crisparkle, going away from this conference still very uneasy in his mind, and very much troubled on behalf of the young man whom he held as a kind of prisoner in his own house, took a memorable night walk.

He walked to Cloisterham Weir.

He often did so, and consequently there was nothing remark-able in his footsteps tending that way. But the preoccupation of his mind so hindered him from planning any walk, or taking heed of the objects he passed, that his first consciousness of being near the

Weir, was derived from the sound of the falling water close at hand.

"How did I come here!" was his first thought, as he stopped.

"Why did I come here!" was his second.

Then, he stood intently listening to the water. A familiar passage in his reading, about airy tongues that syllable men's names, rose so unbidden to his ear, that he put it from him with his hand, as if it were tangible.

It was starlight. The Weir was full two miles above the spot to which the young men had repaired to watch the storm. No search had been made up here, for the tide had been running strongly down, at that time of the night of Christmas Eve, and the likeliest places for the discovery of a body, if a fatal accident had happened under such circumstances, all lay—both when the tide ebbed, and when it flowed again—between that spot and the sea. The water came over the Weir, with its usual sound on a cold starlight night, and little could be seen of it; yet Mr. Crisparkle had a strange idea that something unusual hung about the place.

He reasoned with himself: What was it? Where was it? Put it to the proof. Which sense did it address?

No sense reported anything unusual there. He listened again, and his sense of hearing again checked the water coming over the Weir, with its usual sound on a cold starlight night.

Knowing very well that the mystery with which his mind was occupied, might of itself give the place this haunted air, he strained those hawk's eyes of his for the correction of his sight. He got closer to the Weir, and peered at its well-known posts and timbers. Nothing in the least unusual was remotely shadowed forth. But he resolved that he would come back early in the morning.

The Weir ran through his broken sleep, all night, and he was back again at sunrise. It was a bright frosty morning. The whole composition before him, when he stood where he had stood last night, was clearly discernible in its minutest details. He had surveyed it closely for some minutes, and was about to withdraw his eyes, when they were attracted keenly to one spot.

He turned his back upon the Weir, and looked far away at the sky, and at the earth, and then looked again at that one spot. It caught his sight again immediately, and he concentrated his vision upon it. He could not lose it now, though it was but such a speck in the landscape. It fascinated his sight. His hands began plucking off his coat. For it struck him that at that spot—a corner of the Weir—something glistened, which did not move and come over with the glistening water-drops, but remained stationary.

He assured himself of this, he threw off his clothes, he plunged into the icy water, and swam for the spot. Climbing the timbers, he took from them, caught among their interstices by its chain, a good watch, bearing engraved upon its back, E. D.

He brought the watch to the bank, swam to the Weir again, climbed it, and dived off. He knew every hole and corner of all the depths, and dived and dived and dived, until he could bear the cold no more. His notion was, that he would find the body; he only found a shirt-pin sticking in some mud and ooze.

With these discoveries he returned to Cloisterham, and taking Neville Landless with him, went straight to the Mayor. Mr. Jasper was sent for, the watch and shirt-pin were identified, Neville was detained, and the wildest frenzy and fatuity of evil report arose against him. He was of that vindictive and violent nature, that but for his poor sister, who alone had influence over him, and out of whose sight he was never to be trusted, he would be in the daily commission of murder. Before coming to England he had caused to be whipped to death sundry "Natives"—nomadic persons, encamping now in Asia, now in Africa, now in the West Indies, and now at the North Pole—vaguely supposed in Cloisterham to be always black, always of great virtue, always calling themselves Me, and everybody else Massa or Missie (according to sex), and always reading tracts of the obscurest meaning, in broken English, but always accurately understanding them in the purest mother tongue. He had nearly brought Mrs. Crisparkle's grey hairs with sorrow to the grave. (Those original expressions were Mr. Sapsea's.) He had repeatedly said he would have Mr. Crisparkle's life. He had repeatedly said he would have everybody's life, and become in effect the last man. He had been brought down to Cloisterham, from London, by an eminent Philanthropist, and why? Because that Philanthropist had expressly declared: "I owe it to my fellow-creatures that he should be, in the words of BENTHAM, where he is the cause of the greatest danger to the smallest number."

These dropping shots from the blunderbusses of blunderheadedness might not have hit him in a vital place. But he had to stand against a trained and well-directed fire of arms of precision too. He had notoriously threatened the lost young man, and had, according to the showing of his own faithful friend and tutor who strove so hard for him, a cause of bitter animosity (created by himself, and stated by himself), against that ill-starred fellow. He had armed himself with an offensive weapon for the fatal night, and he had gone off early in the morning, after making preparations for departure. He had been found with traces of blood on him; truly, they might have been wholly caused as he represented, but they might not, also. On a search-warrant being issued for the examination of his room, clothes, and so forth, it was discovered that he had destroyed all his papers, and rearranged all his possessions, on the very afternoon of the disappearance. The watch found at the Weir was challenged by the jeweller as one he had wound and set for Edwin Drood, at twenty minutes past two on that same afternoon; and it had run down, before being cast into the water; and it was the jeweller's positive opinion that it had never been re-wound. This would justify the hypothesis that the watch was taken from him not long after he left Mr. Jasper's house at midnight, in company with the last person seen with him, and that it had been thrown away after being retained some hours. Why thrown away? If he had been murdered, and so artfully disfigured, or concealed, or both, as that the murderer hoped identification to be impossible, except from something that he wore, assuredly the murderer would seek to remove from the body the most lasting, the best known, and the most easily recognizable, things upon it. Those things would be the watch

351

and shirt-pin. As to his opportunities of casting them into the river; if he were the object of these suspicions, they were easy. For, he had been seen by many persons, wandering about on that side of the city—indeed on all sides of it—in a miserable and seemingly half-distracted manner. As to the choice of the spot, obviously such criminating evidence had better take its chance of being found any-where, rather than upon himself, or in his possession. Concerning the reconciliatory nature of the appointed meeting between the two young men, very little could be made of that, in young Landless's favor; for, it distinctly appeared that the meeting originated, not with him, but with Mr. Crisparkle, and that it had been urged on by Mr. Crisparkle; and who could say how unwillingly, or in what ill-conditioned mood, his enforced pupil had gone to it? The more his case was looked into, the weaker it became in every point. Even the broad suggestion that the lost young man had absconded, was rendered additionally improbable on the showing of the young lady from whom he had so lately parted; for, what did she say, with great earnestness and sorrow, when interrogated? That he had, expressly and enthusiastically, planned with her, that he would await the ar-rival of her guardian, Mr. Grewgious. And yet, be it observed, he disappeared before that gentleman appeared.

On the suspicions thus argued and supported, Neville was de-tained and re-detained, and the search was pressed on every hand, and Jasper laboured night and day. But nothing more was found. No discovery being made, which proved the lost man to be dead, it at length became necessary to release the person suspected of having made away with him. Neville was set at large. Then, a consequence ensued which Mr. Crisparkle had too well foreseen. Neville must leave the place, for the place shunned him and cast him out. Even had it not been so, the dear old china shepherdess would have worried herself to death with fears for her son, and with general trepidation occasioned by their having such an inmate. Even had that not been so, the authority to which the Minor Canon deferred officially, would have settled the point.

"Mr. Crisparkle," quoth the Dean, "human justice may err, but it must act according to its lights. The days of taking sanctuary are past. This young man must not take sanctuary with us."

"You mean that he must leave my house, sir?"

"Mr. Crisparkle," returned the prudent Dean, "I claim no authority in your house. I merely confer with you, on the painful necessity you find yourself under, of depriving this young man of the great advantages of your counsel and instruction."

"It is very lamentable, sir," Mr. Crisparkle represented.

"Very much so," the Dean assented.

"And if it be a necessity——" Mr. Crisparkle faltered.

"As you unfortunately find it to be," returned the Dean.

Mr. Crisparkle bowed submissively. "It is hard to prejudge his case, sir, but I am sensible that——"

"Just so. Perfectly. As you say, Mr. Crisparkle," interposed the Dean, nodding his head smoothly, "there is nothing else to be done. No doubt, no doubt. There is no alternative, as your good sense has discovered."

"I am entirely satisfied of his perfect innocence, sir, nevertheless."

"We-e-ell!" said the Dean, in a more confidential tone, and slightly glancing around him, "I would not say so, generally. Not generally. Enough of suspicion attaches to him to—no, I think I would not say so, generally."

Mr. Crisparkle bowed again.

"It does not become us, perhaps," pursued the Dean, "to be partizans. Not partizans. We clergy keep our hearts warm and our heads cool, and we hold a judicious middle course."

"I hope you do not object, sir, to my having stated in public, emphatically, that he will reappear here, whenever any new suspicion may be awakened, or any new circumstance may come to light in this extraordinary matter?"

"Not at all," returned the Dean. "And yet, do you know, I don't think," with a very nice and neat emphasis on those two words: "I *don't think* I would state it, emphatically. State it? Ye-e-es! But emphatically? No-o-o. I *think* not. In point of fact, Mr. Crisparkle, keeping our hearts warm and our heads cool, we clergy need do nothing emphatically."

So, Minor Canon Row knew Neville Landless no more; and he went whithersoever he would, or could, with a blight upon his name and fame.

It was not until then that John Jasper silently resumed his place in the choir. Haggard and red-eyed, his hopes plainly had deserted him, his sanguine mood was gone, and all his worst misgivings had come back. A day or two afterwards, while unrobing, he took his Diary from a pocket of his coat, turned the leaves, and with an impressive look, and without one spoken word, handed this entry to Mr. Crisparkle to read:

"My dear boy is murdered. The discovery of the watch and shirt-pin convinces me that he was murdered that night, and that his jewellery was taken from him to prevent identification by its means. All the delusive hopes I had founded on his separation from his betrothed wife, I give to the winds. They perish before this fatal discovery. I now swear, and record the oath on this page, That I nevermore will discuss this mystery with any human creature, until I hold the clue to it in my hand. That I never will relax in my secresy or in my search. That I will fasten the crime of the murder of my dear dead boy, upon the murderer. And That I devote myself to his destruction."

12

THE DEBATE ON THE "MYSTERY NUMBER" does not proceed in quite so orderly a fashion as one might have hoped: the three investigators back from Cloisterham deliver their reports amidst a babble of eager guesses from those who have already started to discuss Chapter Fifteen and puzzled questions from those who are behind in the reading. Glasnost, as Magistrate Porfiry puts it, has not reached the conference-hall. In short, reader, we are faced with the kind of play that a sports commentator could only describe as rough and scrappy, and the referee himself, Wilmot, seems not to know what to make of it.

Bucket comes forward and, taking the pass from Sally, who intervened to save Ned after she'd got Jasper's secret out of him, states his intention of arresting or at least detaining the latter. But he is tackled by Toad, who says that the woman from the opium-den misunderstood Jasper: Ned, the unknown youth whose name she has heard so often on her client's lips during his opium fits, is not the man that the aforesaid client—i.e. Jasper—was planning, in his aforesaid fits, to strangle and throw from the top of the tower, but, rather, the man he was planning to *save* by throwing someone *else* off the tower.

Archer keeps this idea rolling, but it is sent flying by Popeau, who says scornfully, Oh yes? then how do you explain, my good man, that the name uttered by Jasper has always been that of his nephew and never that of some mysterious other?

Maybe because he didn't know him, says Maigret, stepping in, and possibly even now he doesn't know him, because if Neville . . .

Pooh! Popeau hacks him down, and this foul earns a stern rebuke from the referee. Dupin, backed up by Cuff, takes advantage of this to change the subject: it is his opinion that in Act II, Scene 1 of *Macbeth* there is something curiously similar to . . .

Similar to the title of Chapter Fourteen, Loredana shouts from the bench, eager to make an impression on the referee but forgetting that the witch's words ("When shall we three meet again?") open Act I and not Act II. Besides, as Wilmot points out to her with some embarrassment, every commentator has noticed the quotation from *Macbeth* but no-one has ever found anything in it that throws light on the mystery.

Nonetheless, the young lady has done well to draw

attention to the title, Poirot puts in gallantly, for the title may possibly hold a deeper clue. Besides, I imagine that my colleague Dupin . . .

It is significant, says Dupin, on the ball as ever, that Dickens specially marked the "mystery number," the novel's crucial chapter, with the first line from *Macbeth*. But it is not the line itself that intrigues me; it is, rather, the tragic theme of a murder *committed reluctantly by a husband acting on the instructions of his wife*.

Now Sergeant Cuff, who was on the spot and overheard the end of the dialogue between the Landless twins, maintains, swerving in nimbly, that that exchange can undoubtedly be interpreted as the prelude to a murder *committed reluctantly by a brother acting on the instructions of his sister*. But I leave it to my friend Dupin to show . . .

But the pass is intercepted by the colonel of the Carabinieri, who kicks the argument far from the area, observing that Neville must be in possession of a valid passport, given that he comes from abroad. Or are we to assume, he asks, that he destroyed it along with his other papers?

The question is ridiculed by the incorrigible Popeau, but not by Wilmot, who sees the point: What actual data do we have on the identity of the twins, apart from those given by the unreliable Honeythunder and the twins' own account of themselves? We do not even know that they are brother and sister, since they are not identical.

Then P. Petrovich comes into play, citing the reverse case of Alexei and Nelly in *The Insulted and the Injured,* which gives rise to a whole series of doubts (MARLOWE: Who is the sacristan in fact? WOLFE: How do we know that Jasper and Drood are really uncle and nephew?), and this discussion finishes off the pitch.

The throw-in is taken by Father Brown, who passes to Cuff, who passes to Dupin, who takes up the matter of the "similarities" between the Drood case and the story of Macbeth. Macbeth, like Neville, he argues, after various attempts to draw back, allows himself to be persuaded by his companion (who previously called upon the spirits to "unsex" her [1] to perform "this night's great business"); and in horror at the crime he is about to commit, he observes that tonight "Nature seems dead." Similarly in the MED, when Helena finally persuades him to perform "this night's great business," Neville remarks, "What a strange dead weight there is in the air!" And in both cases, concludes Dupin, shooting for the goal, there is such a violent storm during the night that the chimneys are blown down into the streets. [2]

"Goal! We've won! . . ." Toad shouts wildly, feeling

---

[1] Dupin reminds his colleagues of how Helena furiously tore out her own hair in her attempt to "unsex" herself.

[2] *Macbeth,* II, iii: "Our chimneys were blown down"; *MED,* XIV: "Chimneys topple in the streets."

sure that Dupin's conclusion, which Cuff set up for him, puts the score definitely in Jasper's favour. But not everybody is in agreement, beginning with the referee. A brawl ensues . . .

(Brawling noises, followed by muttering into the microphone, then sudden interruption of the transmission.)

We interrupt this live broadcast in order to assess the state of play from a safe distance, and to supply the reader also with a more ordered if somewhat telegraphic account of the final score.

WILMOT: Interesting analogies with *Macbeth,* but possibly pure coincidence. MED teeming with Shakespearian allusions and derivations of all kinds: e.g. violent scene where Jasper avows to Rosa monstrous love, curously similar to *Hamlet,* Act III, Scene 1, where pale prince *denies* to Ophelia his love with threats & outbursts. Is Jasper pursuing same aim: make her believe him mad?

MAIGRET: Don't know. Previous commentary?

WILMOT, *hesitantly:* Yes, eminent Jasperian defender alluded to yesterday. But would prefer not to influence course of enquiry.

TOAD: Was eminent defender accuser of alleged twins?

WILMOT: No, as I already said, no-one suspected twins before Sergeant Cuff.

TOAD, *Shakespearian:* Hail, brave sergeant! [1]

POIROT: Particularly interesting, Cuff's observation re author's reluctance to show us Helena again with Rosa.

CUFF: And with Neville! Note how brother, from moment of arrest to final departure destination unknown, never once shown talking to sister.

POPEAU: Maybe they quarrelled?

POIROT: Maybe *author,* at this point, cannot have them talk without showing his hand!

CUFF: Exactly. Their dialogue *ante factum* already seems forced, unconvincing, despite novelist's devilish cunning; how can he make them talk *post factum* if guilty? Equally difficult, dialogue of Helena and Rosa. Rosa would wonder how Helena can be so sure of her brother's innocence, given his violent character. Much simpler for author to insert into Grewgious/Jasper scene assurance of Miss Landless's "Defiance of all suspicion and unbounded faith in her brother."

LOREDANA, *greatly struck by Cuff's argument:* Why did the eminent Jasperian defender not note this, Dr Wilmot?

WILMOT: Signorina, I would prefer not . . .

CUFF: In the remaining instalments there will be no more direct Helena/Rosa or Helena/Neville conversations.

---

[1] See *Macbeth,* I, ii.

361

WILMOT: Both right and wrong. I say no more, in order not to influence course of enquiry.

LOREDANA, *losing patience:* Fred!

(Some hasty coughing, some open grinning. Wilmot adjusts tie with Oxbridgian aplomb.)

P. PETROVICH: Jasper's being reduced to a "heap of torn and miry clothes" on learning of his nephew's broken engagement. Only one explanation: culprit horror-struck by the pointlessness of his wicked deed. I appreciate chairman's reluctance to interfere, but wish to know: did Eminent Jasperian Defender find any other explanation?

WILMOT: Yes. He gives a fairly plausible reason why the uncle was so disheartened.

FATHER BROWN: I challenge anyone, defender or not, to explain: 1) The uncle, so anxious about his nephew's safety, waits till dawn before starting his search. 2) Crisparkle doesn't wait for Neville's return from the "reconciliation," but goes to bed and so doesn't know when Neville returns. 3) The first interrogation of Neville is over in an instant, after which the Reverend finds (by mesmerism?) the watch at the Weir, and the shirt-pin at the bottom of the river (!!!); then takes his charge to the Mayor for another interrogation (which *nota bene* the novelist doesn't show; then declares himself "entirely satisfied of his perfect innocence." In short, 4) Helena, Rosa, the Reverend, all have no doubt of Neville's innocence despite everything;

including Grewgious, who saw the sister briefly but never the brother, even from a distance. Come, come! Much too strange! No verisimilitude! I begin to ask myself if the author is able to produce a solution of any kind.

TOAD, *disheartened:* Oh dear!

HOLMES, *spectral:* Alive, he would have been able.

FATHER BROWN, *ignoring interruptions:* With Dr Wilmot's permission, I would like to convey an opinion expressed by my—um—earthly creator.

WILMOT: Go ahead, Father.

FATHER BROWN: As judge in the fictitious trial of Jasper,[1] G. K. Chesterton declared it was impossible to deduce, from the MED, anyone's guilt or innocence, not even whether Drood was alive or dead, because of all the incongruencies and contradictions within the text itself. G. B. Shaw, as jury foreman in this trial, did not hesitate to dismiss the novel on literary grounds, as well, calling it the "gesture by a man who was already three-quarters dead."

P. PETROVICH: Objection! I refuse to recognise any authority in Mr Shaw, who was interested only in the "social" aspect of Dickens's work. Disappointed by the lack of that element in this final novel, Shaw could not appreciate its artistic merits.

---

[1] *The Trial of John Jasper,* stenographic account edited by the Dickens Fellowship, London, 1914.

COLONEL: Absolutely right.

P. PETROVICH: Thank you. With regard to its artistic merits, allow me to give you poet H. W. Longfellow's (1807–82) opinion. He said: "MED is one of Dickens's most beautiful works, even though incomplete." Something more than the gesture of a man three-quarters dead, then! You need only consider such characters as Durdles, Twinkleton, Grewgious, Bazzard, and the opium-den woman, to recognise the mark of a genius of English fiction! You need only consider The Tilted Wagon and its moist baby with one red sock!

Shouts of "Hear hear!" and "Bravo!" Many cluster round P. Petrovich to congratulate him personally, and Father Brown now approaches to express complete agreement. "I quoted Shaw's opinion for the sake of impartiality," he assures him, "but don't share it at all!"

Both men small and round, both untidily dressed, both profoundly religious, both lively and agile despite short legs and arms, they warmly shake hands under Poirot's curious gaze. Poirot is struck by doubt (as Holmes and Dupin immediately deduce from his expression): Is such a close resemblance due purely to chance? Could Chesterton, Poirot wonders, have modelled his famous detective on the St. Petersburg investigator?

Let the reader decide for himself, because Poirot is now immersed in the following thoughts: 1) Dickens delib-

erately patterned the MED after the best-seller by his former friend and new rival, Wilkie Collins. 2) His aim,
according to Forster, was to show the readers how he could
"do it better." But 3) Dickens lacked experience and probably the ability to write a real detective plot; so 4) his
ambitious plan may have backfired, causing the structural
weaknesses noted by Father Brown's "father," despite the
MED's high artistic level. 5) The key to the mystery remains opium, which means the Jekyllian solution is ines-
capable. 6) The evidence gathered by Scotland Yard against
the suspicious twins raises questions but has no significance, being purely circumstantial and unsupported by
anything else.

So we keep going round and round. This is the opinion
also of Maigret, Wolfe, Thorndyke, and even the Latinist
from Juan-les-Pins, who wandered into the Dickens Room
by mistake on his way back from the toilet. Marlowe and
Archer, meanwhile, are pointedly uninterested and sneer
at Loredana, who is absorbed in the contemplation of her
Fred. Fred (Wilmot) proposes everyone adjourn for lunch,
but return at 1500 hours promptly for imprinting and discussion of the August number.

However, as everyone knows or should know, man
proposes and technicians dispose. Here comes a technician
now, to announce that because of technical difficulties imprinting will not be possible until 1600 hours, but the Au-

gust number can be imprinted immediately if all agree. Not all agree; many would like to get the MED out of their head for at least a couple of hours. On the other hand, the July number has been discussed exhaustively, and the questions multiply, and time presses. Wilmot calls for a show of hands, and the motion for immediate imprinting wins, so the next number follows.

CHAPTER XVII

PHILANTHROPY, PROFESSIONAL AND UNPROFESSIONAL

FULL half a year had come and gone, and Mr. Crisparkle sat in a waiting-room in the London chief offices of the Haven of Philanthropy, until he could have audience of Mr. Honeythunder.

In his college-days of athletic exercises, Mr. Crisparkle had known professors of the Noble Art of fisticuffs, and had attended two or three of their gloved gatherings. He had now an opportunity of observing that as to the phrenological formation of the backs of their heads, the Professing Philanthropists were uncommonly like the Pugilists. In the development of all those organs which constitute, or attend, a propensity to "pitch into" your fellow-creatures, the Philanthropists were remarkably favored. There were several Professors passing in and out, with exactly the aggressive air upon them of being ready for a turn-up with any Novice who might happen to be on hand, that Mr. Crisparkle well remembered in the circles of the Fancy. Preparations were in progress for a moral little Mill somewhere on the rural circuit, and other Professors were backing this or that Heavy-Weight as good for such or such speech-making hits, so very much after the manner of the sporting publicans that the intended Resolutions might have been Rounds. In an official manager of these displays much celebrated for his platform tactics, Mr. Crisparkle recognised (in a suit of black) the counterpart of a deceased benefactor of his species, an eminent public character, once known to fame as Frosty-faced Fogo, who in days of yore superintended the formation of the magic circle with the ropes and stakes. There were only three conditions of resemblance wanting between these Professors and those. Firstly, the Philanthropists were in very bad training: much too fleshy, and presenting, both in face and figure, a superabundance of what is known to Pugilistic Experts as Suet Pudding. Secondly, the Philanthropists had not the good temper of the Pugilists, and used worse language. Thirdly, their fighting code stood in great need of revision, as empowering them not only to bore their man to the ropes, but to bore him to the confines of distraction; also to hit him when he was down, hit him anywhere and anyhow, kick him, stamp upon him, gouge him, and maul him behind his back without mercy. In these last particulars the Professors of the Noble Art were much nobler than the Professors of Philanthropy.

Mr. Crisparkle was so completely lost in musing on these similarities and dissimilarities, at the same time watching the crowd which came and went by, always, as it seemed, on errands of antagonistically snatching something from somebody, and never giving anything to anybody: that his name was called before he heard it. On his at length responding, he was shown by a miserably shabby and underpaid stipendiary Philanthropist (who could hardly have done worse if he had taken service with a declared enemy of the human race) to Mr. Honeythunder's room.

"Sir," said Mr. Honeythunder, in his tremendous voice, like a schoolmaster issuing orders to a boy of whom he had a bad opinion, "sit down."

Mr. Crisparkle seated himself.

Mr. Honeythunder, having signed the remaining few score of a few thousand circulars, calling upon a corresponding number of families without means to come forward, stump up instantly, and be Philanthropists, or go to the Devil, another shabby stipendiary Philanthropist (highly disinterested, if in earnest) gathered these into a basket and walked off with them.

"Now, Mr. Crisparkle," said Mr. Honeythunder, turning his chair half round towards him when they were alone, and squaring his arms with his hands on his knees, and his brows knitted, as if he added, I am going to make short work of *you*: "Now, Mr. Crisparkle, we entertain different views, you and I, sir, of the sanctity of human life."

"Do we?" returned the Minor Canon.

"We do, sir."

"Might I ask you," said the Minor Canon: "what are your views on that subject?"

"That human life is a thing to be held sacred, sir."

"Might I ask you," pursued the Minor Canon as before: "what you suppose to be my views on that subject?"

"By George, sir!" returned the Philanthropist, squaring his arms still more, as he frowned on Mr. Crisparkle: "they are best known to yourself."

"Readily admitted. But you began by saying that we took different views, you know. Therefore (or you could not say so) you must have set up some views as mine. Pray, what views *have* you set up as mine?"

"Here is a man—and a young man," said Mr. Honeythunder, as if that made the matter infinitely worse, and he could have easily borne the loss of an old one: "swept off the face of the earth by a deed of violence. What do you call that?"

"Murder," said the Minor Canon.

"What do you call the doer of that deed, sir?"

"A murderer," said the Minor Canon.

"I am glad to hear you admit so much, sir," retorted Mr. Honeythunder, in his most offensive manner; "and I candidly tell you that I didn't expect it." Here he lowered heavily at Mr. Crisparkle again.

"Be so good as to explain what you mean by those very unjustifiable expressions."

"I don't sit here, sir," returned the Philanthropist, raising his voice to a roar, "to be browbeaten."

"As the only other person present, no one can possibly know that better than I do," returned the Minor Canon very quietly. "But I interrupt your explanation."

"Murder!" proceeded Mr. Honeythunder, in a kind of boisterous reverie, with his platform folding of his arms, and his platform nod of abhorrent reflection after each short sentiment of a word. "Bloodshed! Abel! Cain! I hold no terms with Cain. I repudiate with a shudder the red hand when it is offered me."

Instead of instantly leaping from his chair and cheering himself hoarse, as the Brotherhood in public meeting assembled would infallibly have done on this cue, Mr. Crisparkle merely reversed the quiet crossing of his legs, and said mildly: "Don't let me interrupt your explanation—when you begin it."

"The Commandments say no murder. NO murder, sir!" proceeded Mr. Honeythunder, platformally pausing as if he took Mr. Crisparkle to task for having distinctly asserted that they said, You may do a little murder and then leave off.

"And they also say, you shall bear no false witness," observed Mr. Crisparkle.

"Enough!" bellowed Mr. Honeythunder, with a solemnity and severity that would have brought the house down at a meeting, "E—e—nough! My late wards being now of age, and I being released from a trust which I cannot contemplate without a thrill of horror, there are the accounts which you have undertaken to accept on their behalf, and there is a statement of the balance which you have undertaken to receive, and which you cannot receive too soon. And let me tell you, sir, I wish, that as a man and a Minor Canon, you were better employed," with a nod. "Better employed," with another nod. "Bet—ter em—ployed!" with another and the three nods added up.

Mr. Crisparkle rose; a little heated in the face, but with perfect command of himself.

"Mr. Honeythunder," he said, taking up the papers referred to: "my being better or worse employed than I am at present is a matter of taste and opinion. You might think me better employed in enrolling myself a member of your Society."

"Ay, indeed, sir!" retorted Mr. Honeythunder, shaking his head in a threatening manner. "It would have been better for you if you had done that long ago!"

"I think otherwise."

"Or," said Mr. Honeythunder, shaking his head again, "I might think one of your profession better employed in devoting himself to the discovery and punishment of guilt than in leaving that duty to be undertaken by a layman."

"I may regard my profession from a point of view which teaches me that its first duty is towards those who are in necessity and tribulation, who are desolate and oppressed," said Mr. Crisparkle. "However, as I have quite clearly satisfied myself that it is no part of my profession to make professions, I say no more of that. But I owe it to Mr. Neville, and to Mr. Neville's sister (and in a much lower degree to myself), to say to you that I *know* I was in the full possession and understanding of Mr. Neville's mind and heart at the time of this occurrence; and that, without in the least coloring or concealing what was to be deplored in him and required to be corrected, I feel certain that his tale is true. Feeling that certainty, I befriend him. As long as that certainty shall last I will befriend him.

And if any consideration could shake me in this resolve, I should be so ashamed of myself for my meanness that no man's good opinion—no, nor no woman's—so gained, could compensate me for the loss of my own."

Good fellow! Manly fellow! And he was so modest, too. There was no more self-assertion in the Minor Canon than in the schoolboy who had stood in the breezy playing-fields keeping a wicket. He was simply and staunchly true to his duty alike in the large case and in the small. So all true souls ever are. So every true soul ever was, ever is, and ever will be. There is nothing little to the really great in spirit.

"Then who do you make out did the deed?" asked Mr. Honeythunder, turning on him abruptly.

"Heaven forbid," said Mr. Crisparkle, "that in my desire to clear one man I should lightly criminate another! I accuse no one."

"Tcha!" ejaculated Mr. Honeythunder with great disgust; for this was by no means the principle on which the Philanthropic Brotherhood usually proceeded. "And, sir, you are not a disinterested witness, we must bear in mind."

"How am I an interested one?" inquired Mr. Crisparkle, smiling innocently, at a loss to imagine.

"There was a certain stipend, sir, paid to you for your pupil which may have warped your judgment a bit," said Mr. Honeythunder, coarsely.

"Perhaps I expect to retain it still?" Mr. Crisparkle returned, enlightened; "do you mean that too?"

"Well, sir," returned the professional Philanthropist, getting up, and thrusting his hands down into his trousers pockets; "I don't go about measuring people for caps. If people find I have any about me that fit 'em, they can put 'em on and wear 'em, if they like. That's their look out: not mine."

Mr. Crisparkle eyed him with a just indignation, and took him to task thus:

"Mr. Honeythunder, I hoped when I came in here that I might be under no necessity of commenting on the introduction of platform manners or platform manœuvres among the decent forbearances of private life. But you have given me such a specimen of both, that I should be a fit subject for both if I remained silent respecting them. They are detestable."

"They don't suit *you,* I dare say, sir."

"They are," repeated Mr. Crisparkle, without noticing the interruption, "detestable. They violate equally the justice that should belong to Christians, and the restraints that should belong to gentlemen. You assume a great crime to have been committed by one whom I, acquainted with the attendant circumstances, and having numerous reasons on my side, devoutly believe to be innocent of it. Because I differ from you on that vital point, what is your platform resource? Instantly to turn upon me, charging that I have no sense of the enormity of the crime itself, but am its aider and abettor! So, another time—taking me as representing your opponent in other cases—you set up a platform credulity: a moved and seconded and carried unanimously profession of faith in some ridiculous delusion or mischievous imposition. I decline to believe it, and you fall back upon your platform resource of proclaiming that I believe nothing; that because I will not bow down to a false God of our making, I deny the true God! Another time, you make the platform discovery that War is a calamity, and you propose to abolish it by a string of twisted resolutions tossed into the air like the tail of a kite. I do not admit the discovery to be yours in the least, and I have not a grain of faith in your remedy. Again, your platform resource of representing me as revelling in the horrors of a battle field like a fiend incarnate! Another time, in another of your undiscriminating platform rushes, you would punish the sober for the drunken. I claim consideration for the comfort, convenience, and refreshment, of the sober; and you presently make platform proclamation that I have a depraved desire to turn Heaven's creatures into swine and wild beasts! In all such cases your movers, and your seconders, and your supporters—your regular Professors of all degrees—run amuck like so many mad Malays; habitually attributing the lowest and basest motives with the utmost recklessness (let me call your attention to a recent instance in yourself for which you should blush), and quoting figures which you know to be as wilfully onesided as a statement of any complicated account that should be all Creditor side and no debtor, or all Debtor side and no Creditor. Therefore it is, Mr. Honeythunder, that I consider the platform a sufficiently bad example and a sufficiently bad school, even in public life; but hold that, carried into private life, it becomes an unendurable nuisance."

"These are strong words, sir!" exclaimed the Philanthropist.

"I hope so," said Mr. Crisparkle. "Good-morning."

He walked out of the Haven at a great rate, but soon fell into his regular brisk pace, and soon had a smile upon his face as he went along, wondering what the china shepherdess would have said if she had seen him pounding Mr. Honeythunder in the late little lively affair. For Mr. Crisparkle had just enough of harmless vanity to hope that he had hit hard, and to glow with the belief that he had trimmed the Philanthropic jacket pretty handsomely.

He took himself to Staple Inn, but not to P. J. T. and Mr. Grewgious. Full many a creaking stair he climbed before he reached some attic rooms in a corner, turned the latch of their unbolted door, and stood beside the table of Neville Landless.

An air of retreat and solitude hung about the rooms, and about their inhabitant. He was much worn, and so were they. Their sloping ceilings, cumbrous rusty locks and grates, and heavy wooden bins and beams, slowly mouldering withal, had a prisonous look, and he had the haggard face of a prisoner. Yet the sunlight shone in at the ugly garret window which had a penthouse to itself thrust out among the tiles; and on the cracked and smoke-blackened parapet beyond, some of the deluded sparrows of the place rheumatically hopped, like little feathered cripples who had left their crutches in their nests; and there was a play of living leaves at hand that changed the air, and made an imperfect sort of music in it that would have been melody in the country.

The rooms were sparely furnished, but with good store of books.

Everything expressed the abode of a poor student. That Mr. Crisparkle had been either chooser, lender, or donor of the books, or that he combined the three characters, might have been easily seen in the friendly beam of his eyes upon them as he entered.

"How goes it, Neville?"

"I am in good heart, Mr. Crisparkle, and working away."

"I wish your eyes were not quite so large, and not quite so bright," said the Minor Canon, slowly releasing the hand he had taken in his.

"They brighten at the sight of you," returned Neville. "If you were to fall away from me, they would soon be dull enough."

"Rally, rally!" urged the other, in a stimulating tone. "Fight for it, Neville!"

"If I were dying, I feel as if a word from you would rally me; if my pulse had stopped, I feel as if your touch would make it beat again," said Neville. "But I *have* rallied, and am doing famously."

Mr. Crisparkle turned him with his face a little more towards the light.

"I want to see a ruddier touch here, Neville," he said, indicating his own healthy cheek by way of pattern; "I want more sun to shine upon you."

Neville drooped suddenly as he replied in a lowered voice: "I am not hardy enough for that, yet. I may become so, but I cannot bear it yet. If you had gone through those Cloisterham streets as I did; if you had seen, as I did, those averted eyes, and the better sort

377

of people silently giving me too much room to pass, that I might not touch them or come near them, you wouldn't think it quite unreasonable that I cannot go about in the day-light."

"My poor fellow!" said the Minor Canon, in a tone so purely sympathetic that the young man caught his hand: "I never said it was unreasonable: never thought so. But I should like you to do it."

"And that would give me the strongest motive to do it. But I cannot yet. I cannot persuade myself that the eyes of even the stream of strangers I pass in this vast city look at me without suspicion. I feel marked and tainted, even when I go out—as I do only—at night. But the darkness covers me then, and I take courage from it."

Mr. Crisparkle laid a hand upon his shoulder, and stood looking down at him.

"If I could have changed my name," said Neville, "I would have done so. But as you wisely pointed out to me, I can't do that, for it would look like guilt. If I could have gone to some distant place, I might have found relief in that, but the thing is not to be thought of, for the same reason. Hiding and escaping would be the construction in either case. It seems a little hard to be so tied to a stake, and innocent; but I don't complain."

"And you must expect no miracle to help you, Neville," said Mr. Crisparkle, compassionately.

"No, sir, I know that. The ordinary fulness of time and circumstance is all I have to trust to."

"It will right you at last, Neville."

"So I believe, and I hope I may live to know it."

But perceiving that the despondent mood into which he was falling cast a shadow on the Minor Canon, and (it may be) feeling that the broad hand upon his shoulder was not then quite as steady as its own natural strength had rendered it when it first touched him just now, he brightened and said:

"Excellent circumstances for study, anyhow! and you know, Mr. Crisparkle, what need I have of study in all ways. Not to mention that you have advised me to study for the difficult profession of the law, specially, and that of course I am guiding myself by the advice of such a friend and helper. Such a good friend and helper!"

He took the fortifying hand from his shoulder, and kissed it. Mr. Crisparkle beamed at the books, but not so brightly as when he had entered.

"I gather from your silence on the subject that my late guardian is adverse, Mr. Crisparkle?"

The Minor Canon answered: "Your late guardian is a—a most unreasonable person, and it signifies nothing to any reasonable person whether he is *ad*verse or *per*verse, or the *re*verse."

"Well for me that I have enough with economy to live upon," sighed Neville, half wearily and half cheerily, "while I wait to be learned, and wait to be righted! Else I might have proved the proverb that while the grass grows, the steed starves!"

He opened some books as he said it, and was soon immersed in their interleaved and annotated passages, while Mr. Crisparkle sat beside him, expounding, correcting, and advising. The Minor Canon's cathedral duties made these visits of his difficult to accomplish, and only to be compassed at intervals of many weeks. But they were as serviceable as they were precious to Neville Landless.

When they had got through such studies as they had in hand, they stood leaning on the window-sill, and looking down upon the patch of garden. "Next week," said Mr. Crisparkle, "you will cease to be alone, and will have a devoted companion."

"And yet," returned Neville, "this seems an uncongenial place to bring my sister to!"

"I don't think so," said the Minor Canon. "There is duty to be done here; and there are womanly feeling, sense, and courage wanted here."

"I meant," explained Neville, "that the surroundings are so dull and unwomanly, and that Helena can have no suitable friend or society here."

"You have only to remember," said Mr. Crisparkle, "that you are here yourself, and that she has to draw you into the sunlight."

They were silent for a little while, and then Mr. Crisparkle began anew.

"When we first spoke together, Neville, you told me that your sister had risen out of the disadvantages of your past lives as superior to you as the tower of Cloisterham Cathedral is higher than the chimneys of Minor Canon Corner. Do you remember that?"

"Right well!"

"I was inclined to think it at the time an enthusiastic flight. No matter what I think it now. What I would emphasize is, that under the head of Pride your sister is a great and opportune example to you."

"Under *all* heads that are included in the composition of a fine character, she is."

"Say so; but take this one. Your sister has learnt how to govern what is proud in her nature. She can dominate it even when it is wounded through her sympathy with you. No doubt she has suffered deeply in those same streets where you suffered deeply. No doubt her life is darkened by the cloud that darkens yours. But bending her pride into a grand composure that is not haughty or aggressive, but is a sustained confidence in you and in the truth, she has won her way through those streets until she passes along them as high in the general respect as any one who treads them. Every day and hour of her life since Edwin Drood's disappearance, she has faced malignity and folly—for you—as only a brave nature well directed can. So it will be with her to the end. Another and weaker kind of pride might sink broken-hearted, but never such a pride as hers: which knows no shrinking, and can get no mastery over her."

The pale cheek beside him flushed under the comparison and the hint implied in it. "I will do all I can to imitate her," said Neville.

"Do so, and be a truly brave man as she is a truly brave woman," answered Mr. Crisparkle, stoutly. "It is growing dark. Will you go my way with me, when it is quite dark? Mind! It is not I who wait for darkness."

Neville replied that he would accompany him directly. But Mr.

Crisparkle said he had a moment's call to make on Mr. Grewgious as an act of courtesy, and would run across to that gentleman's chambers, and rejoin Neville on his own doorstep if he would come down there to meet him.

Mr. Grewgious, bolt upright as usual, sat taking his wine in the dusk at his open window; his wineglass and decanter on the round table at his elbow; himself and his legs on the windowseat; only one hinge in his whole body, like a bootjack.

"How do you do, reverend sir?" said Mr. Grewgious, with abundant offers of hospitality which were as cordially declined as made. "And how is your charge getting on over the way in the set that I had the pleasure of recommending to you as vacant and eligible?"

Mr. Crisparkle replied suitably.

"I am glad you approve of them," said Mr. Grewgious, "because I entertain a sort of fancy for having him under my eye."

As Mr. Grewgious had to turn his eye up considerably, before he could see the chambers, the phrase was to be taken figuratively and not literally.

"And how did you leave Mr. Jasper, reverend sir?" said Mr. Grewgious.

Mr. Crisparkle had left him pretty well.

"And where did you leave Mr. Jasper, reverend sir?"

Mr. Crisparkle had left him at Cloisterham.

"And when did you leave Mr. Jasper, reverend sir?"

That morning.

"Umps!" said Mr. Grewgious. "He didn't say he was coming, perhaps?"

"Coming where?"

"Anywhere, for instance?" said Mr. Grewgious.

"No."

"Because here he is," said Mr. Grewgious, who had asked all these questions, with his preoccupied glance directed out at window. "And he don't look agreeable, does he?"

Mr. Crisparkle was craning towards the window, when Mr. Grewgious added:

"If you will kindly step round here behind me, in the gloom of the room, and will cast your eye at the second-floor landing window, in yonder house, I think you will hardly fail to see a slinking individual in whom I recognise our local friend."

"You are right!" cried Mr. Crisparkle.

"Umps!" said Mr. Grewgious. Then he added, turning his face so abruptly that his head nearly came into collision with Mr. Crisparkle's: "What should you say that our local friend was up to?"

The last passage he had been shown in the Diary returned on Mr. Crisparkle's mind with the force of a strong recoil, and he asked Mr. Grewgious if he thought it possible that Neville was to be harassed by the keeping of a watch upon him?

"A watch," repeated Mr. Grewgious, musingly. "Ay!"

"Which would not only of itself haunt and torture his life," said Mr. Crisparkle, warmly, "but would expose him to the torment of a perpetually reviving suspicion, whatever he might do, or wherever he might go?"

"Ay!" said Mr. Grewgious, musingly still. "Do I see him waiting for you?"

"No doubt you do."

"Then *would* you have the goodness to excuse my getting up to see you out, and to go out to join him, and to go the way that you were going, and to take no notice of our local friend?" said Mr. Grewgious. "I entertain a sort of fancy for having *him* under my eye to-night, do you know?"

Mr. Crisparkle, with a significant nod, complied, and, rejoining Neville, went away with him. They dined together, and parted at the yet unfinished and undeveloped railway station: Mr. Crisparkle to get home; Neville to walk the streets, cross the bridges, make a wide round of the city in the friendly darkness, and tire himself out.

It was midnight when he returned from his solitary expedition, and climbed his staircase. The night was hot, and the windows of the staircase were all wide open. Coming to the top, it gave him a passing chill of surprise (there being no rooms but his up there) to find a stranger sitting on the window-sill, more after the manner of a venturesome glazier than an amateur ordinarily careful of his neck; in fact, so much more outside the window than inside, as to suggest the thought that he must have come up by the water-spout instead of the stairs.

The stranger said nothing until Neville put his key in his door; then, seeming to make sure of his identity from the action, he spoke:

"I beg your pardon," he said, coming from the window with a frank and smiling air, and a prepossessing address; "the beans."

Neville was quite at a loss.

"Runners," said the visitor. "Scarlet. Next door at the back."

"Oh!" returned Neville. "And the mignonette and wallflower?"

"The same," said the visitor.

"Pray walk in."

"Thank you."

Neville lighted his candles, and the visitor sat down. A handsome gentleman, with a young face, but an older figure in its robustness and its breadth of shoulder; say a man of eight-and-twenty, or at the utmost thirty: so extremely sunburnt that the contrast between his brown visage and the white forehead shaded out of doors by his hat, and the glimpses of white throat below the neckerchief, would have been almost ludicrous but for his broad temples, bright blue eyes, clustering brown hair, and laughing teeth.

"I have noticed," said he; "—my name is Tartar."

Neville inclined his head.

"I have noticed (excuse me) that you shut yourself up a good deal, and that you seem to like my garden aloft here. If you would like a little more of it, I could throw out a few lines and stays between my windows and yours, which the runners would take to directly. And I have some boxes, both of mignonette and wallflower, that I could shove on along the gutter (with a boat-hook I have by me) to your windows, and draw back again when they wanted watering or gardening, and shove on again when they were ship-shape, so that they would cause you no trouble. I couldn't take this liberty without asking your permission, so I venture to ask it. Tartar, corresponding set, next door."

"You are very kind."

"Not at all. I ought to apologise for looking in so late. But having noticed (excuse me) that you generally walk out at night, I thought I should inconvenience you least by awaiting your return. I am always afraid of inconveniencing busy men, being an idle man."

"I should not have thought so, from your appearance."

"No? I take it as a compliment. In fact, I was bred in the Royal Navy and was First Lieutenant when I quitted it. But, an uncle disappointed in the service leaving me his property on condition that I left the Navy, I accepted the fortune and resigned my commission."

"Lately, I presume?"

"Well, I had had twelve or fifteen years of knocking about first. I came here some nine months before you; I had had one crop before you came. I chose this place, because, having served last in a little Corvette, I knew I should feel more at home where I had a constant opportunity of knocking my head against the ceiling. Besides; it would never do for a man who had been aboard ship from his boyhood to turn luxurious all at once. Besides, again: having been accustomed to a very short allowance of land all my life, I thought I'd feel my way to the command of a landed estate, by beginning in boxes."

Whimsically as this was said, there was a touch of merry earnestness in it that made it doubly whimsical.

"However," said the Lieutenant, "I have talked quite enough about myself. It is not my way I hope; it has merely been to present myself to you naturally. If you will allow me to take the liberty I have described, it will be a charity, for it will give me something more to do. And you are not to suppose that it will entail any interruption or intrusion on you, for that is far from my intention."

Neville replied that he was greatly obliged, and that he thankfully accepted the kind proposal.

"I am very glad to take your windows in tow," said the Lieutenant. "From what I have seen of you when I have been gardening at mine, and you have been looking on, I have thought you (excuse me) rather too studious and delicate! May I ask, is your health at all affected?"

"I have undergone some mental distress," said Neville, confused, "which has stood me in the stead of illness."

"Pardon me," said Mr. Tartar.

With the greatest delicacy he shifted his ground to the windows again, and asked if he could look at one of them. On Neville's opening it, he immediately sprang out, as if he were going aloft with a whole watch in an emergency, and were setting a bright example.

"For Heaven's sake!" cried Neville, "don't do that! Where are you going, Mr. Tartar? You'll be dashed to pieces!"

"All well!" said the Lieutenant, coolly looking about him on the housetop. "All taut and trim here. Those lines and stays shall be rigged before you turn out in the morning. May I take this short cut home and say, Good-night?"

"Mr. Tartar!" urged Neville. "Pray! It makes me giddy to see you!"

But Mr. Tartar, with a wave of his hand and the deftness of a cat, had already dipped through his scuttle of scarlet runners without breaking a leaf, and "gone below."

Mr. Grewgious, his bedroom window-blind held aside with his hand, happened at that moment to have Neville's chambers under his eye for the last time that night. Fortunately his eye was on the front of the house and not the back, or this remarkable appearance and disappearance might have broken his rest as a phenomenon. But, Mr. Grewgious seeing nothing there, not even a light in the windows, his gaze wandered from the windows to the stars, as if he would have read in them something that was hidden from him. Many of us would if we could; but none of us so much as know our letters in the stars yet—or seem likely to do it, in this state of existence—and few languages can be read until their alphabets are mastered.

CHAPTER XVIII

A SETTLER IN CLOISTERHAM

AT about this time, a stranger appeared in Cloisterham; a white-haired personage with black eyebrows. Being buttoned up in a tight-ish blue surtout, with a buff waistcoat and grey trousers, he had something of a military air; but he announced himself at the Crozier (the orthodox hotel, where he put up with a portmanteau) as an idle dog who lived upon his means; and he further announced that he had a mind to take a lodging in the picturesque old city for a month or two, with a view of settling down there altogether. Both announcements were made in the coffee-room of the Crozier, to all whom it might, or might not, concern, by the stranger as he stood with his back to the empty fireplace, waiting for his fried sole, veal cutlet, and pint of sherry; and the waiter (business being chronically slack at the Crozier) represented all whom it might or might not concern, and absorbed the whole of the information.

This gentleman's white head was unusually large, and his shock of white hair was unusually thick and ample. "I suppose, waiter," he said, shaking his shock of hair, as a Newfoundland dog might shake his before sitting down to dinner, "that a fair lodging for a single buffer might be found in these parts, eh?"

The waiter had no doubt of it.

"Something old," said the gentleman. "Take my hat down for a moment from that peg, will you? No, I don't want it; look into it. What do you see written there?"

The waiter read: "Datchery."

"Now you know my name," said the gentleman; "Dick Datchery. Hang it up again. I was saying something old is what I should prefer, something odd and out of the way; something venerable, architectural, and inconvenient."

"We have a good choice of inconvenient lodgings in the town, sir, I think," replied the waiter, with modest confidence in its resources that way; "indeed, I have no doubt that we could suit you that far, however particular you might be. But an architectural lodging!" That seemed to trouble the waiter's head, and he shook it.

"Anything Cathedraly now," Mr. Datchery suggested.

"Mr. Tope," said the waiter, brightening, as he rubbed his chin with his hand, "would be the likeliest party to inform in that line."

"Who is Mr. Tope?" inquired Dick Datchery.

The waiter explained that he was the Verger, and that Mrs. Tope had indeed once upon a time let lodgings herself—or offered to let them; but that as nobody had ever taken them, Mrs. Tope's window-bill, long a Cloisterham Institution, had disappeared; probably had tumbled down one day, and never been put up again.

"I'll call on Mrs. Tope," said Mr. Datchery, "after dinner."

So when he had done his dinner, he was duly directed to the spot, and sallied out for it. But the Crozier being an hotel of a most retiring disposition, and the waiter's directions being fatally precise,

390

he soon became bewildered, and went boggling about and about the Cathedral Tower, whenever he could catch a glimpse of it, with a general impression on his mind that Mrs. Tope's was somewhere very near it, and that, like the children in the game of hot boiled beans and very good butter, he was warm in his search when he saw the Tower, and cold when he didn't see it.

He was getting very cold indeed when he came upon a fragment of burial-ground in which an unhappy sheep was grazing. Unhappy, because a hideous small boy was stoning it through the railings, and had already lamed it in one leg, and was much excited by the benevolent sportsmanlike purpose of breaking its other three legs, and bringing it down.

" 'It 'im agin!" cried the boy, as the poor creature leaped; "and made a dint in his wool!"

"Let him be!" said Mr. Datchery. "Don't you see you have lamed him?"

"Yer lie," returned the sportsman. " 'E went and lamed 'isself. I see 'im do it, and I giv' 'im a shy as a Widdy-warning to 'im not to go a bruisin' 'is master's mutton any more."

"Come here."

"I won't; I'll come when yer can ketch me."

"Stay there then, and show me which is Mr. Tope's."

" 'Ow can I stay here and show you which is Topeseses, when Topeseses is t'other side the Kinfreederal, and over the crossings, and round ever so many corners? Stoo-pid! Ya-a-ah!"

"Show me where it is, and I'll give you something."

391

"Come on, then!"

This brisk dialogue concluded, the boy led the way, and by-and-by stopped at some distance from an arched passage, pointing.

"Lookie yonder. You see that there winder and door?"

"That's Tope's?"

"Yer lie; it ain't. That's Jarsper's."

"Indeed?" said Mr. Datchery, with a second look of some interest.

"Yes, and I ain't agoin no nearer 'IM, I tell yer."

"Why not?"

"'Cos I ain't a going to be lifted off my legs and 'ave my braces bust and be choked; not if I knows it and not by 'Im. Wait till I set a jolly good flint a flyin at the back o' 'is jolly old 'ed some day! Now look t'other side the harch; not the side where Jarsper's door is; t'other side."

"I see."

"A little way in, o' that side, there's a low door, down two steps. That's Topeseses with 'is name on a hoval plate."

"Good. See here," said Mr. Datchery, producing a shilling. "You owe me half of this."

"Yer lie; I don't owe yer nothing; I never seen yer."

"I tell you you owe me half of this, because I have no sixpence in my pocket. So the next time you meet me you shall do something else for me, to pay me."

"All right, give us 'old."

"What is your name, and where do you live?"

"Deputy. Travellers' Twopenny, 'cross the green."

The boy instantly darted off with the shilling, lest Mr. Datchery should repent, but stopped at a safe distance, on the happy chance of his being uneasy in his mind about it, to goad him with a demon dance expressive of its irrevocability.

Mr. Datchery, taking off his hat to give that shock of white hair of his another shake, seemed quite resigned, and betook himself whither he had been directed.

Mr. Tope's official dwelling, communicating by an upper stair with Mr. Jasper's (hence Mrs. Tope's attendance on that gentleman), was of very modest proportions, and partook of the character of a cool dungeon. Its ancient walls were massive and its rooms rather seemed to have been dug out of them, than to have been designed beforehand with any reference to them. The main door opened at once on a chamber of no describable shape, with a groined roof, which in its turn opened on another chamber of no describable shape, with another groined roof: their windows small, and in the thickness of the walls. These two chambers, close as to their atmosphere and swarthy as to their illumination by natural light, were the apartments which Mrs. Tope had so long offered to an unappreciative city. Mr. Datchery, however, was more appreciative. He found that if he sat with the main door open he would enjoy the passing society of all comers to and fro by the gateway, and would have light enough. He found that if Mr. and Mrs. Tope, living overhead, used for their own egress and ingress a little side stair that came plump into the Precincts by a door opening outward, to the surprise and inconvenience of a limited public of pedestrians in a narrow way, he would be alone, as in a separate residence. He found the rent moderate, and everything as quaintly inconvenient as he could desire. He agreed therefore to take the lodging then and there, and money down, possession to be had next evening on condition that reference was permitted him to Mr. Jasper as occupying the Gate House, of which, on the other side of the gateway the Verger's hole in the wall was an appanage or subsidiary part.

The poor dear gentleman was very solitary and very sad, Mrs. Tope said, but she had no doubt he would "speak for her." Perhaps Mr. Datchery had heard something of what had occurred there last winter?

Mr. Datchery had as confused a knowledge of the event in question, on trying to recall it, as he well could have. He begged Mrs. Tope's pardon when she found it incumbent on her to correct him in every detail of his summary of the facts, but pleaded that he was merely a single buffer getting through life upon his means as idly as he could, and that so many people were so constantly making away with so many other people, as to render it difficult for a buffer of an easy temper to preserve the circumstances of the several cases unmixed in his mind.

Mr. Jasper proving willing to speak for Mrs. Tope, Mr. Datchery, who had sent up his card, was invited to ascend the postern staircase. The Mayor was there, Mrs. Tope said; but he was not to be regarded in the light of company, as he and Mr. Jasper were great friends.

394

"I beg pardon," said Mr. Datchery, making a leg with his hat under his arm, as he addressed himself equally to both gentlemen; "a selfish precaution on my part and not personally interesting to anybody but myself. But as a buffer living on his means, and having an idea of doing it in this lovely place in peace and quiet, for remaining span of life, beg to ask if the Tope family are quite respectable?"

Mr. Jasper could answer for that without the slightest hesitation.

"That is enough, sir," said Mr. Datchery.

"My friend the Mayor," added Mr. Jasper, presenting Mr. Datchery with a courtly motion of his hand towards that potentate; "whose recommendation is actually much more important to a stranger than that of an obscure person like myself, will testify in their behalf, I am sure."

"The Worshipful the Mayor," said Mr. Datchery, with a low bow, "places me under an infinite obligation."

"Very good people, sir, Mr. and Mrs. Tope," said Mr. Sapsea, with condescension. "Very good opinions. Very well behaved. Very respectful. Much approved by the Dean and Chapter."

"The Worshipful the Mayor gives them a character," said Mr. Datchery, "of which they may indeed be proud. I would ask His Honor (if I might be permitted) whether there are not many objects of great interest in the city which is under his beneficent sway?"

"We are, sir," returned Mr. Sapsea, "an ancient city, and an ecclesiastical city. We are a constitutional city, as it becomes such a city to be, and we uphold and maintain our glorious privileges."

"His Honor," said Mr. Datchery, bowing, "inspires me with a desire to know more of the city, and confirms me in my inclination to end my days in the city."

"Retired from the Army, sir?" suggested Mr. Sapsea.

"His Honor the Mayor does me too much credit," returned Mr. Datchery.

"Navy, sir?" suggested Mr. Sapsea.

"Again," repeated Mr. Datchery, "His Honor the Mayor does me too much credit."

"Diplomacy is a fine profession," said Mr. Sapsea, as a general remark.

"There, I confess, His Honor the Mayor is too many for me," said Mr. Datchery, with an ingenuous smile and bow; "even a diplomatic bird must fall to such a gun."

Now, this was very soothing. Here was a gentleman of a great—not to say a grand—address, accustomed to rank and dignity, really setting a fine example how to behave to a Mayor. There was something in that third-person style of being spoken to, that Mr. Sapsea found particularly recognisant of his merits and position.

"But I crave pardon," said Mr. Datchery. "His Honor the Mayor will bear with me, if for a moment I have been deluded into occupying his time, and have forgotten the humble claims upon my own, of my hotel, the Crozier."

"Not at all, sir," said Mr. Sapsea. "I am returning home, and if you would like to take the exterior of our cathedral in your way, I shall be glad to point it out."

"His Honor the Mayor," said Mr. Datchery, "is more than kind and gracious."

As Mr. Datchery, when he had made his acknowledgments to Mr. Jasper, could not be induced to go out of the room before the Worshipful, the Worshipful led the way down stairs; Mr. Datchery following with his hat under his arm, and his shock of white hair streaming in the evening breeze.

"Might I ask His Honor," said Mr. Datchery, "whether that gentleman we have just left is the gentleman of whom I have heard in the neighbourhood as being much afflicted by the loss of a nephew, and concentrating his life on avenging the loss?"

"That is the gentleman. John Jasper, sir."

"Would His Honor allow me to inquire whether there are strong suspicions of any one?"

"More than suspicions, sir," returned Mr. Sapsea, "all but certainties."

"Only think now!" cried Mr. Datchery.

"But proof, sir, proof, must be built up stone by stone," said the Mayor. "As I say, the end crowns the work. It is not enough that Justice should be morally certain; she must be immorally certain—legally, that is."

"His Honor," said Mr. Datchery, "reminds me of the nature of the law. Immoral. How true!"

"As I say, sir," pompously went on the Mayor, "the arm of the law is a strong arm, and a long arm. That is the way *I* put it. A strong arm and a long arm."

"How forcible!——And yet, again, how true!" murmured Mr. Datchery.

"And without betraying what I call the secrets of the prison-house," said Mr. Sapsea; "the secrets of the prison-house is the term I used on the bench."

"And what other term than His Honor's would express it?" said Mr. Datchery.

"Without, I say, betraying them, I predict to you, knowing the iron will of the gentleman we have just left (I take the bold step of calling it iron, on account of its strength), that in this case the long arm will reach, and the strong arm will strike.——This is our cathedral, sir. The best judges are pleased to admire it, and the best among our townsmen own to being a little vain of it."

All this time Mr. Datchery had walked with his hat under his arm, and his white hair streaming. He had an odd momentary appearance upon him of having forgotten his hat, when Mr. Sapsea now touched it; and he clapped his hand up to his head as if with some vague expectation of finding another hat upon it.

"Pray be covered, sir," entreated Mr. Sapsea; magnificently implying: "I shall not mind it, I assure you."

"His Honor is very good, but I do it for coolness," said Mr. Datchery.

Then Mr. Datchery admired the cathedral, and Mr. Sapsea pointed it out as if he himself had invented and built it; there were a few details indeed of which he did not approve, but those he glossed over, as if the workmen had made mistakes in his absence. The cathedral disposed of, he led the way by the churchyard, and stopped to extol the beauty of the evening—by chance—in the immediate vicinity of Mrs. Sapsea's epitaph.

"And by-the-by," said Mr. Sapsea, appearing to descend from an elevation to remember it all of a sudden; like Apollo shooting down from Olympus to pick up his forgotten lyre; "*that* is one of our small lions. The partiality of our people has made it so, and strangers have been seen taking a copy of it now and then. I am not a judge of it myself, for it is a little work of my own. But it was troublesome to turn, sir; I may say, difficult to turn with elegance."

Mr. Datchery became so ecstatic over Mr. Sapsea's composition that, in spite of his intention to end his days in Cloisterham, and therefore his probably having in reserve many opportunities of copying it, he would have transcribed it into his pocket-book on the spot, but for the slouching towards them of its material producer and perpetuator, Durdles, whom Mr. Sapsea hailed, not sorry to show him a bright example of behaviour to superiors.

"Ah, Durdles! This is the mason, sir; one of our Cloisterham worthies; everybody here knows Durdles. Mr. Datchery, Durdles; a gentleman who is going to settle here."

"I wouldn't do it if I was him," growled Durdles. "We're a heavy lot."

"You surely don't speak for yourself, Mr. Durdles," returned Mr. Datchery, "any more than for His Honor."

"Who's His Honor?" demanded Durdles.

"His Honor the Mayor."

"I never was brought afore him," said Durdles, with anything but the look of a loyal subject of the mayoralty, "and it'll be time enough for me to Honor him when I am. Until which, and when, and where:

> "Mister Sapsea is his name,
> England is his nation,
> Cloisterham's his dwelling-place,
> Aukshneer's his occupation."

Here, Deputy (preceded by a flying oyster-shell) appeared upon the scene, and requested to have the sum of threepence instantly "chucked" to him by Mr. Durdles, whom he had been vainly seeking up and down, as lawful wages overdue. While that gentleman, with his bundle under his arm, slowly found and counted out the money, Mr. Sapsea informed the new settler of Durdles's habits, pursuits, abode, and reputation. "I suppose a curious stranger might come to see you, and your works, Mr. Durdles, at any odd time?" said Mr. Datchery upon that.

"Any gentleman is welcome to come and see me any evening if he brings liquor for two with him," returned Durdles, with a penny between his teeth and certain halfpence in his hands. "Or if he likes to make it twice two, he'll be doubly welcome."

"I shall come. Master Deputy, what do you owe me?"

"A job."

"Mind you pay me honestly with the job of showing me Mr. Durdles's house when I want to go there."

Deputy, with a piercing broadside of whistle through the whole gap in his mouth, as a receipt in full for all arrears, vanished.

The Worshipful and the Worshipper then passed on together until they parted, with many ceremonies, at the Worshipful's door; even then, the Worshipper carried his hat under his arm, and gave his streaming white hair to the breeze.

Said Mr. Datchery to himself that night, as he looked at his white hair in the gas-lighted looking-glass over the coffee-room chimneypiece at the Crozier, and shook it out: "For a single buffer, of an easy temper, living idly on his means, I have had a rather busy afternoon!"

CHAPTER XIX

SHADOW ON THE SUN-DIAL

AGAIN Miss Twinkleton has delivered her valedictory address, with the accompaniments of white wine and pound cake, and again the young ladies have departed to their several homes. Helena Landless has left the Nuns' House to attend her brother's fortunes, and pretty Rosa is alone.

Cloisterham is so bright and sunny in these summer days, that the cathedral and the monastery-ruin show as if their strong walls were transparent. A soft glow seems to shine from within them, rather than upon them from without, such is their mellowness as they look forth on the hot corn-fields and the smoking roads that distantly wind among them. The Cloisterham gardens blush with ripening fruit. Time was when travel-stained pilgrims rode in clattering parties through the city's welcome shades; time is when wayfarers, leading a gipsy life between haymaking time and harvest, and looking as if they were just made of the dust of the earth, so very dusty are they, lounge about on cool doorsteps, trying to mend their unmendable shoes, or giving them to the city kennels as a hopeless job, and seeking others in the bundles that they carry, along with their yet unused sickles swathed in bands of straw. At all the more public pumps there is much cooling of bare feet, together with much bubbling and gurgling of drinking with hand to spout on the part of these Bedouins; the Cloisterham police meanwhile looking askant from their beats with suspicion, and manifest impatience that the intruders should depart from within the civic bounds, and once more fry themselves on the simmering highroads.

· On the afternoon of such a day, when the last cathedral service is done, and when that side of the High Street on which the Nuns' House stands is in grateful shade, save where its quaint old garden opens to the west between the boughs of trees, a servant informs Rosa, to her terror, that Mr. Jasper desires to see her.

If he had chosen his time for finding her at a disadvantage, he could have done no better. Perhaps he has chosen it. Helena Landless is gone, Mrs. Tisher is absent on leave, Miss Twinkleton (in her amateur state of existence) has contributed herself and a veal pie to a picnic.

"Oh why, why, why, did you say I was at home!" cries Rosa, helplessly.

The maid replies, that Mr. Jasper never asked the question. That he said he knew she was at home, and begged she might be told that he asked to see her.

"What shall I do, what shall I do?" thinks Rosa, clasping her hands.

Possessed by a kind of desperation, she adds in the next breath that she will come to Mr. Jasper in the garden. She shudders at the thought of being shut up with him in the house; but many of its windows command the garden, and she can be seen as well as heard there, and can shriek in the free air and run away. Such is the wild idea that flutters through her mind.

She has never seen him since the fatal night, except when she was questioned before the Mayor, and then he was present in gloomy watchfulness, as representing his lost nephew and burning to avenge him. She hangs her garden-hat on her arm, and goes out. The moment she sees him from the porch, leaning on the sun-dial, the old horrible feeling of being compelled by him, asserts its hold upon her. She feels that she would even then go back, but that he draws her feet towards him. She cannot resist, and sits down, with her head bent, on the garden-seat beside the sun-dial. She cannot look up at him for abhorrence, but she has perceived that he is dressed in deep mourning. So is she. It was not so at first; but the lost has long been given up, and mourned for, as dead.

He would begin by touching her hand. She feels the intention and draws her hand back. His eyes are then fixed upon her, she knows, though her own see nothing but the grass.

"I have been waiting," he begins, "for some time, to be summoned back to my duty near you."

After several times forming her lips, which she knows he is closely watching, into the shape of some other hesitating reply, and then into none, she answers: "Duty, sir?"

"The duty of teaching you, serving you as your faithful musicmaster."

"I have left off that study."

"Not left off, I think. Discontinued. I was told by your guardian that you discontinued it under the shock that we have all felt so acutely. When will you resume?"

"Never, sir."

"Never? You could have done no more if you had loved my dear boy."

"I did love him!" cries Rosa, with a flash of anger.

"Yes; but not quite—not quite in the right way, shall I say? Not in the intended and expected way. Much as my dear boy was, unhappily, too self-conscious and self-satisfied (I'll draw no parallel between him and you in that respect) to love as he should have loved, or as any one in his place would have loved—must have loved!"

She sits in the same still attitude, but shrinking a little more.

"Then, to be told that you discontinued your study with me, was to be politely told that you abandoned it altogether?" he suggested.

"Yes," says Rosa, with sudden spirit. "The politeness was my guardian's, not mine. I told him that I was resolved to leave off, and that I was determined to stand by my resolution."

"And you still are?"

"I still am, sir. And I beg not to be questioned any more about it. At all events, I will not answer any more; I have that in my power."

She is so conscious of his looking at her with a gloating admiration of the touch of anger on her, and the fire and animation it brings with it, that even as her spirit rises, it falls again, and she struggles with a sense of shame, affront, and fear, much as she did that night at the piano.

"I will not question you any more, since you object to it so much; I will confess."

"I do not wish to hear you, sir," cries Rosa, rising.

This time he does touch her with his outstretched hand. In shrinking from it, she shrinks into her seat again.

"We must sometimes act in opposition to our wishes," he tells her in a low voice. "You must do so now, or do more harm to others than you can ever set right."

"What harm?"

"Presently, presently. You question *me*, you see, and surely that's not fair when you forbid me to question you. Nevertheless, I will answer the question presently. Dearest Rosa! Charming Rosa!"

She starts up again.

This time he does not touch her. But his face looks so wicked and menacing, as he stands leaning against the sun-dial—setting, as it were, his black mark upon the very face of day—that her flight is arrested by horror as she looks at him.

"I do not forget how many windows command a view of us," he says, glancing towards them. "I will not touch you again, I will come no nearer to you than I am. Sit down, and there will be no mighty wonder in your music-master's leaning idly against a pedestal and speaking with you, remembering all that has happened and our shares in it. Sit down, my beloved."

She would have gone once more—was all but gone—and once more his face, darkly threatening what would follow if she went, has stopped her. Looking at him with the expression of the instant frozen on her face, she sits down on the seat again.

"Rosa, even when my dear boy was affianced to you, I loved you madly; even when I thought his happiness in having you for his wife was certain, I loved you madly; even when I strove to make him more ardently devoted to you, I loved you madly; even when he gave me the picture of your lovely face so carelessly traduced by him, which I feigned to hang always in my sight for his sake, but worshipped in torment for years, I loved you madly. In the distasteful work of the day, in the wakeful misery of the night, girded by sordid realities, or wandering through Paradises and Hells of visions into which I rushed, carrying your image in my arms, I loved you madly."

If anything could make his words more hideous to her than they are in themselves, it would be the contrast between the violence of his look and delivery, and the composure of his assumed attitude.

"I endured it all in silence. So long as you were his, or so long as I supposed you to be his, I hid my secret loyally. Did I not?"

This lie, so gross, while the mere words in which it is told are so true, is more than Rosa can endure. She answers with kindling indignation: "You were as false throughout, sir, as you are now. You were false to him, daily and hourly. You know that you made my life unhappy by your pursuit of me. You know that you made me afraid to open his generous eyes, and that you forced me, for his own trusting, good, good sake, to keep the truth from him, that you were a bad, bad man!"

His preservation of his easy attitude rendering his working features and his convulsive hands absolutely diabolical, he returns, with a fierce extreme of admiration:

"How beautiful you are! You are more beautiful in anger than in repose. I don't ask you for your love; give me yourself and your hatred; give me yourself and that pretty rage; give me yourself and that enchanting scorn; it will be enough for me."

Impatient tears rise to the eyes of the trembling little beauty, and her face flames; but as she again rises to leave him in indignation, and seek protection within the house, he stretches out his hand towards the porch, as though he invited her to enter it.

"I told you, you rare charmer, you sweet witch, that you must stay and hear me, or do more harm than can ever be undone. You asked me what harm. Stay, and I will tell you. Go, and I will do it!"

Again Rosa quails before his threatening face, though innocent of its meaning, and she remains. Her panting breathing comes and goes as if it would choke her; but with a repressive hand upon her bosom, she remains.

"I have made my confession that my love is mad. It is so mad that, had the ties between me and my dear lost boy been one silken thread less strong, I might have swept even him from your side when you favored him."

A film comes over the eyes she raises for an instant, as though he had turned her faint.

"Even him," he repeats. "Yes, even him! Rosa, you see me and you hear me. Judge for yourself whether any other admirer shall love you and live, whose life is in my hand."

"What do you mean, sir?"

"I mean to show you how mad my love is. It was hawked through the late inquiries by Mr. Crisparkle, that young Landless had confessed to him that he was a rival of my lost boy. That is an inexpiable offence in my eyes. The same Mr. Crisparkle knows under my hand that I have devoted myself to the murderer's discovery and destruction, be he who he might, and that I determined to discuss the mystery with no one until I should hold the clue in which to entangle the murderer as in a net. I have since worked patiently to wind and wind it round him; and it is slowly winding as I speak."

"Your belief, if you believe in the criminality of Mr. Landless, is not Mr. Crisparkle's belief, and he is a good man," Rosa retorts.

"My belief is my own; and I reserve it, worshipped of my soul! Circumstances may accumulate so strongly *even against an innocent man*, that, directed, sharpened, and pointed, they may slay him. One wanting link discovered by perseverance against a guilty man, proves his guilt, however slight its evidence before, and he dies. Young Landless stands in deadly peril either way."

"If you really suppose," Rosa pleads with him, turning paler, "that I favor Mr. Landless, or that Mr. Landless has ever in any way addressed himself to me, you are wrong."

He puts that from him with a slighting action of his hand and a curled lip.

"I was going to show you how madly I love you. More madly now than ever, for I am willing to renounce the second object that has arisen in my life to divide it with you; and henceforth to have no object in existence but you only. Miss Landless has become your bosom friend. You care for her peace of mind?"

"I love her dearly."

"You care for her good name?"

"I have said, sir, I love her dearly."

"I am unconsciously," he observes, with a smile, as he folds his hands upon the sun-dial and leans his chin upon them, so that his talk would seem from the windows (faces occasionally come and go there) to be of the airiest and playfulest: "I am unconsciously giving offence by questioning again. I will simply make statements, therefore, and not put questions. You do care for your bosom friend's good name, and you do care for her peace of mind. Then remove the shadow of the gallows from her, dear one!"

"You dare propose to me———"

"Darling, I dare propose to you. Stop there. If it be bad to idolize you, I am the worst of men; if it be good, I am the best. My love for you is above all other love, and my truth to you is above all other truth. Let me have hope and favor, and I am a forsworn man for your sake."

Rosa puts her hands to her temples, and, pushing back her hair, looks wildly and abhorrently at him, as though she were trying to piece together what it is his deep purpose to present to her only in fragments.

"Reckon up nothing at this moment, angel, but the sacrifices that I lay at those dear feet, which I could fall down among the vilest ashes and kiss, and put upon my head as a poor savage might. There is my fidelity to my dear boy after death. Tread upon it!"

With an action of his hands, as though he cast down something precious.

"There is the inexpiable offence against my adoration of you. Spurn it!"

With a similar action.

"There are my labors in the cause of a just vengeance for six toiling months. Crush them!"

With another repetition of the action.

"There is my past and my present wasted life. There is the desolation of my heart and my soul. There is my peace; there is my despair. Stamp them into the dust, so that you take me, were it even mortally hating me!"

The frightful vehemence of the man, now reaching its full height, so additionally terrifies her as to break the spell that has held her to the spot. She swiftly moves towards the porch; but in an instant he is at her side, and speaking in her ear.

"Rosa, I am self-repressed again. I am walking calmly beside you to the house. I shall wait for some encouragement and hope. I shall not strike too soon. Give me a sign that you attend to me."

She slightly and constrainedly moves her hand.

"Not a word of this to any one, or it will bring down the blow, as certainly as night follows day. Another sign that you attend to me."

She moves her hand once more.

"I love you, love you, love you. If you were to cast me off now—but you will not—you would never be rid of me. No one should come between us. I would pursue you to the death."

The handmaid coming out to open the gate for him, he quietly pulls off his hat as a parting salute, and goes away with no greater show of agitation than is visible in the effigy of Mrs. Sapsea's father opposite. Rosa faints in going up-stairs, and is carefully carried to her room, and laid down on her bed. A thunderstorm is coming on, the maids say, and the hot and stifling air has overset the pretty dear; no wonder; they have felt their own knees all of a tremble all day long.

CHAPTER XX

DIVERS FLIGHTS

ROSA no sooner came to herself than the whole of the late interview was before her. It even seemed as if it had pursued her into her insensibility, and she had not had a moment's unconsciousness of it. What to do, she was at a frightened loss to know: the only one clear thought in her mind, was, that she must fly from this terrible man.

But where could she take refuge, and how could she go? She had never breathed her dread of him to any one but Helena. If she went to Helena, and told her what had passed, that very act might bring down the irreparable mischief that he threatened he had the power, and that she knew he had the will, to do. The more fearful he appeared to her excited memory and imagination, the more alarming her responsibility appeared: seeing that a slight mistake on her part, either in action or delay, might let his malevolence loose on Helena's brother.

Rosa's mind throughout the last six months had been stormily confused. A half-formed, wholly unexpressed suspicion tossed in it, now heaving itself up, and now sinking into the deep; now gaining palpability, and now losing it. Jasper's self-absorption in his nephew when he was alive, and his unceasing pursuit of the inquiry how he came by his death, if he were dead, were themes so rife in the place,

413

that no one appeared able to suspect the possibility of foul play at his hands. She had asked herself the question, "Am I so wicked in my thoughts as to conceive a wickedness that others cannot imagine?" Then she had considered, Did the suspicion come of her previous recoiling from him before the fact? And if so, was not that a proof of its baselessness? Then she had reflected, "What motive could he have, according to my accusation?" She was ashamed to answer in her mind, "The motive of gaining *me*!" And covered her face, as if the lightest shadow of the idea of founding murder on such an idle vanity were a crime almost as great.

She ran over in her mind again, all that he had said by the sun-dial in the garden. He had persisted in treating the disappearance as murder, consistently with his whole public course since the finding of the watch and shirt-pin. If he were afraid of the crime being traced out, would he not rather encourage the idea of a voluntary disappearance? He had even declared that if the ties between him and his nephew had been less strong, he might have swept "even him" away from her side. Was that like his having really done so? He had spoken of laying his six months' labours in the cause of a just vengeance at her feet. Would he have done that, with that violence of passion, if they were a pretence? Would he have ranged them with his desolate heart and soul, his wasted life, his peace, and his despair? The very first sacrifice that he represented himself as making for her, was his fidelity to his dear boy after death. Surely these facts were strong against a fancy that scarcely dared to hint itself. And yet he was so terrible a man! In short, the poor girl (for what could she know of the criminal intellect, which its own professed students perpetually misread, because they persist in trying to reconcile it with the average intellect of average men, instead of identifying it as a horrible wonder apart), could get by no road to any other conclusion than that he *was* a terrible man, and must be fled from.

She had been Helena's stay and comfort during the whole time. She had constantly assured her of her full belief in her brother's innocence, and of her sympathy with him in his misery. But she had never seen him since the disappearance, nor had Helena ever spoken one word of his avowal to Mr. Crisparkle in regard of Rosa, though as a part of the interest of the case it was well known far and wide. He was Helena's unfortunate brother, to her, and nothing more. The assurance she had given her odious suitor was strictly true, though it would have been better (she considered now) if she could have restrained herself from so giving it. Afraid of him as the bright and delicate little creature was, her spirit swelled at the thought of his knowing it from her own lips.

But where was she to go? Anywhere beyond his reach, was no reply to the question. Somewhere must be thought of. She determined to go to her guardian, and to go immediately. The feeling she had imparted to Helena on the night of their first confidence, was so strong upon her—the feeling of not being safe from him, and of the solid walls of the old convent being powerless to keep out his ghostly following of her—that no reasoning of her own could calm her terrors. The fascination of repulsion had been upon her so long, and now culminated so darkly, that she felt as if he had power to bind her by a spell. Glancing out at window, even now, as she rose to dress, the sight of the sun-dial on which he had leaned when he declared himself, turned her cold, and made her shrink from it, as though he had invested it with some awful quality from his own nature.

She wrote a hurried note to Miss Twinkleton, saying that she had sudden reason for wishing to see her guardian promptly, and had gone to him; also, entreating the good lady not to be uneasy, for all was well with her. She hurried a few quite useless articles into a very little bag, left the note in a conspicuous place, and went out, softly closing the gate after her.

It was the first time she had ever been in Cloisterham High Street alone. But knowing all its ways and windings very well, she hurried straight to the corner from which the omnibus departed. It was, at that very moment, going off.

"Stop and take me, if you please, Joe. I am obliged to go to London."

In less than another minute she was on her road to the railway, under Joe's protection. Joe waited on her when she got there, put her safely into the railway carriage, and handed in the very little bag after her, as though it were some enormous trunk, hundredweights heavy, which she must on no account endeavour to lift.

"Can you go round when you get back, and tell Miss Twinkleton that you saw me safely off, Joe?"

"It shall be done, Miss."

"With my love, please, Joe."

"Yes, Miss—and I wouldn't mind having it myself!" But Joe did not articulate the last clause; only thought it.

Now that she was whirling away for London in real earnest, Rosa was at leisure to resume the thoughts which her personal hurry had checked. The indignant thought that his declaration of love soiled her; that she could only be cleansed from the stain of its impurity by appealing to the honest and true; supported her for a time against her fears, and confirmed her in her hasty resolution. But as the evening grew darker and darker, and the great city impended nearer and nearer, the doubts usual in such cases began to arise. Whether this was not a wild proceeding after all; how Mr. Grewgious might regard it; whether she should find him at the journey's end; how she would act if he were absent; what might become of her, alone, in a place so strange and crowded; how if she had but waited and taken counsel first; whether, if she could now go back, she would not do it thankfully: a multitude of such uneasy speculations disturbed her, more and more as they accumulated. At length the train came into London over the housetops; and down below lay the gritty streets with their yet un-needed lamps aglow, on a hot light summer night.

"Hiram Grewgious, Esquire, Staple Inn, London." This was all

Rosa knew of her destination; but it was enough to send her rattling away again in a cab, through deserts of gritty streets, where
many people crowded at the corners of courts and byways to get
some air, and where many other people walked with a miserably
monotonous noise of shuffling feet on hot paving-stones, and
where all the people and all their surroundings were so gritty and
so shabby.

There was music playing here and there, but it did not enliven
the case. No barrel-organ mended the matter, and no big drum beat
dull care away. Like the chapel bells that were also going here and
there, they only seemed to evoke echoes from brick surfaces, and
dust from everything. As to the flat wind instruments, they seemed
to have cracked their hearts and souls in pining for the country.

Her jingling conveyance stopped at last at a fast-closed gateway
which appeared to belong to somebody who had gone to bed very
early, and was much afraid of housebreakers; Rosa, discharging her
conveyance, timidly knocked at this gateway, and was let in, very
little bag and all, by a watchman.

"Does Mr. Grewgious live here?"

"Mr. Grewgious lives there, Miss," said the watchman, pointing
further in.

So Rosa went further in, and, when the clocks were striking
ten, stood on P. J. T.'s doorstep, wondering what P. J. T. had done
with his street door.

Guided by the painted name of Mr. Grewgious, she went up-
stairs and softly tapped and tapped several times. But no one an-

swering, and Mr. Grewgious's door-handle yielding to her touch, she went in, and saw her guardian sitting on a window-seat at an open window, with a shaded lamp placed far from him on a table in a corner.

Rosa drew nearer to him in the twilight of the room. He saw her, and he said in an under-tone: "Good Heaven!"

Rosa fell upon his neck, with tears, and then he said, returning her embrace:

"My child, my child! I thought you were your mother!"

"But what, what, what," he added, soothingly, "has happened? My dear, what has brought you here? Who has brought you here?"

"No one. I came alone."

"Lord bless me!" ejaculated Mr. Grewgious. "Came alone! Why didn't you write to me to come and fetch you?"

"I had no time. I took a sudden resolution. Poor, poor Eddy!"

"Ah, poor fellow, poor fellow!"

"His uncle has made love to me. I cannot bear it," said Rosa, at once with a burst of tears, and a stamp of her little foot; "I shudder with horror of him, and I have come to you to protect me and all of us from him, if you will?"

"I will!" cried Mr. Grewgious, with a sudden rush of amazing energy. "Damn him!

> "Confound his politics,
> Frustrate his knavish tricks!
> On Thee his hopes to fix?
> Damn him again!"

After this most extraordinary outburst, Mr. Grewgious, quite beside himself, plunged about the room, to all appearance undecided whether he was in a fit of loyal enthusiasm, or combative denunciation.

He stopped and said, wiping his face: "I beg your pardon, my dear, but you will be glad to know I feel better. Tell me no more just now, or I might do it again. You must be refreshed and cheered. What did you take last? Was it breakfast, lunch, dinner, tea, or supper? And what will you take next? Shall it be breakfast, lunch, dinner, tea, or supper?"

The respectful tenderness with which, on one knee before her, he helped her to remove her hat, and disentangle her pretty hair from it, was quite a chivalrous sight. Yet who, knowing him only on the surface, would have expected chivalry—and of the true sort, too: not the spurious—from Mr. Grewgious?

"Your rest too must be provided for," he went on; "and you shall have the prettiest chamber in Furnival's. Your toilet must be provided for, and you shall have everything that an unlimited head chambermaid—by which expression I mean a head chambermaid not limited as to outlay—can procure. Is that a bag?" he looked hard at it; sooth to say, it required hard looking at to be seen at all in a dimly-lighted room: "and is it your property, my dear?"

"Yes, sir. I brought it with me."

"It is not an extensive bag," said Mr. Grewgious, candidly, "though admirably calculated to contain a day's provision for a canary bird. Perhaps you brought a canary bird?"

420

Rosa smiled, and shook her head.

"If you had he should have been made welcome," said Mr. Grewgious, "and I think he would have been pleased to be hung upon a nail outside and pit himself against our Staple sparrows; whose execution must be admitted to be not quite equal to their intention. Which is the case with so many of us! You didn't say what meal, my dear. Have a nice jumble of all meals."

Rosa thanked him, but said she could only take a cup of tea. Mr. Grewgious, after several times running out, and in again, to mention such supplementary items as marmalade, eggs, water-cresses, salted fish, and frizzled ham, ran across to Furnival's without his hat, to give his various directions. And soon afterwards they were realised in practice, and the board was spread.

"Lord bless my soul!" cried Mr. Grewgious, putting the lamp upon it, and taking his seat opposite Rosa; "what a new sensation for a poor old Angular bachelor, to be sure!"

Rosa's expressive little eyebrows asked him what he meant?

"The sensation of having a sweet young presence in the place that whitewashes it, paints it, papers it, decorates it with gilding, and makes it Glorious!" said Mr. Grewgious. "Ah me! Ah me!"

As there was something mournful in his sigh, Rosa, in touching him with his tea-cup, ventured to touch him with her small hand too.

"Thank you, my dear," said Mr. Grewgious. "Ahem! Let's talk."

"Do you always live here, sir?" asked Rosa.

"Yes, my dear."

"And always alone?"

"Always alone; except that I have daily company in a gentleman by the name of Bazzard; my clerk."

"*He* doesn't live here?"

"No, he goes his ways after office hours. In fact, he is off duty here, altogether, just at present; and a Firm down stairs with which I have business relations, lend me a substitute. But it would be extremely difficult to replace Mr. Bazzard."

"He must be very fond of you," said Rosa.

"He bears up against it with commendable fortitude if he is," returned Mr. Grewgious, after considering the matter. "But I doubt if he is. Not particularly so. You see, he is discontented, poor fellow."

"Why isn't he contented?" was the natural inquiry.

"Misplaced," said Mr. Grewgious, with great mystery.

Rosa's eyebrows resumed their inquisitive and perplexed expression.

"So misplaced," Mr. Grewgious went on, "that I feel constantly apologetic towards him. And he feels (though he doesn't mention it) that I have reason to be."

Mr. Grewgious had by this time grown so very mysterious, that Rosa did not know how to go on. While she was thinking about it Mr. Grewgious suddenly jerked out of himself for the second time:

"Let's talk. We were speaking of Mr. Bazzard. It's a secret, and moreover it is Mr. Bazzard's secret; but the sweet presence at my table makes me so unusually expansive, that I feel I must impart it in inviolable confidence. What do you think Mr. Bazzard has done?"

"Oh dear!" cried Rosa, drawing her chair a little nearer, and her mind reverting to Jasper, "nothing dreadful, I hope?"

"He has written a play," said Mr. Grewgious, in a solemn whisper. "A tragedy."

Rosa seemed much relieved.

"And nobody," pursued Mr. Grewgious in the same tone, "will hear, on any account whatever, of bringing it out."

Rosa looked reflective, and nodded her head slowly; as who should say: "Such things are, and why are they!"

"Now, you know," said Mr. Grewgious, "*I* couldn't write a play."

"Not a bad one, sir?" asked Rosa, innocently, with her eyebrows again in action.

"No. If I was under sentence of decapitation, and was about to be instantly decapitated, and an express arrived with a pardon for the condemned convict Grewgious if he wrote a play, I should be under the necessity of resuming the block and begging the executioner to proceed to extremities,—meaning," said Mr. Grewgious, passing his hand under his chin, "the singular number, and this extremity."

Rosa appeared to consider what she would do if the awkward supposititious case were hers.

"Consequently," said Mr. Grewgious, "Mr. Bazzard would have

a sense of my inferiority to himself under any circumstances; but when I am his master, you know the case is greatly aggravated."

Mr. Grewgious shook his head seriously, as if he felt the offence to be a little too much, though of his own committing.

"How came you to be his master, sir?" asked Rosa.

"A question that naturally follows," said Mr. Grewgious. "Let's talk. Mr. Bazzard's father, being a Norfolk farmer, would have furiously laid about him with a flail, a pitchfork, and every agricultural implement available for assaulting purposes, on the slightest hint of his son's having written a play. So the son, bringing to me the father's rent (which I receive), imparted his secret, and pointed out that he was determined to pursue his genius, and that it would put him in peril of starvation, and that he was not formed for it."

"For pursuing his genius, sir?"

"No, my dear," said Mr. Grewgious, "for starvation. It was impossible to deny the position that Mr. Bazzard was not formed to be starved, and Mr. Bazzard then pointed out that it was desirable that I should stand between him and a fate so perfectly unsuited to his formation. In that way Mr. Bazzard became my clerk, and he feels it very much."

"I am glad he is grateful," said Rosa.

"I didn't quite mean that, my dear. I mean that he feels the degradation. There are some other geniuses that Mr. Bazzard has become acquainted with, who have also written tragedies, which likewise nobody will on any account whatever hear of bringing out, and these choice spirits dedicate their plays to one another in a highly panegyrical manner. Mr. Bazzard has been the subject of one of these dedications. Now, you know, *I* never had a play dedicated to *me*!"

Rosa looked at him as if she would have liked him to be the recipient of a thousand dedications.

"Which again, naturally, rubs against the grain of Mr. Bazzard," said Mr. Grewgious. "He is very short with me sometimes, and then I feel that he is meditating 'This blockhead is my master! A fellow who couldn't write a tragedy on pain of death, and who will never have one dedicated to him with the most complimentary congratulations on the high position he has taken in the eyes of posterity!' I reflected beforehand: 'Perhaps he may not like this,' or 'He might take it ill if I asked that,' and so we get on very well. Indeed, better than I could have expected."

"Is the tragedy named, sir?" asked Rosa.

"Strictly between ourselves," answered Mr. Grewgious, "it has a dreadfully appropriate name. It is called The Thorn of Anxiety. But Mr. Bazzard hopes—and I hope—that it will come out at last."

It was not hard to divine that Mr. Grewgious had related the Bazzard history thus fully, at least quite as much for the recreation of his ward's mind from the subject that had driven her there, as for the gratification of his own tendency to be social and communicative. "And now, my dear," he said at this point, "if you are not too tired to tell me more of what passed to-day—but only if you feel quite able——I should be glad to hear it. I may digest it the better, if I sleep on it to-night."

Rosa, composed now, gave him a faithful account of the interview. Mr. Grewgious often smoothed his head while it was in progress, and begged to be told a second time those parts which bore on Helena and Neville. When Rosa had finished, he sat, grave, silent, and meditative, for a while.

"Clearly narrated," was his only remark at last, "and, I hope, clearly put away here," smoothing his head again: "See, my dear," taking her to the open window, "where they live! The dark windows over yonder."

"I may go to Helena to-morrow?" asked Rosa.

"I should like to sleep on that question to-night," he answered, doubtfully. "But let me take you to your own rest, for you must need it."

With that, Mr. Grewgious helped her to get her hat on again, and hung upon his arm the very little bag that was of no earthly use, and led her by the hand (with a certain stately awkwardness, as if he were going to walk a minuet) across Holborn, and into Furnival's Inn. At the hotel door, he confided her to the Unlimited head chambermaid, and said that while she went up to see her room, he would remain below, in case she should wish it exchanged for another, or should find that there was anything she wanted.

Rosa's room was airy, clean, comfortable, almost gay. The Unlimited had laid in everything omitted from the very little bag (that is to say, everything she could possibly need), and Rosa tripped down the great many stairs again, to thank her guardian for his thoughtful and affectionate care of her.

"Not at all, my dear," said Mr. Grewgious, infinitely gratified; "it is I who thank you for your charming confidence and for your charming company. Your breakfast will be provided for you in a neat, compact, and graceful little sitting-room (appropriate to your figure), and I will come to you at ten o'clock in the morning. I hope you don't feel very strange indeed, in this strange place."

"Oh no, I feel so safe!"

"Yes, you may be sure that the stairs are fire-proof," said Mr. Grewgious, "and that any outbreak of the devouring element would be perceived and suppressed by the watchman."

"I did not mean that," Rosa replied. "I mean, I feel so safe from him."

"There is a stout gate of iron bars to keep him out," said Mr. Grewgious, smiling, "and Furnival's is fire-proof and specially watched and lighted, and *I* live over the way!" In the stoutness of his knight-errantry, he seemed to think the last-named protection all-sufficient. In the same spirit, he said to the gate-porter as he went out, "If some one staying in the hotel should wish to send across the road to me in the night, a crown will be ready for the messenger." In the same spirit, he walked up and down outside the iron gate for the best part of an hour, with some solicitude: occasionally looking in between the bars, as if he had laid a dove in a high roost in a cage of lions, and had it on his mind that she might tumble out.

Nothing occurred in the night to flutter the tired dove, and the dove arose refreshed. With Mr. Grewgious when the clock struck ten in the morning, came Mr. Crisparkle, who had come at one plunge out of the river at Cloisterham.

"Miss Twinkleton was so uneasy, Miss Rosa," he explained to her, "and came round to Ma and me with your note, in such a state of wonder, that, to quiet her, I volunteered on this service by the very first train to be caught in the morning. I wished at the time that you had come to me; but now I think it best that you did *as* you did, and came to your guardian."

"I did think of you," Rosa told him; "but Minor Canon Corner was so near him——"

"I understand. It was quite natural."

"I have told Mr. Crisparkle," said Mr. Grewgious, "all that you told me last night, my dear. Of course I should have written it to him immediately; but his coming was most opportune. And it was particularly kind of him to come, for he had but just gone."

"Have you settled," asked Rosa, appealing to them both, "what is to be done for Helena and her brother?"

"Why really," said Mr. Crisparkle, "I am in great perplexity. If even Mr. Grewgious, whose head is much longer than mine and who is a whole night's cogitation in advance of me, is undecided, what must I be!"

The Unlimited here put her head in at the door—after having rapped, and been authorized to present herself—announcing that a gentleman wished for a word with another gentleman named Cri-

428

sparkle, if any such gentleman were there. If no such gentleman were there, he begged pardon for being mistaken.

"Such a gentleman is here," said Mr. Crisparkle, "but is engaged just now."

"Is it a dark gentleman?" interposed Rosa, retreating on her guardian.

"No, Miss, more of a brown gentleman."

"You are sure not with black hair?" asked Rosa, taking courage.

"Quite sure of that, Miss. Brown hair and blue eyes."

"Perhaps," hinted Mr. Grewgious, with habitual caution, "it might be well to see him, reverend sir, if you don't object. When one is in a difficulty, or at a loss, one never knows in what direction a way out may chance to open. It is a business principle of mine, in such a case, not to close up any direction, but to keep an eye on every direction that may present itself. I could relate an anecdote in point, but that it would be premature."

"If Miss Rosa will allow me then? Let the gentleman come in," said Mr. Crisparkle.

The gentleman came in; apologised, with a frank but modest grace, for not finding Mr. Crisparkle alone; turned to Mr. Crisparkle, and smilingly asked the unexpected question: "Who am I?"

"You are the gentleman I saw smoking under the trees in Staple Inn a few minutes ago."

"True. There I saw you. Who else am I?"

Mr. Crisparkle concentrated his attention on a handsome face, much sunburnt; and the ghost of some departed boy seemed to rise, gradually and dimly, in the room.

The gentleman saw a struggling recollection lighten up the Minor Canon's features, and smiling again, said: "What will you have for breakfast this morning? You are out of jam."

"Wait a moment!" cried Mr. Crisparkle, raising his right hand. "Give me another instant! Tartar!"

The two shook hands with the greatest heartiness, and then went the wonderful length—for Englishmen—of laying their hands each on the other's shoulders, and looking joyfully each into the other's face.

"My old fag!" said Mr. Crisparkle.

"My old master!" said Mr. Tartar.

"You saved me from drowning!" said Mr. Crisparkle.

"After which you took to swimming, you know!" said Mr. Tartar.

"God bless my soul!" said Mr. Crisparkle.

"Amen!" said Mr. Tartar.

And then they fell to shaking hands most heartily again.

"Imagine," exclaimed Mr. Crisparkle, with glistening eyes: "Miss Rosa Bud and Mr. Grewgious, imagine Mr. Tartar, when he was the smallest of juniors, diving for me, catching me, a big heavy senior, by the hair of the head, and striking out for the shore with me like a water-giant!"

"Imagine my not letting him sink, as I was his fag!" said Mr. Tartar. "But the truth being that he was my best protector and

430

friend, and did me more good than all the masters put together, an irrational impulse seized me to pick him up, or go down with him."

"Hem! Permit me, sir, to have the honor," said Mr. Grewgious, advancing with extended hand, "for an honor I truly esteem it. I am proud to make your acquaintance. I hope you didn't take cold. I hope you were not inconvenienced by swallowing too much water. How have you been since?"

It was by no means apparent that Mr. Grewgious knew what he said, though it was very apparent that he meant to say something highly friendly and appreciative.

If Heaven, Rosa thought, had but sent such courage and skill to her poor mother's aid! And he to have been so slight and young then!

"I don't wish to be complimented upon it, I thank you, but I think I have an idea," Mr. Grewgious announced, after taking a jog-trot or two across the room, so unexpected and unaccountable that they had all stared at him, doubtful whether he was choking or had the cramp. "I *think* I have an idea. I believe I have had the pleasure of seeing Mr. Tartar's name as tenant of the top set in the house next the top set in the corner?"

"Yes, sir," returned Mr. Tartar. "You are right so far."

"I am right so far," said Mr. Grewgious. "Tick that off," which he did, with his right thumb on his left. "Might you happen to know the name of your neighbour in the top set on the other side of the party-wall?" coming very close to Mr. Tartar, to lose nothing of his face, in his shortness of sight.

431

"Landless."

"Tick that off," said Mr. Grewgious, taking another trot, and then coming back. "No personal knowledge, I suppose, sir?"

"Slight, but some."

"Tick that off," said Mr. Grewgious, taking another trot, and then coming back. "Nature of knowledge, Mr. Tartar?"

"I thought he seemed to be a young fellow in a poor way, and I asked his leave—only within a day or so—to share my flowers up there with him; that is to say, to extend my flower-garden to his windows."

"Would you have the kindness to take seats?" said Mr. Grewgious. "I *have* an idea!"

They complied; Mr. Tartar none the less readily, for being all abroad; and Mr. Grewgious, seated in the centre, with his hands upon his knees, thus stated his idea, with his usual manner of having got the statement by heart.

"I cannot as yet make up my mind whether it is prudent to hold open communication under present circumstances, and on the part of the fair member of the present company, with Mr. Neville or Miss Helena. I have reason to know that a local friend of ours (on whom I beg to bestow a passing but a hearty malediction, with the kind permission of my reverend friend) sneaks to and fro, and dodges up and down. When not doing so himself, he may have some informant skulking about, in the person of a watchman, porter, or suchlike hanger-on of Staple. On the other hand, Miss Rosa very naturally wishes to see her friend Miss Helena, and it would seem important that at least Miss Helena (if not her brother too, through her) should privately know from Miss Rosa's lips what has occurred, and what has been threatened. Am I agreed with generally in the views I take?"

"I entirely coincide with them," said Mr. Crisparkle, who had been very attentive.

"As I have no doubt I should," added Mr. Tartar, smiling, "if I understood them."

"Fair and softly, sir," said Mr. Grewgious; "we shall fully confide in you directly, if you favor us with your permission. Now, if our local friend should have any informant on the spot, it is tolerably clear that such informant can only be set to watch the chambers in the occupation of Mr. Neville. He reporting, to our local friend, who comes and goes there, our local friend would supply for himself, from his own previous knowledge, the identity of the parties. Nobody can be set to watch all Staple, or to concern himself with comers and goers to other sets of chambers: unless, indeed, mine."

"I begin to understand to what you tend," said Mr. Crisparkle, "and highly approve of your caution."

"I needn't repeat that I know nothing yet of the why and wherefore," said Mr. Tartar; "but I also understood to what you tend, so let me say at once that my chambers are freely at your disposal."

"There!" cried Mr. Grewgious, smoothing his head triumphantly. "Now we have all got the idea. You have it, my dear?"

"I think I have," said Rosa, blushing a little as Mr. Tartar looked quickly towards her.

"You see, you go over to Staple with Mr. Crisparkle and Mr. Tartar," said Mr. Grewgious; "I going in and out and out and in, alone, in my usual way; you go up with those gentlemen to Mr. Tartar's rooms; you look into Mr. Tartar's flower-garden; you wait for Miss Helena's appearance there, or you signify to Miss Helena that you are close by; and you communicate with her freely, and no spy can be the wiser."

"I am very much afraid I shall be——"

"Be what, my dear?" asked Mr. Grewgious, as she hesitated. "Not frightened?"

"No, not that," said Rosa, shyly; —"in Mr. Tartar's way. We seem to be appropriating Mr. Tartar's residence so very coolly."

"I protest to you," returned that gentleman, "that I shall think the better of it for evermore, if your voice sounds in it only once."

Rosa not quite knowing what to say about that, cast down her eyes, and turning to Mr. Grewgious, dutifully asked if she should put her hat on? Mr. Grewgious being of opinion that she could not do better, she withdrew for the purpose. Mr. Crisparkle took the opportunity of giving Mr. Tartar a summary of the distresses of Neville and his sister; the opportunity was quite long enough, as the hat happened to require a little extra fitting on.

Mr. Tartar gave his arm to Rosa, and Mr. Crisparkle walked, detached, in front.

"Poor, poor Eddy!" thought Rosa, as they went along.

Mr. Tartar waved his right hand as he bent his head down over Rosa, talking in an animated way.

"It was not so powerful or so sun-browned when it saved Mr. Crisparkle," thought Rosa, glancing at it; "but it must have been very steady and determined even then."

Mr. Tartar told her he had been a sailor, roving everywhere for years and years.

"When are you going to sea again?" asked Rosa.

"Never!"

Rosa wondered what the girls would say if they could see her crossing the wide street on the sailor's arm. And she fancied that the passers-by must think her very little and very helpless, contrasted with the strong figure that could have caught her up and carried her out of any danger, miles and miles without resting.

She was thinking further, that his far-seeing blue eyes looked as if they had been used to watch danger afar off, and to watch it without flinching, drawing nearer and nearer: when, happening to raise her own eyes, she found that he seemed to be thinking something about *them*.

This a little confused Rosebud, and may account for her never afterwards quite knowing how she ascended (with his help) to his garden in the air, and seemed to get into a marvellous country that came into sudden bloom like the country on the summit of the magic bean-stalk. May it flourish for ever!

PART FOUR

THE LAST NUMBER

13.

I T SHOULD NOW BE THE FOURTH
DAY of the convention, reader. We
should already be discussing the last number. But in fact
it's still yesterday afternoon, and we're on a sight-seeing
coach making its way along Via Ostiense towards the "historic centre" of the city. At this very moment we are passing the Basilica of San Paolo. What has brought about this
spatial-temporal glitch?

To explain it, we must step back half an hour: and that
is to 1500 hours. All the members of our group meet up
again in the Dickens Room. The speakers take their places
at the table. The chairman opens the session. Then enters
a new dark-haired hostess. Wearing big round glasses which
give her the air of a model who has turned to teaching,
she announces that the coach is waiting outside to take
them on their tour.

What coach? What tour?

There follows a lively exchange between Loredana and
the new arrival (named Antonia), from which it emerges

that each work-group has the right to a guided tour of the city, and that today it is the Drood group's turn.

LOREDANA, *pointing to the members:* But they've already been imprinted. They all have the August number in their heads.

ANTONIA: No one said anything to me about a number. I was told to take everyone to the Roman Forum and then to St Peter's. Come on, it's lovely out! You don't want to keep them cooped up on a day like this!

The Latinist from Juan-les-Pins, who has permanently joined the Dickensians out of disgust for his colleague from Pirna, suggests a compromise: The debate could be held on board the coach, which surely has a microphone.

Two microphones, Antonia says: one for herself as a guide, the other at the disposal of any group-member who wishes to use it.

And so here we are, aboard the coach, leaving behind us not only the pompous Basilica (pompous, as Antonia quite rightly points out, on account of the wretched "restoration" it underwent in the pre-Japanese era, after the fire of 1823) but also Chapter Seventeen, remarkable for its pages on Honeythunder but on the whole of less interest clue-wise.

"However," Cuff says, "we mustn't overlook the fact that for the first time Dickens makes Crisparkle express some slight reservation as regards his belief in young Landless. Six months earlier, Crisparkle told the Dean that he was entirely satisfied of his perfect innocence; now he says he is certain of it, but adds that he'll continue to befriend him 'as long as that certainty shall last.' Mightn't that suggest that the author is trying to cover himself?"

"Well, of course," Loredana puts in, with feminine logic. "The Canon has realised that Neville's sister is making up to him, and he's thinking of the scene his mother will make if he lets himself get trapped."

"Quite right," says the colonel of the Carabinieri. "Because we mustn't forget—and Signorina Loredana has done well to remind us of it—that Mrs. Crisparkle does not at all approve of her son's indulgence towards the accused. She was convinced, remember, of the boy's dangerous nature from the start! And that may already have been the author covering himself."

"Excuse me, please," Antonia interrupts. The doubts regarding Neville's innocence as well as her own tirade against the Basilica on the left have prevented her from directing their attention to the Pagan Sepulchre that the coach has just passed on the right. According to the pious legend, she tells them now, it was there, in the tomb of the matron Lucina, that St Paul the Apostle was secretly buried, after being beheaded near the Tre Fontane, not far from the U&O.

The trippers all pay respectful attention, but a natural

441

association with the tomb of the matron Sapsea immediately brings the discussion back to the MED and Chapter
Eighteen.

" 'That most discussed chapter of any book of modern
times,' " says Dr Wilmot, "as the Droodist J. Y. Watt put
it, exaggerating perhaps, but making a real point nonetheless.[1] For on no question is there such total disagreement
among the scholars as on the identity of Datchery, the
mysterious and obviously disguised character who settles
in Cloisterham to observe Jasper."

"I'll bet he's that . . . what's his name? . . . the clerk
of Mr Grewgious that we saw in Chapter Eleven and who
. . . that's it: Bazzard. I'll bet Datchery is Bazzard," says
Antonia.

This declaration is greeted by an astounded silence,
and the driver himself turns round to look at her, risking
a collision with the lorry he's overtaking.

"But how do you . . . what do you know about . . ."
Loredana finally stammers out. "Don't tell me you've read
this MED yourself? Or are *you* telepathic too?"

The truth is simpler than that, reader. Knowing that
she was assigned to take the Drood group out, and wishing
to share in their interests, the conscientious hostess pre-

---

[1] John Y. Watt, *A Student's Study on Edwin Drood*, undated but 1913.

pared herself by a subliminal imprinting of the entire book. And, as Dr Wilmot now compliments her, her hypothesis is by no means a fanciful one.

The editor of *The Dickensian* explains that 33.7% of the scholars believe Datchery to be Bazzard. But, he adds, a good 20% think he is Helena in disguise, or Neville; 16%, Tartar; and another 16% see him as Drood himself, who is not dead and has now returned to unmask his uncle. The remaining 14.3% are divided between: a) the ubiquitous Grewgious; b) a detective sent by Grewgious, but who is not Bazzard; c) a detective not sent by anyone, but who has heard about the case and has come to look into it on his own account; d) Dickens himself, making a personal and surprising appearance at the end as the deus ex machina of the whole plot;[1] e) a stranger destined to remain a stranger, since the MED, once again, is too incoherent to allow any reasonable conclusions to be drawn. This final point of view, Wilmot says, is held by G. K. Chesterton; while Cecil Chesterton (who defended Jasper in the mock trial in 1914) was a "Bazzardian."[2]

LOREDANA: Antonia's right, it must be Bazzard. At any

---

[1] This intriguing hypothesis was advanced by the English scholar W. W. Robson (*Times Literary Supplement*, Number 4206).
[2] The Bazzard hypothesis finds support in the fact that the clerk is "off duty here just at present," when Rosa arrives in London.

rate, he knows his stuff as a detective, seeing as he's already got onto Durdles and the Sapsea tomb with its crazy tablet.

ANTONIA: Meanwhile we have now reached—you will see it on your left—the Pyramid of Caius Cestius, which is 37 metres in height and contains a sepulchral cell of 4 × 6 metres, in which Belzoni would have run no risk of getting stuck. Its inscription . . .

LATINIST, *anxious to make an impression on Antonia:* It is in Augustean characters and tells us that C. Cestius (who died in 12 B.C.) was a member of the College of the *Septemviri epulones*, the organizers of sacred banquets, and that it took 330 days to build his tomb.

WILMOT: You may also be interested to know that during his stay in Rome in 1845, described in *Pictures from Italy* (1846), Dickens enjoyed a moonlit view of this same pyramid . . .

ANTONIA: . . . which together with the nearby Porta San Paolo (the ancient *Porta Ostiense*) forms one of the most picturesque sights of Rome.

WILMOT: Nor did he fail to brood on the adjoining Protestant Cemetery, where Shelley's ashes are laid, and Keats's bones.

As for the reader, we trust he will not fail to admire the thoroughness of the Japanese, under whose auspices a perfect inter-disciplinary fusion has been achieved between

tourism, culture, and restoration. The remark that Marlowe and Archer make to Antonia, as an opening gambit,
seems a little less appropriate: "With all this creep-show
talk of tombs, I wouldn't lay much on Drood's still being
alive." [1]

Antonia, finding the remark in dubious taste, does not
reply. She prefers to engage in an animated conversation
with the Latinist about Titus Livy's *First Decade* (which she
also learnt by heart subliminally). Meanwhile, the coach
has turned in to Piazza Albania, which is choked with traffic,
so the others take this opportunity to discuss Chapter
Nineteen with its menacing "shadow on the sun-dial."

LOREDANA: What a beast!

DUPIN: Not if we accept the hypothesis that Jasper is
merely feigning madness to Rosa, so that the real culprit
or culprits will underestimate him as an investigator. The
analogy with the scene between Hamlet and Ophelia, from
this point of view, strikes me as of the utmost importance.
And if we add to this the similarities with *Macbeth*, which
would seem to incriminate the two Landlesses . . .

POIROT: But, according to Jasper's eminent defender,

---

[1] The cynical Bucket has already indicated one reason for considering
Drood dead, though a third of all Droodists think him alive. The strongest
argument in favour of death appears to us to be the ring with diamonds
and rubies that Dickens had him put inside his waistcoat pocket: what
could the purpose of this ring be, if not to identify the corpse half-
consumed by the quicklime?

if I've understood correctly, the Landless twins are *not* the murderers.

WILMOT: No, according to him . . . But I might as well tell you that the defender I spoke of is Sir Felix Aylmer, a well-known actor and theatrical scholar, whose book *The Drood Case* in 1964 revolutionised MED studies.

TOAD, *to himself:* Thank God we're getting somewhere at last! But I have a nasty feeling . . .

WILMOT: According to Aylmer, the murderer is none of the characters we've already met. He's a fanatic, a kind of terrorist who has come from the Middle East, to pay Edwin out, in accordance with Mahometan custom, for the grave affront that his father (who, as we know, lived there) committed against Islam . . .

ALL, *including Antonia and the Latinist, who look up from their discussion of* First Decade: The Rushdie Case!

WILMOT: Let's not be over-hasty. Aylmer proposed the religious hypothesis as a first possibility, observing that the stones in the ring in Edwin's possession could have come from the sacrilegious sacking of Mecca in 1813, in which European officers in the service of Mehemet Ali took part . . .

ALL, *excluding Antonia, who does not know Collins, but including, mysteriously, the Latinist:* But that would be exactly the same plot as *The Moonstone*! With the opium and all the rest!

446

WILMOT: Quite. And therefore Aylmer, judging that such barefaced plagiarism was impossible on Dickens's part, falls back on the family vendetta; Drood's father, he says, gravely affronted an Islamic nobleman, whose descendants have sworn to avenge themselves on his son, on December 24, the anniversary of the affront. Jasper, who knew all about the threat overhanging Edwin and had prepared a plan to thwart it, is not Edwin's uncle but his half-brother (on his mother's side), while the woman in the opium-den is Rosa's grandmother. Rosa's father, remember . . .

TOAD: All right, all right, that's enough! I knew it: out of the frying-pan and into the fire. First, a murderer who against all the rules is the prime suspect; and now, a murderer who was never suspected for the simple reason that we didn't know of his existence! . . . This is going too far! Poirot, say something, for heaven's sake!

POIROT: There is no doubt that when the murderer is a totally unknown person, the crime loses much of its . . . er . . . *charme*. The classic case is that of the passing vagabond, which we have already considered. But if Aylmer is right . . .

TOAD: There's no difference whatsoever: some fellow we've never seen or heard of! A perfect stranger!

POIROT: Not so perfect. Inspector Maigret has already suspected his existence and his intentions.

MAIGRET: I merely suggested a reason why Jasper kept

saying his nephew's name in his opium dreams, even though the enemy he imagined himself killing was someone else. It could be that the uncle knew of the existence of this enemy, knew of his murderous intentions towards his nephew, but did not yet know his name.

POIROT: In other words: Jasper has known for some time that *someone*, on the night of December 24, will try to kill his nephew, but he doesn't know *who*. Later, with the arrival of the twins, he begins to suspect that the assassin is Neville, but he can't be sure.

ANTONIA: That makes no sense. If Jasper knows of the threat and has even prepared a plan to thwart it, why on earth does he go blissfully to bed that night, leaving Drood to take a walk with his presumed killer?

WILMOT: Aylmer's explanation is somewhat involved, but it does stand up, in its own way. I certainly wouldn't exclude the possibility that Dickens had in mind something along these lines, given the fondness of his public for stories of murky family history, especially if set against an Anglo-colonial background. So, according to Aylmer . . .

The explanation is truly involved, reader. So we hereby furnish the following telegraphic summary:

Islamic family passes blame from father to son, condemns Edwin to death by sacred law of vengeance, but sentence cannot be carried out—another sacred law—so long as Edwin is engaged to Rosa. Rosa's father, you see, although Edwin's father's friend, behaves nobly to Islamic family and wins their unswerving protection for self and descendants, and all relatives of descendants. Assassin must therefore first determine whether Edwin and Rosa are still engaged. Only if not, can he proceed. Jasper stirs up Neville not only to make him give himself away (if he is the assassin) but also to see whether the two lovebirds are still in love. Convinced (erroneously) that they are, and certain the assassin will respect the sacred law, he goes blissfully to bed. Question: How does assassin learn engagement broken off? Explanation: He overheard the entire Rosa/Edwin conversation, while Jasper, detained at the cathedral for Vespers, saw only the final affectionate kiss and took it for love.

DRIVER, *who has been listening, having nothing else to do, since the coach is still held up in Piazza Albania:* What a story!

Should the reader ever find himself in a midsummer traffic jam in Rome, barely moving from Piazza Albania along the Viale Aventino, there will be no point in his staying on the right. On the right, in the direction of the Circus Maximus, there is nothing for him to see apart from the appalling modern Palazzo della FAO with the adjoining Ministry for Post and Telegraphs. But by keeping as far as

449

possible to the left, he will have an unobstructed view of the marvellous southeastern ruins of the Palatine at sunset, unless it is already dark.

In this case, the sun has not yet set, but the spectacle is still impressive. Antonia, with help from the Latinist, provides commentary on it; describes the Domitian constructions to the west, the arches of Septimius Severus (20 to 30 metres high) to the south, and the site of the famous *Septizonium* to the south-east. But Toad allows nobody to enjoy the spectacle. "*Questa e quella, per me pari sono,*" he croaks querulously from *Rigoletto*. ("This one or that one, it's all the same to me!" Meaning, the "Jekyllian" solution or that of the unknown assassin.) And adds that the reappearance of Lascar Sal in Chapter Twenty-two leaves no alternative.

But Chapter Twenty-two hasn't been imprinted yet, the reader will object. How do they come to be talking of it already? We forgot to explain that the traffic in the Viale Aventino remained stationary for so long, that the debate on the August number petered out. Thorndyke, with regard to the "shadow on the sun-dial," had drawn their attention to Jasper's hypnotic power; simply by staring at Rosa, he was able not only to paralyse her but even to force her, towards the end of their conversation, twice to give him a sign of assent. Dupin then insisted on the derivation of this scene from *Hamlet*, demonstrating how Jasper, here and there, expresses himself in iambic pentameter.[1] And Sergeant Cuff reminded everybody that he had foreseen (with Wilmot's "partial" nod) that the author would not present us with any further private conversations between Helena and Rosa. Nor, it goes without saying, between Helena and Neville.

"Six months have gone by since that fatal night," the sergeant said. "We've reached the last page of the fifth number. And the three *have not talked to one another again*, at least not in our presence. A situation that could hardly be prolonged without the reader growing suspicious."

COLONEL: Quite right!

CUFF: So Dickens finds a clever way out, and implying that careless talk costs lives, he has Grewgious come out with innocent sounding words along the lines: "I can't as yet make up my mind whether it is prudent in the present situation for Miss Rosa to hold open communication with Miss Helena and Mr. Neville. On the other hand, Miss Rosa naturally wishes to see her friend, and it would seem important that at least Miss Helena (if not her brother too, through her) should privately know from Miss Rosa's lips what has occurred, and what has been threatened."

TOAD: Hear, hear!

---

[1] The meticulous Poirot confirmed that he had counted nine such lines. This one especially is Shakespearian in its wording: "I shall not strike too soon. Give me a sign / that you attend to me."

CUFF: Which, in my opinion, is as much as to say: "As author, I don't see how I can have these three talk without letting the cat out of the bag. Yet the reader is bound to suspect something, if I go on like this. So in the next number Rosa will talk to Helena. But, with a twist or two on my part, connected with Jasper's machinations, the promised 'private conversation' will be held anything but privately."

What is this twist or two? The coach-trippers' curiosity as to subsequent developments had grown so acute, that Loredana finally radio-phoned through to the U&O: Would it be possible to proceed immediately with the tele-imprinting of the next number via the simultaneous-translation headphones in the coach?

In no time at all, the subliminal impulses were transmitted to the coach, and even before the Palatine was in sight, the work-group had all sub-listened to the entire September number: the one that Dickens, June 8, 1870, left unfinished on the sixth- or seventh-from-last page, and which the reader will now find overleaf.

LOREDANA: But . . .

Oh yes, just a moment, reader. In the heat of the debate and the sightseeing, we forgot two or three other points that it would be well to mention now:

A. Chapter Twenty is entitled "Divers Flights." Loredana explains, for those not familiar with English, that the word "flight" has two meanings, one connected with the idea of movement through air and the other with escape. The divers flights, therefore, are: Rosa's escape from Cloisterham; the arrival of her train in London, which speeds "over the housetops" (the track being elevated at this point); and her ascension to the "garden in the air" of the providential Mr Tartar.

B. Speaking of the window-to-window conversation between Tartar and the "poor student," P. Petrovich jokingly referred to "Kafka's theft." Why? Because Kafka, an assiduous reader of Dickens (whose "opulence and great, careless prodigality" he exalted in a diary note), was almost certainly influenced by this episode in the balcony-to-balcony conversations between Karl and the "poor student" in *Amerika*.

C. The Latinist, in his increasingly animated conversation with Antonia, declared himself to be a great admirer of Wilkie Collins. How strange (she remarked) for a scholar from Juan-les-Pins! The fact is (he said) that I was first drawn to Latin by my love for the protagonist of a Collins novel. Ah (Antonia at once asked), and what was the title of the novel, and what was the protagonist's name? He blushed, however, and said nothing, so this point will have to be cleared up later.

CHAPTER XXI

A GRITTY STATE OF THINGS
COMES ON

MR. TARTAR's chambers were the neatest, the cleanest, and the best ordered chambers ever seen under the sun, moon, and stars. The floors were scrubbed to that extent, that you might have supposed the London blacks emancipated for ever, and gone out of the land for good. Every inch of brass work in Mr. Tartar's possession was polished and burnished, till it shone like a brazen mirror. No speck, nor spot, nor spatter soiled the purity of any of Mr. Tartar's household gods, large, small, or middle-sized. His sitting-room was like the admiral's cabin, his bath-room was like a dairy, his sleeping-chamber, fitted all about with lockers and drawers, was like a seedsman's shop; and his nicely-balanced cot just stirred in the midst, as if it breathed. Everything belonging to Mr. Tartar had quarters of its own assigned to it: his maps and charts had their quarters; his books had theirs; his brushes had theirs; his boots had theirs; his clothes had theirs; his case-bottles had theirs; his telescopes and other instruments had theirs. Everything was readily accessible. Shelf, bracket, locker, hook, and drawer were equally within reach, and were equally contrived with a view to avoiding waste of room, and providing some snug inches of stowage for something that would have exactly fitted nowhere else. His gleaming little service of plate was so arranged upon his sideboard as that a slack salt-spoon would have instantly betrayed itself; his toilet implements were so arranged upon his dressing-table as that a toothpick of slovenly deportment could have been reported at a glance. So with the curiosities he had brought home from various voyages. Stuffed, dried, repolished, or otherwise preserved, according to their kind; birds, fishes, reptiles, arms, articles of dress, shells, seaweeds, grasses, or memorials of coral reef; each was displayed in its especial place, and each could have been displayed in no better place. Paint and varnish seemed to be kept somewhere out of sight, in constant readiness to obliterate stray finger-marks wherever any might become perceptible in Mr. Tartar's chambers. No man-of-war was ever kept more spick and span from careless touch. On this bright summer day, a neat awning was rigged over Mr. Tartar's flower-garden as only a sailor could rig it; and there was a sea-going air upon the whole effect, so delightfully complete, that the flower-garden might have appertained to stern-windows afloat, and the whole concern might have bowled away gallantly with all on board, if Mr. Tartar had only clapped to his lips the speaking-trumpet that was slung in a corner, and given hoarse orders to have the anchor up, look alive there, men, and get all sail upon her!

Mr. Tartar doing the honors of this gallant craft, was of a piece with the rest. When a man rides an amiable hobby that shies at nothing and kicks nobody, it is only agreeable to find him riding it with a humorous sense of the droll side of the creature. When the

man is a cordial and an earnest man by nature, and withal is perfectly fresh and genuine, it may be doubted whether he is ever seen
to greater advantage than at such a time. So Rosa would have naturally thought (even if she hadn't been conducted over the ship with
all the homage due to the First Lady of the Admiralty, or First Fairy
of the Sea), that it was charming to see and hear Mr. Tartar half
laughing at, and half rejoicing in, his various contrivances. So Rosa
would have naturally thought, anyhow, that the sunburnt sailor showed
to great advantage when, the inspection finished, he delicately withdrew out of his admiral's cabin, beseeching her to consider herself
its Queen, and waving her free of his flower-garden with the hand
that had had Mr. Crisparkle's life in it.

"Helena! Helena Landless! Are you there?"

"Who speaks to me? Not Rosa?" Then a second handsome face
appearing.

"Yes, my darling!"

"Why, how did you come here, dearest?"

"I—I don't quite know," said Rosa with a blush; "unless I am
dreaming!"

Why with a blush? For their two faces were alone with the other
flowers. Are blushes among the fruits of the country of the magic
beanstalk?

"*I* am not dreaming," said Helena, smiling. "I should take more
for granted if I were. How do we come together—or so near together—so very unexpectedly?"

Unexpectedly indeed, among the dingy gables and chimney-pots of P. J. T.'s connection, and the flowers that had sprung from the salt sea. But Rosa, waking, told in a hurry how they came to be together, and all the why and wherefore of that matter.

"And Mr. Crisparkle is here," said Rosa, in rapid conclusion; "and could you believe it? Long ago, he saved his life!"

"I could believe any such thing of Mr. Crisparkle," returned Helena, with a mantling face.

(More blushes in the beanstalk country!)

"Yes, but it wasn't Mr. Crisparkle," said Rosa, quickly putting in the correction.

"I don't understand, love."

"It was very nice of Mr. Crisparkle to be saved," said Rosa, "and he couldn't have shown his high opinion of Mr. Tartar more expressively. But it was Mr. Tartar who saved him."

Helena's dark eyes looked very earnestly at the bright face among the leaves, and she asked, in a slower and more thoughtful tone:

"Is Mr. Tartar with you now, dear?"

"No; because he has given up his rooms to me—to us, I mean. It *is* such a beautiful place!"

"Is it?"

"It is like the inside of the most exquisite ship that ever sailed. It is like—it is like——"

"Like a dream?" suggested Helena.

Rosa answered with a little nod, and smelled the flowers.

Helena resumed, after a short pause of silence, during which she seemed (or it was Rosa's fancy) to compassionate somebody: "My poor Neville is reading in his own room, the sun being so very bright on this side just now. I think he had better not know that you are so near."

"Oh, I think so too!" cried Rosa very readily.

"I suppose," pursued Helena, doubtfully, "that he must know by-and-by all you have told me; but I am not sure. Ask Mr. Crisparkle's advice, my darling. Ask him whether I may tell Neville as much or as little of what you have told me as I think best."

Rosa subsided into her state-cabin, and propounded the question. The Minor Canon was for the free exercise of Helena's judgment.

"I thank him very much," said Helena, when Rosa emerged again with her report. "Ask him whether it would be best to wait until any more maligning and pursuing of Neville on the part of this wretch shall disclose itself, or to try to anticipate it: I mean, so far as to find out whether any such goes on darkly about us?"

The Minor Canon found this point so difficult to give a confident opinion on, that, after two or three attempts and failures, he suggested a reference to Mr. Grewgious. Helena acquiescing, he betook himself (with a most unsuccessful assumption of lounging indifference) across the quadrangle to P. J. T.'s, and stated it. Mr. Grewgious held decidedly to the general principle, that if you could steal a march upon a brigand or a wild beast, you had better do it; and he also held decidedly to the special case, that John Jasper was a brigand and a wild beast in combination.

Thus advised, Mr. Crisparkle came back again and reported

to Rosa, who in her turn reported to Helena. She, now steadily pursuing her train of thought at her window, considered thereupon.

"We may count on Mr. Tartar's readiness to help us, Rosa?" she inquired.

O yes! Rosa shyly thought so. O yes, Rosa shyly believed she could almost answer for it. But should she ask Mr. Crisparkle? "I think your authority on the point as good as his, my dear," said Helena, sedately, "and you needn't disappear again for that." Odd of Helena!

"You see, Neville," Helena pursued after more reflection, "knows no one else here: he has not so much as exchanged a word with any one else here. If Mr. Tartar would call to see him openly and often; if he would spare a minute for the purpose, frequently; if he would even do so, almost daily; something might come of it."

"Something might come of it, dear?" repeated Rosa, surveying her friend's beauty with a highly perplexed face. "Something might?"

"If Neville's movements are really watched, and if the purpose really is to isolate him from all friends and acquaintance and wear his daily life out grain by grain (which would seem to be the threat to you), does it not appear likely," said Helena, "that his enemy would in some way communicate with Mr. Tartar to warn him off from Neville? In which case, we might not only know the fact but might know from Mr. Tartar what the terms of the communication were."

"I see!" cried Rosa. And immediately darted into her state-cabin again.

Presently her pretty face reappeared, with a greatly heightened colour, and she said that she had told Mr. Crisparkle, and that Mr. Crisparkle had fetched in Mr. Tartar, and that Mr. Tartar—"who is waiting now in case you want him," added Rosa, with a half look back, and in not a little confusion between the inside of the state-cabin and out—had declared his readiness to act as she had suggested, and to enter on his task that very day.

"I thank him from my heart," said Helena. "Pray tell him so."

Again not a little confused between the Flower Garden and the Cabin, Rosa dipped in with her message, and dipped out again with more assurances from Mr. Tartar, and stood wavering in a divided state between Helena and him, which proved that confusion is not always necessarily awkward, but may sometimes present a pleasant appearance.

"And now, darling," said Helena, "we will be mindful of the caution that has restricted us to this interview for the present, and will part. I hear Neville's moving too. Are you going back?"

"To Miss Twinkleton's?" asked Rosa.

"Yes."

"O, I could never go there any more; I couldn't indeed, after that dreadful interview!" said Rosa.

"Then where *are* you going, pretty one?"

"Now I come to think of it, I don't know," said Rosa. "I have settled nothing at all yet, but my guardian will take care of me. Don't be uneasy, dear. I shall be sure to be somewhere."

(It did seem likely.)

"And I shall hear of my Rosebud from Mr. Tartar?" inquired Helena.

"Yes, I suppose so; from——" Rosa looked back again in a flutter, instead of supplying the name. "But tell me one thing before we part, dearest Helena. Tell me that you are sure, sure, sure, I couldn't help it."

"Help it, love?"

"Help making him malicious and revengeful. I couldn't hold any terms with him, could I?"

"You know how I love you, darling," answered Helena, with indignation; "but I would sooner see you dead at his wicked feet."

"That's a great comfort to me! And you will tell your poor brother so, won't you? And you will give him my remembrance and my sympathy? And you will ask him not to hate me?"

With a mournful shake of the head, as if that would be quite a superfluous entreaty, Helena lovingly kissed her two hands to her friend, and her friend's two hands were kissed to her; and then she saw a third hand (a brown one) appear among the flowers and leaves, and help her friend out of sight.

The reflection that Mr. Tartar produced in the Admiral's Cabin by merely touching the spring knob of a locker and the handle of a drawer, was a dazzling enchanted repast. Wonderful macaroons,

461

glittering liqueurs, magically preserved tropical spices, and jellies of celestial tropical fruits; displayed themselves profusely at an instant's notice. But Mr. Tartar could not make time stand still; and time, with his hardhearted fleetness, strode on so fast, that Rosa was obliged to come down from the Beanstalk country to earth, and her guardian's chambers.

"And now, my dear," said Mr. Grewgious, "what is to be done next? To put the same thought in another form; what is to be done with you?"

Rosa could only look apologetically sensible of being very much in her own way, and in everybody else's. Some passing idea of living, fireproof, up a good many stairs in Furnival's Inn for the rest of her life, was the only thing in the nature of a plan that occurred to her.

"It has come into my thoughts," said Mr. Grewgious, "that as the respected lady, Miss Twinkleton, occasionally repairs to London in the recess, with the view of extending her connexion, and being available for interviews with metropolitan parents, if any—whether, until we have time in which to turn ourselves round, we might invite Miss Twinkleton to come and stay with you for a month?"

"Stay where, sir?"

"Whether," explained Mr. Grewgious, "we might take a furnished lodging in town for a month, and invite Miss Twinkleton to assume the charge of you in it for that period?"

"And afterwards?" hinted Rosa.

"And afterwards," said Mr. Grewgious, "we should be no worse off than we are now."

"I think that might smooth the way," assented Rosa.

"Then let us," said Mr. Grewgious, rising, "go and look for a furnished lodging. Nothing could be more acceptable to me than the sweet presence of last evening, for all the remaining evenings of my existence; but these are not fit surroundings for a young lady. Let us set out in quest of adventures, and look for a furnished lodging. In the meantime, Mr. Crisparkle here, about to return home immediately, will no doubt kindly see Miss Twinkleton and invite that lady to co-operate in our plan."

Mr. Crisparkle, willingly accepting the commission, took his departure; Mr. Grewgious and his ward set forth on their expedition.

As Mr. Grewgious's idea of looking at a furnished lodging was to get on the opposite side of the street to a house with a suitable bill in the window, and stare at it; and then work his way tortuously to the back of the house, and stare at that; and then not go in, but make similar trials of another house, with the same result; their progress was but slow. At length he bethought himself of a widowed cousin, divers times removed, of Mr. Bazzard's, who had once solicited his influence in the lodger world, and who lived in Southampton Street, Bloomsbury Square. This lady's name, stated in uncompromising capitals of considerable size on a brass door-plate, and yet not lucidly as to sex or condition, was BILLICKIN.

Personal faintness, and an overpowering personal candour, were the distinguishing features of Mrs. Billickin's organization. She came

languishing out of her own exclusive back parlor, with the air of
having been expressly brought-to for the purpose, from an accu-
mulation of several swoons.

"I hope I see you well, sir," said Mrs. Billickin, recognizing her
visitor with a bend.

"Thank you, quite well. And you, ma'am?" returned Mr. Grewgious.

"I am as well," said Mrs. Billickin, becoming aspirational with
excess of faintness, "as I hever ham."

"My ward and an elderly lady," said Mr. Grewgious, "wish to
find a genteel lodging for a month or so. Have you any apartments
available, ma'am?"

"Mr. Grewgious," returned Mrs. Billickin, "I will not deceive
you; far from it. I *have* apartments available."

This, with the air of adding: "Convey me to the stake, if you
will; but while I live, I will be candid."

"And now, what apartments, ma'am?" asked Mr. Grewgious,
cosily. To tame a certain severity apparent on the part of Mrs. Billickin.

"There is this sitting-room—which call it what you will, it is
the front parlor, Miss," said Mrs. Billickin, impressing Rosa into the
conversation: "the back parlor being what I cling to and never part
with; and there is two bedrooms at the top of the 'ouse with gas
laid on. I do not tell you that your bedroom floors is firm, for firm
they are not. The gas-fitter himself allowed that to make a firm job,
he must go right under your jistes, and it were not worth the outlay

464

as a yearly tenant so to do. The piping is carried above your jistes, and it is best that it should be made known to you."

Mr. Grewgious and Rosa exchanged looks of some dismay, though they had not the least idea what latent horrors this carriage of the piping might involve. Mrs. Billickin put her hand to her heart, as having eased it of a load.

"Well! The roof is all right, no doubt," said Mr. Grewgious, plucking up a little.

"Mr. Grewgious," returned Mrs. Billickin, "if I was to tell you, sir, that to have nothink above you is to have a floor above you, I should put a deception upon you which I will not do. No, sir. Your slates WILL rattle loose at that elewation in windy weather, do your utmost, best or worst! I defy you, sir, be you what you may, to keep your slates tight, try how you can." Here Mrs. Billickin, having been warm with Mr. Grewgious, cooled a little, not to abuse the moral power she held over him. "Consequent," proceeded Mrs. Billickin, more mildly, but still firmly in her incorruptible candour: "consequent it would be worse than of no use for me to trapse and travel up to the top of the 'ouse with you, and for you to say, 'Mrs. Billickin, what stain do I notice in the ceiling, for a stain I do consider it?' and for me to answer, 'I do not understand you, sir.' No sir; I will not be so underhand. I *do* understand you before you pint it out. It is the wet, sir. It do come in, and it do not come in. You may lay dry there, half your lifetime; but the time will come, and it is best that you should know it, when a dripping sop would be no name for you."

Mr. Grewgious looked much disgraced by being prefigured in this pickle.

"Have you any other apartments, ma'am?" he asked.

"Mr. Grewgious," returned Mrs. Billickin, with much solemnity, "I have. You ask me have I, and my open and my honest answer air, I have. The first and second floors is wacant, and sweet rooms."

"Come, come! There's nothing against *them*," said Mr. Grewgious, comforting himself.

"Mr. Grewgious," replied Mrs. Billickin, "pardon me, there is the stairs. Unless your mind is prepared for the stairs, it will lead to inevitable disappointment. You cannot, Miss," said Mrs. Billickin, addressing Rosa, reproachfully, "place a first floor, and far less a second, on the level footing of a parlor. No, you cannot do it, Miss, it is beyond your power, and wherefore try?"

Mrs. Billickin put it very feelingly, as if Rosa had shown a head-strong determinatioin to hold the untenable position.

"Can we see these rooms, ma'am?" inquired her guardian.

"Mr. Grewgious," returned Mrs. Billickin, "you can. I will not disguise it from you, sir, you can."

Mrs. Billickin then sent into her back parlor for her shawl (it being a state fiction, dating from immemorial antiquity, that she could never go anywhere without being wrapped up), and having been enrolled by her attendant, led the way. She made various genteel pauses on the stairs for breath, and clutched at her heart in the drawing-room as if it had very nearly got loose, and she had caught it in the act of taking wing.

"And the second floor?" said Mr. Grewgious, on finding the first satisfactory.

"Mr. Grewgious," replied Mrs. Billickin, turning upon him with ceremony, as if the time had now come when a distinct understanding on a difficult point must be arrived at, and a solemn confidence established, "the second floor is over this."

"Can we see that too, ma'am?"

"Yes, sir," returned Mrs. Billickin, "it is open as the day."

That also proving satisfactory, Mr. Grewgious retired into a window with Rosa for a few words of consultation, and then asking for pen and ink, sketched out a line or two of agreement. In the meantime Mrs. Billickin took a seat, and delivered a kind of Index to, or Abstract of, the general question.

"Five-and-forty shillings per week by the month certain at the time of year," said Mrs. Billickin, "is only reasonable to both parties. It is not Bond Street nor yet St. James's Palace; but it is not pretended that it is. Neither is it attempted to be denied— for why should it?—that the Arching leads to a Mews. Mewses must exist. Respecting attendance; two is kep', at liberal wages. Words *has* arisen as to tradesmen, but dirty shoes on fresh hearth-stoning was attributable, and no wish for a commission on your orders. Coals is either *by* the fire, or *per* the scuttle." She emphasized the prepositions as marking a subtle but immense difference. "Dogs is not viewed with faviour. Besides litter, they gets stole, and sharing suspicions is apt to creep in, and unpleasantness takes place."

By this time Mr. Grewgious had his agreement-lines, and his earnest-money, ready. "I have signed it for the ladies, ma'am," he said, "and you'll have the goodness to sign it for yourself, Christian and Surname, there, if you please."

"Mr. Grewgious," said Mrs. Billickin in a new burst of candour, "no, sir! You must excuse the Christian name."

Mr. Grewgious stared at her.

"The door-plate is used as a protection," said Mrs. Billickin, "and acts as such, and go from it I will not."

Mr. Grewgious stared at Rosa.

"No, Mr. Grewgious, you must excuse me. So long as this 'ouse is known indefinite as Billickin's, and so long as it is a doubt with the riff-raff where Billickin may be hidin', near the street door or down the airy, and what his weight and size, so long I feel safe. But commit myself to a solitary female statement, no, Miss! Nor would you for a moment wish," said Mrs. Billickin, with a strong sense of injury, "to take that advantage of your sex, if you was not brought to it by inconsiderate example."

Rosa reddening as if she had made some most disgraceful attempt to overreach the good lady, besought Mr. Grewgious to rest content with any signature. And accordingly, in a baronial way, the sign-manual BILLICKIN got appended to the document.

Details were then settled for taking possession on the next day but one, when Miss Twinkleton might be reasonably expected; and Rosa went back to Furnival's Inn on her guardian's arm.

Behold Mr. Tartar walking up and down Furnival's Inn, checking himself when he saw them coming, and advancing towards them!

"It occurred to me," hinted Mr. Tartar, "that we might go up the river, the weather being so delicious and the tide serving. I have a boat of my own at the Temple Stairs."

"I have not been up the river for this many a day," said Mr. Grewgious, tempted.

"I was never up the river," added Rosa.

Within half an hour they were setting this matter right by going up the river. The tide was running with them, the afternoon was charming. Mr. Tartar's boat was perfect. Mr. Tartar and Lobley (Mr. Tartar's man) pulled a pair of oars. Mr. Tartar had a yacht, it seemed, lying somewhere down by Greenhithe; and Mr. Tartar's man had charge of this yacht, and was detached upon his present service. He was a jolly favored man, with tawny hair and whiskers, and a big red face. He was the dead image of the sun in old woodcuts, his hair and whiskers answering for rays all round him. Resplendent in the bow of the boat, he was a shining sight, with a man-of-war's man's shirt on—or off, according to opinion—and his arms and breast tattoo'd all sorts of patterns. Lobley seemed to take it easily, and so did Mr. Tartar; yet their oars bent as they pulled, and the boat bounded under them. Mr. Tartar talked as if he were doing nothing, to Rosa who was really doing nothing, and to Mr. Grewgious who was doing this much that he steered all wrong; but what did that matter, when a turn of Mr. Tartar's skilful wrist, or a mere grin of Mr. Lobley's over the bow, put all to rights! The tide bore them on in the gayest and most sparkling manner, until they stopped to dine in some everlastingly green garden, needing no matter-of-fact identification here; and then the tide obligingly turned—being devoted to that party alone for that day; and as they floated idly among some osier beds, Rosa tried what she could do in the rowing way, and came off splendidly, being much assisted; and Mr. Grewgious tried what he could do, and came off on his back, doubled up with an oar under his chin, being not assisted at all. Then there was an interval of rest under boughs (such rest!) what time Mr. Lobley mopped, and, arranging cushions, stretchers, and the like, danced the tight rope the whole length of the boat like a man to whom shoes were a superstition and stockings slavery; and then came the sweet return among delicious odours of limes in bloom, and musical ripplings; and, all too soon, the great black city cast its shadow on the waters, and its dark bridges spanned them as death spans life, and the everlastingly green garden seemed to be left for everlasting, unregainable and far away.

"Cannot people get through life without gritty stages, I wonder!" Rosa thought next day, when the town was very gritty again, and everything had a strange and an uncomfortable appearance of seeming to wait for something that wouldn't come. No. She began to think, that, now the Cloisterham school days had glided past and gone, the gritty stages would begin to set in at intervals and make themselves wearily known!

Yet what did Rosa expect? Did she expect Miss Twinkleton? Miss Twinkleton duly came. Forth from her back parlor issued the

Billickin to receive Miss Twinkleton, and War was in the Billickin's eye from that fell moment.

Miss Twinkleton brought a quantity of luggage with her, having all Rosa's as well as her own. The Billickin took it ill that Miss Twinkleton's mind, being sorely disturbed by this luggage, failed to take in her personal identity with that clearness of perception which was due to its demands. Stateliness mounted her gloomy throne upon the Billickin's brow in consequence. And when Miss Twinkleton, in agitation taking stock of her trunks and packages, of which she had seventeen, particularly counted in the Billickin herself as number eleven, the B found it necessary to repudiate.

"Things cannot too soon be put upon the footing," said she, with a candour so demonstrative as to be almost obtrusive, "that the person of the 'ouse is not a box nor yet a bundle, nor a carpet bag. No, I am 'ily obleeged to you, Miss Twinkleton, nor yet a beggar."

This last disclaimer had reference to Miss Twinkleton's distractedly pressing two and sixpence on her, instead of the cabman.

Thus cast off, Miss Twinkleton wildly inquired, "which gentleman" was to be paid? There being two gentlemen in that position (Miss Twinkleton having arrived with two cabs), each gentleman on being paid held forth his two and sixpence on the flat of his open hand, and, with a speechless stare and a dropped jaw, displayed his wrong to heaven and earth. Terrified by this alarming spectacle, Miss Twinkleton placed another shilling in each hand; at the same time appealing to the law in flurried accents, and recounting her luggage this time with the two gentlemen in, who caused the total to come out complicated. Meanwhile the two gentlemen, each looking very hard at the last shilling grumblingly, as if it might become eighteenpence if he kept his eyes on it, descended the doorsteps, ascended their carriages, and drove away, leaving Miss Twinkleton on a bonnet-box in tears.

The Billickin beheld this manifestation of weakness without sympathy, and gave directions for "a young man to be got in" to wrestle with the luggage. When that gladiator had disappeared from the arena, peace ensued, and the new lodgers dined.

But the Billickin had somehow come to the knowledge that Miss Twinkleton kept a school. The leap from that knowledge to the inference that Miss Twinkleton set herself to teach *her* something, was easy. "But you don't do it," soliloquised the Billickin; "*I* am not your pupil, whatever she," meaning Rosa, "may be, poor thing!"

Miss Twinkleton on the other hand, having changed her dress and recovered her spirits, was animated by a bland desire to improve the occasion in all ways, and to be as serene a model as possible. In a happy compromise between her two states of existence, she had already become, with her workbasket before her, the equally vivacious companion with a slight judicious flavouring of information, when the Billickin announced herself.

"I will not hide from you, ladies," said the B, enveloped in the shawl of state, "for it is not my character to hide neither my motives nor my actions, that I take the liberty to look in upon you to express a 'ope that your dinner was to your liking. Though not Professed but Plain, still her wages should be a sufficient object to her to stimilate to soar above mere roast and biled."

"We dined very well indeed," said Rosa, "thank you."

"Accustomed," said Miss Twinkleton, with a gracious air which to the jealous ears of the Billickin seemed to add "my good woman"— "Accustomed to a liberal and nutritious, yet plain and salutary diet, we have found no reason to bemoan our absence from the ancient city, and the methodical household, in which the quiet routine of our lot has been hitherto cast."

"I did think it well to mention to my cook," observed the Billickin with a gush of candour, "which I 'ope you will agree with, Miss Twinkleton, was a right precaution, that the young lady being used to what we should consider here but poor diet, had better be brought forward by degrees. For, a rush from scanty feeding to generous feeding, and from what you may call messing to what you may call method, do require a power of constitution, which is not often found in youth, particular when undermined by boarding-school!"

It will be seen that the Billickin now openly pitted herself against Miss Twinkleton, as one whom she had fully ascertained to be her natural enemy.

"Your remarks," returned Miss Twinkleton, from a remote moral eminence, "are well meant, I have no doubt; but you will permit me to observe that they develop a mistaken view of the subject, which can only be imputed to your extreme want of accurate information."

473

"My information," retorted the Billickin, throwing in an extra syllable for the sake of emphasis at once polite and powerful: "My information, Miss Twinkleton, were my own experience, which I believe is usually considered to be a good guidance. But whether so or not, I was put in youth to a very genteel boarding-school, the mistress being no less a lady than yourself, of about your own age or it may be some years younger, and a poorness of blood flowed from the table which has run through my life."

"Very likely," said Miss Twinkleton, still from her distant eminence; "and very much to be deplored. Rosa, my dear, how are you getting on with your work?"

"Miss Twinkleton," resumed the Billickin, in a courtly manner, "before retiring on the Int, as a lady should, I wish to ask of yourself as a lady, whether I am to consider that my words is doubted?"

"I am not aware on what ground you cherish such a supposition," began Miss Twinkleton, when the Billickin neatly stopped her.

"Do not, if you please, put suppositions betwixt my lips, where none such have been imparted by myself. Your flow of words is great, Miss Twinkleton, and no doubt is expected from you by your pupils, and no doubt is considered worth the money. *No* doubt, I am sure. But not paying for flows of words, and not asking to be favored with them here, I wish to repeat my question."

"If you refer to the poverty of your circulation," began Miss Twinkleton, when again the Billickin neatly stopped her.

"I have used no such expressions."

"If you refer then to the poorness of your blood."

"Brought upon me," stipulated the Billickin, expressly, "at a boarding-school."

"Then," resumed Miss Twinkleton, "all I can say, is, that I am bound to believe on your asseveration that it is very poor indeed. I cannot forbear adding, that if that unfortunate circumstance influences your conversation, it is much to be lamented, and it is eminently desirable that your blood were richer. Rosa, my dear, how are you getting on with your work?"

"Hem! Before retiring, Miss," proclaimed the Billickin to Rosa, loftily cancelling Miss Twinkleton, "I should wish it to be understood between yourself and me that my transactions in future is with you alone. I know no elderly lady here, Miss, none older than yourself."

"A highly desirable arrangement, Rosa, my dear," observed Miss Twinkleton.

"It is not, Miss," said the Billickin, with a sarcastic smile, "that I possess the Mill I have heard of, in which old single ladies could be ground up young (what a gift it would be to some of us!), but that I limit myself to you totally."

"When I have any desire to communicate a request to the person of the house, Rosa, my dear," observed Miss Twinkleton, with majestic cheerfulness, "I will make it known to you, and you will kindly undertake, I am sure, that it is conveyed to the proper quarter."

"Good-evening, Miss," said the Billickin, at once affectionately and distantly. "Being alone in my eyes, I wish you good-evening with best wishes, and do not find myself drove, I am truly 'appy to say, into expressing my contempt for any indiwidual, unfortunately for yourself, belonging to you."

The Billickin gracefully withdrew with this parting speech, and from that time Rosa occupied the restless position of shuttlecock between these two battledores. Nothing could be done without a smart match being played out. Thus, on the daily-arising question of dinner, Miss Twinkleton would say, the three being present together:

"Perhaps, my love, you will consult with the person of the house, whether she can procure us a lamb's fry; or, failing that, a roast fowl."

On which the Billickin would retort (Rosa not having spoken a word), "If you was better accustomed to butcher's meat, Miss, you would not entertain the idea of a lamb's fry. Firstly, because lambs has long been sheep, and secondly, because there is such things as killing-days, and there is not. As to roast fowls, Miss, why you must be quite surfeited with roast fowls, letting alone your buying, when you market for yourself, the agedest of poultry with the scaliest of legs, quite as if you was accustomed to picking 'em out for cheapness. Try a little inwention, Miss. Use yourself to 'ousekeeping a bit. Come now, think of somethink else."

To this encouragement, offered with the indulgent toleration of a wise and liberal expert, Miss Twinkleton would rejoin, reddening:

"Or, my dear, you might propose to the person of the house a duck."

"Well, Miss!" the Billickin would exclaim (still no word being spoken by Rosa), "you do surprise me when you speak of ducks! Not to mention that they're getting out of season and very dear, it really strikes to my heart to see you have a duck; for the breast, which is the only delicate cuts in a duck, always goes in a direction which I cannot imagine where, and your own plate comes down so miserably skin-and-bony! Try again, Miss. Think more of yourself and less of others. A dish of sweetbreads now, or a bit of mutton. Somethink at which you can get your equal chance."

Occasionally the game would wax very brisk indeed, and would be kept up with a smartness rendering such an encounter as this quite tame. But the Billickin almost invariably made by far the higher score; and would come in with side hits of the most unexpected and extraordinary description, when she seemed without a chance.

All this did not improve the gritty state of things in London, or the air that London had acquired in Rosa's eyes of waiting for something that never came. Tired of working and conversing with Miss Twinkleton, she suggested working and reading: to which Miss Twinkleton readily assented, as an admirable reader, of tried powers. But Rosa soon made the discovery that Miss Twinkleton didn't read fairly. She cut the love scenes, interpolated passages in praise of female celibacy, and was guilty of other glaring pious frauds. As an instance in point, take the glowing passage: "Ever dearest and best adored, said Edward, clasping the dear head to his breast, and drawing the silken hair through his caressing fingers, from which he suffered it to fall like golden rain; ever dearest and best adored, let us fly from the unsympathetic world and the sterile coldness of the stony-hearted, to the rich warm Paradise of Trust and Love." Miss Twinkleton's fraudulent version tamely ran thus: "Ever engaged to me with the consent of our parents on both sides, and the approbation of the silver-haired rector of the district, said Edward, respectfully raising to his lips the taper fingers so skilful in embroidery, tambour, crochet, and other truly feminine arts; let me call on thy papa 'ere to-morrow's dawn has sunk into the west, and propose a suburban establishment, lowly it may be, but within our means, where he will be always welcome as an evening guest, and where every arrangement shall invest economy, and constant interchange of scholastic acquirements, with the attributes of the ministering angel to domestic bliss."

As the days crept on and nothing happened, the neighbours began to say that the pretty girl at Billickin's, who looked so wistfully and so much out of the gritty windows of the drawing-room, seemed to be losing her spirits. The pretty girl might have lost them but for the accident of lighting on some books of voyages and sea-adventure. As a compensation against their romance, Miss Twinkleton, reading aloud, made the most of all the latitudes and longitudes, bearings, winds, currents, offsets, and other statistics (which she felt to be none the less improving because they expressed nothing whatever to her); while Rosa, listening intently, made the most of what was nearest to her heart. So they both did better than before.

CHAPTER XXII

THE DAWN AGAIN

ALTHOUGH Mr. Crisparkle and John Jasper met daily under the Cathedral roof, nothing at any time passed between them bearing reference to Edwin Drood after the time, more than half a year gone by, when Jasper mutely showed the Minor Canon the conclusion and the resolution entered in his Diary. It is not likely that they ever met, though so often, without the thoughts of each reverting to the subject. It is not likely that they ever met, though so often, without a sensation on the part of each that the other was a perplexing secret to him. Jasper as the denouncer and pursuer of Neville Landless, and Mr. Crisparkle as his consistent advocate and protector, must at least have stood sufficiently in opposition, to have speculated with keen interest on the steadiness and next direction of the other's designs. But neither ever broached the theme.

False pretence not being in the Minor Canon's nature, he doubtless displayed openly that he would at any time have revived the subject, and even desired to discuss it. The determined reticence of Jasper, however, was not to be so approached. Impassive, moody, solitary, resolute, so concentrated on one idea, and on its attendant fixed purpose, that he would share it with no fellow-creature, he lived apart from human life. Constantly exercising an Art which brought him into mechanical harmony with others, and which could not have been pursued unless he and they had been in the nicest mechanical relations and unison, it is curious to consider that the spirit of the man was in moral accordance or interchange with nothing around him. This indeed he had confided to his lost nephew, before the occasion for his present inflexibility arose.

That he must know of Rosa's abrupt departure, and that he must divine its cause, was not to be doubted. Did he suppose that he had terrified her into silence, or did he suppose that she had imparted to any one — to Mr. Crisparkle himself, for instance — the particulars of his last interview with her? Mr. Crisparkle could not determine this in his mind. He could not but admit, however, as a just man, that it was not, of itself, a crime to fall in love with Rosa, any more than it was a crime to offer to set love above revenge.

The dreadful suspicion of Jasper which Rosa was so shocked to have received into her imagination, appeared to have no harbour in Mr. Crisparkle's. If it ever haunted Helena's thoughts, or Neville's, neither gave it one spoken word of utterance. Mr. Grewgious took no pains to conceal his implacable dislike of Jasper, yet he never referred it, however distantly, to such a source. But he was a reticent as well as an eccentric man; and he made no mention of a certain evening when he warmed his hands at the Gate House fire, and looked steadily down upon a certain heap of torn and miry clothes upon the floor.

Drowsy Cloisterham, whenever it awoke to a passing reconsideration of a story above six months old and dismissed by the bench of magistrates, was pretty equally divided in opinion whether John Jasper's beloved nephew had been killed by his treacherously passionate rival, or in an open struggle: or had, for his own purposes, spirited himself away. It then lifted up its head, to notice that the bereaved Jasper was still ever devoted to discovery and revenge; and then dozed off again. This was the condition of matters, all round, at the period to which the present history has now attained.

The Cathedral doors have closed for the night; and the Choir Master, on a short leave of absence for two or three services, sets his face towards London. He travels thither by the means by which Rosa travelled, and arrives, as Rosa arrived, on a hot, dusty evening.

His travelling baggage is easily carried in his hand, and he repairs with it, on foot, to a hybrid hotel in a little square behind Aldersgate Street, near the General Post Office. It is hotel, boarding-house, or lodging-house, at its visitor's option. It announces itself, in the new Railway Advertisers, as a novel enterprise, timidly beginning to spring up. It bashfully, almost apologetically, gives the traveller to understand that it does not expect him, on the good old constitutional hotel plan, to order a pint of sweet blacking for his drinking, and throw it away; but insinuates that he may have his boots blacked instead of his stomach, and maybe also have bed, breakfast, attendance, and a porter up all night, for a certain fixed charge. From these and similar premises, many true Britons in the lowest spirits deduce that the times are levelling times, except in the article of high roads, of which there will shortly be not one in England.

He eats without appetite, and soon goes forth again. Eastward and still eastward through the stale streets he takes his way, until he reaches his destination: a miserable court, specially miserable among many such.

He ascends a broken staircase, opens a door, looks into a dark stifling room, and says: "Are you alone here?"

"Alone, deary; worse luck for me and better for you," replies a croaking voice. "Come in, come in, whoever you be: I can't see you till I light a match, yet I seem to know the sound of your speaking. I am acquainted with you, ain't I?"

"Light your match, and try."

"So I will, deary, so I will; but my hand that shakes, as I can't lay it on a match all in a moment. And I cough so, put my matches where I may, I never find 'em there. They jump and start, as I cough and cough, like live things. Are you off a voyage, deary?"

"No."

"Not seafaring?"

"No."

"Well, there's land customers, and there's water customers. I'm a mother to both. Different from Jack Chinaman t'other side the court. He ain't a father to neither. It ain't in him. And he ain't got the true secret of mixing, though he charges as much as me that has, and more if he can get it. Here's a match, and now where's the candle? If my cough takes me, I shall cough out twenty matches afore I gets a light."

. But she finds the candle, and lights it before the cough comes on. It seizes her in the moment of success, and she sits down rocking herself to and fro, and gasping at intervals, "Oh, my lungs is awful bad, my lungs is wore away to cabbage-nets!" until the fit is over. During its continuance she has had no power of sight, or any other power not absorbed in the struggle; but as it leaves her, she begins to strain her eyes, and as soon as she is able to articulate, she cries, staring:

"Why, it's you!"

"Are you so surprised to see me?"

"I thought I never should have seen you again, deary. I thought you was dead, and gone to Heaven."

"Why?"

"I didn't suppose you could have kept away, alive, so long, from the poor old soul with the real receipt for mixing it. And you are in mourning too! Why didn't you come and have a pipe or two of comfort? Did they leave you money, perhaps, and so you didn't want comfort?"

"No!"

"Who was they as died, deary?"

"A relative."

"Died of what, lovey?"

"Probably, Death."

"We are short to-night!" cries the woman, with a propitiatory laugh. "Short and snappish, we are! But we're out of sorts for want of a smoke. We've got the all-overs, haven't us, deary? But this is the place to cure 'em in; this is the place where the all-overs is smoked off!"

"You may make ready then," replies the visitor, "as soon as you like."

He divests himself of his shoes, loosens his cravat, and lies across the foot of the squalid bed, with his head resting on his left hand.

"Now, you begin to look like yourself," says the woman, approvingly. "Now, I begin to know my old customer indeed! Been trying to mix for yourself this long time, poppet?"

"I have been taking it now and then in my own way."

"Never take it your own way. It ain't good for trade, and it ain't good for you. Where's my inkbottle, and where's my thimble, and where's my little spoon? He's going to take it in a artful form now, my deary dear!"

Entering on her process, and beginning to bubble and blow at the faint spark enclosed in the hollow of her hands, she speaks from time to time, in a tone of snuffling satisfaction, without leaving off. When he speaks, he does so without looking at her, and as if his thoughts were already roaming away by anticipation.

"I've got a pretty many smokes ready for you, first and last, haven't I, chuckey?"

"A good many."

"When you first come, you was quite new to it; warn't ye?"

484

"Yes, I was easily disposed of, then."

"But you got on in the world, and was able by-and-by to take your pipe with the best of 'em, warn't ye?"

"Ay. And the worst."

"It's just ready for you. What a sweet singer you was when you first come! Used to drop your head, and sing yourself off, like a bird! It's ready for you now, deary."

He takes it from her with great care, and puts the mouth-piece to his lips. She seats herself beside him, ready to refill the pipe. After inhaling a few whiffs in silence, he doubtingly accosts her with:

"Is it as potent as it used to be?"

"What do you speak of, deary?"

"What should I speak of, but what I have in my mouth?"

"It's just the same. Always the identical same."

"It doesn't taste so. And it's slower."

"You've got more used to it, you see."

"That may be the cause, certainly. Look here." He stops, becomes dreamy, and seems to forget that he has invited her attention. She bends over him, and speaks in his ear.

"I'm attending to you. Says you just now, look here. Says I now, I am attending to ye. We was talking just before of your being used to it."

"I know all that. I was only thinking. Look here. Suppose you had something in your mind; something you were going to do."

"Yes, deary; something I was going to do?"

485

"But had not quite determined to do."

"Yes, deary."

"Might or might not do, you understand."

"Yes." With the point of a needle she stirs the contents of the bowl.

"Should you do it in your fancy, when you were lying here doing this?"

She nods her head. "Over and over again."

"Just like me! I did it over and over again. I have done it hundreds of thousands of times in this room."

"It's to be hoped it was pleasant to do, deary."

"It *was* pleasant to do!"

He says this with a savage air, and a spring or start at her. Quite unmoved, she retouches and replenishes the contents of the bowl with her little spatula. Seeing her intent upon the occupation, he sinks into his former attitude.

"It was a journey, a difficult and dangerous journey. That was the subject in my mind. A hazardous and perilous journey, over abysses where a slip would be destruction. Look down, look down! You see what lies at the bottom there?"

He has darted forward to say it, and to point at the ground, as though at some imaginary object far beneath. The woman looks at him, as his spasmodic face approaches close to hers, and not at his pointing. She seems to know what the influence of her perfect quietude will be; if so, she has not miscalculated it, for he subsides again.

"Well; I have told you, I did it, here, hundreds of thousands of times. What do I say? I did it millions and billions of times. I did it so often, and through such vast expanses of time, that when it was really done, it seemed not worth the doing, it was done so soon."

"That's the journey you have been away upon?" she quietly remarks.

He glares at her as he smokes; and then, his eyes becoming filmy, answers: "That's the journey."

Silence ensues. His eyes are sometimes closed and sometimes open. The woman sits beside him, very attentive to the pipe, which is all the while at his lips.

"I'll warrant," she observes, when he has been looking fixedly at her for some consecutive moments, with a singular appearance in his eyes of seeming to see her a long way off, instead of so near him: "I'll warrant you made the journey in a many ways, when you made it so often?"

"No, always in one way."

"Always in the same way?"

"Ay."

"In the way in which it was really made at last?"

"Ay."

"And always took the same pleasure in harping on it?"

"Ay."

For the time he appears unequal to any other reply than this lazy monosyllabic assent. Probably to assure herself that it is not the assent of a mere automaton, she reverses the form of her next sentence.

"Did you never get tired of it, deary, and try to call up something else for a change?"

He struggles into a sitting posture, and retorts upon her: "What do you mean? What did I want? What did I come for?"

She gently lays him back again, and, before returning him the instrument he has dropped, revives the fire in it with her own breath; then says to him, coaxingly:

"Sure, sure, sure! Yes, yes, yes! Now, I go along with you. You was too quick for me. I see now. You come o' purpose to take the journey. Why, I might have known it, through its standing by you so."

He answers first with a laugh, and then with a passionate setting of his teeth: "Yes, I came on purpose. When I could not bear my life, I came to get the relief, and I got it. It WAS one! It WAS one!" This repetition with extraordinary vehemence, and the snarl of a wolf.

She observes him very cautiously, as though mentally feeling her way to her next remark. It is: "There was a fellow-traveller, deary."

"Ha ha ha!" He breaks into a ringing laugh, or rather yell.

"To think," he cries, "how often fellow-traveller, and yet not know it! To think how many times he went the journey, and never saw the road!"

The woman kneels upon the floor, with her arms crossed on the coverlet of the bed, close by him, and her chin upon them. In this crouching attitude, she watches him. The pipe is falling from his mouth. She puts it back, and laying her hand upon his chest, moves him slightly from side to side. Upon that he speaks, as if she had spoken.

"Yes! I always made the journey first, before the changes of colours and the great landscapes and glittering processions began. They couldn't begin till it was off my mind. I had no room till then for anything else."

Once more he lapses into silence. Once more she lays her hand upon his chest, and moves him slightly to and fro, as a cat might stimulate a half-slain mouse. Once more he speaks, as if she had spoken.

"What? I told you so. When it comes to be real at last, it is so short that it seems unreal for the first time. Hark!"

"Yes, deary. I'm listening."

"Time and place are both at hand."

He is on his feet, speaking in a whisper, and as if in the dark.

"Time, place, and fellow-traveller," she suggests, adopting his tone, and holding him softly by the arm.

"How could the time be at hand unless the fellow-traveller was? Hush! The journey's made. It's over."

"So soon?"

"That's what I said to you. So soon. Wait a little. This is a vision. I shall sleep it off. It has been too short and easy. I must have a better vision than this; this is the poorest of all. No struggle, no consciousness of peril, no entreaty—and yet I never saw *that* before." With a start.

"Saw what, deary?"

"Look at it! Look what a poor, mean, miserable thing it is! *That* must be real. It's over!"

He has accompanied this incoherence with some wild unmeaning gestures; but they trail off into the progressive inaction of stupor, and he lies a log upon the bed.

The woman, however, is still inquisitive. With a repetition of her catlike action she slightly stirs his body again, and listens; stirs again, and listens; whispers to it, and listens. Finding it past all rousing for the time, she slowly gets upon her feet, with an air of disappointment, and flicks the face with the back of her hand in turning from it.

But she goes no further away from it than the chair upon the hearth. She sits in it, with an elbow on one of its arms, and her chin upon her hand, intent upon him. "I heard ye say once," she croaks under her breath, "I heard ye say once, when I was lying where you're lying, and you were making your speculations upon me, 'Unintelligible!' I heard you say so, of two more than me. But don't ye be too sure always; don't ye be too sure, beauty!"

Unwinking, cat-like, and intent, she presently adds: "Not so potent as it once was? Ah! Perhaps not at first. You may be more right there. Practice makes perfect. I may have learned the secret how to make ye talk, deary."

He talks no more, whether or no. Twitching in an ugly way from time to time, both as to his face and limbs, he lies heavy and silent. The wretched candle burns down; the woman takes its expiring end between her fingers, lights another at it, crams the guttering frying morsel deep into the candlestick, and rams it home with the new candle, as if she were loading some ill-savoured and unseemly weapon of witchcraft; the new candle in its turn burns down; and still he lies insensible. At length what remains of the last candle is blown out, and daylight looks into the room.

It has not looked very long, when he sits up, chilled and shaking, slowly recovers consciousness of where he is, and makes himself ready to depart. The woman receives what he pays her with a grateful "Bless ye, bless ye, deary!" and seems, tired out, to begin making herself ready for sleep as he leaves the room.

But seeming may be false or true. It is false in this case, for, the moment the stairs have ceased to creak under his tread, she glides after him, muttering emphatically: "I'll not miss ye twice!"

There is no egress from the court but by its entrance. With a weird peep from the doorway, she watches for his looking back. He does not look back before disappearing, with a wavering step. She follows him, peeps from the court, sees him still faltering on without looking back, and holds him in view.

He repairs to the back of Aldersgate Street, where a door immediately opens to his knocking. She crouches in another doorway, watching that one, and easily comprehending that he puts up temporarily at that house. Her patience is unexhausted by hours. For sustenance she can, and does, buy bread within a hundred yards, and milk as it is carried past her.

He comes forth again at noon, having changed his dress, but carrying nothing in his hand, and having nothing carried for him. He is not going back into the country, therefore, just yet. She follows him a little way, hesitates, instantaneously turns confidently, and goes straight into the house he has quitted.

"Is the gentleman from Cloisterham indoors?"

"Just gone out."

"Unlucky. When does the gentleman return to Cloisterham?"

"At six this evening."

"Bless ye and thank ye. May the Lord prosper a business where a civil question, even from a poor soul, is so civilly answered!"

"I'll not miss ye twice!" repeats the poor soul in the street, and not so civilly. "I lost ye last, where that omnibus you got into nigh your journey's end plied betwixt the station and the place. I wasn't so much as certain that you even went right on to the place. Now, I know ye did. My gentleman from Cloisterham, I'll be there before ye and bide your coming. I've swore my oath that I'll not miss ye twice!"

Accordingly, that same evening the poor soul stands in Cloisterham High Street, looking at the many quaint gables of the Nuns' House, and getting through the time as she best can until nine o'clock; at which hour she has reason to suppose that the arriving omnibus passengers may have some interest for her. The friendly darkness, at that hour, renders it easy for her to ascertain whether this be so or not; and it is so, for the passenger not to be missed twice arrives among the rest.

"Now, let me see what becomes of you. Go on!"

An observation addressed to the air. And yet it might be addressed to the passenger, so compliantly does he go on along the High Street until he comes to an arched gateway, at which he unexpectedly vanishes. The poor soul quickens her pace; is swift, and close upon him entering under the gateway; but only sees a postern staircase on one side of it, and on the other side an ancient vaulted room, in which a large-headed, grey-haired gentleman is writing, under the odd circumstances of sitting open to the thoroughfare and eyeing all who pass, as if he were toll-taker of the gateway: though the way is free.

"Halloa!" he cries in a low voice, seeing her brought to a standstill: "who are you looking for?"

"There was a gentleman passed in here this minute, sir."

"Of course there was. What do you want with him?"

"Where do he live, deary?"

"Live? Up that staircase."

"Bless ye! Whisper. What's his name, deary?"

"Surname Jasper, Christian name John. Mr. John Jasper."

"Has he a calling, good gentleman?"

"Calling? Yes. Sings in the choir."

"In the spire?"

"Choir."

"What's that?"

Mr. Datchery rises from his papers, and comes to his doorstep. "Do you know what a cathedral is?" he asks, jocosely.

The woman nods.

"What is it?"

She looks puzzled, casting about in her mind to find a definition, when it occurs to her that it is easier to point out the substantial object itself, massive against the dark-blue sky and the early stars.

"That's the answer. Go in there at seven to-morrow morning, and you may see Mr. John Jasper, and hear him too."

"Thank ye! Thank ye!"

The burst of triumph in which she thanks him, does not escape the notice of the single buffer of an easy temper living idly on his means. He glances at her; clasps his hands behind him, as the wont of such buffers is; and lounges along the echoing precincts at her side.

"Or," he suggests, with a backward hitch of his head, "you can go up at once to Mr. Jasper's rooms there."

The woman eyes him with a cunning smile, and shakes her head.

"Oh! You don't want to speak to him?"

She repeats her dumb reply, and forms with her lips a soundless "No."

"You can admire him at a distance three times a day, whenever you like. It's a long way to come for that, though."

The woman looks up quickly. If Mr. Datchery thinks she is to be so induced to declare where she comes from, he is of a much easier temper than she is. But she acquits him of such an artful thought, as he lounges along, like the chartered bore of the city, with his uncovered grey hair blowing about, and his purposeless hands rattling the loose money in the pockets of his trousers.

The chink of the money has an attraction for her greedy ears. "Wouldn't you help me to pay for my travellers' lodging, dear gentleman, and to pay my way along? I am a poor soul, I am indeed, and troubled with a grievous cough."

"You know the travellers' lodging, I perceive, and are making directly for it," is Mr. Datchery's bland comment, still rattling his loose money. "Been here often, my good woman?"

"Once in all my life."

"Ay, ay?"

They have arrived at the entrance to the Monks' Vineyard. An appropriate remembrance, presenting an exemplary model for imitation, is revived in the woman's mind by the sight of the place. She stops at the gate, and says energetically:

"By this token, though you mayn't believe it, that a young gentleman gave me three and sixpence as I was coughing my breath away on this very grass. I asked him for three and sixpence, and he gave it me."

"Wasn't it a little cool to name your sum?" hints Mr. Datchery, still rattling. "Isn't it customary to leave the amount open? Mightn't it have had the appearance, to the young gentleman—only the appearance—that he was rather dictated to?"

"Lookee here, deary," she replies, in a confidential and persuasive tone, "I wanted the money to lay it out on a medicine as does me good, and as I deal in. I told the young gentleman so, and he gave it me, and I laid it out honest to the last brass farden. I want to lay out the same sum in the same way now; and if you'll give it me, I'll lay it out honest to the last brass farden again, upon my soul!"

"What's the medicine?"

"I'll be honest with you beforehand, as well as after. It's opium."

Mr. Datchery, with a sudden change of countenance, gives her a sudden look.

"It's opium, deary. Neither more nor less. And it's like a human creetur so far, that you always hear what can be said against it, but seldom what can be said in its praise."

Mr. Datchery begins very slowly to count out the sum demanded of him. Greedily watching his hands, she continues to hold forth on the great example set him.

"It was last Christmas Eve, just arter dark, the once that I was here afore, when the young gentleman gave me the three and six."

Mr. Datchery stops in his counting, finds he has counted wrong, shakes his money together, and begins again.

"And the young gentleman's name," she adds, "was Edwin."

Mr. Datchery drops some money, stoops to pick it up, and reddens with the exertion as he asks:

"How do you know the young gentleman's name?"

"I asked him for it, and he told it me. I only asked him the two questions, what was his Chris'en name, and whether he'd a sweetheart? And he answered, Edwin, and he hadn't.''

Mr. Datchery pauses with the selected coins in his hand, rather as if he were falling into a brown study of their value, and couldn't bear to part with them. The woman looks at him distrustfully, and with her anger brewing for the event of his thinking better of the gift; but he bestows it on her as if he were abstracting his mind from the sacrifice, and with many servile thanks she goes her way.

John Jasper's lamp is kindled, and his Lighthouse is shining when Mr. Datchery returns alone towards it. As mariners on a dangerous voyage, approaching an iron-bound coast, may look along the beams of the warning light to the haven lying beyond it that may never be reached, so Mr. Datchery's wistful gaze is directed to this beacon, and beyond.

His object in now revisiting his lodging, is merely to put on the hat which seems so superfluous an article in his wardrobe. It is half-past ten by the cathedral clock, when he walks out into the Precincts again; he lingers and looks about him, as though, the enchanted hour when Mr. Durdles may be stoned home having struck, he had some expectation of seeing the Imp who is appointed to the mission of stoning him.

In effect, that Power of Evil is abroad. Having nothing living to stone at the moment, he is discovered by Mr. Datchery in the unholy office of stoning the dead, through the railings of the churchyard. The Imp finds this a relishing and piquing pursuit; firstly, because their resting-place is announced to be sacred; and secondly,

497

because the tall headstones are sufficiently like themselves, on their beat in the dark, to justify the delicious fancy that they are hurt when hit.

Mr. Datchery hails him with: "Halloa, Winks!"

He acknowledges the hail with: "Halloa, Dick!" Their acquaintance seemingly having been established on a familiar footing.

"But I say," he remonstrates, "don't yer go a making my name public. I never means to plead to no name, mind yer. When they says to me in the Lock-up, a going to put me down in the book, 'What's your name?' I says to them 'Find out.' Likeways when they says 'What's your religion?' I says, 'Find out.'"

Which, it may be observed in passing, it would be immensely difficult for the State, however statistical, to do.

"Asides which," adds the boy, "there ain't no family of Winkses."

"I think there must be."

"Yer lie, there ain't. The travellers give me the name on account of my getting no settled sleep and being knocked up all night; whereby I gets one eye roused open afore I've shut the other. That's what Winks means. Deputy's the nighest name to indict me by: but yer wouldn't catch me pleading to that, neither."

"Deputy be it always, then. We two are good friends; eh, Deputy?"

"Jolly good."

"I forgave you the debt you owed me when we first became acquainted, and many of my sixpences have come your way since; eh, Deputy?"

"Ah! And what's more, yer ain't no friend o' Jarsper's. What did he go a histing me off my legs for?"

"What indeed! But never mind him now. A shilling of mine is going your way to-night, Deputy. You have just taken in a lodger I have been speaking to; an infirm woman with a cough."

"Puffer," assents Deputy, with a shrewd leer of recognition, and smoking an imaginary pipe, with his head very much on one side and his eyes very much out of their places: "Hopeum Puffer."

"What is her name?"

" 'Er Royal Highness the Princess Puffer."

"She has some other name than that; where does she live?"

"Up in London. Among the Jacks."

"The sailors?"

"I said so; Jacks. And Chayner men. And hother Knifers."

"I should like to know, through you, exactly where she lives."

"All right. Give us 'old."

A shilling passes; and, in that spirit of confidence which should pervade all business transactions between principals of honor, this piece of business is considered done.

"But here's a lark!" cries Deputy. "Where did yer think 'Er Royal Highness is a goin' to, to-morrow morning? Blest if she ain't a goin' to the KIN-FREE-DER-EL!" He greatly prolongs the word in his ecstasy, and smites his leg, and doubles himself up in a fit of shrill laughter.

"How do you know that, Deputy?"

"Cos she told me so just now. She said she must be hup and

hout o' purpose. She ses, 'Deputy, I must 'ave a early wash, and make myself as swell as I can, for I'm a goin' to take a turn at the KIN-FREE-DER-EL!' " He separates the syllables with his former zest, and, not finding his sense of the ludicrous sufficiently relieved by stamping about on the pavement, breaks into a slow and stately dance, perhaps supposed to be performed by the Dean.

Mr. Datchery receives the communication with a well-satisfied though a pondering face, and breaks up the conference. Returning to his quaint lodging, and sitting long over the supper of bread and cheese and salad and ale which Mrs. Tope has left prepared for him, he still sits when his supper is finished. At length he rises, throws open the door of a corner cupboard, and refers to a few uncouth chalked strokes on its inner side.

"I like," says Mr. Datchery, "the old tavern way of keeping scores. Illegible, except to the scorer. The scorer not committed, the scored debited with what is against him. Hum; ha! A very small score this; a very poor score!"

He sighs over the contemplation of its poverty, takes a bit of chalk from one of the cupboard shelves, and pauses with it in his hand, uncertain what addition to make to the account.

"I think a moderate stroke," he concludes, "is all I am justified in scoring up;" so, suits the action to the word, closes the cupboard, and goes to bed.

A brilliant morning shines on the old city. Its antiquities and ruins are surpassingly beautiful, with the lusty ivy gleaming in the sun, and the rich trees waving in the balmy air. Changes of glorious light from moving boughs, songs of birds, scents from gardens, woods, and fields—or, rather, from the one great garden of the whole cultivated island in its yielding time—penetrate into the Cathedral, subdue its earthy odour, and preach the Resurrection and the Life. The cold stone tombs of centuries ago grow warm; and flecks of brightness dart into the sternest marble corners of the building, fluttering there like wings.

Comes Mr. Tope with his large keys, and yawningly unlocks and sets open. Come Mrs. Tope, and attendant sweeping sprites. Come, in due time, organist and bellows-boy, peeping down from the red curtains in the loft, fearlessly flapping dust from books up at that remote elevation, and whisking it from stops and pedals. Come sundry rooks, from various quarters of the sky, back to the great tower; who may be presumed to enjoy vibration, and to know that bell and organ are going to give it them. Come a very small and straggling congregation indeed: chiefly from Minor Canon Corner and the Precincts. Come Mr. Crisparkle, fresh and bright; and his ministering brethren, not quite so fresh and bright. Come the Choir in a hurry (always in a hurry, and struggling into their nightgowns at the last moment, like children shirking bed), and comes John Jasper leading their line. Last of all comes Mr. Datchery into a stall, one of a choice empty collection very much at his service, and glancing about him for Her Royal Highness the Princess Puffer.

The service is pretty well advanced before Mr. Datchery can

discern Her Royal Highness. But by that time he has made her out, in the shade. She is behind a pillar, carefully withdrawn from the Choir Master's view, but regards him with the closest attention. All unconscious of her presence, he chants and sings. She grins when he is most musically fervid, and—yes, Mr. Datchery sees her do it!—shakes her fist at him behind the pillar's friendly shelter.

Mr. Datchery looks again to convince himself. Yes, again! As ugly and withered as one of the fantastic carvings on the under brackets of the stall seats, as malignant as the Evil One, as hard as the big brass eagle holding the sacred books upon his wings (and, according to the sculptor's representation of his ferocious attributes, not at all converted by them), she hugs herself in her lean arms, and then shakes both fists at the leader of the Choir.

And at that moment, outside the grated door of the Choir, having eluded the vigilance of Mr. Tope by shifty resources in which he is an adept, Deputy peeps, sharp-eyed, through the bars, and stares astounded from the threatener to the threatened.

The service comes to an end, and the servitors disperse to breakfast. Mr. Datchery accosts his last new acquaintance outside, when the Choir (as much in a hurry to get their bedgowns off, as they were but now to get them on) have scuffled away.

"Well, mistress. Good-morning. You have seen him?"

"*I've* seen him, deary; *I've* seen him!"

"And you know him?"

"Know him! Better far, than all the Reverend Parsons put together know him."

Mrs. Tope's care has spread a very neat, clean breakfast ready
for her lodger. Before sitting down to it, he opens his corner-
cupboard door; takes his bit of chalk from its shelf; adds one thick
line to the score, extending from the top of the cupboard door to
the bottom; and then falls to with an appetite.

14.

W̲E HAD REACHED THE CIRCUS MAX-
IMUS and the smoke-wreathed scene
in the opium-den, amidst which Toad's last hopes evapo-
rated.

"It's either the one," our uncompromising aesthete of
crime says, "or the other. Either Jasper relives the murder
of his nephew in a opium haze, the murder he so often
dreamt of and finally committed; or Aylmer's right and
Jasper doesn't relive anything, but continues to imagine
that he has killed the unknown assassin, who in fact fled
after strangling Drood and either hiding the corpse or destroying it.[1] Whichever the truth, the Drood case loses all
its appeal—at least for me."

Dupin and Cuff do not give up so easily.

---

[1] In Aylmer's "reconstruction," the unknown assassin believes he has killed
Drood, having strangled him with the silk scarf he previously removed
from Jasper. But Drood then regained consciousness and, finding the scarf
round his neck, concluded it was his uncle who had tried to kill him, so
he fled immediately to Egypt, not to return until the happy ending.

"The only thing that's clear," says Dupin, "is that the author has prevented, and continues to prevent, any of the protagonists from engaging in a discussion of the case. Jasper, first of all, has sworn that he will not discuss it again 'with any human creature' until he finds the murderer himself. Crisparkle refuses on principle to harbour such suspicion against anyone. Rosa can't prevent herself from suspecting Jasper, but has scruples about admitting it even to herself. Grewgious does not hide his 'implacable dislike' of that shady character, but he 'never referred it, however distantly, to such a source' as murder. Helena, for her part, has decided not to talk to her friend about her brother's 'infatuation,' and the author uses this excuse to have her say nothing at all on the subject. As for the brother himself, he has set so keenly to his studies that he never lifts his head from his books, except to pay homage to Crisparkle and declare himself 'marked and tainted, but innocent.' Now," Dupin continues, "this state of affairs has lasted six months. At which point, Dickens himself, as Cuff quite rightly says, must have realised that he couldn't continue like this without arousing suspicion. Hence his promise of a 'private conversation' between Helena and Rosa. But Cuff also foresaw . . ."

A chorus of maddened car-horns interrupts the speaker and makes the whole work-group jump up from their seats. What's happened? The driver has been paying more attention to the Drood case than to the vehicles in front of him, and has thus drawn the understandable ire of those behind him. But the momentary gap is quickly filled, and now they are motionless again, in Piazza di Porta Capena. The coach (Antonia tells them) will try to turn into Via dei Cerchi, along the valley of the Circus Maximus, where, as everyone knows, the Rape of the Sabine Women took place.

"Yes," says Cuff. "I also foresaw that the author would wriggle out of it with another trick, another display of his extraordinary conjuring talent. What happens in fact? He manages to pass off as a private conversation between Helena and Rosa what is actually a very public one, for though it takes place between two windows, everyone else is listening in, including 'poor Neville.' The result? A merry little operetta scene, in which they talk about everything and everybody—except the reason they're all there. Drood's mysterious disappearance is never mentioned. His very name seems to have become taboo."

DRIVER: Obviously, Professor, this Dickens doesn't want to tie himself down.

CUFF: Exactly. The circumstances in which Drood disappears are far from clear, and the author makes quite sure that the subject is not brought up again. All the information we have comes from that first interrogation of Neville, from which we learnt that he returned home at ten past midnight, after spending a few minutes with Drood on the

506

river bank. The rest is a total mystery. The official enquiry took place without our even knowing it: we learn that it did take place only because, six months later, Rosa says in passing that she, too, was called to testify.

DRIVER: I'd say, Professor, the author didn't call us so he wouldn't have to answer our questions.

DUPIN: Quite. Why, we could have asked at the enquiry, did Crisparkle not wait up for his charge? Could it be that he suddenly felt a great drowsiness after drinking the herb tea that his mother (or so he believed) left on his bedside table? And ever-anxious Jasper, whose window remained illuminated until dawn. Why did he wait so long before hurrying out in search of his nephew? Could he, too, have fallen irresistibly asleep? As for Helena, we are told that she normally shared a room with Rosa; therefore, if she went out that night, Rosa would have certainly noticed. But the college is empty for the Christmas holidays, so perhaps Helena found some pretext for changing rooms . . . These are circumstances that any enquiry, even one conducted by Sapsea, could not have failed to clear up. Instead . . .

It's always a mistake to engage any taxi- or coach-driver in conversation. He's turned round again to contribute to the discussion and neglected to nudge forwards another six feet. When the honking dies down, Superintendent Battle speaks.

"In the last chapter of the last number, Dickens himself sums up the situation and blandly concludes: 'This was the condition of matters, all round, at the period to which the present history has now attained.' In fact, he's given us no all-round picture of the condition of matters, and we haven't attained anything. Cuff and Dupin put their finger on the problem we're faced with: *To find circumstantial proof of someone's guilt, when all the evidence has been kept hidden and practically every party is prevented from speaking.*"

"An unusual problem," says the driver as he starts to turn into Via dei Cerchi.

"A common problem, in Mafia-related crimes," the colonel of the Carabinieri answers him sharply.

The Mafia hypothesis cheers the trippers, and their mood brightens, also because the turning manœuvre into Via dei Cerchi is executed with complete success. The coach now proceeds at a fair speed between the slopes of the Palatine and those of Aventine Hill, which, however, on this side offers nothing of greater interest than the absurd Monument to Gius. Mazzini Sitting in Meditation (1949) on a huge marble plinth with statues and high-reliefs.

"Dickens," Wilmot says, "was an admirer of the great Genoese idealist, whom he knew in person and whose Clerkenwell School (for Italian organ-grinder boys in the streets of London) he supported generously."

508

But we are now approaching the Forum Boarium (the most ancient market in Rome, predating its own foundation) and the immediate problem is how to reach the Roman Forum. Should they cross this market (now Piazza della Bocca della Verità, one of the most interesting and picturesque sights of the city, but also one of the most congested), and continue along Via del Teatro di Marcello, to face the unknown hazards of Piazza Venezia? Or would it be better to attempt a daring short cut along Via S. Giovanni Decollato, Via della Consolazione, and Via del Carcere Tulliano?

The Bocca della Verità (the Mouth of Truth, an ancient drain-cover carved in the shape of a great face; it is traditionally supposed to bite off the hands of liars) appears to attract many of the party, including Loredana, who remarks that if only they could get Jasper to put his hand inside, the case would be solved.

"Not necessarily," Wolfe objects, "since the Jekyllians claim there are two Jaspers: a good and honest one, and a wicked liar. How would the old drain-cover distinguish between them?"

It is therefore decided to attempt the road towards S. Giovanni Decollato. It is extremely narrow, but the sixteenth-century church (which belonged to the Florentine Fraternity, who tended those under death-sentence) is of interest to the Drood group for its Historic Chamber.

"This chamber," Antonia explains, "contains objects relating to various executions, including that of Beatrice Cenci (called the "beautiful parricide") and her brother Giacomo. And who knows, that dark family history (the subject of Shelley's famous tragedy) might inspire someone with some new idea on the Landless twins."

The driver manages to pull up in a little lay-by off the road, but unfortunately the church turns out to be closed. Antonia thus has to content herself with pointing out the façade and informing the group that the cloisters hold seven mass-graves for executed paupers: six for men, one for women.

"Happy days," Marlowe and Archer remark, neither of them pleased with the necrological turn the sight-seeing has taken.

Dr Wilmot then calls attention to the wall opposite and a rusty grating behind which an ancient ruined court-yard can be seen.

"It was probably there," he tells them, "that on March 8, 1845, Dickens climbed onto a heap of old cart-wheels to witness the execution of a country robber who'd beaten a German countess to death."

"Bavarian," specifies the Carabinieri colonel, who re-members the case perfectly. "The poor woman was on a pilgrimage to Rome, inadvisedly on foot and alone, and the murderer, a young man from near Viterbo, with no previous convictions, killed her with a stick in order to possess himself of her money and valuables. He made the mistake of giving some of the valuables to his wife, who in her worry told her confessor about it. Who in turn . . . I don't know if Dickens mentions this . . ."

"He does," Wilmot assures him.

". . . who in turn, then, spoke to our officers in Viterbo. After which the law obviously had to take its course."

"The beheading took place on this very spot," the editor of *The Dickensian* continues, "and in his *Pictures from Italy,* Dickens describes it in macabre, even sadistic, detail. He notes, for example, that although the guillotine worked perfectly, the victim's neck disappeared, having retracted partly into the head and partly into the trunk."

"How awful!" Loredana and Antonia exclaim in disgust, while the driver gives a quick shudder and drives off.

The uneasy silence that follows is broken by Magistrate P. Petrovich.

"I know *Pictures from Italy* very well," he says, "and I must confess that the description of the execution of that poor wretch has always disturbed me. Not only because Dickens, once an opponent of capital punishment, later became a firm advocate of it. And not only because of the silly little joke he makes, probably due to his anti-Papism, about St. John the Baptist. No, what unsettles me is his moralistic contempt for the crowd who came there to 'abandon themselves wholly to pleasure.' But, then, why did *he* come, actually arriving three hours early to be sure of a good view? 'Ah, but I'm not like them!' he must have said to himself on that occasion, as he did on so many other—too many other—occasions in his life. Which, of course, does not diminish my boundless admiration for him as an artist."

"These are difficult things to discuss in a coach . . ." Wilmot begins, with understandable discomfort.

But Inspector Bucket, who has been reflecting on the murder of the Bavarian countess, brings them back to the Drood case.

"After killing Edwin with his heavy stick," he observes (lifting his index finger to his ear, as if to hear suggestions), "Nèville might have stripped the body of its valuables in order to simulate a robbery. Then, after throwing the shirt-pin and watch into the Weir, he might have given the ring to Helena, knowing that she would never do what the peasant woman from Viterbo did, and go and confess everything to the Reverend Crisparkle. But perhaps the author did intend to have her confess in the end?"

This ingenious *perhaps* wins Toad's immediate approval. There can be doubt about it, he says with satisfaction; it's clear that Dickens based the case of the pseudo-Cingalese twins on that of the man from Viterbo, the only difference being that in this instance Helena, too, will mount the scaffold. Let's not forget—he adds—that in the cloisters for the executed there's a grave for women as well.

The colonel of the Carabinieri is not so sure.

"The jewel that the Viterbo villain gave his wife was a ring," he says, "but probably of little value, certainly without any diamonds or rubies. Besides, when I said that he killed her with a stick, I didn't make myself clear: in committing his crime, the murderer of the Teutonic tourist did not employ some makeshift offensive weapon in his possession; he used the victim's own pilgrim's staff. The differences between the two cases are considerable."

"Ah," rejoins Toad, "but when Neville shows his stick to his alleged sister, he says that it's a pilgrim's staff. The sinister allusion is all too clear."

Meanwhile, the coach has come out into Piazza della Consolazione, under the south slope of the Capitol, and Antonia points to a rocky outcrop on the western cliff.

"It was from that place," she says, "that they hurled those found guilty of treason and other infamies. Scholars are agreed that Tarpeian Rock was named after the daughter of the consul Sp. Tarpeius, the first to be so hurled before he was crushed beneath the shields of the Sabines."

LOREDANA *smiles:* And whose body would we see shattered on the ground if we could share Jasper's dreams in the opium-den? I remember he says "It's over!" presumably as he looks down from the top of the tower.

CUFF *recalls:* Doesn't he also say: "So soon"? Or is that the woman in the opium-den? At any rate they are also the words Helena uses, when she talks to Neville before the crime: "Think how soon it will be over."

P. PETROVICH: If it's of any interest, that is similar to what Dickens writes in at the end of the description of the Roman execution: "The show was over."

The more serious Dickensians find this interesting, but Marlowe and Archer are getting irritated: "This is a sightseeing tour, isn't it? Do we have to drag Dickens and the MED into everything?"

ANTONIA *reassures them:* If the traffic in Via della Consolazione permits, we'll soon be arriving at the famous Tullianum, also known as the Mamertine Prison: the name of which does not derive, as was once believed, from Servius Tullius, but from a *tullus* (spring of water) which issued and in fact still issues there, for which reason it was originally used as a cistern. The Tullianum wasn't converted into a prison until Republican days, when they added a cell on top for those condemned to death, among whom were Vercingetorix (who was beheaded), Jugurtha (strangled) and Catiline's accomplices (*"vixerunt,"* said Cicero). All this has nothing to do with Dickens or the MED.

DR WILMOT *smiles:* Up to a point. According to his illustrator, Fildes,[1] it would seem that Dickens's idea was to set the novel's final scene in a condemned cell, and that he was planning to visit the jail in Maidstone by way of research. There is no doubt, however, that he visited the Mamertine, the upper cell of which (later converted into the Chapel of S. Pietro in Carcere) particularly attracted him for the "rusty daggers, knives, pistols, clubs, divers instruments of violence" that had been employed for various murders, and were hung there still "fresh from use" to propitiate Heaven.

Everyone laughs at Antonia's error, including Antonia herself, and she instructs the driver to bear right and turn into Via delle Grazie, forgetting about the Mamertine. They draw up at a side entrance (normally closed, but open now at Antonia's bidding) to the Roman Forum.

---

[1] We will see, later, the cover Fildes designed for the MED, as well as the famous engraving "The Empty Chair."

15.

I F A VISITOR TO THE ROMAN FORUM were to descend now into that narrow underground space incorrectly known as Romulus's Tomb but nonetheless containing, underneath a slab of black marble (the famous Lapis Niger), genuine remains from the Age of Kings, he would surprise Antonia and the Latinist intent on deciphering that enigmatic inscription on the broken pyramidal stele. Apart from the so-called "fibula of Preneste" (probably a forgery), it is without doubt the earliest-known Latin inscription. But where are the others?

Climbing back up to the surface, the visitor might recognise the man lighting his pipe under the Arch of Septimius Severus as Inspector Maigret, and he might also identify Holmes and his friend Watson in the two tourists leaning over the *Millarium aureum* (near the *Umbilicus Urbis*) in order to learn the distances between Rome and the principal cities of the Empire. But we doubt whether he would know Thorndyke and Dr Fell, to say nothing of the obscure Popeau, in the trio who have just entered the Curia (where the Senate used to meet) in order to admire those solemn Anaglypha Traiani, believed to have once adorned the tribune of the Rostra.

As for the rest of the Drood work-group, they've grown tired of waiting for Antonia, and have dispersed into smaller groups here and there: some towards the Basilica Aemilia and the Temple of Antoninus and Faustina, some towards the House of the Vestal Virgins, and others further off, in the direction of the Arch of Titus. What chance do we have now of discovering if the spirit of the place has worked on anyone, inspiring him with some conclusion to the mystery of the MED?

"A mystery of mysteries, a mystery squared!" we hear Hastings exclaim as he follows Poirot amidst the picturesque remains of marble monuments that form a little labyrinth near the Fountain of Juturna. The Belgian investigator replies ironically, "Why not cubed?" and regards the cube-shaped altar dedicated to the *Genius aquarum*.

Thus far, Poirot's contributions to the case have been modest, to say the least; his quip, perhaps, derives from embarrassment more than anything. This exchange with Captain Hastings, however, is interrupted by Dupin, who approaches them from the Rostra, quoting the speech Antony delivered there in perfect English against Caesar's assassins: "Friends, Romans, countrymen . . ."

"On these very Rostrums," he also recalls, "they ex-hibited Cicero's head, after Antony had him murdered by hired killers. Mind you, Antony wasn't the monster of cruelty that he's sometimes made out to be. Once again, as in *Macbeth,* the instigator was his wife, who didn't hesitate to thrust a nail through the great orator's tongue."

An allusion to Helena's true nature?

We now cross the Vicus Tuscus and enter the ancient Law Courts, or Basilican Julia, where the police and carabinieri (the three Scotland Yard men and the Colonel) are talking to the Bench (Magistrate P. Petrovich). This improvised "summit" is not concerned with the MED, however. They are discussing the eternal problem of criminals, whom the police do their best to lock up and the law never tires of setting free again on various pretexts. Incidentally, the Colonel asks, what was Dickens's opinion on this subject?

P. PETROVICH: Dickens deplored the morbid sympathy for criminals of all kinds that he felt was being fostered in Victorian society. Indeed, as he puts it in the MED, the "average intellect of average men" must be clearly distinguished from the "criminal intellect," which is "a horrible wonder apart." His ideas of justice were thus very simple: he urged hanging for those guilty of murder, and life-imprisonment for all other criminals, from highwaymen to hen-thieves and common hoodlums, if they were recidivists.

WILMOT, *who approaches with Loredana:* As for vagabonds, not to mention false ones . . .

POIROT, *who is passing along the Vicus Tuscus with Hastings:* What false vagabonds?

WILMOT: The ones he describes with inimitable humour in his notes on Piazza di Spagna, where he is interested not in the "eighteenth-century scenic flight of steps"—he hated the Baroque—nor in P. Bernini's Barcaccia Fountain, but in the individuals of uncertain social extraction who, dressed as drovers, pilgrims, brigands, and shepherds from the Roman Campagna, hang about on the steps offering their services as models to foreign painters. He calls them "the falsest vagabonds in the world," because, he says, they have "no counterparts in Rome or any other part of the habitable globe."

LOREDANA: What about real vagabonds? Surely he didn't want *them* sentenced to life-imprisonment?

WILMOT: No, and in some of his novels he treats them with a certain indulgence. But we know that the ones that passed in front of his house in Gadshill, on the Dover road, he considered to be "a cursed plague." The very sight of them infuriated him. So much so, in fact, that he actually had an underground passage built to reach his property on the other side of the road, to avoid being accosted while crossing over.

519

HASTINGS: We all have our failings, even the greatest geniuses. I remember on the Somme, the commander of my brigade, a fellow of unquestionable courage . . .

Hastings's military reminiscences are guaranteed to break up any party. A few seconds later, everyone remembers something he has neglected to see—the Temple of Vesta, the Temple of Divus Romulus,[1] or the interesting collections of the Antiquarium Forense—and they all disperse.

Antonia and the Latinist, meanwhile, have finally emerged from the depths, and a little further on they stop by a stone plinth with a dedicatory inscription. What lies behind this persistent epigraphic interest? Could there be some connection with Sapsea, we wonder as we approach them. But this inscription concerns a victory by someone (name chiselled away) in the war against the Goths, and it is soon apparent that the couple's thoughts are far from the Drood case.

"The date is towards the end of the Roman Empire of the West," the Latinist is explaining. "The great Stilicho, with his victory over Radagaisus at Fiesole (403), managed to stem the Gothic invasion. But then he fell into disgrace with Honorius and was put to death (408): As you can see, they even removed his name from this stone (for *damnatio memoriae*). With no more obstacle in Alaric's way, Rome

---

[1] Maxentius's son, who died in childhood in 307 and was deified.

520

fell into his hands (410). This is the tragic background against which Wilkie Collins . . .

"Yes?" Antonia says encouragingly, hanging on his every word.

". . . against which, in his juvenile novel, as I was saying earlier, he set the story of a Roman maiden, the beautiful Antonina . . ."

"Antonina!" exclaims Antonia, clinging to the young scholar in her emotion.

After this, the dialogue becomes so sickly-sweet that we are induced, for discretion's sake, to hurry back to the middle of the Forum and the central stretch of the Sacred Way.[1] This stretch, which slopes slightly upwards from the Vicus Tuscus, was once called the Clivus Sacer. It is here that the course of events takes an odd turn.

What could have been the cause, reader? The influence of an ancient prophecy, such as the one that made the legendary M. Curtius hurl both himself and his horse into this nearby *lacus,* now named after him? Or the influence of some magic-religious cult associated with the Sacred Fig-Tree that stands beside the *lacus*? Or with the *matronae*

---

[1] We will learn later from other members of the group, who unashamedly eavesdropped, that the above-mentioned novel is entitled *Antonina, or the Fall of Rome,* and that the Latinist is so keen on Wilkie Collins that he has read all his novels, even the feeblest of them, and is always happy to recount their plots to anyone who will listen.

veneficae recorded by Livy, who were summoned to the Forum by a *viator* (messenger) and confessed to having poisoned the wells with mysterious potions? Whatever the truth, Marlowe's and Archer's behaviour, as they descend the afore-mentioned Clivus, cannot be accounted for by any natural explanation.

Their conduct so far has been perfectly natural if not altogether above reproach. For example, they tried (unsuccessfully) to chat up a couple of female tourists, who were not even particularly attractive. Then we heard them ask a custodian if it was possible to buy anything stronger than orangeade or mineral water in the Forum. But now we see them flitting like crazed flies around the "ruins of private buildings of the Republican Age" which flank the Clivus. As if possessed, they run back and forth between the rectangular remains of a brick floor and the foundation of a building formed of small rooms placed on either side of intersecting corridors.

What are they looking for? When Holmes goes up and asks them this, they seem to awaken from a trance and admit they have no idea. Holmes's brow darkens, and we at once understand why.

The reader will recall the singular phenomenon provoked by the first subliminal transmission. Someone (the lady from Arezzo?) fell into a kind of hypnotic state, which was accompanied by hallucinations; and someone else

(Holmes, yes, Holmes) said that "certain matters," although they had no apparent connection with the Drood case, "perturbed him greatly." Now, as we know, Holmes once called up the spirit of Dickens to find out who the murderer was; but Boz said that he would rather the truth did not come to light. It is clear, then, that Holmes would be alarmed by any paranormal manifestation during the convention, and this one, an unmistakable incidence of clairvoyance, is especially worrisome.

Because, let's be frank: it is not likely that two such detectives as Marlowe and Archer, courageous but hardly what one would call cultured, would know enough archaeology even to distinguish between the Temple of Saturn and the Basilica of Maxentius. Yet they were irresistibly drawn towards that brick floor and the building with small rooms on either side of intersecting corridors. Who or what informed their sub-conscious that the first was once an inn (identified in 1908 by Boni thanks to the remains of its wine-shop), and the second (discovered later by Bartoli) a brothel?

Now that they have returned to their senses, the two men hurriedly leave the group and the Forum. They will pursue their hedonistic research in town, and make their own way back to the hotel tomorrow morning.

This is but the first of such manifestations. Antonia has the sudden intuition that the carved bases on either side of the Lapis Niger do not support two "crouching lions," as Boni believed, but two large dogs. Wolfe, whom we come across in the Antiquarium Forense, is fascinated by a little *urceus* (pitcher) which was discovered with other fragments in the Archaic Necropolis and now sits in a glass case by a window. "The jug!" we hear him murmur dazedly. Inspector Bucket and Superintendent Battle have been seized by an urge to visit Piazza di Spagna in order to determine the real nature of the vagabonds loitering there. And Popeau, beneath the Arch of Titus, points an accusatory finger at a shabby, bearded individual with an old kitbag by his side, seated on the steps of the Temple of Jupiter Stator. "Murderer! Murderer!" we hear him repeat as if in a dream, but with such conviction that the colonel of the Carabinieri orders an officer passing by to check the suspect's papers.

Well, the reader will scarcely believe it, but the man actually turns out to be a *false vagabond,* a writer by profession, with ample means of support, who has come to the Forum to seek inspiration for a new novel set in the Augustan age.

The Latinist finds nothing strange in this.

"The young Collins," he says, "also came to these ruins for inspiration, and there's no evidence that he was well dressed. Especially since he didn't know Antonina yet!"

"Maybe he, too, had an old kitbag," says Antonia coquettishly.

But Antonia and the Latinist did not take part in yesterday morning's session, and so know nothing of the mysterious vision that occurred there, concerning dogs, a jug next to a window, and a false vagabond who was the real murderer. When Loredana tells them, they, too, fall silent in amazement.

16.

I T IS NINE A.M., READER. The participants are all making their way towards the Dickens Room. But let us step back in time, to see how yesterday's sightseeing concluded. The tour was supposed to end with a visit to St Peter's and the Sistine Chapel, with its magnificent Japanese-sponsored restorations.

They had almost reached the Basilica, when the driver suffered a sudden attack of revulsion. The hostesses called him to task: Did he doubt the magnificent results of the restorations?

It wasn't that, he said. He just couldn't take Michelangelo's frescoes, especially the ones on the rear wall. They turned his stomach.

"You mean the Last Judgement? Do you find it too . . . too *overcharged*?" the two women asked him.

He didn't know, because he'd never seen it; nonetheless he abhorred it—he explained in a strange voice—"as a typical example of pre-Baroque, heralding the intolerable

abortions that Bernini and his friends left all over Rome."
And with this, he made a dangerous U-turn, to join the
Trastevere road and drive back to the U&O.

Antonia and Loredana were prepared to argue with
him, but Dr Wilmot in a low voice advised them not to.
Wilmot did not return to the subject until that evening,
after dinner in the hotel, when the atmosphere was more
relaxed.

"It was another paranormal event," he said. "I don't
know if anyone noticed, but . . ."

"Yes." Porfiry Petrovich nodded. "I couldn't say whether
it was by extrasensory perception or what, but when the
driver flew into that anti-Michelangelo, anti-Baroque
tirade, he was merely repeating Dickens's own thoughts
on the subject. In the *Pictures* . . ."

"And not only in the *Pictures,*" the editor of *The Dickensian* said. "The same opinion (a rather misguided one, to
tell the truth, like all his opinions on the figurative arts) is
to be found in a letter from Rome to his friend and biographer, Forster."

At these words, Holmes struck the table and declared
that there could no longer be any doubt: It was Dickens's
own spirit that was producing these manifestations, to warn
them to leave the Drood case alone.

"Which means we're getting near the truth," the Carabinieri colonel observed shrewdly.

527

But Gideon Fell, an expert in cases of spirits that turned out to be something other than spirits, put forward a different hypothesis: The driver, in the pay of industrial rivals of the sponsors, could have simulated his trance in order to throw the enquiry into confusion.

"Yes, but what about the other manifestations?" asked Maigret, who didn't believe in spirits either, but didn't see how the suppositious rivals of the sponsors were able to transform Marlowe and Archer into learned archaeologists, or to summon up dogs, jugs, and false vagabonds in order to throw the members of the group off the scent.

Father Brown offered a more plausible explanation, pointing out first of all that the Church (and Dickens, too) has always disapproved of spiritualism and the practices connected with it.

"However," he went on, "that should not prevent us from acknowledging that the human mind possesses *natural* faculties that we know little about as yet, such as the so-called powers of telepathy. In yesterday's session, we ourselves became involved in a complex albeit confused psychic interchange, in which fragments of one person's thoughts were transmitted to another's. The same thing may have happened again this afternoon."

TOAD: But the driver . . .

F. BROWN: The driver, I quite agree, could hardly have known Dickens's rash opinion of the Baroque and Michel-

angelo's late work. But Dr Wilmot and Magistrate Petrovich did know it! There was thus no need to disturb the
spirit of Dickens in order to . . .

P. PETROVICH: But I wasn't thinking of any such thing
just then.

WILMOT: Nor was I. I had put Dickens's views on the
subject completely out of my mind, given their relative,
um, irrelevance.

F. BROWN: Which makes this even more probable. In
certain circumstances, it's what the person has forgotten
or considers to be unimportant that becomes the object of
unconscious transmission.

COLONEL: Yes.

F. BROWN: Let's take the case of those . . . public
facilities, as I might call them, which attracted our colleagues, though little more than a heap of stones. Am I
wrong in assuming that someone among us, perhaps our
friend the Latinist, knew exactly what those buildings had
been used for? And thus it was he who unconsciously informed . . .

LATINIST, *heatedly, under Antonia's raised eyebrows:* Quite
unconsciously! Apart from the graffiti that are sometimes
discovered in them, I take no interest in such . . .

F. BROWN: No doubt. But let's turn to the dogs, the
jug, and the false vagabond. These, too, may derive from
unconscious telepathy. But with a few differences. First of

all, they appear to be connected with the MED, despite the fact that they are not mentioned there. In the second place, they were repeated. Finally, we don't know where they come from — that is, *who transmitted them,* although the prime suspect here is, of course, Dr Wilmot.

WILMOT, *finding everyone looking at him suspiciously:* But I . . .

F. BROWN: I know what you're going to say. You didn't take part in the telepathic exchange yesterday, since you weren't imprinted. But someone else in the room may have *picked up* those fragments of your thoughts and transmitted them.

COLONEL: I have information to the effect that a lady wearing no identification badge was seen leaving the room in a hurry. I could arrange for her to be found and brought to the station for questioning. We could also have her confront the accused . . . Dr Wilmot, I mean.

F. BROWN: I would say that Dr Wilmot should first probe his memory. Perhaps the author was planning to use those dogs, that jug, etc., in the final solution. And there might be evidence — indirect — or some allusion of Dickens's that Dr Wilmot felt unimportant and thus put out of his mind.

P. PETROVICH: They could also be elements that some Droodist used in his *own* solution, with no basis in the text, such as the hired assassin proposed by Aylmer, or the umbrella that the American, Kerr,[1] introduced in his famous burlesque solution.

It was on this umbrella, reader, that last night's discussion concluded. In his confusion, Dr Wilmot would have probably liked to begin searching his memory at once, but we saw Loredana tugging him away by the sleeve, while Antonia did the same with the Latinist, who was telling Hastings the plot of *The Haunted Hotel,* a late novel by Wilkie Collins.[2] Apart from a few who stayed up chatting, everybody went to bed.

With regard to this morning's session, the reader must be prepared for a disappointment. No light was thrown on the enigma of the telepathy. Although Dr Wilmot continued his self-examination into the small hours (as his rather drained appearance testifies), he failed to recall anything that connected the paranormal events with the MED, or with any of the literature on the MED. He therefore doubts that he was the agent of the phenomenon. "I might have forgotten dogs or jugs," he says, "but a false vagabond, well, I think I'd remember him."

Whatever the answer, he adds, now that we have fin-

---

[1] O. C. Kerr (pseudonym of R. H. Newell), *The Cloven Foot,* New York, 1870. According to Kerr, Jasper not only lost his memory of the murder but also his umbrella. So when he finds it again . . .
[2] *The Haunted Hotel, or A Mystery of Modern Venice,* London, 1878.

ished examining all six instalments, it would be best to pass on to the secondary documents. The most important being:

a) Dickens's notes, which we have already referred to, on the structure and chapter division of the novel's first six numbers;

b) the cuts, corrections, and additions made by the author on the manuscript or the proofs; and

c) the so-called "Sapsea fragment": i.e., a few manuscript pages of uncertain date, which recount the arrival in Cloisterham of a certain Poker, who tries to ingratiate himself with Sapsea in order to obtain information on Drood's disappearance. It is clearly a first rough version of the character of Datchery, whom Dickens then re-created completely, and it offers no clues as to the real identity of Datchery.

"It goes without saying," states Wilmot, "that all serious Droodists have carefully combed this material in the hope of finding corroboration for their various hypotheses. But, in my opinion, so far not one has come up with any clue worth the name."

Methodical Popeau still would like the material to be transmitted forthwith. But everyone else is happy to take the chairman's word for it and pass on to further matters.

"Especially since time is running out!" shouts Toad.[1]

"The rest of the documentary evidence," Dr Wilmot continues therefore, "consists of the various 'confidential revelations' that Dickens is supposed to have made to his relatives and closest friends. There is, for example, the reference already cited of 'suspense to the end.' There is Fildes's statement about the setting of the last scene in the condemned cell. There is Wills's[2] statement on the 'serious difficulties' the author said he was having with the plot while working on the sixth number: difficulties that Wills believed aggravated his condition of exhaustion and perhaps helped to hasten his end. And there is the much-discussed testimony of Forster, on which all the 'Jekyllian' reconstructions are based; according to which Dickens confided to his friend and biographer that: 1) the culprit was Jasper, and 2) the surprise ending would consist in Jasper's description of his nephew's murder in close detail, but as if he had no idea that he was the murderer."

TOAD: Forster was a charlatan, a pompous, meddling fool! He claimed to be on such close terms with the nov-

---

[1] Tomorrow, reader, is already the fifth and final day of the work-sessions, since Saturday will be devoted to parties and celebrations, and on Sunday everyone goes home.
[2] The sub-editor of the magazine *All the Year Round,* which took over from *Household Words* in 1859.

elist that Dickens told him everything. So when Forster didn't know, he guessed, or just brazenly invented things. Dickens even threw him out of the house for this once. I move that his testimony be struck from the record.

WILMOT: And various other people claimed to have received "confidences" with regard to Drood's death or the true identity of Bazzard. The only conclusion one can really draw is that Dickens, pestered by inquisitive people on all sides and trusting nobody, chose to "reveal" to each one the first thing that entered his head.

POIROT: Even to the Queen?

Poirot's question takes everyone by surprise, including ourselves. What does the Belgian investigator know of the relations between Dickens and Queen Victoria? The smile on the face of Magistrate P. Petrovich, the only Dickens expert in the room apart from the editor of *The Dickensian*, helps us guess the truth. Our step back in time at the beginning of this chapter was not sufficient. Last night, after everyone went to bed, we reported that a few people stayed up chatting. But, sleepy ourselves, we passed up the chance to listen in, feeling it could not be relevant to the Drood case. But it is clear now that Poirot (perhaps judging that Wilmot, so engrossed in Loredana, is no longer to be relied on, or perhaps merely wanting to speed things up) subjected Porfiry Petrovich to a quick cross-examination.

It is too late to find out just what he asked him. But Petrovich, among other things, must have related the picturesque little anecdote that Wilmot now recounts.

WILMOT: In March 1870, when the first number of the MED was already eagerly awaited by everybody, Queen Victoria received the author at Buckingham Palace. Dickens supposedly promised her, as a joke, that she would have each number "much earlier than common mortals." But there was also a rumour (which might well have been spread deliberately, to increase sales) that he had promised to let her know the solution of the mystery in advance.[1] It is a fact that the author dedicated a bound edition of his works to her on that occasion; and that at the beginning of June, while he was finishing the sixth number, Her Majesty wrote to him from Balmoral to tell him of the "beautiful effect" that the volumes made on a shelf in her living room. Perhaps a way of reminding him of his promise?

LOREDANA, *to Wilmot, beside herself in her veneration for the English Royal Family:* Her Majesty! This is wonderful! Why didn't you tell us before?

ANTONIA,[2] *to the scholar from Juan-les-Pins, whose republi-*

---

[1] This could be important. It meant that if someone did not want the secret of the MED to be revealed, he could not wait until the last moment to stop it.

[2] It goes without saying that Antonia, after her involvement in the manifestations yesterday, was authorised by the sponsors to join the Drood work-group permanently.

535

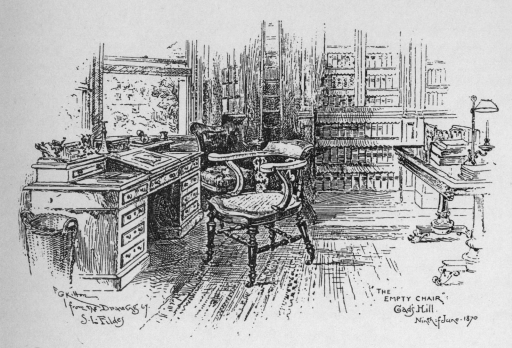

"THE
EMPTY CHAIR".
Gads Hill.
Ninth of June 1870

Figure 1.

can sentiments she has now adopted: I don't see the difference
between her and common mortals, do you?

The editor of *The Dickensian* ignores the interruption.
He signals to an attendant in a black apron, then turns to
the screen that has taken the place of the blackboard at
the front of the room.

"But the letter from Balmoral Castle," he continues,
"did not reach Gadshill until June 10, the day after . . .
Figure 1, please."

The lights go out, and on the screen appears "The

536

Empty Chair," the famous drawing by Luke Fildes, engraved by F. G. Kitton, which adorns the dining- or living-rooms of so many old English boarding-houses.

A respectful hush falls on the darkened room. Dr Wilmot's voice rings out as clear and professorial as ever, but there is a waver of emotion in it as he tells of the last days of Dickens.

"During the month of May, which he had spent in London, the circulatory problems from which he suffered worsened. He had got behind in writing the sixth number, which was to be delivered to the printer June 10. But in the peace of Gadshill his health improved. Every morning he went to work in the little chalet of the 'Wilderness,' the wood he owned on the other side of Dover Road, and he would not return until the afternoon, when he had filled a good many pages.

"Possibly he had resolved the difficulties he had mentioned to Wills a few days earlier. At any rate his prodigious inventive powers, the 'opulence and great, careless prodigality' that Kafka particularly admired in him, showed no signs of flagging. One need only consider, in these very last pages, the unsurpassable ebullience of the scene between Deputy and Datchery near the ancient tombs. It was only through blindness, through total incomprehension, that Shaw could have called this novel the work of a man 'already three-quarters dead.' And as for Wilkie Collins, it

was certainly personal rancour that lay behind his venom-
ous description of the MED as 'Dickens' last laboured effort, the melancholy work of a worn-out brain.'

"On June 7, only about fifteen pages were needed to
complete the sixth number. The writer gave himself half a
day's rest. He took Mamie and Georgina [1] for a walk, drove
in the carriage to Rochester to post a few letters, and came
back with some Chinese lanterns which, despite his lame-
ness (he also suffered from oedema of the left foot and
hand), he hung up in the garden himself.

"The next day, he was at work in the chalet again,
where he wrote and corrected another half-dozen pages.
'Tomorrow I'll have finished,' he said to his sister-in-law
when he returned. As usual, he then sat in his study, at
the desk we now see before us, to go through his correspondence. It was five p.m. Towards half-past six he went
into the dining-room. His sister-in-law (Mamie wasn't there;
she had gone to see her sister in London) saw him stagger
as he entered, his face contracted in a grimace of pain. He
had been feeling bad for at least an hour, he told her, as
he sank into a chair. Then he began to make random, dis-
connected remarks. He stood up, saying that he must go

---

[1] His elder daughter and sister-in-law, respectively, with whom the writer
lived since his separation from his wife. His other daughter, Kate, was
married to Wilkie Collins's brother and lived in London.

at once to London; but, overcome by dizziness again, he fell senseless.

"Despite prompt assistance from the local physician, Dr Steele, and the aid of two eminent specialists who were sent for from London, Dickens did not regain consciousness. The diagnosis was a brain haemorrhage. He died on the afternoon of June 9. In this drawing by his friend and illustrator, Luke Fildes, we can see his study exactly as he had left it the day before: with the unposted letters and the 'empty chair' moved away from the desk . . . Lights, please."

17.

"WAITING FOR POIROT," jokes Loredana while Dr Wilmot looks meaningfully at his pocket-watch, which tells him it is a quarter past three.

Poirot, usually so punctual, is late for the afternoon session. This is all the more annoying, since, as Toad once again remarks, "Time is running out! We have to present our conclusions by tomorrow evening. Mind you, if the culprit turns out to be Jasper or the unknown assassin, don't expect my signature."

But it is not only Poirot (whose friend Hastings denies all knowledge of his whereabouts) who is late. Dr Thorndyke and the colonel of the Carabinieri are also missing. As is . . . no, here comes the Collinsian Latinist, together with Antonia.

At three-twenty the chairman opens the session regardless, nodding to the attendant to take up his position at the projector, as he did this morning.

"The last document we must examine," he says, "is

the cover illustration, which Fildes drew for the MED to precise instructions from the author. The illustration is the same for all the numbers, as I believe I've already told you. To make up for this, as J. Cuming Walters put it so concisely, 'No two Droodists have ever given the same explanation of it.'[1] Figure 2, please."

After the sense of melancholy that the "Empty Chair" left in everybody, the cover of the MED, with its cluster of animated scenes, has more of a humorous effect. Maigret's and Dupin's remarks, however, which open the discussion, are less frivolous than one might expect.

MAIGRET: The young couple leaving the cathedral, in the top left-hand corner, would seem to reassure the Victorian reader that the story will have a happy and matrimonial ending. But who are the happy couple? If we are to judge by Jasper's expression, as he watches them, gnawing his fingers (assuming it is Jasper, on the right, next to the Dean and the Minor Canon), then the bride must be Rosa, who has crowned her dream of love with Mr. Tartar. Except that, traditionally, the wedding takes place *after* the murderer has been unmasked. What, then, is Jasper doing there? He should have been executed by now, or at least be sitting in the condemned cell.

DUPIN: If we take up the suggestions of the last issue,

[1] J. Cuming Walters, *The Complete MED,* London, 1912.

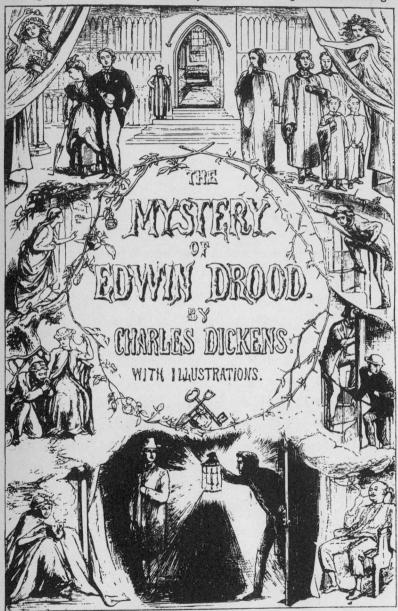

THE

MYSTERY

OF

EDWIN DROOD.

BY

CHARLES DICKENS.

WITH ILLUSTRATIONS.

LONDON: CHAPMAN & HALL, 193, PICCADILLY.

Advertisements to be sent to the Publishers, and ADAMS & FRANCIS, 59, Fleet Street, E.C.

[The right of Translation is reserved.]

Figure 2.

a truly happy ending would have to be *doubly* matrimonial: Rosa and Tartar on one side, Helena and Crisparkle on the other. The illustrator would hardly have missed such an opportunity! From which we can conclude that things go very differently, and that the condemned cell contains not Jasper but Helena and her wretched alleged brother.

TOAD: Pray to God it be so!

P. PETROVICH: But note that all the episodes illustrated on the cover, apart from the one in the middle at the bottom, are literally set in an opium-haze, for they are all framed by the clouds rising from the pipes of the two smokers in the lower corners, the opium-den woman and, symmetrically, the Chinaman from the rival den. The scene at the top, therefore . . .

WILMOT: Yes, almost all the Jekyllians make this point, at least as far as the scene at the top is concerned. That is to say, it isn't a real scene but Jasper's nightmare: under the influence of the opium, he's oppressed by the thought of Rosa's and Edwin's wedding day, and so begins to plan his crime. As for the two little scenes on the left, it makes no difference whether they're dreams or not: in the first, a girl, probably Rosa, is reading one of the "LOST" notices posted in and around Cloisterham after Drood's disappearance; in the second, Jasper is kneeling at Rosa's feet, declaring his love for her.

LIEUTENANT: What about the scene on the right?

The lights come back on, allowing us to pick out the Lieutenant in the first row; he entered in the dark and took the seat usually occupied by his superior officer. ("Lieutenant Mattei," he says, introducing himself with a courteous bow. "The Colonel apologises, but official duties have detained him in the barracks. He sent me to keep him up to date with the course of the enquiry.") We take the opportunity to look around the room, but neither Poirot nor Thorndyke has turned up. The lights dim again.

WILMOT: In the scene on the right, it can't be Jasper taking his nephew up the tower to strangle him and throw him down, either in a dream or reality. Because in that case who would the third man be? Therefore it must be a true scene set at the *end* of the investigation, although Datchery is not recognisable. According to Wilson, whose theory we've already discussed, the three on the spiral staircase are Neville, Crisparkle, and Grewgious, and they're following Datchery to the top of the tower, where they intend to surprise Jasper, who has compulsively returned to the scene of the crime.

BUCKET: These Jekyllians pull out the opium whenever it suits them, but forget all about it when it doesn't.

BATTLE: Exactly. Wasn't it Wilson who used the opium to argue Jasper's split-personality, but who said that the final confession would be torn from him by Helena, through hypnosis, because otherwise the plagiarism from Collins would be too obvious? It's the same here: the scene at the top is explained by the opium clouds at the bottom; but not the scene on the right, because that doesn't fit his interpretation. No, this makes things too easy!

LIEUTENANT MATTEI, *instantly winning Toad's approval:* Yes, too easy.

WILMOT: Let's go to the drawing in the middle at the bottom. This is the favourite of those who believe Jasper is the murderer: the anti-Jasperians, you might say. They are by no means all Jekyllians; many of them feel that Jasper is simply a villain, a "wicked man" whose drug-addiction serves as no excuse.

LIEUTENANT MATTEI, *at once losing Toad's approval:* Quite right.

SERGEANT CUFF: I can imagine how the anti-Jasperians read this, and up to a point I agree. The man with the lantern is Jasper, and he's entering Mrs Sapsea's tomb, to open the coffin and check its contents.

WILMOT: Yes, he's worked out that Datchery is an investigator whom Grewgious has put on his track, and he's also learnt about the ring, thanks to his habit of constant spying and eavesdropping. He rightly fears that the ring may have remained intact amidst the calcified remains that he hid in the tomb, so he's come to remove it.

DUPIN: But Datchery, who is of course Bazzard, was not so clumsy as to let this crucial secret out by mistake.

It was by design that he conferred with Grewgious near the Cathedral, raising his voice enough for Jasper to over-hear. So when Jasper takes the bait and that very night approaches with his lantern, Datchery is there waiting for him, phantom-like and menacing.

WILMOT: Some of Jasper's defenders wriggle out of this with various ingenious explanations,[1] but this is in fact the interpretation of his most influential accusers. But, as I have already mentioned, they are not all agreed on the identity of the mysterious investigator. Some believe Datchery to be . . . Helena. Others say he is Bazzard. The ghostly figure in the tomb is not Bazzard, however, but Helena *disguised as Drood,* or, rather *as Drood's ghost.* In this way she adds the effect of surprise to her hypnotic powers and so obtains the confession.

P. PETROVICH, *clearing his throat:* Ahem, I don't know what the legal value would be of a confession obtained under such circumstances. But whoever the ghostly indi-vidual is, if the scene really is set in Mrs Sapsea's tomb, Jasper's appearance there tells very strongly against him.

CUFF: Why?

The question, delivered in a firm voice, is like a gaunt-let thrown. Everyone immediately understands that the high-

---

[1] Aylmer, for example, claims that this scene does not take place in the Sapsea tomb but at some other location, where Jasper meets Neville or a different individual whom he suspects is the unknown assassin.

ranking Scotland Yard officer has his own counter-explanation. This counter-explanation (the chairman says, smiling) will certainly be less fantastic than those offered by
other defenders in the past. Less fantastic but far more
elaborate, which makes it a pity that Thorndyke and Poirot
are not present to hear it.

"And therefore," continues Wilmot, while the lights
are turned back on, which confirms that the two seats are
still empty, "as it is already late, I suggest we adjourn until
tomorrow, when we may hope . . ."

"By all means," says Cuff, no less courteously. "But
what I have to say is by no means elaborate. I merely
wished to remind the defenders that Jasper, as he never
tires of repeating, *is investigating matters too.* Why, then, should
his meeting another investigator in Mrs Sapsea's tomb 'tell
very strongly against him'? No, my idea is that from the
moment of this encounter, Datchery begins to glimpse the
truth as well, and so secretly joins forces with Jasper to
unmask the real murderers.

TOAD, *highly excited:* I move that we at once present the
sponsors with this irrefutable solution! The murderers are
the two sinister Cingalese twins. Jasper is as innocent as a
new-born babe!

HOLMES, *lugubriously:* May be, and I would be only too
happy if it were so . . . But in that case why should the
author have said, in his message from beyond, that he did

547

not wish the secret to come to light? . . . No, Drood's disappearance conceals something far more sinister! Besides, I fail to see what connection there is . . .

He breaks off. His detective instinct is clearly struggling with the promise made to Dickens's ghost. At last Holmes shakes his head and refuses to go on. Everyone accepts Dr Wilmot's suggestion and prepares to leave the room.

But Loredana, who appears to be struck by a professional doubt, does not leave the platform.

"I don't understand," she says at last. "It's so uncharacteristic for two such well-mannered people as Mr Poirot and Mr Thorndyke to have stayed away like this without even taking the trouble to notify us."

ANTONIA, *from her seat, to Loredana:* I don't understand either. Or maybe I do, all too well. You don't think . . .

LOREDANA: Oh, of course!

ANTONIA: Wait here, then, while I go and see.

The participants, accustomed to the ways of big international hotels, have all guessed the truth before Antonia returns with folded slips of paper, which are recognisable as the light-blue forms for telephone messages at the reception desk. There is also a telex.

"They're all urgent, all addressed to Dr Frederick Wilmot in the Dickens Room," Loredana says, flipping through

548

them and handing them to the chairman in order of arrival, "and all were sitting there at the reception desk."

"*O tempora,*" the Latinist remarks on everybody's behalf.

Dr Wilmot reads them aloud. "1415 hours, telephone message from Rome from Mr Poirot and Mr Thorndyke: *Making outside enquiries on D. case. Will probably arrive late. Please excuse. Proceed in our absence.* 1445 hours, telephone from Spoleto, Perugia: *Unable to return before evening.* 1530 hours, telephone from Monte S. Savino, Arezzo, from Mr Poirot: *Returning tomorrow morning.* 1600 hours, telex from Pisa: *Hope to return tomorrow afternoon—Thorndyke.*"

Everyone naturally turns to Hastings and Thorndyke's colourless lawyer-companion, Astley.

What do they mean by "outside enquiries"? And why at Spoleto? And why at Monte San Savino? And Pisa? Could there be some connection between its famous tower, so brilliantly described in the *Pictures,* and the tower of Cloisterham? Furthermore, why does Poirot announce his return for tomorrow morning, while Thorndyke "hopes" to return tomorrow afternoon?

Hastings repeats, though with embarrassment (he is probably not telling the truth), that he did not even know Poirot intended to leave the U&O; and Astley limits himself to a formal "no comment."

Suspicions then fall on the Latinist, who had been seen talking at length with Poirot after the morning session, and on Antonia as well. (The two had a "rather sheepish air," according to Popeau, when they arrived late for the afternoon session.) Others, noting the simultaneous disappearance of the colonel, accost Lieutenant Mattei; but the latter announces that he must return to barracks at once and takes his leave with a curt military bow.

The remainder of the evening passes in wild and playful conjectures: such as Maigret's idea that Spoleto, with its festival, might throw light on some of the MED's many allusions to theatrical works. But most people apparently decided to keep their theories to themselves. Monte San Savino, after all, must have suggested something to somebody. And who could have failed to notice the unusual speed with which the two investigators traveled, indicating some extraordinary means of transportation. As for Pisa, its significance is perfectly clear—at least to us—in the light of Thorndyke's movements and his "hope" of returning before tomorrow afternoon.

As for the rest, all we can do is wait until tomorrow morning.

18.

THE D. CASE may call for 'outside enquiries,' but a little punctuality would do no harm either," says the editor of *The Dickensian* in some irritation, as he re-examines the blue slips of paper from yesterday. "Besides, Poirot did ask us to proceed without him. So, since there seem to be no further messages,[1] I would suggest . . ."

"Quite right," says the colonel of the Carabinieri, who has arrived with his customary punctuality, and pretends not to notice the curious eyes directed towards him from all sides.

"We might begin," says Magistrate Petrovich, "by recapitulating and comparing the main theses. Of which I believe there are three."

"Four," Maigret corrects him. "Let's not forget the false vagabond."

---

[1] No further messages have arrived so far, reader. Should any come, Antonia is poised at the reception desk, ready to bring them at once to our attention. So it strikes us, too, as a good idea to begin now.

"Ah, well . . ." The accuser of Raskolnikov smiles. "But why not forget him? We know that in the Cloisterham of the novel, as in Rochester in reality, there was a continual to and fro of tramps on their way from Gravesend to Dover and vice versa. Now, on the grounds of . . . well, literary absurdity, as one might put it, we've ruled out the idea that Drood was assaulted and killed by a true vagabond, for theft, like the poor pilgrim countess on her way to Rome. But what if the murderer were the unknown Oriental assassin disguised as an Occidental vagabond? I know that this would still not satisfy our friend Toad, but it is by no means impossible. It is a variation, however, on the theme of the unknown assassin, and so the main theses remain three in number."

"They can be reduced even to two," says Dupin, "because . . ."

"One moment, one moment," the chairman cuts in, "let's first state what these three are. Otherwise we'll get confused."

"Absolutely right," says Colonel D'Attilio (at last we are provided his name).

By common accord, then, Dr Wilmot is asked to expound the three main theses.

THESIS A

This is the thesis put forward by Wilson and later refined by Forsyte: Not only is Jasper the murderer, but his motive and modus operandi are precisely as expected. Jasper's jealousy of Rosa and hatred for his nephew is so intense that he plans to strangle him and in addition hurl him from the top of the tower; after which he will decompose the body in the quicklime and hide the bones in the Sapsea tomb. But Datchery/Bazzard will identify the bones thanks to the ring, and the uncle-murderer will finally confess.

The obvious objection to this thesis is that the mystery is no mystery, for we already know everything. The answer to the objection: The mystery lies in Jasper's split-personality, which will be dramatically revealed to the reader only at the end.

The main criticism of this answer, made by the supporters of Thesis B: However dramatic the revelation of Jasper's split-personality may be, the public, who has already been introduced, by Wilkie Collins, to the mystery novel, will be terribly disappointed. Dickens could not have been so simple as to fail to see this.

If I may add a criticism of my own (Wilmot says), the motive of jealousy, whether or not it is connected with a split-personality, is completely out of proportion with the ferocity of the modus operandi. Why should Jasper, not content with disposing of his nephew in order to gain access to Rosa, want to vent his rage on the corpse as well? Why must he see him struggling and pleading at his feet[1] before strangling him? After all, it is *he* who is the betrayer; it is not as if Drood perfidiously stole the girl from him!

Therefore, if the murderer really is Jasper, there has to be a deeper motive. And here is where the real mystery might lie. I would remind you of the subtle question put at the very beginning by Colonel D'Attilio: "The opium-addict, who left the den at dawn, doesn't get to the cathedral until that afternoon, when he arrives all out of breath for the service. This means that he can't have left London before one o'clock. Where was he and what was he doing until that time?" The author doesn't tell us, and we let it pass the first time. There might be nothing to it. But the same thing is repeated in the last chapter: Once again Jasper leaves the den at dawn, but as the author deliberately stresses (without, however, giving us a word of explanation), he doesn't set out for Cloisterham again until six p.m. It is thus clear that Jasper has some business in London that has nothing to do with opium. What does it have

---

[1] As Jasper says to the opium-den woman, referring to his "fellow-traveller" on the tower.

to do with Drood? A question that the supporters of Thesis A would do well to consider.

THESIS B

This is the thesis of the "unknown hired assassin," developed by Aylmer, who gives two possibilities: 1) the family vendetta of Muslim origin; 2) a terrorist action in response to a grave affront committed by Drood's father against Islam. Aylmer opts for the family vendetta, since in the other case the plagiarism of *The Moonstone* would be too blatant.

Anyway, in Thesis B, as we saw yesterday, the plan concocted by Jasper is designed entirely to protect Drood and not to harm him. What is particularly interesting and even persuasive is the explanation of the "ghostly cry" that Durdles heard on the night of Christmas Eve *the previous year*. On that night too (the anniversary of the grave affront to the family), an unknown assassin was in Cloisterham; but, finding Drood still engaged to Rosa, he postponed the execution. Even so, he ascended the cathedral tower to reconnoitre the territory, and accidentally fell, letting out the aforementioned cry. Jasper, who not only heard the cry but also the crash, found the corpse, guessed that it must be the assassin, and threw it into the river. This accident inspired his ruthless plan of action in dealing with the assassin that would come the following year. As for

555

Jasper's mysterious business in London, Aylmer's explanation ties in neatly with his thesis: Being Egyptian on his mother's side, Jasper speaks the language perfectly and furthermore is olive-skinned; thus he has been able to infiltrate the Islamic community around the port-district of London, in the hope of identifying the new assassin when he arrives.

THESIS C

WILMOT: This is what we might call the Scotland Yard thesis. It was formulated by Sergeant Cuff, with the assistance of his colleagues Inspector Bucket and Superintendent Battle. I believe it now has the added support of Dupin, Inspector Maigret, and of course our friend Toad. For the first time in the history of MED criticism, the two Landlesses are identified as the murderers.

TOAD: The choice is between the so-called twins and the false vagabond! I totally reject both Thesis A and Thesis B. Nor do I see how the three theses could be reduced to two, in the words of our friend Dupin.

MAIGRET: Actually, they can be reduced to one.

DUPIN: Possibly, but before we synthesise, let us analyse. Well, then. Thesis B and our Thesis C both involve a hired assassin. But in B, the assassin is unknown to everybody, including the reader, since he is none of the characters we have met. A most unsatisfactory device, for it is against all the rules of Father Knox [1] for a criminal case to be solved by bringing in a complete stranger at the last moment. In C, on the other hand, the assassin is unknown only temporarily; it will finally be revealed that he—or, rather, they—figured in the novel from the very beginning.

To sum up, one might say that the two theses complement one another, although naturally several things remain to be explained. For example, Aylmer insists that Drood is not dead but has fled in the belief that it was Jasper who wanted to kill him. But we say he *is* dead and that his remains, with the ring, lie in the Sapsea tomb. How did they get there? That is what must find out. Meanwhile I'll just observe that in both cases we have an inadequate, bungling assassin. Aylmer's is supposed to be an expert strangler, but he leaves Drood merely choked. Our killer, instead of proceeding ritually as his iron-willed fanatical sister would have him do, kills half-heartedly and haphazardly with a walking stick.

TOAD: Excellent.

DUPIN: As for the question of motive, a family vendetta and religious fanaticism need not be mutually exclusive. We do not think—as Aylmer does, and as do the sup-

---

[1] Monsignor Ronald Knox (1888–1957), Roman Catholic priest and classical scholar, laid down the "Ten Commandments of Detection" in 1928.

porters of Thesis A—that Dickens would have allowed the question of plagiarism to deter him from choosing the plot that suited him best. After the relative lack of success of his previous novel and the striking success of *The Moonstone,* his feelings of jealousy towards his former protégé, collaborator, and friend had turned into bile and contempt. "A skilful craftsman, and not even that skilful," as he said to his sub-editor, Wills. He was writing his own mystery now, and probably wanted to show his public that he could do it better: perhaps using the very same ingredients.

F. BROWN: I fear this could well be the truth. Anyone who knows the human heart—and especially the artist's heart—can imagine, from that snatch of dialogue with Wills, what Dickens's interior monologue must have been: "Oh? I'm in decline, am I? Worn-out, finished? I'll show that wind-bag and everyone else! They want a mystery, do they? Very well, I'll teach them how to write a mystery, a *great* mystery, and I'll do it using the same ingredients as that puffed-up pen-pusher, that third-rate scribbler! I'll dignify them, give them life, create real characters, real settings, real atmosphere, drama, suspense, and, by Jove, real prose!" Yes, it is quite possible that the MED grew out of this rage and this pride; this desire to humiliate the hack, to eliminate the parvenu with one sweep of the lion's paw. Honour, old affection, scruples—all forgotten. If such things as Jasper's drugs and the terrorist duo appear to be

558

plagiarised from *The Moonstone,* so much the better: it will be a deliberate, mocking plagiarism.

P. PETROVICH: I began by supporting Thesis A. Jasper's split-personality, which anticipates Jekyll, symbolising the struggle between Good and Evil, struck me (and indeed strikes me still) as worthier of Dickens's pen. However, so far the author has shown us only the Evil side of Jasper: what about the Good side? The struggle, it seems to me, is rather slow in getting off the ground.

So I don't rule out my support for Thesis C, provided the Grand Guignol "family vendetta of Muslim origin" could be eliminated. Something similar to the Rushdie case would be more interesting, as well as more in character with what we know of the Landlesses. Besides, there is no need for us to limit ourselves to ritual terrorism of Islamic or Hindu origin (the latter represented by the well-known *Vama çara,* or Way of the Left Hand). It was in March 1869 that the twenty-year-old Netchaev arrived in Geneva, to propagate that explosive *Revolutionary Catechism,* a book much admired by Bakunin. It stirred young people of every nation to the wildest forms of terrorism. Might not Dickens have taken inspiration from this? In August that same year, he wrote to Forster: "I have a very curious and new idea for my new story. Not a communicable idea (or the interest of the book would be gone), but a very strong one, though difficult to work."

TOAD: Hear, hear!

F. BROWN, N. WOLFE, G. FELL *say nothing, but from their faces it is clear that they, too, are beginning to favour Thesis C.*

SERGEANT CUFF: The "family vendetta of Muslim origin" doesn't satisfy us at Scotland Yard either. A terrorist action of the Netchaev-Bakunin kind, or such as the one planned against Rushdie, strikes us as far more in keeping with the character of Helena (the classic fanatic who'll stick at nothing) and Neville (the classic backslider). Think of the new meaning this would give to the "evil report" that the author inserts in Chapter Sixteen: those rumours that Neville would be capable of almost anything "but for his poor sister, who alone had influence over him, and out of whose sight he was never to be trusted."

And there's the business of the papers that Neville destroys before his attempted flight. What papers, if it's a family vendetta? What need would there be for him to bring papers over from Ceylon? Whereas it's typical of the political terrorist to lumber himself with pamphlets and booklets of subversive propaganda (though not Netchaev's *Revolutionary Catechism,* since in 1842 it didn't exist yet).

Finally, notice that in Thesis B, although Neville is not the assassin, Jasper *suspects* he is. Which explains both Jasper's behaviour towards him and the kind of understanding (re Rosa's engagement) that seems to exist between the two and which I myself had already assumed to exist. But if we do away with the family vendetta idea, we'll need some other link between Edwin's execution and the breaking of the engagement.

TOAD: We'll find it!

WILMOT: Or the computer will. But we should work on the solution in its broad outline.

Things don't look good, reader. The morning session is over and the afternoon one has begun, and still no sign of either Poirot or Thorndyke. The participants are beginning to wonder what contribution the two could make anyway. By now, Thesis C has the support of the majority, even though it has not yet been fully expounded.

"In my opinion," Dupin is saying, "the main problem still to be solved is the one I referred to this morning. If Drood did not survive, contrary to what Aylmer believes, and his remains are found in the Sapsea tomb along with the ring, how did they get there? Perhaps the Landlesses put them there to incriminate Jasper, knowing of his plan to thwart the unknown assassin. But how could they have known of his plan?

"The explanation may be less difficult than it at first seems; it also removes an improbability that none of our predecessors noticed. You will remember that on the night of the crime, for all their anxiety about their young charges, neither Jasper nor the Reverend Crisparkle waited up for them. My hypothesis is that Neville has carefully drugged both with the laudanum he found in Mrs Crisparkle's medicine-closet. Then Helena (who, as I further suggested, changed bedrooms in order to be able to leave the college unobserved) slips into the Gate House to check that the drug is working. There she finds Jasper, who under the effect of the drug falls into his usual monologue and thus unwittingly reveals his plan to her!

"Helena takes the key to the tomb and runs to the river. There she finds Neville, who has killed Drood, albeit not ritually. But what's done is done. She pockets the watch and the pin (which she will throw into the weir the next day) but purposely leaves the ring, to identify the body. The two of them (the young woman has the strength of a man) carry the corpse into Durdles's yard and plunge it into the quick-lime. They then pull out the remains and hide them in the coffin, which Jasper previously unscrewed."[1]

CUFF: As for Datchery/Bazzard, after his encounter with Jasper in the tomb, he directs his enquiries along different lines. Unlike Rosa, Crisparkle, Grewgious, and the rest—

---

[1] All this business with the quick-lime and the carrying of the corpse might strike the reader as exceptionally difficult. But as S. Netchaev explains (words which apply to the religious fanatic as well): "The terrorist must have only one science, that of destruction. To this end he will study engineering, physics, chemistry, even medicine."

and unlike all who have analysed the Drood case before us—Bazzard is not under the mawkish, twisted influence of Helena. Once Jasper has convinced him with his frank explanation, the two will work together to get a confession out of the Landlesses—and they will succeed. But I believe Inspector Maigret has a word to say on this.

MAIGRET: One might think that Neville would be the first to confess, given his weak character and his leanings towards penitence. But in Victorian England a murderer, however sincere his confession, could not hope to escape the death-sentence. Neville knows perfectly well that he'll go to the gallows regardless (and remember how in Chapter Nineteen Jasper prophetically casts their shadow over his sister as well).[1] His weakness could thus result in a stubborn silence. His sister (or "sister") is stubborn for different reasons. Remember Thesis A, in which Jasper's confession is wrested from him by Helena's hypnotic powers. As she says to Rosa, she doesn't fear Jasper's power because she feels that she is stronger than he. But it's possible that in a final trial of hypnotic strength Jasper might come out on top. Thus it would be Helena who confesses under hypnosis; and she would confess in precisely the way Thesis A (based on what Dickens supposedly revealed to

---

[1] "You do care for her peace of mind," he says to Rosa. "Then remove the shadow of the gallows from her!"

Forster) says Jasper will confess: recounting everything in detail, but as if describing another man's crime. This is why I said that the three theses can be reduced to one.

POIROT: But you also mentioned a fourth thesis, Inspector, which we could name Thesis D.

THESIS D

Yes, reader. None of those present, absorbed as they were by the fascinating conclusions of Thesis C, noticed Poirot's arrival. He has been there for some time, in fact, but stayed discreetly by the door.[1] Nobody shows any sign of surprise; nobody asks him premature questions. They know it would be in vain.

The only remark comes from Colonel D'Attilio.

"Thesis D," he says. "Quite right."

MAIGRET, *to Poirot while the latter takes his seat:* I deduce that you have sublistened to us, *cher ami.* You know therefore that I was referring to the false vagabond. And from your messages I deduce that you have been with Thorndyke to the district of Arezzo, after which Thorndyke went to the Pisa airport, from which he no doubt left for London.

DUPIN: I would further deduce the complicity of Col-

---

[1] Also, on his return, he first went to the Technicians' Room to sublisten to the minutes of the last two sessions.

onel D'Attilio, who was also absent yesterday afternoon. Because there is no way one can be in Rome at 1415, in Spoleto at 1445, in the district of Arezzo at 1530, and in Pisa at 1600, without the use of a helicopter belonging to the Carabinieri.

D'ATTILIO: One can hide nothing from you, Dupin. I admit that I supplied the helicopter, at Poirot's request, after taking a statement from the relatives of the lady whose brother, by her own admission, is a senior consultant in Arezzo.

As for the reader, he will be able to deduce the importance that Poirot eventually attributed to the telepathic hallucinations of this lady. But when? What persuaded Poirot to trouble the Carabinieri for a helicopter so he could pursue external enquiries with Thorndyke in that direction?

POIROT, *as if reading our minds:* In an investigation, as we all know, it is not the frank admissions but almost always the lies, the things omitted or suppressed, that put us onto the right track. Our enquiry into the Drood case is no exception to this rule. Almost immediately I suspected that one of us was concealing the truth; later, that there were two such people. But it was not until yesterday morning that I obtained definite proof. I proceeded at once, therefore . . .

POPEAU, *his spiteful voice rising above the exclamations of surprise from all:* What proof? What are you talking about? Have you gone mad?

POIROT: Thank you. When someone asks me this, it generally means that the case is solved. As for the proof, well, it is a matter of: *Videntes non vident.*

LATINIST: *Videntes non vident et audientes non audiunt.* Eyes have they, and see not. They have ears, and hear not.

POIROT: Yes, you all had the proof before your eyes, and didn't see it. Someone, and I'm afraid I'm referring to Porfiry Petrovich, also had ears to hear and heard not. But more of this later. I was saying that, having obtained the proof, I at once informed the Carabinieri. And they, in the person of our Colonel D'Attilio . . .

D'ATTILIO: Soon identified the wanted woman. She belongs to a distinguished Arezzo family, and, it appears, attended the convention out of mere curiosity. From the telephone statement we took from her relatives, it also emerged that on Tuesday afternoon the lady returned to Monte San Savino, where the family live, still in a mentally agitated state, talking of dogs, jugs, windows, and false-vagabond murderers. That same evening, eluding the surveillance of her family, she proceeded to Spoleto, where she was found late that night raving amidst the ruins of the ancient theatre. According to local witnesses, she mentioned, among other things, a fatal Scottish owl and an Italian mouse-trap.

DUPIN, *enigmatically:* This fits Thesis C.

POIROT: Exactly. Before proceeding to Monte San Savino, we therefore touched down at Spoleto, where the witnesses confirmed what has just been said. One of them also told us that according to the deranged woman, the owl and trap were linked to a murder. She apparently shouted several times: "That's why he killed him!"

DUPIN: But this does not fit Thesis C!

POIROT: But it does fit Thesis D. We ourselves saw the patient—or, rather, the telepath—and, despite her brother's objections to a formal interrogation were able to obtain a description, if somewhat vague, of the murderer. Strangely, for a vagabond, whether true or false, he *wore glasses.* It was on hearing this that I finally saw the light.

HOLMES, *as pale as a ghost:* No! . . . Poirot, in God's name, no!

POIROT: I'm sorry, Holmes. You know that when I seek the truth, I do not stop half-way.

WILMOT, *curtly:* Gentlemen, may I remind you that we have very little time. And I don't think this convention is the most suitable place for deductions based on telepathy and spiritualism.

POIROT, *no less curtly:* No doubt, Dr Wilmot. We would have all preferred to base our deductions on the facts, if you had not deliberately kept them from us.

LOREDANA: This is outrageous! Unheard of! It's . . . it's crazy!

POIROT: I can only answer you as I did Popeau, my dear girl. As far as spiritualism is concerned, it was in fact my utter scepticism towards it that first made me suspect Holmes. It could not possibly be a question of spirits. But if a detective of his calibre was convinced that Dickens did not want the truth about the Drood case to come out, there had to be a definite reason. Holmes, as we know, had studied the case long before us. And, I told myself, he must have reached conclusions that frightened him. Must have unconsciously dismissed them from his mind and replaced them with the story of the spiritualist séance. But his memory, to judge by his remarks a moment ago, has now returned to him.

HOLMES *sits silently, head bowed, ignoring his colleagues' stares and Watson's whispered questions.*

WILMOT *sits grim-faced, also silent, ignoring Loredana's anguished questions.*

POIROT: But let us return to Monte San Savino. Or, rather, let us leave it again. To Thorndyke en route to London via Pisa, and myself to Rome, where I spent this morning in biographical and bibliographical research. *First-hand* research.

TOAD: Very wise, seeing that here we can't trust anyone.

POIROT: I followed several trails, and you will have to bear with me while I go over them all. Let's begin with the theatre. It is clear that the "fatal Scottish owl" that had insinuated itself into the mind of the lady from Arezzo, and which originated, without any doubt, from Holmes's or Wilmot's mind, was the "owl, the fatal bellman" that Lady Macbeth hears while her husband is killing the unfortunate Duncan.

DUPIN: Perfectly clear.

POIROT: It is no less clear that the "Italian mouse-trap" refers to "The Mouse-Trap" in *Hamlet,* the fictional Italian tragedy that the prince has the travelling company of actors perform before his murderous stepfather and his own "most pernicious" mother. Now, Dupin had already pointed out the persistent allusions in the MED to both *Hamlet* and *Macbeth.* And he had also noted how in both tragedies (indeed, in all three, if we include the fictional one, where the murderer is called Lucianus) we have a criminal couple that corresponds, in ruthlessness—especially the woman—to our couple, Helena and Neville. But he had not paid sufficient attention, it struck me, to the question of the *play within the play.*

COL. D'ATTILIO, F. BROWN, P. PETROVICH, LATINIST and OTHERS: Maybe because we get such an overdose of that stuff nowadays.

POIROT: I quite agree. But the fact is, the MED teems

with theatrical allusions, beginning with the macabre-grotesque pantomime "How Do You Do To-morrow?" of the false Italian clown Signor Jacksonini. The neo-detective Bazzard (there is no doubt that he is Datchery) is himself a playwright, an unusual occupation for a solicitor's clerk, in those days at any rate. I think it unlikely that all this was not intended to lead towards something decidedly theatrical, in the latter part of the MED.

DUPIN: You mean, Bazzard would resort to a play within a play to unmask the murderers?

POIROT: More that Dickens, in the finale, would resort to a *play within the novel*. This, I think, was the new idea, the twist, the surprise that the novelist—who was always so keen on theatre—had up his sleeve for the readers.

POPEAU, *sarcastically:* Did the lady from Arezzo tell you this as well?

POIROT: No, it was my Latinist friend. But in a way Inspector Maigret had already stumbled on the truth, when he remarked that at the end, *whoever it was who confessed,* the confession would take that special form that Dickens had mentioned to Forster. A story that the murderer narrates or writes, as if the action and the characters were purely imaginary. A kind of script for a sensational drama. But perhaps our friend from Juan-les-Pins can explain things better than I.

ANTONIA, *very proud:* You'll see, he's wonderful!

LATINIST, *also proud, but containing it:* A brother and sister of uncertain nationality, perhaps of gipsy origin, and who indeed may not even be brother and sister, plan to kill an Englishman. The brother has qualms and would like to back out, but she insists ruthlessly. It is she in fact who devises the murder-plan: the body will be destroyed chemically and the remains hidden in a secret, inaccessible place. And so it happens, and for several months no-one knows whether it was a voluntary disappearance or a crime. But the place was not so secret and inaccessible as they thought! The remains are identified thanks to an object that the chemical agent could not destroy.

ANTONIA: Isn't he wonderful!

LATINIST: At this point, a relative of the murdered man turns up, who is actively involved in theatre. He suggests to the "sister," who possesses mesmeric powers and is a prey to dark fancies, that she should write him a script for a sensational drama of the Elizabethan kind. She does this, and the result is a perfect theatrical reconstruction of the crime, played out, as in *Hamlet,* by characters who differ from their originals only by name.

ANTONIA, *while the Latinist takes his seat again in satisfaction:* I think he's wonderful!

LOREDANA: I don't understand. What's so wonderful

about it? All François *(the Latinist's name)* has done is give us a summary of the complete plot of the MED according to Thesis C.

POIROT: So it would seem. But he has also given us, as I myself have managed to check by consulting the rare volume, a very faithful summary of the plot of *The Haunted Hotel,* a novel by Wilkie Collins which came out in 1878.

Poirot has no mysterious powers of divination, reader. The fact that he went and looked up that mediocre and practically unknown novel by Collins, which no MED scholar had ever concerned himsellf with before,[1] is due to his having overheard the conversation between the Collinsian Latinist and Hastings the other evening. And that is why he himself stayed and chatted so long with the Latinist before leaving.

It is easy to imagine the difficulty Poirot found himself in after this discovery. Ruling out pure and simple coincidence, there were only three possibilities. The first was that Collins had reconstructed the plot of the MED himself, including the theatrical twist, and used it for his book

---

[1] Perhaps because of the misleading title. There are no ghosts in the story; the "haunting" refers to the protagonist's mesmeric powers. It is curious that many Droodists have insisted, instead, on the much more tenuous resemblances between the MED and another book by Collins, *Miss or Mrs?,* of 1871.

(with different settings and trappings).[1] But why should he do this, if he considered the MED "the melancholy work of a worn-out brain"? The second possibility: Dickens himself revealed the plot to his former friend and collaborator. But, again, why on earth should Dickens do this, fearing Collins, though he called him a hack, as a rival? And the third possibility . . .

POIROT: The third possibility is that the original twist and its development *were Collins's*; that Collins himself had spoken of them to Dickens before their relations deteriorated; and that Dickens, in his boundless egotism, coolly appropriated them.

The reader will no doubt imagine that at this point the room resounded with protests and shocked cries. He would be wrong. A dazed silence fell on the Drood work-group. And in that silence, Poirot continued his exposition, his voice neutral, his tone factual.

POIROT: This explains many things. It explains, for example, a second, most singular point of similarity between the MED and Collins's novel. In the latter, the script that the murderer is supposed to hand over to the person who

---

[1] In Collins's novel, the murderess already has theatrical leanings and writes her drama-confession under auto-suggestion, whereas Helena, according to Thesis C, will write hers under the hypnotic influence of Jasper. But it is possible that she too has literary ambitions, a far from uncommon phenomenon among terrorists.

commissioned it *breaks off half-way*—at the point where the crime has been committed but the murderer's (murderers') subsequent movements remain to be told. The playwright is in fact found on the floor, beside her manuscript, *having died of a brain haemorrhage.* The manuscript itself, written in an increasingly confused hand, reveals all the *"signs of an overwrought brain."* Shall we now look at Figure 3, which is to be found in Forster's volume, but which Dr Wilmot did not think it appropriate to show us?

The attendant with the projector, who has entered without our noticing, projects Figure 3. And Loredana, as in a dream, dims the lights.

POIROT: You see. We have here the last tormented page of the MED and, below it, for comparison, a clear manuscript page from *Oliver Twist.* But we also have here *a story that breaks off half-way,* we have *the "signs of an overwrought (or worn-out) brain,"* and we have, on the same day, a death *from brain haemorrhage.* I have no doubt that in Collins's ghost-ridden novel (whose only ghosts were in the author's head), this terrible triple allusion was inspired by Figure 3 and the obsessive, inextinguishable hatred that Collins still harboured for Dickens: the man who had not only humiliated and insulted him, but had also stolen his plot and the central idea of the play within the novel. I have my doubts, however, about the "brain haemorrhage." Shall we look at Figure 1 again for a moment?

A brilliant morning shines on the old city. Its antiquities and ruins are surpassingly beautiful, with the lusty ivy gleaming in the sun, and the rich trees waving in the balmy air. Changes of glorious light from moving boughs, songs of birds, scents from gardens, woods, and fields — or, rather, from the one great garden of the whole cultivated island in its yielding time — penetrate into the Cathedral, subdue its earthy odour, and preach the Resurrection and the Life. The cold stone tombs of centuries ago grow warm, and flecks of brightness dart into the sternest marble corners of the building, fluttering there like wings.

Comes Mr. Tope with his large keys, and yawning unlocks and sits open. Comes Mrs. Tope and attendant sweeping sprites. Comes, in due time, attendant shadow from the tower, Mr. Jasper keeping aloof from the rest, while great with the Precincts. Come rooks from various quarters of the sky, with great ostentation, and flop down that tall and organ are about to give it tongue. Comes a very dusty congregation; chaff from Minor Canon Corner and the Precincts. Come Mr. Crisparkle, fresh and bright; only his ministering between comes the choir in a hurry (always in a hurry), and a slovenly child chucking children hustling into their gowns at the last moment; and comes John Jasper reading their ... Last of all comes Mr. Datchery, who ... choir, very much at his service and glancing about him for Her Royal Highness the Princess Puffer.

The service is pretty well advanced before Mr. Datchery can discern the Royal Highness. But by that time he has made her out, in the shade. She is behind a pillar, careful to keep out of the choir-master's view, but regards him with the closest attention. All unconscious of her chunky and sings. She watches him as he is most musical fervid, and ... yes, Mr. Datchery sees her do it — shakes her fist at him, behind the pillar's friendly shelter.

"No" — replied the Dodger "not here. for this aint the shop for justice, besides which my attorney is a breakfasting this morning with the Wice President of the House of Commons, but I shall have something to say, and so will he and so will a wery numerous and respectable circle of acquaintance as'll make them beaks wish they'd never been born, or that they'd got their footman to hang 'em up to their own afore they let 'em come out this morning to try it on upon me. I'll—'

"There: he's fully committed" interposed the clerk. "Take him away."

Figure 3.

At this point, reader, the silence is almost palpable. But one can sense that the tension is about to snap. While we wait, and everybody's eyes are fixed on the screen, let's have a look at Figure 1 ourselves, on page 536. Had a good look? But now a strangled cry from Loredana:

"The jug!!! . . ."

POIROT: Quite. By the window. The jug of water that Dickens always kept on his desk, and which Dr Wilmot apparently forgot all about. You will recall that when we taxed him, he admitted calmly, "I might have forgotten dogs or jugs, but a false vagabond, well, I think I'd remember him." The classic trick of admitting to what hardly matters in order better to deny what really matters! He knew he couldn't get out of showing us the famous Figure 1; but he reckoned that nobody would notice the jug. And he would have been right, had it not been for . . . ahem, Hercule Poirot, who thus obtained the concrete proof, the final link in the chain.

POPEAU: Proof of what? Link in what chain? What's all this got to do with the Drood case?

POIROT: Nothing, at least not directly. Drood's murderers have already been rumbled by Scotland Yard, with the help of Dupin. We are now considering Thesis D, which does not concern the Drood case but the crime of the false vagabond.

WILMOT, *having come to a decision:* All right, Poirot. But could we talk about it alone, for a moment?

POIROT: Certainly, *cher ami.* But maybe Holmes would like . . .

HOLMES: Yes, I should be present, too.

The three men go into the corridor, where we hasten to join them. They are talking quietly and calmly. Holmes nods several times with satisfaction, and the chairman's expression relaxes somewhat. Dr Wilmot then goes off to a telephone box; he comes back two minutes later, and they all return to the Dickens Room, where Poirot resumes his account.

POIROT: When I said that Dr Wilmot had deliberately withheld the facts from us, I did not intend to accuse him of having deceived us from the beginning. Just like Holmes, after dimly intuiting the truth about the D. case, he unconsciously dismissed it from his mind. But then he began to remember, perhaps when he saw the jug enlarged on the screen. That is why immediately afterwards he tried, though clumsily, to suppress the incident of the dogs.

WILMOT: Why clumsily? I merely refrained from mentioning the incident.

POIROT: Too late, however. When you described the afternoon of rest that Dickens allowed himself on June 7, the day before his death, you were on the point of telling us about the dogs. But suddenly, you couldn't say the names Don and Linda. So you told us that on the afternoon in question Dickens "took *Mamie and Georgina* for a walk," his elder daughter and sister-in-law. But the slight hesitation that followed the "took" was not slight enough to escape Hercule Poirot! Nor could he fail to notice the incongruity of the expression "take for a walk" applied to an elderly writer, sick and lame, accompanying two robust women on a stroll. And in fact, as I discovered in the course of my research this morning, it was Don and Linda that Dickens took for a walk, the two big guard-dogs (a Newfoundlander and a Saint Bernard) which were kept chained in his garden. Mamie wasn't even there, having gone to London to visit her sister, Kate.

P. PETROVICH: It's true! Odd that I didn't notice, even though I've read Forster's book and remember his description of that day perfectly.

POIROT: So you, too, averted your eyes from the terrible truth. There is no doubt that the telepathic lady from Arezzo was referring to those two guard-dogs when she transmitted the thought, *thats why the dogs didnt.* "Didn't" what? For constructors like ourselves, it should not be too difficult to complete this fragment. "That's why the dogs didn't . . ."

LOREDANA, *almost inaudibly:* "That's why the dogs didn't bark."

POIROT: And why should they have barked?

LOREDANA, *as before:* Because of the false vagabond, who came into the garden and approached the window with his phial of poison.

POIROT: And why didn't they bark?

LOREDANA *buries her face in her hands and doesn't reply.*

ANTONIA, *plucking up courage:* Because the vagabond was not only false, he was also known to the dogs, though they hadn't seen him recently.

POIROT: Exactly. Collins, before he—

POPEAU, *staggered:* Collins? You don't mean to say Dickens was murdered? And that it was Collins who did it?

POIROT: But of course, *cher ami.*

POPEAU, *showing himself to be the kind of plodding policeman who gets there long after everyone else:* Ça alors!

POIROT: As I was saying, Collins, before he and Dickens fell out, was a frequent visitor to Gadshill. And so not only did the dogs know him well, but he was well acquainted with his former friend's habits. He knew that Dickens, in the summer, worked in the chalet of the "Wilderness" and stayed there until the afternoon, when he would come back and see to his correspondence in his study on the ground-floor. He knew about the jug on the desk, by the window. And finally, he knew from Kate Dickens, who had married his brother Charles, that her

579

father's health had deteriorated and that there was a threat of brain haemorrhage hanging over him. Collins's modus operandi was therefore extremely simple, if we except the glasses. He was in fact very short-sighted and had to keep them on, even at the risk of being recognised through his vagabond disguise, while he loitered on the Gadshill road near the house, waiting for the right moment. The right moment came when Georgina left the afternoon-post on the desk, changed the water in the jug, and withdrew to her rooms upstairs. Mamie, as we know and as he also knew, was not at home. The only risk was that Dickens might arrive before he had time to pour the contents of the phial into the jug and disappear.[1] Dickens, however, hard at work writing the page we've just seen, did not return until late.

MARLOWE, *taking advantage of Poirot's dramatic pause:* Very clever, Poirot. But where's the proof? You talk of poison, yet the symptoms described by Dr Steele, and by the two specialists who came running from London, match those of brain haemorrhage.

POIROT: But Dickens *would* die from a brain haemorrhage if the poison used were digitalin. It is well-known that the glycosides of digitalis produce a powerful and rapid

---

[1] True, the victim might not drink from the jug, though he kept it on the desk because of the various pills that he had to take during the course of the day. But if anybody else drank from it, the effects would not be lethal.

increase in blood pressure. In Dickens's state of health, it would have taken only a few centigrams to cause the rupture of an aneurysm.

ARCHER: Well, how about a few centigrams of evidence while you're at it? No jury would convict Collins on that pile of circumstantial guesswork. We need some concrete proof!

POIROT: Of course. And that is why Dr Thorndyke has gone to London. But we don't need to wait for his return—he has clearly been held up by some air-strike. The telex he sent me this morning consists of just one word, but it is eloquent enough for anyone who has guessed the purpose of his journey.[1] *He draws the telex from his pocket and hands it to the editor of* The Dickensian. It is for your eyes only, Dr Wilmot; as soon as you have read it, you may destroy it.

---

[1] It is obvious that from London Thorndyke went to Gadshill. There, disguised as a vagabond, he managed to approach the window of Dickens's study (which has not been altered, because the house is a museum) and remove the jug from the desk for the instant needed to extract the dregs, which he later analysed in his own laboratory. It is equally obvious that the word in the telegram is DIGITALIN.

EPILOGUE

The D. case, reader, was thus the Dickens case.

Poirot's further punctilious clarifications are of little interest. We cannot, however, pass over one melancholy hypothesis he posits: When Dickens spoke to Wills of the difficulties he was having with the plot, he was perhaps alluding to feelings of remorse, feelings that had persuaded him to change his ending and give up the idea of the play within the novel. Collins, who had recognised the product of his own ingenuity from the first instalment,[1] could not have known this. Thus, exactly like Jasper in Thesis A, he proceeded with the murder, unaware that his hated rival had already left the field.

---

[1] Another possibility: It was Dickens himself who told Collins, claiming (and by now, in his egomania, thoroughly convinced of the fact) that it was his own idea. We can point to similar brazen behaviour on his part in a related case. In mid-1869, another contributor to *All the Year Round,* R. Lytton, sent Dickens the first episode of a story of his, vexingly like the MED in the relations between an uncle and nephew. Dickens turned it down, saying that the theme was too reminiscent of a story already published. No analyst of the MED has found any trace of such a story.

As to the defence of Collins, we cannot report in full the Latinist's passionate peroration, in which he praised the writer's mild nature and long devotion to Dickens, referred to the painful ailments that had led to his self-destruction with opium, and described Dickens's "increasingly shameful" treatment of his former friend. He went so far as to conclude: "If Wilkie really did kill him, I don't blame him!"

But let us return to that mini-conference between Wilmot, Holmes, and Poirot in the corridor. Or, rather: let Poirot himself tell us, with one of his classic, clinching wrap-ups.

From the very beginning *(Poirot says)* our debate was plagued, as it were, by the question of plagiarism. There was Dickens's plagiarism of *The Moonstone,* which completely misled our predecessors instead of putting them on the right track. There was the alleged, and no less misleading, derivation of the character of Jekyll from that of Jasper, with the added complication of two further acts of plagiarism on Stevenson's part: the story of the uncle who plans to make his nephew fall from the tower, in *Kidnapped,* and the derivation of the character of Utterson from that of Grewgious, which Dickens in turn may have taken from Sterne. We also saw how Dickens drew on certain scenes from *Macbeth* and *Hamlet*: with the double aim of providing us with subtle clues that pointed to the Landlesses, and of preparing us for the final twist of the play within the novel.

But so far *(Poirot continues)* we remain in the realm of literary imitation and pure fiction. The plagiarism becomes serious, and the coincidence curious indeed, when we see reality imitating fiction. Here, for example, we find the most real of detectives, *moi,* the inimitable Poirot, discovering that he is the unwitting imitation of a . . . well, a somewhat dubious detective, one Popeau! And we find the main road of Gadshill suddenly peopled with imaginary— nay, doubly imaginary—"men in buckram," in a sort of prelude to the real vagabonds (among whom one who is real enough, though false) who will pass along it on that fatal June 8, 1870.

Was it entirely by chance *(Poirot asks himself)* that I was reminded of those men in buckram when Dr Wilmot told us about Dickens's house and garden in that locality? As you know, I do not believe in supernatural premonitions, but I certainly had the impression then of something inexplicably sinister. I began to reflect on Holmes's supernatural fears, and to wonder whether they might not have some basis in fact.

But let us leave the house of Gadshill *(Poirot resumes after a pause for effect)* and pass on to the castle of Elsinore, where the "second-degree" fiction of the play within the play is celebrated in Act Three. Here we see an actor impersonating a murderer, Lucianus, in an Italian tragedy (the murdered man is Gonzago). He enters the victim's garden furtively, with "Thoughts black, hands apt, drugs fit, and time agreeing," and pours his poison into the victim's ear. For additional details we need only look at the "real" scene in Act One, where the ghost of the victim, after stating that the murderer knew his "custom always of the afternoon," specifies that the poison was "hebenon," the "leperous distilment" of which "holds such an enmity with blood of man."

Scholars *(Poirot adds after another pause)* have not been able to identify the plant Shakespeare calls hebenon. And I don't know whether *Digitalis purpurea* would have any deleterious effect if instilled into the ear. But reality is so strikingly foreshadowed in that fictitious scene that I am inclined to think that *Hamlet* inspired Collins not only with the plot of his novel but also with the method of his crime. Unless . . .

This time, Poirot pauses for so long that everybody starts when suddenly he cries, in the ghost's own words:

O, horrible! O, horrible! most horrible!

And there is still a tremor of fear in his voice as he concludes:

"Unless Holmes and Hamlet are right, when they say there are more things in heaven and earth than . . . than are dreamt of in the philosophy of Hercule Poirot."

WILMOT, *to the audience:* Bearing in mind this possibility, not to mention the horror that Thesis D would arouse in the breasts of our sponsors, I have asked the technicians to eliminate every reference to it from the electronic minutes of the session. Poirot, Holmes, and I have given our solemn word, furthermore, that we will not speak of this to anyone. May we ask the same of you?

TOAD, *his voice hoarser than anyone has ever heard it:* I will be the first to give you my word. Let's make do with Thesis C, the conclusions of which are more than any critic dreamt of in his Droodist philosophy.

There is no need to add, reader, that all those present, including Loredana, Antonia, the Latinist, and Thorndyke (who arrived just a moment ago), all quickly followed Toad's example. And you have also probably guessed, reader, that, notwithstanding the cover of the MED, there will be not one but two weddings. Between whom, we leave it to you to imagine.